Nytstars

by

Jo-Anne Sieppert

PITTSBURGH, PENNSYLVANIA 15222

ISBN: 978-1-4349-9389-2
Library of Congress Control Number: 2008941109

Printed in the United States of America

First Printing

For more information or to order additional books, please contact:
RoseDog Books
701 Smithfield Street
Pittsburgh, Pennsylvania 15222
U.S.A.
1-800-834-1803
www.dorrance.com

CHAPTER ONE

TYLER

"Well, well, well," Mrs. Suzanne said in her typical snarling voice, which made the hairs on the back of Tyler Leeds's neck stand up as she walked down the row of desks in the classroom, returning the class's English papers on poems and their hidden meanings. "Mr. Leeds, another D. Should I have expected anything better, really?" she muttered under her breath, but, of course, loudly enough for Tyler to hear.

She shoved the paper on Tyler's desk and shot him the usual disapproving look that she liked to give him any chance she got. Tyler really had no idea why she had never liked him, but then again, neither did many people, so he did not really care.

Tyler was and always had been what you might call a loner. He had suffered from nightmares since he was very young. "Even as an infant, his sleeps were always uneasy, tossing and fidgeting in his crib, crying and screaming. I tried everything: feeding him, rocking him—I even tried letting him sleep in my bed with me, but nothing ever worked," his mom would explain to doctors and specialists over and over. Tyler's constant sleepless nights had taken a toll on him; he had become moody and distant. The dark circles under his bloodshot eyes, his pale skin, his shaggy hair, and his scruffy clothes gave him the appearance of an old man. He quite often fell asleep in class or at lunch, which made him a target for taunting and bullying from his peers. His only real friend was his brother Michael; other than that, he had no one. No one to just hang out with and do what other thirteen-year-old boys did; instead, he mostly hung out by himself, practicing his karate or kicking a soccer ball around the yard with his brother.

He didn't like school at all, and it seemed like school didn't really like him either. Tyler showed up for class and sat in the back of the room, spending most of his time staring out of the window. Mrs. Suzanne was the teacher Tyler disliked the most, and the feeling was mutual. Mrs. Suzanne did not hide her feelings toward Tyler at all. She would pick him out over the rest of the class and do everything she could to make the time he spent in her classroom miserable.

"Well, most of you did an okay job on your papers," Mrs. Suzanne said, smirking.

Tyler rolled his eyes and continued to stare out the window at the overgrown oak tree on the front lawn of the school—the tree that was often the focus of his attention, with the branch that was shaped like a staircase. Tyler would imagine that the staircase led to a secret world where nobody knew who he was, where he wasn't different from everybody else—a world anywhere other than here.

"Well, I hope you are all putting the finishing touches on your poems. They are due Monday, first thing, and we will be reading them aloud to the class, so please make sure you have them ready—no excuses. You will also need to have a copy written in good handwriting to hand in to me. I will be grading you on both your oral and your...Mr. Leeds...Mr. Leeds!" Mrs. Suzanne yelled as she noticed Tyler had fallen asleep on his desk. "Mr. Leeds, naptime is over."

Tyler sat up quickly, opened his eyes, and saw that the whole class was staring and laughing at him.

"Well, I'm glad you are awake now, Mr. Leeds—I'm sorry to disturb your nappy-wappy!" Mrs. Suzanne spat. "Well, thank you for volunteering to go first on Monday morning with your poem reading, Mr. Leeds. I'm sure it will be unimpressive as usual."

Tyler opened his mouth to shout back at her, but the bell rang to signal the end of the class. Mrs. Suzanne glared at him, then turned her back to him in a satisfied sort of way. Tyler grabbed his books and stormed out of the room, past the group of so-called popular kids known as "the Gang" that were hanging out in the hallway, giggling and pointing at him as he walked by. Tyler ignored them as they pretended to be asleep and snored at him.

He reached his locker, shoved his books inside, and pulled out his gym bag. Another subject he disliked; not that there was a subject he really did like, but gym was one of the worst. It wasn't that Tyler wasn't good at gym, or sports, for that matter—in fact, he really quite enjoyed them—but what he didn't enjoy was always being the last one picked for the teams, or the complaining from the team that had to pick him. He didn't mind running laps; he was the fastest in the class. In fact, he could run fast for longer than anyone else, so he always finished first, usually fast enough that he would be the first one to the changing room and would finish showering before the other boys came in. Tyler couldn't wait to go home; however, he still had to get through gym, his last class of the day that Thursday.

Mr. Stolts, the gym teacher, was an older man with completely white hair, a mustache that was badly in need of a trim, a stomach that hung over the top of the jogging pants that were like his uniform, and a shirt that was once white but was now gray and sweat-stained under the arms. Mr. Stolts wasn't a mean teacher; he was more an unobservant teacher. Either he truly didn't notice the Gang being mean to the other students, or he just didn't care to get involved. Gym class went the same way every time: the Gang always picked the popular kids first for the teams, and today was no exception.

"Okay, kids, come on, get a move on, we haven't got all day. Pick your teams so you can go play soccer outside," Mr. Stolts said as he picked up the gym bag with all the pinnies in it and headed for the door leading to the soccer field.

Conner Jakins was the class bully and the leader of the Gang. He was tall, with dark brown hair and equally dark eyes. Like everyone in the popular crowd, he always wore the coolest brand-name clothes, taking much pride in displaying to everyone how rich his family was. He was definitely the most popular kid in class, either because everyone really liked him or because everyone was just scared of him, but when he made a joke everyone laughed just the same. If he didn't like you, well, neither did anyone else. The entire class seemed to follow his every move, like sheep following the flock.

"Who knew nobody would want you on their team, hey, Naps?" Conner called mockingly at Tyler. The whole class laughed, following the flock. "Well, too bad for you, Chase, he is on your side; I hope he doesn't fall asleep in the middle of the field."

Chase Powart, Conner Jakins's best friend and ally, was tall like Conner, with blue eyes and black hair that was always perfectly styled. Chase was like Conner's clone. The two of them together caused constant trouble, picking on anyone they wanted to, which was mostly Tyler. They were popular, rich, good-looking—well, at least they thought so. "The leaders of the flock," as Tyler referred to them, were each just as mean as the other.

"Man, I swear we had him last time," Chase complained, looking at Tyler with an expression of disgust and annoyance on his face.

"Oh, well, you get him this time as well then. Aren't you lucky?" Conner teased.

The two teams followed Mr. Stolts outside and onto the soccer field. "Okay, you know the drill: one side over there, the other over there," Mr. Stolts said, pointing to either side of the field. "Chase, your side can wear the pinnies," he shouted as he pulled the pinnies out of the gym bag along with the soccer ball.

"This sucks, we get Naps and we have to wear the pinnies," Chase said, giving Tyler a push from behind as he stormed past.

Tyler just ignored him, grabbed a pinnie, and put it on. Both teams set up on either side of the field. As usual, Chase and Conner were the center forwards. Dean Minns was in net for Chase's side, and Greg Daniels was in net for Conner's side, also as usual. Most of the girls, who didn't like to play, were the subs. They never really subbed in; they were more like the spectators. (Mr. Stolts didn't seem to care who played what, or even if everyone played, yet they all somehow got a grade at the end of term.) Mr. Stolts sort of played referee—well, he blew the whistle when the game started, and when anyone scored, if he noticed.

The whistle blew and everyone on the field began to play. Tyler just waited for the ball to come close to him. He didn't really want to do anything; he wished he could just sit on the sides like the girls and watch, but he knew if he did, it would just give them something else to tease him about. Conner came running toward Tyler with the ball. Tyler knew he could easily get the ball away from Conner, but he didn't, pretending to try to get the ball then just watching as Conner ran past him toward the goal. Conner scored the first goal of the game.

"Thanks, loser," Conner shot at Tyler as he walked past him, smiling like he had just scored a goal for the World Cup. The way the class played, you would think they were going to win a medal or something.

After a few minutes, Chase scored the first goal for their team. He gave the whole team a high five, except for Tyler. Tyler spent most of the game trying to keep away from the play, and was checking his watch, counting down the time left in the class, when suddenly Conner ran right into him, knocking him flat on the ground, and kept running right past him without any acknowledgment and scored the next goal.

"Could you be any more of a loser, Naps? Man, your mom must be so ashamed," Conner said, giving him a kick as he walked past. Tyler got to his feet and glared at Conner. Tyler was mad; he could feel his insides boiling with anger.

"Aw, did I make you mad, Naps? What are you going to do, snore at me?"

Everyone on the field started to laugh. Mr. Stolts blew the whistle for the game to begin again, and Chase kicked the ball to his teammate on the right, but Tyler rushed up the field and got the ball first.

"What are you doing, Naps?" Chase called after him, but Tyler didn't hear; he kept on running with the ball toward Greg Daniels.

Conner, still in shock, ran toward Tyler. "You wish, loser," he said, as he tried every soccer trick he knew to get the ball away from Tyler. He even tried to dive on the ground, trying to knock Tyler off his feet. Tyler simply dodged out of the way, keeping the ball. Three more players from Conner's team tried to get the ball away from Tyler; they all failed. Tyler kicked the ball as hard as he could on the net, and scored.

Everyone just stared at him. No one had ever seen him even attempt to play before, let alone take the ball all the way to the net, around four players, including Conner, and score. Tyler looked at his classmates, and instantly he was filled with embarrassment. He had no idea what had just come over him. He glanced around the field at the faces full of judgment, and without saying a word, he ran from the field and headed for the changing room. Even Mr. Stolts was amazed; he didn't even try to stop Tyler from leaving class early. Tyler quickly showered, dressed, and grabbed his stuff from his locker, before anyone else did.

"Hey, Ty," Michael said as he walked out of his class and saw Tyler waiting for him. "Cool, you got let out early?"

"Yeah, something like that," Tyler said as he followed his brother to his locker, hoping they wouldn't run into Conner and Chase on their way out the doors.

"Ah, tomorrow's Friday—thank goodness," Michael said as he filled his backpack with books. "See you tomorrow, Brandon. Don't forget to study, Chris—big test tomorrow," Michael called to his friends, and the boys headed home together.

Michael, fourteen, had strawberry blond hair and deep blue eyes. He kept his hair well-groomed and, as far as Tyler could tell, sprayed on enough cologne in the morning for at least ten guys. Tyler often got annoyed waiting for Michael to get ready in the morning before school. "Just throw something on, Mike; really, nobody cares what you look like," Tyler would moan. "Maybe nobody, including yourself, cares what *you* look like, but I have a reputation to uphold," Michael would respond. All the work seemed to pay off, at least; Michael was almost always surrounded by smiling or giggling girls who blushed profusely when Michael smiled back at them. Unlike Tyler, Michael was quite popular with both the other kids in the school and the teachers. Tyler didn't really mind; he had actually gotten used to being different from everyone, and he quite despised the sheep of the school.

That night, Tyler got into bed and lay down. He was going to try to stay awake as long as he could, and when he knew he couldn't stay awake any longer, he would shut his eyes for only a few minutes at a time, in hopes of avoiding another long night full of terrifying nightmares. He set the alarm on his watch to go off every ten minutes, the same as he did every night; unfortunately, the alarm on his watch was not very loud, so he usually slept through it.

Mrs. Leeds came into the boys' room, gave them each a goodnight kiss, and went out, closing the door. Mrs. Leeds was a short woman; in fact, Michael and Tyler had already passed her height. She had long brown hair and the same deep blue eyes as both Michael and Tyler, in which Tyler could see her sadness when she said goodnight to him. She knew he would have nightmares; she also knew she couldn't do anything to help him sleep. Tyler had tried everything, but nothing worked, and now he didn't even want his mother to come to him when he woke up screaming in the night. "Mom, please, I am too old to have my mommy rocking me back to sleep. I need to deal with this on my own," Tyler would groan.

Tyler reached under his pillow for his flashlight and turned it on. He stared at the top bunk, trying unsuccessfully to think of something other than sleep. All he could think about was closing his eyes and falling into a deep sleep, a sleep without any dreams, without any monsters, ghosts, or death. How he longed for just one full night of sleep, uninterrupted sleep; he couldn't remember the last time he had slept all the way through a night.

"Are you awake, Ty?" Michael asked from the top bunk.

"You know I am, Mike," Tyler grunted.

"I know, sorry—just checking. Are you going to try and sleep tonight at all?" Mike asked.

"Why do you care? I won't disturb you, if that's what you're worried about." Tyler rolled over in bed and turned off the flashlight.

"I wasn't worried about that, I was just asking. Never mind. Goodnight." Michael also rolled over, closed his eyes, and drifted off to sleep.

As he lay in his bed, Tyler began to feel cold, so he pulled his blankets up to his chin. He looked around his room, checking for anything—or, better yet, nothing. It wasn't long before he noticed a strange shadow on the wall across the room. The shadow looked like a large, hooded figure, larger than a normal person, and definitely larger than anyone in the house. Tyler wasn't sure what it was from; it didn't look familiar to him at all. He searched the room to find what was making the shadow, but to his surprise, there was nothing that resembled the shape anywhere. There was an icy chill in the room; maybe the window was open, Tyler thought to himself.

"Michael...Hey, Mike, are you awake?" Tyler whispered to Michael, who was asleep on the top bunk. When Michael didn't answer, Tyler decided to get up and check the window himself. Feeling a little scared, Tyler held on tightly to his flashlight, just in case. Slowly, he crept to the window. To his surprise, the window was closed, but there was still a draft.

"Where is that draft coming from?" Tyler said quietly to himself. He turned around and headed for the door, taking one more look over his shoulder to see if the shadow was still on the wall. To his relief, it had vanished. Tyler reached for the handle of his bedroom door, but quickly removed his hand—the door handle was like ice, so cold it sent a chilling feeling rushing through his entire body. Tyler ran quickly, jumping back into bed and pulling the covers all the way over his head. He lay there for a while, not moving or making any noise. There was a noise coming from the other side of his bedroom door. It was a loud ripping noise, as if someone was standing on the other side of the door ripping up paper. Tyler closed his eyes as tightly as he could and put his hands up over his ears, whispering to himself, "It's just a dream, it's just a dream." He took his hands down again in hopes that the sound had gone, but instead, it had become louder. Tyler knew something was wrong; the door handle was cold as ice, and who was making that sound? He just knew it wasn't his parents.

"Mike! Psst...Mike!" he whispered. Michael didn't answer—he was still asleep. Tyler was on his own to face whatever was on the other side of the door. He reached for the door handle again, this time with his pajama sleeve over his hand. As fast as he could, he opened the door. When he looked into the hallway, everything seemed normal—except the cold. He was shivering all over, so much so that he could hardly stand still. The light was still on in the hall and the TV was still on downstairs.

Maybe Mom or Dad left a window open or the heating broke, Tyler hoped as he continued down the hall. The hallway was filled with beautiful pictures of ocean views and city skylines, all from places that Mrs. Leeds wanted to go. There was an empty spot at the end of the hall where Mrs. Leeds's favorite picture usually hung. The picture was of an old castle that was said to be located near where she lived in England when she was a little girl. The castle was spectacular: it was surrounded by beautiful, manicured gardens filled with perfect flowers and tall trees acting like a wall around the castle grounds. The castle was brilliantly old and full of character. There was no sun shining in the background—only gray clouds. The castle was said to have been deserted for years, but if you looked closely enough and wanted to see it, you could see a girl standing in one of the windows on the top floor in the left tower. Mrs. Leeds said the girl was the daughter of the family that used to live in the castle, but she had died in the castle when she was only twelve. Murdered—nobody ever found out who did it, Tyler remembered. The family had been so grief-stricken that they just left the castle one night, never to return—but the ghost of the little girl never left. Mrs. Leeds had heard the story of the castle when she was a little girl; she had loved it so much that her father had bought the painting for her.

Mom has never taken that picture down; I wonder why she took it down tonight, Tyler thought. As he reached the top of the stairs, he tried to listen to see if he could hear anything. Again he heard what he thought was a ripping sound. Was that the picture? Tyler thought as he stood frozen with fear at the top of the stairs. What was going on down there? What should he do? Should he shout for his mom and dad? Was it too late? Had something already happened to them? Terrible thoughts were going through Tyler's head. He imagined walking down the stairs and seeing his parents dead or dying a terrible death, blood splattered all over the place. Tyler shivered with fear, closed his eyes, and turned around, ready to walk back to bed, but he couldn't—he knew he had to go downstairs. He had to see for himself. Slowly and quietly, he tiptoed down the stairs, holding tight to the railing, forcing himself to move each step. When he reached the bottom step, he paused, took a deep breath, and tiptoed into the living room, his heart pounding like a drum in his chest.

He gasped. There in the middle of the room was an elf—an ugly, mean-looking elf that stood about the same height as Tyler but was obviously much, much older. The elf was rather large around the middle. He was wearing very old and tatty-looking clothes: his pants had holes in the knees and were covered in dirt, and they were too small, coming down just a little past his knees, and were frayed at the ends from wear. He wasn't wearing any shoes or socks. The elf's feet were quite large compared to the rest of his body; his toenails were long and yellow like they hadn't been cut or even washed in a very long time, if ever. He had only four toes on each foot, which were short, fat, and covered in hair. His shirt looked like it may once have been white, but now it was covered in filth that had turned it a dingy gray color, with patches of mud and blood on it. The shirt was also covered in rips and tears, and just like his pants, his shirt was too small. The elf's bulging stomach was dirty and hairy; it showed in the gap between his pants and his shirt.

Tyler stared at the elf's face, which was covered in wrinkles and moles. There were little patches of hair covering his face. His teeth were as yellow as his toenails, with little pieces of food and paper stuck between them. He was missing at least three teeth that Tyler could see from where he was standing. His nose was long and crooked; there was hair coming out of it as well. His eyes were black and bugged out of his head. There was a long, tangled black mass of hair on the elf's head, which was most likely home to many bugs from the look and smell of it.

All around the elf were enormous and hairy black spiders, much bigger than normal spiders: they were almost as big as the elf, with eyes a deep, piercing red, teeth yellow and razor-sharp. They moved quickly, making bone-chilling tapping sounds with all eight legs, which stretched out over their bodies, then bent downward to the floor. The spiders were most definitely under the elf's command.

Tyler was frozen, petrified with fear. He didn't like even little spiders, so he was pretty sure that these giant spiders were not going to be any more to his liking. The spiders were looking right at Tyler, but they didn't move; the elf hadn't moved either. Can they see me? Tyler thought to himself as he stood perfectly still, watching them, waiting for them to do something—anything.

"NOSH TROSH TRESH," the elf finally commanded to the spiders. They headed for the stairs. Tyler quickly shut his eyes; he expected the spiders to attack him, to rip his body limb from limb…but they didn't. When he was sure they had passed by, he opened his eyes again and looked at the elf. The elf was now walking around in circles, rubbing his tummy hungrily, yet he still showed no sign that he had noticed Tyler. Maybe he was invisible, or maybe this was just the elf's way of torturing him, making him wait, not knowing what was going to happen to him or his family—after all, Tyler hadn't even tried to run away.

Tyler heard a rush and scattering, then suddenly the familiar tapping he knew to be the hairy spider legs rushing past him. They were carrying more pictures from the upstairs hallway; they dropped them on the floor at the elf's feet, who greedily devoured them in seconds after ripping them to shreds. The elf then looked at the spiders once more, and growled similar words he had used to send them to get the pictures. "NOSH LOSHTA KOSHY." Once again the spiders headed up the stairs; Tyler assumed they were going for another picture.

The elf finally turned and looked at Tyler. For the first time he actually seemed to acknowledge that he was standing there—not that Tyler minded that he hadn't been noticed.

"You ungry?" the elf said in a gruff voice.

Tyler shook his head, somewhat terrified. "I, err…no."

The elf stared at Tyler with an angry look on his face. "Well, me friends are—they will feast."

"Your…your friends?" Tyler hoped he wasn't meaning more elves; they didn't have many pictures left.

"Spiders, me friends, are ungry."

Tyler wasn't sure what the spiders ate, and he wasn't sure that he wanted to know. Then all of a sudden, he heard piercing screams coming from the bedrooms upstairs. Tyler turned to run, but the elf was suddenly in front of him.

"No, you stay here—unless you want to be eaten too?"

Tyler was horrified. "NO, THEY CAN'T! THEY CAN'T EAT THEM!" Tyler yelled at the elf, who refused to move out of the way. Out of the corner of his eye, Tyler saw the spiders coming down the stairs with his mom, his dad, and Michael held tightly in their teeth. They were screaming, waving their arms and legs, trying desperately to get free of the spiders' clutches.

"YOU PUT THEM DOWN!" Tyler was now trying to push the elf out of the way; he had to help his family. The spider that was holding Tyler's dad dropped him on the ground, pinning him down with its two front legs so he couldn't move; the other spiders then did the same. All the while, Tyler was frantically trying to figure out how to help them.

"ROSHDA!" cried the elf.

The spiders opened their mouths wide and bent down towards their feast.

"NOOOOO!" Tyler screamed.

Just then, he felt a familiar hand on his shoulder and heard someone calling his name.

"Tyler! Tyler, wake up! It's just a dream, Tyler—wake up." Michael now had both his hands on Tyler's shoulders and was shaking him gently, trying to wake him up. It had been a nightmare; there was no elf, no spiders. Tyler pushed his covers off and jumped out of bed.

"The picture…I need to see if it's still there, just to make sure." Tyler was white and shaking all over.

"I'll check—you get back into bed," Michael insisted as he gave Tyler a light push so he would get back into bed without any argument. "Which picture?"

"The one of the castle on the end—you know, Mom's favorite."

Michael walked to the end of the hallway, where Mrs. Leeds's favorite picture hung as always, just as Michael knew it would be. He went back into the bedroom.

"The picture is fine, Tyler, I promise. They all are—I checked each one. It was only a dream; there is nothing to worry about. Besides, you know I wouldn't let anything happen to you—I'm your big brother," Michael said, puffing out his chest.

"Thanks, Mike."

Tyler was now determined to stay awake all night. He turned on his flashlight and grabbed a book to read. After what felt like hours, he saw a faint light coming from the window. The light looked as if it were coming from the tree branch just outside. Tyler set his book aside and walked slowly over to the window. He could feel his heart beginning to pound faster. He wasn't sure if he wanted to know what the light was; what if he just stayed in bed and ignored it? But he couldn't ignore it—he had to see what it was.

It's just a light. Don't be such a baby, it's just a light. It's not like a light can hurt you, Tyler told himself as he walked toward the window. He couldn't just ignore the light; he knew he would have to check it out. But what if the elf wasn't a dream? What if he was outside?

"I must be brave…I…I must be brave…" Tyler stammered to himself as he walked to the window. He took a deep breath, wiped the sweat from his forehead, and pulled back the curtains slowly, terrified the whole time of what he might see. He looked out: there was nothing. He let out a big sigh of relief.

"Man, do I need to calm down. It's all in my head. Boy, am I a wimp sometimes," Tyler said to himself as he stood in front of the window. He took one last look out of the window—only this time, the tree branch wasn't empty. There, right in front of him, close enough to touch, was a large man, just sitting there. Why was he there on the tree branch—was he a burglar? He didn't move or even try to run away.

Tyler didn't know what to do. He just stared out the window at the man, just in case he had imagined him there, but there he was, dressed in a long, hooded, black cloak that covered him from his head to his feet. Tyler looked for a face, but it was too dark, and the hood on his cloak seemed to be casting a dark shadow over where his face should be. The dark, hooded figure leaned slightly forward toward Tyler, who stood frozen. A curious part of him didn't want to move; he was somewhat intrigued by the dark figure—terrified but intrigued.

The man began to stand up very slowly. He was very tall, yet he never hit his head on any of the branches in the tree. Tyler was almost hypnotized by his terrifying presence. His heart was beating so hard and so loudly, he was sure the whole house could hear it thumping. He desperately wanted to shout to Michael, but when he opened his mouth to scream, nothing came out. He tried to turn and run, but his feet seemed to be glued to the floor. The dark figure held out his right hand—it looked like he was trying to reach Tyler through the glass. Tyler tried once more to call out to Michael, but again nothing came out; his heart was pounding so hard that at any moment it was going to come right through his chest. The figure on the branch reached out further; his hand began to come through the glass. The glass just seemed to melt away, at any moment the man's long, giant, ghastly hand would grab Tyler, and there would be nothing he could do. Tyler felt helpless, terrified—and curious, which frightened him just as much.

Tyler opened his mouth to make a final attempt to scream, but it was no use: the tiny noise that he did make was not loud enough for anyone to hear. Then he felt the man's strong, icy grip pulling hard on his arm. He tugged so hard that he pulled Tyler right out of the window, which melted away to let Tyler fall. He finally screamed, but it was too late—nobody could save him now. Any second now, he would hit the ground.

"Tyler, wake up, it's me," he heard Michael shout as he was shaking him to wake him up. Tyler sat up in bed, looked at Michael, and lay back down on his pillow.

"Michael, go look out the window, please." Tyler knew it had only been a dream, but he always had to check, just in case. Michael didn't mind; he had shared a room with Tyler long enough so that he almost wished that just once Tyler hadn't been dreaming, and there really was a monster or something.

Michael walked over to the window, not having the slightest idea what he was looking for. He pulled back the curtains and took a deep breath, just in case he did see something. All he could see was the tree in front of the window. He looked across the street at the rows of houses that were always there. The street was exactly the way it should be in the middle of the night: the houses were dark and quiet, filled with their sleeping families. The leaves on the trees blew peacefully in the gentle breeze that drenched the night; there was a blanket of dew covering the street. Michael looked into the back yard and still saw nothing unusual: their soccer nets that they hadn't put away, the neighbor's cat walking sleepily along the fence, and a few birds perched motionless in a tree, but that was it. Michael closed the curtains and turned around to look at Tyler.

"What did you see?" he asked Tyler, who knew from the look on his face Michael had seen nothing.

"Nothing. I'm sorry for waking you. Go back to sleep—it must have been a dream. I should have known," Tyler mumbled.

"You know, it's almost five o'clock already—how about some early-morning video games?" Michael suggested, knowing that if Tyler went back to sleep again, he would just have another nightmare.

Tyler was relieved; he didn't want to go back to sleep again either. They sat in front of their TV and played video games until it was time to get ready for school. It didn't seem to be too long before they heard their mom downstairs in the kitchen, making breakfast. They hurriedly got dressed and headed down the stairs to the kitchen.

"Did you have a good sleep? Nightmare free, I hope." Mrs. Leeds had a desperate look on her face; Tyler couldn't bear to let her down, so he lied.

"Yeah, nightmare free all night." Tyler looked at the floor as he lied to his mom; he knew she would know he was lying if she was looking right at him. The boys ate their breakfasts and left for school.

CHAPTER TWO

THE MYSTERIOUS BLUE

"Once you have finished the book you are reading, class, I expect a three-page book report with a title page," said Mrs. Lang said to Tyler's history class. Mrs. Lang was a tall, thin woman who looked about a hundred years old, with gray hair she wore in a tight bun on the top of her head and gold-rimmed glasses that sat on the end of her nose no matter how many times she pushed them up. She wore hand-knitted cardigans that she made herself, with long gray or black skirts that hung to her ankles, and dingy white blouses with ruffled collars, half-untucked and spattered with coffee stains. She always wore sensible shoes and very rarely wore a smile on her face, yet no matter how old or unhappy she looked, she was the most understanding teacher Tyler had had so far. She never judged him, and never got angry when he fell asleep in class. Mrs. Lang knew all about Tyler's nightmares and how little he slept, so when he did fall asleep, even if it was in her class, she just left him alone. She told him what he had missed after class. This helped Tyler's history grades but did nothing but hurt his problem with his classmates.

"I will assign you a book to read. When I call out your name, please come to the front of the class and collect your book," Mrs. Lang continued. "Conner," Mrs. Lang began. "Chris, Michelle, Devin." Mrs. Lang continued down the class list, but she hadn't noticed that Tyler was asleep at his desk. "Tyler...Tyler." She looked around the group of students who were still gathered in front of her desk. Then the entire class turned and stared at Tyler, who was not-so-peacefully sleeping.

"No—get off! No!" Tyler was shouting in his sleep.

Mrs. Lang walked quickly over to his desk and tapped him on the back. "Wake up, Tyler. Wake up," she said, desperately trying to wake him up before Conner Jakins and his gang made too much of a fuss.

Tyler jumped, opened his eyes, and was shocked to see Mrs. Lang standing over him. He saw the entire class staring and laughing at him; he was used to it by now—this wasn't the first time it had happened. Tyler rubbed his eyes and looked at Mrs. Lang.

"I'm sorry, Mrs. Lang, I didn't get much sleep last night. What were you saying?"

Tyler ignored all of the laughing and taunting. Mrs. Lang looked at Tyler sympathetically, smiled, and said, "It's your turn to come up and get your book for your book report."

Mrs. Lang returned to her desk, Tyler following behind her. As he walked past the other desks in the room, he could feel everyone's eyes staring at him. A group of girls were giggling in the corner; they pointed at Tyler and mouthed, "No...No...Get off me..." Conner and Chase were sitting in the middle row of the aisle down which Tyler was walking. As soon as Tyler got close, Conner stuck his foot out and tripped him. Tyler fell to the ground; the entire class started laughing as Chase shouted over everyone's noise, "NO...NO...GET OFF ME...MOMMY! HELP, MOMMY!"

"That will be enough, class, settle down. Class, settle down," Mrs. Lang shouted at her class. "Conner and Chase, go down to the principal's office; you can tell him your joke and see if he finds it funny."

Conner and Chase gave Tyler a look that he knew all too well to mean that he was going to pay for that.

"Now if we may continue with the rest of the class without any more interruptions...or will you all join Conner and Chase in detention?"

The rest of the morning went quite smoothly for Tyler. When it was lunchtime, he ate his lunch with Michael and his friend Brandon like he did every day, only today, instead of going to play soccer with them in the field after they had finished eating, he stayed behind at the bench. He didn't want Michael to know that Conner and Chase were going to be looking for him soon.

"Why aren't you coming to play soccer? Are you feeling okay?" Michael asked.

"I'm fine—I just have some work to do, that's all."

"Now I know you're lying; you never turn down soccer to do homework. Come on out..." But before he had the chance to finish his sentence, Conner and Chase turned up.

"I should have known you would have your big brother here to protect you. You really are a big baby," Conner taunted.

"Why don't you get your mommy as well?" Chase joined in.

Michael moved in between Tyler and Conner. "I'm not here to protect Tyler; we're going to play soccer, if you don't mind." Michael stared at Conner and Chase.

"So, big brother, are you going to fight his battle for him?" Conner asked as he pushed Michael. Michael didn't even have the chance to retaliate—Tyler pushed Conner so hard he fell to the ground. Tyler put his foot on Conner's chest so he couldn't move, while Michael moved in front of Chase so he wouldn't be able to interfere. Tyler looked down at Conner.

"I don't need my big brother or anyone else to protect me, but I do need you to get lost." Tyler moved his foot off of Conner's chest and stepped out of the way so he could walk past.

"This isn't over, Tyler—I will get you. You can dream about that if you like," Conner said as he and Chase walked away.

Michael turned to look at Tyler. Brandon just stood there, a little shocked

"Well, at least you know your karate class is paying off, right?" Brandon joked.

"What was all that about?" Michael finally asked.

"It was nothing, just Conner and Chase being jerks as usual," Tyler said, picking up his backpack and walking away.

Michael stood in front of him so he couldn't go any further. "It was nothing? They were looking for a fight! Why? What happened?"

Tyler sighed. "I fell asleep in Mrs. Lang's class. I must have had a dream or something, because when I woke up, Mrs. Lang was standing in front of me and the whole class was laughing at me, and, well, you know Conner and Chase—they took it too far. Mrs. Lang got mad at them and sent them to the principal's office. I don't know what happened from there, but it probably wasn't too good for them, and now, surprise, they're mad at me. Who cares, anyway—they have to bully someone, don't they?"

Michael shook his head. "Those two need to be taught a lesson. One of these days, we will get them back in a major way—you can count on that, Tyler." Michael yawned and sat back down at the table. "Okay, let's give soccer a miss today. I'm a little tired, anyway," he said through another yawn.

After lunch was over, they headed back to their classes for the rest of the afternoon. Tyler did his best to stay awake in class, especially in the classes he had with Conner and Chase. The afternoon went fairly quickly and before long, the day's final bell rang. Everyone went to their lockers except Conner and Chase, who went to the office for their detention. Tyler grabbed his bag and went to find Michael and Brandon

"I can't take it anymore—I need to sleep. At soccer today, I fell asleep on the field. It might not have been so bad, but I used the ball as my pillow," Michael told Brandon as they walked home from school together.

"Well, you could always get some earplugs, or a cork for Tyler," laughed Brandon.

"Somehow I don't think my mom and dad would like that too much. Don't forget, we're going to the library later."

"Oh, yeah, homework," replied Brandon.

"Hey, why didn't you wait for me?" Tyler asked, running up to them quite out of breath.

Michael looked at Brandon in hopes that he would have a good excuse, but he didn't. "I'm sorry, Tyler, I just forgot. I'm a little tired."

Tyler looked away; he knew Michael didn't sleep very well because he kept him awake. "Sorry, Michael…I, uh…I…"

"Hey, it wasn't you—I just couldn't get comfy," Michael lied.

"Hi, boys, how was your day? Don't forget, we're going shopping after supper," Mrs. Leeds said as Michael and Tyler walked through the front door.

"Mom, I told Brandon I would go to the library with him tonight," Michael said.

"That's okay—we can go shopping early, right after supper. It won't take too long, and then I'll take you and Brandon to the library."

"Okay," Michael groaned, a little disappointed that he would still have to go shopping.

Mrs. Leeds, Michael, and Tyler cleaned the table after supper and off they went.

"I thought we could try this little shop. Someone at work told me she went there and found some really great stuff."

"Whatever, Mom, shopping is shopping. Let's just get it done."

Mrs. Leeds smiled and parked the car. They walked down the street and stopped outside a little shop called "The Mysterious Blue."

"This is it! What do you think?"

Michael and Tyler glanced at each other and sighed; neither of them were too thrilled at the sight of the shop. The outside looked like an old house that had been deserted for years. Most of the windows were cracked, those that were not were so dirty you couldn't see through them. The roof needed to be replaced; there were shingles missing all over. The chimney was missing so many bricks, it looked like it wouldn't make it through another windy day. Yet there was just something about the Mysterious Blue that made you want to go inside. The front door was red, and unlike the rest of the exterior, it looked like new, with a big wrought iron handle and a star-shaped doorknocker.

Michael looked around at the gardens surrounding the shop. There were no flowers in the garden, or grass—just some overgrown weeds bursting through the concrete. In the garden were a few clay statues of strange-looking creatures with eyes that seemed to be glaring at the front door.

Tyler looked at a large statue that stood almost seven feet tall; it looked to be guarding the entrance to the shop. Tyler froze with fear. He had seen that statue before, only when he saw it, it wasn't a statue—it was a man, and he was standing on a branch in the tree outside Tyler's window. Tyler was about to walk over to it for a closer look when Mrs. Leeds spoke.

"I don't think a garden statue would make a good birthday present. She doesn't have a garden; she lives in an apartment. And besides, that thing's huge—not to mention ugly."

The large statue's shadowy face seemed to alter its expression. It now looked angry, or insulted, as if it had actually heard Mrs. Leeds's comment. But it was just a statue—how could it? It seemed as though Tyler was the only one who had noticed. Tyler stared at Mrs. Leeds as if seeing her for the first time.

"You okay, Ty?" she asked, concerned.

"What? Uh, I…yep, I'm, uh…"

"Okay, let's get going. I don't have all night," Mike jumped in quickly.

Mrs. Leeds followed Tyler and Michael as they stepped up to the front door.

"It all seems a little strange, Mom, don't you think?" Michael said, taking another look at the shabby, rundown-looking garden. "I mean, really, this place looks like a dump. I can't see you finding anything nice here."

Mrs. Leeds just smiled. "Don't be so quick to judge, Michael; things are not always what they seem. It's what's on the inside that counts," she said as she gave an urging nod to Tyler to open the door.

Tyler rubbed his hand over the star-shaped doorknocker; a chill ran through his body. He shivered, now filled with curiosity that seemed to be pulling him into the shop, yet fear was holding him back. He had no idea why; after all, it was just a shop. Tyler opened the front door and stepped inside.

Michael's mouth dropped open with amazement. He couldn't believe how right his mom had been. The outside was nothing like the inside of the shop; it was as if they were standing in a different shop completely. All of the walls were painted an awesome fire red that soaked you in a warm and cozy feeling. There was a magnificent gold molding running around the floor and ceiling. Lining the walls were mesmerizing pictures of brilliant castles and families dressed like royalty from at least a hundred years ago.

Tyler noticed that one of the pictures looked familiar. "Hey, Mike, isn't that the same as Mom's picture?"

Michael took a quick glance at the picture. "No, I don't think so," he said as he continued to stare around the room.

Tyler took another look at the picture "You're right, this window up here looks like you can see in the castle…into a hallway, I think…I can't really tell, although it…"

"Since when did you become so interested in lousy old pictures?" Michael teased.

"I'm not, I was just looking," Tyler said defensively as his face turned red.

"I'm just bugging you, Ty. Let's go look around."

The shop smelled old and damp, yet was surprisingly warm. On the far wall was a large, beautiful fireplace with a cast-iron guard in front of it shaped like a castle with two rounded towers, one on either end. The mantelpiece was also large, and was covered with old photographs in black and white of very distinguished-looking people. The floors were a dark wood that creaked as you walked. All around the room was old-fashioned furniture that showed its wear: chairs in which you could imagine many people had sat, a desk at which someone had so obviously worked, dining tables that had been hosts to many a meal. The shop had three levels; each one was filled with shelves towering all the way to the ceiling, oversized wardrobes with large doors covered with paintings of children, bookshelves filled with old, dusty books with titles neither Tyler nor Michael had ever heard of. There were smaller shelves in rows, which were cluttered with what looked like junk to Michael and Tyler. It was all very old and dusty; none of it looked like anything they would want for their birthdays. There were vases, lamps, jewelry boxes, and fancy bowls. They walked up to the winding staircase to look around the top level. It smelled just like the first. It wasn't very well-lit upstairs, so Tyler stuck close to Michael.

"Don't go too far, you two," said Mrs. Leeds from the bottom of the stairs.

"We won't leave the shop," Tyler replied. He walked around a shelf toward Michael, but something caught his eye on another shelf. He walked slowly toward a star that looked out of place in the shop. Everything else in the shop was old, yet the star at which Tyler was looking appeared new—there was no dust or dirt on it at all.

"Hmmm, why are you here, I wonder? You don't seem to belong here," Tyler whispered to himself. As he held it in both hands, the star became warm and started to get brighter. The star was only small; Tyler held it tight in his hands, trying to hide the light, but when he opened his hands again, the light was still there. Tyler quickly put the star back down on the shelf. As soon as he took his hands off of it, the light faded as quickly as it had appeared. Tyler looked over his shoulders, then picked it up again in both hands. Just as before, the star became warm and started to light up. Tyler returned the star to the shelf a second time and walked away to find Michael, but after two steps, he turned back and picked up the star again. Once more, like magic, the star began to light up. Tyler studied the star, but there was no light bulb, no on-off switch—nothing. He put the star on the shelf again and watched the light drift away. Tyler looked around to see if he could find Michael.

"Michael! Pssst…Mike, where are you?" Tyler whispered. When he finally saw Michael at the other end of the shop, he shouted, "Hey, Mike, come look at this!"

Michael jumped, almost dropping the glass jar he was holding. "This place is creepy, don't you think? I mean, it feels like we're being watched, and not in that 'I think you're stealing' kind of way, either. It's more like a…uh, I don't know, like weird creepy, you know what I mean?"

Tyler was just about to agree when they saw their mom coming up the stairs.

"Don't touch anything, boys—it all looks very expensive and very old. You wouldn't want to break anything," their mom whispered.

"You should not be so quick to judge," said a voice from behind the shelf. "More often than not, things are not what they seem, especially in this shop. Be careful what you see, and for that matter, be careful what sees you."

Michael quickly looked behind the shelf. "There's nobody there! I mean, they're gone…uh, I…uh, I think they're gone." Michael looked at Tyler, who was staring at the star.

"I'm sure it was the shop owner. Well, let's hurry up and pick something so we can get you to the library," said Mrs. Leeds as she looked around quickly for the first thing she could buy for her friend. Michael and Tyler, who had picked up the star, followed their mom back down the stairs. Across the room, they spotted another spiral staircase. As they walked toward it, they noticed a draft coming from the bottom. Michael had begun to walk down the stairs when he heard his mom say to Tyler, "What is that in your hand? I thought I asked you not to touch."

Tyler held tightly to the star; he was very intrigued by it. "Mom, could we have this star for our room? It's really cool. Please, Mom, please?" Tyler begged.

"I don't think so, Tyler. It's probably expensive," said Mrs. Leeds as she took the star from Tyler and placed it on the shelf at the top of the stairs.

They all walked down the spiral staircase. An icy chill came over Michael and Tyler. They looked at each other to see if they had both felt it; a slight nod at each other assured them that they both had. The bottom floor was especially creepy. There were cobwebs all over the ceiling and shelves, and both Michael and Tyler had that same feeling that someone was watching them as they looked around. Tyler could not stop thinking about the star; for some reason, he knew he just had to have it. He tried asking his mom again.

"Mom, please, could we have that star? It will look really great in our room. I could do extra chores, dishes every night, anything."

"I don't know, Tyler. There's no price tag. I don't know how much it is; we'll have to ask. I'm going to look over there. You boys stay together, and don't touch anything." Michael and Tyler nodded to their mom, who smiled and walked away.

"I don't think it will be too expensive," Tyler grumbled.

"Are you kidding? Look at all the stuff in here—it's all expensive. I bet it's..." Michael began, but before he could finish his sentence, the voice returned from behind a shelf.

"Destiny has no price tag. When one is meant to have something, no amount of money will stop him from having it—especially when one has wandered into the Mysterious Blue just in time. We have been waiting for the two of you for a while now. We were beginning to think you wouldn't be coming."

"What do mean, 'waiting for us'? We are just here shopping—are you talking to us?" Michael asked as he looked to see who, in fact, he was asking. Once again, Michael quickly went to the other side of the shelf to see who was there, but once again, there was nobody. The star that Tyler wanted so desperately was sitting on the shelf. "I thought Mom put that star on the shelf upstairs. Did you bring it down, Tyler?" But before Tyler could answer, they heard a voice again.

"Hello, boys—I have been waiting for you two. I see you found your destiny, Tyler," said a little old lady. She was shorter than Tyler, with long, wavy, silver hair down past her waist. She smiled at Michael and Tyler with a warm, loving smile that sent a feeling of comfort through Tyler.

"We are just looking, thank you," Michael said as he pulled on Tyler's arm and quickly went back upstairs to meet Mrs. Leeds, who was placing a small jewelry box on the counter.

"This will be it, thank you," she said.

"But Mom, please, the star," begged Tyler once more.

"Okay, okay—and the star."

"Thanks, Mom," Tyler whispered.

"The boys were meant to have that star—you'll see," said the lady.

"I'll go get it," Tyler suggested. But to everyone's surprise, the lady had it in her hand. She put it in a bag and handed it to Tyler, giving another bag with the gift in it to Mrs. Leeds, and they left the Mysterious Blue.

"That was a neat shop, wasn't it, boys?" Mrs. Leeds asked as they left the shop and headed back to the car. "Weird, different, and maybe a little creepy, but neat."

Michael and Tyler just looked at each other; they were still puzzled by what the old lady had said. Was she talking to them? Neither of them had seen anyone else in the shop—but what did she mean?

"So, what do you think all that was about?" Michael asked as he watched Tyler examining the star as if he expected it to jump up and down or sing a song or something.

"She was just a lonely old lady; she probably tells stories to everybody that comes into the shop. I wouldn't worry about it," Tyler lied in a voice that sounded unlike his own.

"So what do you need to do at the library?" Mrs. Leeds asked, unknowingly interrupting a conversation Michael and Tyler didn't really want to have in the car where their mom could hear anyway.

"We're doing a science project on the solar system."

"Maybe you could use that star Tyler had to have. It would make a good model for your project," said Mrs. Leeds.

Tyler looked up at Michael and whispered, "I think it's the star that wanted me."

When they pulled up to the library, Brandon was waiting outside. Mrs. Leeds parked the car and they all went inside.

"How was shopping?" Brandon asked with a smile.

Michael looked around to make sure his mom wasn't close enough to hear. "I'm not sure. Have you ever been to a little shop called 'Mysterious Blue'?"

"Never heard of it," replied Brandon.

"Well, that's one weird shop—trust me, you're not missing anything." Michael told Brandon all about the strange voice from behind the shelf, and about the little old lady. "I know it sounds strange and unreal, but I swear it was as though that lady had known us forever. She seemed so familiar to me, but we have never met—trust me, I would remember meeting someone that strange. Not to mention Tyler was acting really weird in the store, and not just little brother kind of weird either—this was weird-weird. I can't remember the last time he begged my mom to buy him something from the store. It was as if he could not leave without that star."

"How's the book-hunting coming, boys?" Mrs. Leeds asked, surprising the boys.

"Uh...it's...uh, fine, Mom, thanks."

"Okay. Well, I would like to leave as soon as you have all you need, okay?"

"Okay, Mom, we're almost done." Michael and Brandon quickly picked out a handful of books each, checking only that they were on the solar system.

"Did you find any good books?" Mrs. Leeds asked Tyler when they found him curled up in a large armchair with a book, but he didn't answer. At first it just seemed that he was so involved in his book that he didn't hear her—that is, until Michael put his hand on Tyler's shoulder.

"Hey, bookworm," he joked.

Tyler jumped out of the chair, dropping his book and knocking Michael to the ground. Everyone just stared at Tyler.

"Uh...uh, sorry, I was dreaming. I think I must have fallen asleep."

Brandon laughed, until Tyler shoved him.

"Okay, boys, how about we get going?" Mrs. Leeds said, stepping between Tyler and Brandon to avoid a fight.

They all left the library. Mrs. Leeds dropped Brandon off first, then they went home. Tyler and Michael ran upstairs to their room, and as soon as they walked in, Michael closed the door behind them, after checking to make sure their mom hadn't followed them.

"Okay, spill it—what is with the star? Why did you want it so bad? You're not starting a new collection of old lady knickknacks, are you?"

Tyler was stumped. "I don't know, to be honest—I just like it, I guess."

Michael, unconvinced, just stared at him.

Mrs. Leeds walked into the room. "Boys, you should think about going to bed soon. It's getting late."

Tyler's stomach did a flip—the same flip it usually did when he was told it was bedtime. Michael kissed his mom on the cheek and went to brush his teeth. Tyler, on the other hand, was not so willing. He began with the excuse that he was hungry, and then he was thirsty...all the usual excuses. He really did not want to go to bed; he knew that as soon as he went to sleep, he would have terrible nightmares.

CHAPTER THREE

A PAINFUL, FIERY DEATH

Finally, when his mom would accept no more excuses, Tyler went to his room, crawled into his bed, and closed his eyes. He lay awake for what felt like hours, staring at the bottom of Michael's bunk. His eyes were getting heavy, his mind full of nothing, his body numb…finally his eyes fell shut.

Tyler felt a warm, gentle breeze over his face. He jerked his eyes open, finding himself in a large, open field. Jumping to his feet, Tyler looked around, trying to figure out were he was. The grass was greener than he had ever seen, like a green blanket, covering for miles. There were no flowers, trees, birds, bugs, or anything, yet even though it was so empty, everything seemed so perfect. The breeze suddenly died; it was neither hot nor cold, and silence drenched the field.

"Where am I?" Tyler said to himself. "Hello? Is anyone here? Something is wrong, I can feel it." Tyler suddenly felt helpless, scared, and alone; he had no idea why he was there, or how he got there. I must be dreaming, he thought, pinching his arm to try to wake himself up. Nothing happened, so he did it again, harder—still nothing.

"I don't get it. Where am I?" He turned around, then around again. "Grass, nothing but grass," Tyler grumbled. "Wait, what's that?"

Far off in the distance was a tiny speck of white against the almost navy blue sky. The white speck got closer and closer, all the while growing bigger…then it vanished, just like that—gone. Tyler frantically yet unsuccessfully searched the sky. He took a few steps, and suddenly, from out of nowhere, an enormous dragon swooshed down toward him letting out a piercing roar, so loud that Tyler couldn't help but cover his ears, ducking just in time, and the dragon flew out of sight. Tyler's eyes frantically searched the sky. Far away in the distance, there was a glimpse of what seemed to be the dragon, returning getting closer and closer. The creature really was exquisite, Tyler couldn't help but be somewhat hypnotized by the dragon, it was deadly beautiful like nothing Tyler had ever seen. Tyler had seen dragons in books and movies before but this was different, he was terrified, he wanted to run he knew he it was dangerous this was a dragon, a real life fire-breathing dragon. The dragon's enormous tail was swishing back and forth; the great white dragon opened its gigantic mouth, baring its long sharp dagger like teeth. Tyler was shaking with fear, panic-stricken looking around for a stick or something, anything to give him a chance to save himself, but there was nothing This was it; there was no way for him to protect himself. It was hopeless; there was nothing around him but grass. The dragon was now so close, Tyler's nose burned with the hot smell of smoke. It was getting harder to breathe. Tyler gasped, and looked deep into the dragon's mouth; he could see the flames igniting at the back of its throat. He knew that, any second now, that would be his painful, fiery death. The flames erupted into a great fireball. Tyler was drenched in a thick, black smoke, unable to see anything, coughing and waving his hands to try to break through the smoke. Tyler stumbled as he felt his body getting hotter and hotter. His skin felt like it was just going to melt right off. He was so hot, his entire body was dripping with sweat. He couldn't bear it any longer. He screamed as his body slumped to the floor; the pain was excruciating. Exhausted, he closed his eyes and...

"Tyler...Tyler, are you asleep already?" Michael asked.

Tyler jumped up, his body shaking, his heart pounding. "The dragon—what happened to the dragon?" Tyler asked, not really knowing whom he was asking or if they even heard him. He was dizzy and disoriented. Tyler fell back down in his bed.

"You were just dreaming, Tyler—there was no dragon. Are you okay?"

"I'm fine," Tyler lied.

"Tyler, how did she know your name?" Michael questioned. "Why would they hide behind the shelf? Who were they hiding from? Not us, surely—why would anyone need to hide from us? All I know is that the old lady seemed to think that we were really important for some reason, and that that star may be more important than you think."

"Why would you think the star is important? It's just a star," Tyler said, none too convincingly.

"Wait—if it's just a star, then why did you have to have it, and why did the old lady want you to have it so bad?"

"Like Mom said, she was probably lonely. I bet she tells that story to everyone that goes into the store," Tyler lied.

"Sure. Well, I don't agree with you, but whatever." Michael yawned, rolled over, and went back to sleep. It wasn't long before Tyler was asleep again as well.

"HELP...HELP..." Tyler heard screaming coming from downstairs. Instantly, he jumped out of bed and looked in the top bunk for Michael, but it was empty.

"HELP...TYLER, HELP ME." It was Michael. Tyler ran downstairs, his heart pounding so hard his chest hurt—what would he find? He paused on the bottom step, took a deep breath, and quietly walked into the living room. There in the middle of the room was a man wearing a long, black, hooded cloak. He was facing the fireplace, where there was a small fire burning.

"Who are you?" Tyler asked, looking around the room to see if anyone else was there. Tyler couldn't see Michael anywhere. "Michael! Michael, can you hear me?" Tyler shouted.

"He can't hear you, Tyler. Only you can hear him."

"Who are you, why are you here, and what do you want?" Tyler demanded.

"I want you to come with me, Tyler" the man stated.

"Why would I come with you?"

"You still don't know, do you? The way they all have been talking about you, I expected more. I have to say, Tyler, I am disappointed in you." The man's words burned Tyler.

"What are you talking about?" Tyler snapped.

The man now seemed irritated. "You are powerful, Tyler, or at least you will be if you come with me. Your powers are inside you; I will teach you how to reach them. Tyler, trust me."

Tyler stared at the man in the cloak. "Powerful? Me? What are you talking about? I am not powerful! You're wrong—you have to be."

The man in the cloak turned slowly. "How dare you? I am never wrong," the man bellowed. "My name is Candor; I am a great Nyt lord. I was sent here to find you, with orders to take you to the King of Darkness."

"Why? What does the King of Darkness want with me? And where is Michael? If it's me that he wants, why did you take Michael? Why didn't you just come and take me?" Tyler asked.

"It is not that simple—our people cannot just come into your world and take Lyts," Candor said. His voice had a powerful tone that sent a shiver down Tyler's spine.

"What do you mean, 'my world'? What world are you from? And what powers do you think I have?" Tyler asked, unsure if he really wanted to know the answer. There was a long silence. Tyler looked around the room again for some kind of sign as to where Michael could possibly be.

Finally, Candor looked at Tyler. "I am from the World of Darkness—a world where all your worst fears are reality, a world where nobody is safe. That's why I am here to have you join the dark army: so you can be safe, forever."

Tyler stared at Candor. "Why me? And what do you mean, 'safe forever'? Safe from what? What army could I possibly join?"

"No more questions," Candor spat.

"I want to see my brother. Where is he? I want to see him."

"You will," Candor insisted.

"I want to see my brother now," Tyler yelled.

"You will see your brother when I say it is time. You need to get your things together—we are leaving." Candor stepped closer to Tyler; he was a very large man, about seven feet tall. Tyler was frightened yet intrigued, but he knew he couldn't leave his brother.

"No," Tyler spat at Candor. "I am not going anywhere without my brother. Now where is he?"

Candor was now furious. "Nobody disobeys me without feeling the consequences." Candor raised his left hand; in it was a black circle on a chain. Candor began to say words that Tyler didn't understand.

"Node lays Sloane…Node lays Sloane."

Tyler felt his whole body fall to the ground. He was overcome with excruciating pain all over his body, as if there was a ton of bricks on top of him. The room began to spin. Tyler felt very hot, so hot his blood could have boiled. All of a sudden, he began to fall. There was no end to the fall; he just kept falling and falling. There was nothing around him. Everything was black; he was still in so much pain that he just wanted to hit the ground, or anything, just to stop falling.

With a jolt, Tyler sat up and opened his eyes. Panic fell over his entire body. Where was he? He felt as though he was somewhere familiar. A cool breeze blew over him; he looked around and realized that he was in his back yard. How did he get there? Was it all just another nightmare, or was this real? Tyler stood up, walked back toward the house, and stopped. He had the feeling that someone was watching him, but when he looked around, there was nobody anywhere in sight. Everything was still and quiet; the sky was blacker than ever, and covered with a blanket of millions of stars. One star in particular seemed so bright and so close, as if he could have reached out his hand and grabbed it from the sky.

What is wrong with me? All I want is to sleep without a single nightmare, just one night, Tyler thought to himself as he stood on the doorstep looking up at the sky.

Tyler opened the door and went inside. He went straight into the living room; there was no fire in the fireplace, so he turned to go upstairs to bed. Out of the corner of his eye, he noticed the chair was facing the fireplace, which it usually didn't.

"Hello," he whispered, frozen on the step, hoping nobody would answer. Nobody did, so he continued up the stairs. Halfway up, something was telling him to go back; he needed to see for himself that the chair was empty. He took a deep breath, turned around, and very slowly walked downstairs. Tyler still had that strange feeling of somebody watching him. His heart began to beat faster and faster again as he slowly went back toward the chair. He took a deep breath; his chest was throbbing from his pounding heart and the deep breath felt like it would choke him. He put his hand on the back of the chair and quickly turned it around. Tyler took a step back. He felt all the blood drain from his face; there on the chair was the star, glowing extremely brightly.

"What is this doing here? It was in my bedroom—this is silly, that star being on the chair doesn't mean anything, and maybe Dad was looking at it and left it on the chair."

Tyler ran quietly upstairs into his room and looked on the top bunk; he almost fell off when he saw that Michael wasn't there.

"It wasn't a dream; he was gone—really gone."

Now he was panicked; where could Candor have taken Michael, and why? What could the King of Darkness possibly want with him? He was just a regular kid—well, except the nightmares.

"What am I going to do? How am going to find Michael? Where do I look?"

Tyler felt sick. He had no idea what to do, and he didn't think his parents would believe him. And why should they? He hardly believed it himself. Scared and confused, he turned and ran to the stairs, but he tripped on the rug and began to fall—but not once did he feel the stairs as he was falling.

All of a sudden, Tyler sat up; he was in bed. "It was a dream," he said again. He took a deep breath, slid out of bed, and stood on the edge of his bed so he could see into Michael's, and there he was, still asleep. Tyler sighed with relief and got back into bed.

"It was all a dream. I knew it," Tyler said to himself, looking at the clock. It was 7:00 a.m., so he lay awake until Michael woke up, going over his dream in his head. Could it have meant something? Was it more than a dream? Tyler now found himself questioning all of his dreams. Were they more than just nightmares? Could they be messages or something?

"Another world…is it possible? Could there really be other worlds?" Tyler said to himself.

"How was your sleep?" Michael asked Tyler as he climbed down the ladder from his bed.

"Um, fine," Tyler lied. He didn't want to tell Michael about his dream, or about Candor; he didn't want to risk any chance of his mom hearing. It was a good thing he waited, because moments later, their mom came up the stairs.

"Good morning, boys. How was your sleep?"

Tyler lied once again as he looked at the ground, forced a smile, and said, "Fine."

"We're almost ready, Mom. We'll be right down," Michael said, breaking the uncomfortable silence. They got dressed and headed downstairs for breakfast.

"I'll race you," said Michael at the top of the stairs, and they ran down the stairs, through the living room, and into the kitchen, and sat down. Mrs. Leeds gave them each a plateful of pancakes.

"So, what are you boys going to do today?" she asked.

"We're going to the park to play soccer with some friends," Michael said quickly.

Tyler looked curiously at Michael. He didn't know anything about playing soccer at the park, but from the kick under the table from Michael he knew to go along with it.

"Yep, soccer," Tyler agreed.

"Okay, but I'm going to Auntie Karen's house after work for a little while, if anyone wants to come with me."

"No, thanks," Michael replied quickly so Tyler didn't have a chance to say anything. "Say hi to Auntie Karen for us, though."

Mrs. Leeds looked suspiciously at them. "You're not up to anything you shouldn't be, are you?" she asked them.

"No," they both said at the same time.

"Fine, I will trust you—just make sure you stay together. I don't want you to leave Tyler by himself, Michael."

"You should know me better than that, Mom."

Michael and Tyler ate their breakfasts quickly, put their dishes in the sink, grabbed their soccer gear, gave their mom a kiss goodbye, and ran out the door. They both had so much to tell each other. Tyler wanted to tell Michael all about last night's dream; it had just felt different compared to his usual nightmares. He had the distinct feeling that it was more than just a dream, but he didn't know why. But before Tyler even had the chance to say anything, Michael began to question Tyler about the star again.

"So, are you going to be honest with me now and tell me what you think about that star? I know you know more—or feel more—than you're saying, don't you? It's not just a star, is it? You wouldn't have made such a big deal about Mom buying it for you. No, there is definitely something… And what do think that woman meant about how important we are and our destiny and all that? How did she know your name? Come on, Tyler, talk to me, I—"

"Michael, give me a chance to answer, will you? Yeah, I think there is more to the star."

"Then why didn't you say so last night when I asked you?"

"I don't know; I just felt like it wasn't the right time to. Anyway, I had a dream last night…"

Michael turned away. "You don't have to talk about it if you don't want to."

"No, it's important. Well, at least I think might be."

Tyler didn't know whether Michael would find it important or not, but he did. Tyler told Michael all about his dream, and how real it had sounded when he heard Michael's voice coming from downstairs, and how terrified he had felt when he looked in the top bunk and Michael wasn't there. Tyler could tell from the look of fear and curiosity on Michael's face that he was taking him seriously, so he continued.

"It felt so real. I have never had a dream so real. It means something, I'm sure of it; there is no way it was just a dream. No way."

Michael was shocked; it took him a few minutes before he said a word.

"I don't really know what to say, Tyler. Do you think your dream has anything to do with the star?" Michael questioned.

"The star was on the chair when I went back downstairs to check."

"To check what?" Michael asked.

"To check if it was a dream or not. You know, to see if Candor was sitting in the chair."

Michael was concerned by Tyler's dream. It did sound like it could have been real, but it was strange. Really…another world, great lords of the night, the King of Darkness? It all seemed so surreal.

"So are you going to tell me where we're going?" Tyler asked as they turned the corner.

Michael had to tell Tyler, even though he knew Tyler wouldn't like it.

"Okay, but you have to promise not to freak out."

To Michael's relief, Brandon came walking toward them. "Hey, what's up, guys?" he said as he shoved the last piece of Pop-Tart into his mouth. Brandon was quite short for his age and rather chubby. He had dirty blonde hair that always looked messy, and wore glasses that were often broken and clothes that were always too big. Brandon was a good friend to Michael. He never minded Tyler hanging around; he knew how close Michael and Tyler were, and he knew all about Tyler's nightmares. Brandon never questioned why he had to go to the Leedses' house for sleepovers and Michael never came to his house. Fortunately, Brandon was a very heavy sleeper and was never awoken when Tyler woke up from a nightmare.

"Hey, Brandon—Michael was just about to tell me where we are going today."

"Perfect," Brandon said happily. "I'm in the mood for an adventure!"

"Shopping," Michael stated, trying to sound innocent.

"Shopping? You want to go shopping? For what?" Tyler asked, disappointed and annoyed.

"Why do you want to go shopping?" Brandon moaned.

Michael had a thrilled look on his face. "The question is not why I want to go shopping—it's where."

"Okay, so where do you want to go shopping?"

From the look on Tyler's face, he had figured it out. Brandon, on the other hand, had no idea, and Tyler didn't say anything. He was waiting for Michael to answer.

Michael looked at Tyler and said, "The Mysterious Blue."

"Why do you want to go there?" Brandon moaned once again.

"Old dump? How do you know if it's an old dump or not? You said you had never been!" Tyler snapped. He felt the need to defend the Mysterious Blue.

"Sorry, I didn't mean anything. I just…I'm sorry."

Tyler ignored Brandon's apology. "I want to go back to the store without Mom there; I want to try and talk to that old lady again, to see if she can tell us what she meant yesterday. I also want to ask her about the star. She might know something about it—something that could help us."

Michael was right: Tyler did freak out.

"Are you mad?" Tyler yelled at Michael. Brandon, who was digging in his backpack, was startled; he dropped his chocolate milk, spilling it all over the ground.

"What do you think Mom will say if she finds out we went back to that shop? And what do you think that lady is going to say—that the star is a magical portal to another world or something? I'm not going."

Michael knew they had to go back to that shop. He knew they needed answers, and the Mysterious Blue seemed like the most obvious place to get them—especially when that's where it all started in the first place.

"Michael does have a good point, Tyler. Besides, your mom won't find out unless you tell her."

"That's right. I know that star is special; we just have to find out why, and why you had to have it."

Brandon saw the unsure look on Tyler's face. "What will it hurt, Ty? Let's say we go there and find out nothing—the star is just an ornament, and the lady is just a lonely, crazy old lady. Then what? You haven't lost anything."

Michael and Tyler both stared at Brandon, amazed and stunned at what he had just said.

"Wow, Brandon, that was so unlike you," Michael teased. "You're right—there is nothing to lose."

Brandon pulled out a notebook and a pen. "Can you write that down for me? The part where you said that I'm right?"

Tyler shook his head.

"Don't you think you should have brought the star with you?" Brandon asked. "What if the lady isn't there? Or what if she doesn't remember you?" That was more like the sort of thing that Brandon usually said.

"Haven't you been listening to me at all?" Michael spat at Brandon. "I don't think that she sold very many people their destiny."

"You're right. Sorry," Brandon said quietly.

The three boys headed toward the bus stop. They hadn't been there long before the bus arrived.

"Do you at least know which stop to get off at?" Tyler asked Michael.

"I, um…well, I think so," he replied.

CHAPTER FOUR

BACK TO THE BLUE

The bus was almost full when the three of them walked on. Brandon sat next to a man in a business suit. The man was carrying a briefcase and staring intently at a folder he was holding in his hand labeled "Month End". Brandon tried to read the file over his shoulder until the man turned around and shot Brandon a look that meant, *Mind your own business*.

Tyler was sitting next to a lady who seemed quite strange; she was wearing a very large knitted sweater that, being at least two sizes too big, looked as though it wasn't hers. She had big black boots on that also seemed too big. Her skirt was brown and held up by a rope belt. Her hair was long and scraggly. The lady was muttering to herself while she stared out the window. Tyler tried hard to listen to what she was saying without leaning too close; she had a distinct smell of damp old newspaper and cats that made Tyler's nose curl.

"Sleep…must get sleep…just one hour…sleep…must get sleep…just one hour…sleep…" the lady muttered to herself over and over again.

Tyler was alarmed at first, but then he felt somewhat relieved to know that someone else was having sleep problems also. It was as if he wasn't alone anymore; just knowing that there was at least one other person that couldn't sleep well kind of gave him a sense of comfort. Tyler debated whether he should say something to the lady or not. He could ask her why she didn't sleep; maybe she would have some different ideas to help him sleep. But it was too late— just as Tyler had gotten up the nerve to talk to the lady, Michael shouted, "Come on, guys, this is our stop. Let's go."

Tyler looked at the lady; it was too late, he had missed his chance. But the lady grabbed his arm, pulled him closer to her, and whispered in his ear: "Follow your destiny, so we all can sleep."

Tyler, who was holding his nose from the smell of her breath, stared at her. "What do you mean? How do you know...what do you know?"

Tyler felt a tug on his other arm. "Come on, we're going to miss our stop. Let's go," Michael insisted as he pulled Tyler off the bus.

Tyler stared at the lady as he was being dragged off the bus.

"That lady knew something," Tyler said, staring at the bus as it pulled away.

"What?"

"I don't know what...she just knew something." But it was too late now; she was gone.

They walked around the corner and down the street to the front gate outside the Mysterious Blue. The boys didn't say a word; they stood outside the gate and stared at the shop. Finally Michael grabbed the gate, turned around to Tyler, and said, "Are you ready for some answers?"

"I think so." Tyler looked at Brandon, who looked as though he might throw up. "You all right?"

"Maybe I should wait outside—you know, to keep watch, just in case."

"Keep watch for what, exactly? It's not like we're doing anything wrong," Michael said as he slowly pushed the gate open for them to enter the garden and proceed to the front door.

"I just mean to watch for...um... Okay, let's go," Brandon sputtered. He was not sure what the boys were hoping to find. He wasn't sure if he wanted to find anything, but he did know he would have to go with them—they would never leave him outside.

Michael looked at Brandon, knowing why he wanted to stay outside. "There's nothing to worry about, I'm sure. Besides, you said yourself that Tyler's karate classes were paying off." Michael smiled at Tyler, who shook his head and put his hand on Brandon's shoulder.

"Don't worry—I'll protect you from the little old lady in the shop."

They all laughed, including Brandon. Michael went through the gate first, followed by Brandon. Tyler paused for a minute, took a deep breath, looked at the familiar statue, and said quietly to himself, "Let's find our destiny." He followed Michael and Brandon down the path to the front door.

Tyler stared once again at the big red door with the star doorknocker on it. He moved in front of Michael and Brandon and rubbed his hand over the star. Michael and Brandon didn't say anything; they just watched as Tyler stared at the door and the star as if he were the only one there. Tyler put his hand on the doorknocker; once again, the same feeling as before sent a shiver down his spine, as if someone had walked over his grave. Tyler reached for the handle and turned it—a vision of Candor standing in front of the fireplace in his living room, the dragon, the elf, then the star, all rushed through his head in one pounding, painful vision. Tyler stumbled backward.

"What's wrong?" Michael asked.

Tyler shook his head. The pain left as quickly as it had come. "Nothing...I'm fine. Let's go."

Tyler opened the door and they all went inside. The door slammed itself shut behind them. They all spun around, looking at the door, then looking at each other without saying a word.

"Wow, this is exactly how you described it. It's really cool." Brandon's mouth hung open with amazement.

"Let's make sure we all stay together, okay? No wandering off," Michael said to them both, but mostly meaning Tyler; he wasn't worried about Brandon moving more than an inch away from his side. As they walked through the shop, they looked at all the familiar-looking things that they had seen the last time they were there.

"Hello…is anyone here?" Michael called as they headed for the spiral staircase to go downstairs.

There was a familiar draft coming from the basement. Tyler shivered and looked desperately downstairs. He wasn't sure why he felt so desperate to find answers; he just felt like time was running out.

Out of the corner of his eye, Michael spotted a shadow behind a shelf. He moved toward it, followed closely by Brandon and Tyler. When he looked behind the shelf, nobody was there and the shadow had gone. They walked around the entire basement, but they didn't see any sign of the little old lady.

"We should check each level—she could be anywhere."

"Maybe she isn't here today. It could be her day off." Michael and Tyler glared at Brandon; they knew he had only said that out of fear.

As they made their way back up the stairs, Tyler saw something shining on a shelf in the back of the room. He waited until the other two were almost all the way up the stairs before he snuck off to see what it was. The shelf from which the light had been coming was empty, and the light seemed to have vanished.

"Hello? Is there anyone here? My name is Tyler—I was in yesterday."

At first, nobody answered, so he turned around and headed back toward the stairs.

"I know who you are," said a small voice behind the shelf.

Tyler took a deep breath, closed his eyes, and turned around. He opened his eyes and jumped back, surprised; there, standing right in front of him, was a very shy, very pretty girl.

"Excuse me?" Tyler said, looking around to see if the girl was alone.

"I know who you are. You're Tyler. We have been waiting for you. You are here to find your destiny, to help us."

Tyler was stunned. "Who are you? How do you know who I am, or why I'm here?"

The girl looked around as if someone might be listening. "My name is Sara. I live with my grandma; we…um…we take care of the Mysterious Blue. We have been waiting for you for a long time. We were beginning to think you would never find your destiny. Everyone has been very worried."

"Sara, have you finished your chores?" said a familiar voice. Tyler whipped his head around in surprise, and saw the old lady standing right behind him.

"No, Grandma, sorry—I will go and finish them right now." Sara smiled at Tyler and walked toward a door that Tyler had never noticed before.

"I see you met my granddaughter," the old lady said to Tyler with a warm and inviting smile on her face. "She is a very sweet girl; she has been so very good to me."

Tyler was staring at the little old lady with his mouth open in complete shock. There was something very strange going on and he couldn't wait any longer to find out what it was.

"I'm sorry, I don't mean to be rude, but can you tell me what you're talking about when you say 'my destiny'?" Who are you? How do you know me? What is so special about that star? Who is Candor, and—" Before Tyler could go on, the old lady interrupted him, with her hands waving slightly in front of his face.

"Slow down, Tyler, or you will get me all confused. Now, first things first: my name is Lodiss and like I said already, Sara is my granddaughter, and that star is special because that star will take you to your destiny. You really have no idea who you are?"

Tyler was confused; of course he knew who he was. He was Tyler Leeds…but what did that matter?

"I don't really know what you're talking about…who I really am?"

Lodiss shook her head in disbelief. "Do you know who your grandparents were?"

Tyler felt suddenly uncomfortable; his grandparents had died over a year ago. Besides, what could his grandparents possibly have to do with any of this?

"They both died in bed, in their sleep. Why? What do you mean, 'Do I know who they were'?"

Lodiss shook her head again. This time, however, she looked saddened by Tyler's answer. "You never knew anything?" she asked Tyler, who was more confused now than ever.

Tyler turned around and walked a few steps away from Lodiss with his hands on his head, pacing back and forth for a while before finally stopping in front of her. He took a deep breath, swallowed the huge lump in his throat, and stared at her.

"There is a lot to tell me, isn't there?" he asked in a slow, deep voice unlike his own.

Lodiss put her hand on his, looked deep into his eyes, and began. "I'm sorry your grandparents never had the chance to tell you themselves. I know they wanted to; they were waiting until you were ready. It was unfortunate that they died when they did. Your grandparents were heroes, Tyler—you must know that. They were so much more than just your grandparents. You were named after your grandfather, right? Tyler was his middle name. You have more than just a name in common: he also was a Nytstar."

"He was a what?" Tyler asked.

"A Nytstar—it's like a wizard of the night."

Tyler was quiet for a moment while he tried to believe what Lodiss was saying. Finally, when he was convinced that Lodiss was telling him a tale, he kind of laughed.

"I'm a wizard? Me… This must be a joke."

Lodiss didn't seem to notice his laugh—or she just didn't care. "No," she said as she continued, "I never said you were a wizard. A Nytstar and a wizard are two different things."

Tyler laughed again; this time, it was somewhat forced. "I, uh…I'm sorry."

"There is no need to apologize. How would you know if nobody has told you?"

Tyler was starting to feel bad for laughing. Lodiss was being nice, even though Tyler wasn't sure whether to believe her or not.

"A Nytstar wears a special necklace. You can't always see it; sometimes it is invisible. You just need to know how to make it unseen."

Suddenly Tyler heard footsteps coming down the spiral staircase. Without turning to see who it was, Lodiss said, "Oh, good, your brother is here—he too should hear this."

"Is he a Nytstar too?" Tyler asked hopefully.

"Of course he is. You both possess the powers."

Michael's mouth dropped open in surprise. "I obviously missed an important part of the conversation." Michael looked at Tyler, then his eyes shifted curiously to Lodiss. "What 'powers' do we both posses?"

Brandon stood beside his friends in silence, his tense body and anxious expression showing that he would rather be anywhere other than standing in the lower level of the Mysterious Blue.

Michael listened intently to every word Lodiss said as she filled him in on what she had already told Tyler.

"Now, about your necklaces…"

"Wait," Tyler interrupted. "Do my nightmares have anything to do with all this?"

Lodiss's expression changed quickly; her smile fell and a shocked, sad expression was left in its place. She tried not to look Tyler in the eyes as she fiddled with her fingers before she finally spoke.

"You've had nightmares since you were a baby. They have gotten worse, haven't they?" Lodiss asked.

Tyler looked at Michael and Brandon, not really wanting to answer in front of them, but he did anyway. "Yes, they have gotten worse, but how did you know?"

Lodiss grabbed a chair from the back wall and motioned to Tyler, Michael, and Brandon to do the same.

"You had better sit down while I tell you this," Lodiss said, smiling. "Tyler, your nightmares are showing you the other world. You are not just any Nytstar, Tyler—that is why you have nightmares and Michael doesn't. Your grandfather was a great Nytstar; you are the one that will follow in your grandfather's footsteps, and you are the one that will rise above all other Nytstars. That is your destiny."

Michael's eyes, which had been watching every word and every move that Lodiss made, now focused on Tyler, who looked more confused than ever.

"I don't understand—why me? Why not Michael? He is the oldest; he should be the one to follow in our grandfather's footsteps, not me." Tyler stopped suddenly, having just realized that he had no idea what footsteps she was talking about. "I don't understand all this. I'm sorry, I just think you have mistaken us for someone else. We are just kids—we know nothing about any of this. I mean, really, another world, magic powers... It all sounds unreal. I...just...I don't know," Tyler said, his voice slightly cracking.

Lodiss smiled at Tyler and Michael, a sort of sad smile. She sighed, got up from her chair, and walked over to the counter. She reached behind it and pulled out an old, dusty-looking book. Lodiss blew the dust off the top and wiped it clean with the sleeve of her sweater.

"This book will tell you everything you boys need to know. And if you need to know anything that is not in the book, simply ask it," Lodiss said in a matter-of-fact way.

"*Ahem*...I do have a name, you know. You don't have to call me 'it'; that is very rude."

Brandon almost fell off his chair when he saw that it was the book talking. Tyler and Michael stared at the book in amazement.

"Of course—I'm sorry, you're right. How rude of me. This is Michael and Tyler Leeds." Lodiss turned the book toward Michael and Tyler. The book was marvelous: it had a dark red velvet cover, with gold trim running all the way around its front and back. In each corner was a circle, which Tyler recognized straight away as being very similar to the one Candor wore around his neck when he saw him in his dream. The book was unlike any they had ever seen before; in the middle of the front page was a face, a face that moved and talked just like any other face did—any face, that is, that was attached to a head, and not a book.

"Michael and Tyler Leeds, really? You are the grandchildren of Simon and Clair Leeds. Why, of course you are."

Tyler moved forward toward the book. He reached out to touch it, but pulled his hand back; he wasn't sure it was safe. He wasn't sure if it was real.

"You're...you're...a...talking book," Tyler stumbled to say.

Lodiss sat back down in her chair and handed the book to Michael, who was a little unsure whether to take it, but when Lodiss smiled and nodded to him, he reached out, took the book, and rested it on his knee.

"Michael, how nice to finally meet you. Your grandparents told me a lot about both of you. Their death was such a tragedy. A lot of Nytstars were worried that it would all be over when they died; because neither of your parents are Nytstars, there was no one to take over where your grandparents left off."

Michael was studying the book very closely. He seemed to be so interested in the book that he had forgotten about anything else. Tyler gave him a nudge to encourage him to ask the book questions; Michael looked at Tyler and saw from the look on Tyler's face exactly what the nudge was for.

"What do we call you?" Michael asked timidly.

"Nomad," the book replied, then waited patiently for the string of questions he knew he was about to be asked.

"Nomad, how did you know our grandparents?"

Nomad had an expression on his face that looked as if he was trying to scowl, but was not doing a very good job. "I was your grandfather's book. I taught him everything, the same as his father, and his father, and his father, and…yes, well, I am sure you get the idea. I also helped Simon—I mean, your grandfather—develop the Dreamencers," Nomad explained, full of pride.

"What are the Dreamencers?" Michael asked eagerly.

"They are like the Nytpolice," Nomad answered.

"Why do the Nytstars need police?" Michael shot back.

"The Dreamencers protect all Nytstars, and everything else that lives in the Dark World, against the King of Darkness, and his army of darkness."

Tyler, who hadn't been able to look at Nomad since he began talking about his grandfather, now stared right at him, overwhelmed with shock. Lodiss was sitting across from Michael and Tyler; she was watching the book, and them, very closely. Michael remembered Tyler's dream about the King of Darkness and Candor. Michael watched Tyler, waiting for him to tell Nomad about his dream, but Tyler said nothing. He looked at Nomad and closed his eyes; he expected that when he opened them, he would wake up, and this would all have been a dream, just another one of his nightmares—only this dream wasn't scary. Tyler opened his eyes and stared down at Nomad.

"You have already met Candor; he tried to trick you into going with him. He told you the King of Darkness wanted you to join his army, that night in your dream," Nomad stated.

Tyler glanced at Michael and Lodiss, then returned his stare to Nomad. "How did you know that? How do you know what I dream?" Tyler asked in a whisper.

"I know more than what is written on my pages. You boys will learn also, and I will teach you everything. I thought, however, from the bruise on your arm, that you would have realized that they are not just dreams."

Tyler grasped his arm, remembering pinching it, trying to wake himself up from his dream about the dragon.

"Teach us what, Nomad? All we really know so far is what you and Lodiss have just told us," Michael explained.

"You boys each have a necklace that you were given by your grandparents—that necklace is the key to your powers."

"We were never given a necklace by our grandparents," Michael and Tyler said together.

Lodiss looked at them and smiled. "Well, of course your grandparents hadn't given them to you yet. They are not toys; they hold a lot of powers. It could have been very dangerous if they had given them to you when you were too young to know how to use them," Lodiss said with a little laugh.

"I'm sorry to say, Lodiss, we still don't know how to use them," Michael said, feeling somewhat embarrassed.

"Well, of course you don't know how to use them yet. We have just met! I'm good, but I'm not that good," Nomad laughed.

"I will return in a moment," Lodiss said as she walked toward the stairs. Michael and Tyler nodded, and she disappeared. Tyler fidgeted in his chair; Michael just stared at the book and Brandon looked blankly around the room.

"Wow, powers and a necklace—that sounds very nice. Are we going home soon?" Brandon asked in a whisper. This just annoyed Michael, so he ignored it and continued to examine the book.

"So why doesn't Michael have nightmares like I do? You said we both have the powers—why am I the only one?"

"You are different people, Tyler. You have something that most other Nytstars don't have, and you were not even supposed to have it."

Just then, Lodiss returned, carrying two boxes: one was wrapped in blue paper with a small silver bow on top, the other wrapped in black paper with a gold bow on top.

Tyler looked at Lodiss and the boxes in her hand for a moment, then turned back to Nomad.

"What do I have that other Nytstars don't have?" Tyler shot at Nomad before Lodiss had a chance to say anything.

"You have the mark."

"What mark are you talking about?" Tyler snapped.

"You have the mark of Dramess: the mark on the bottom of your foot that looks like a star. The mark of Dramess is an ancient Triss that was cast upon an ancestor of yours hundreds and hundreds of years ago. A Triss is kind of like a charm. When Alaford Leedsonath saved Dramess's only infant son years ago, Dramess repaid him by putting a Triss on him. He put a mark on his foot shaped like a star. The Triss Dramess used was ancient; it had not been used in centuries, as it is one of the most powerful and complicated Trisses of all. The Triss can be fatal to the Nytstar who casts it. Dramess transferred all of his powers, his kingdom, and his throne to Alaford Leedsonath, binding their Oltes together, thus Alaford became one of the most powerful Nytstars ever. You now have that mark. The mark is passed on through your sons to their sons and their sons. The mark will only stop when there are no more sons."

Tyler pulled off his left shoe and sock. He could feel everyone's eyes staring at him; they all wanted to see the mark. Tyler looked at the bottom of his foot as if seeing it for the first time. He had always thought the mark was a birthmark; he could never have imagined it to be anything more.

"But wait," Tyler shouted suddenly, "my grandfather never had a son; he only had daughters, two of them."

"That's why the King of Darkness wants you so badly on his side. You're special; you were never supposed to have the mark, but you do. Tyler, you are a king of the Nyt"

Lodiss took the book from Michael's knee and set it down next to her. "I think it is time we gave the boys their necklaces, don't you, Nomad?" Lodiss asked the book, who didn't look too happy to be sitting on the floor.

"Yes, I think you may be right, Lodiss. Now listen closely: you boys must promise us that you will never take these off, no matter what. With great power comes great responsibility. You will have to read all of my pages and learn all there is to know about being a Nytstar. As you will soon discover, you already have the powers; you just need to learn how to use them. One of the most important things you need to know is that not everybody can know about our world; it is paramount that our world remains a secret." Nomad turned his eyes towards Brandon, who sank even deeper into his chair. "Those few who have been chosen and trusted with our secret would be very foolish not to keep it a secret; the consequences would be unbearably painful."

Brandon knew Nomad was talking to him. He nodded slightly and turned his head.

Lodiss handed Tyler and Michael their boxes: the box wrapped in the blue wrapping paper was for Michael, and the box in the black paper was for Tyler. The boys gave each other a very excited look, like the ones they gave each other on Christmas morning when they first saw all the presents under the tree. Michael opened his first; in the box was a very old-looking wooden jewelry box, which he opened very slowly, trying to wait for Tyler to catch up— but Tyler seemed to be frozen. Michael couldn't wait any longer, so he opened the box and stared at the necklace inside, looking somewhat disappointed. Tyler finally finished pulling off the black paper and opened the box to see his old-looking jewelry box inside. Tyler had almost exactly the reaction that Michael had had: disappointment.

"This necklace is full of powers? Are you sure?" Tyler asked as he examined the necklace more closely.

"You are very quick to judge," Nomad said, sounding a little cross.

Michael took out the necklace and began to examine every inch thoroughly. He must have turned it over ten times before he noticed the writing on the back, and quietly he read it to himself: "Mr. Michael Leeds: Intellect, Precision, and Determination." Michael looked up, grinning; he was quite pleased with what was written on the back of his necklace. Everyone had always commented on how smart and determined he was. He drifted off, lost in thought. Even as a small boy, he always had to do everything before everybody else: he walked when he was six months old; he was potty-trained at twelve months; he could ride a two-wheeler when he was only three years old; at four he was reading, spelling, and doing math. There's no doubt about it, Michael thought to himself a little big-headedly, those words definitely describe me.

Tyler just stared at the necklace in his hand. It didn't seem like anything more than a necklace; the chain was a regular-looking chain, with a clasp and what Tyler thought was a regular-looking pendant. The pendant was a black circle, with stars that seemed to come and go depending on how the light shone on it. Tyler held the chain out toward Lodiss, who suddenly went quite pale; she looked as if at any moment she might faint.

"Can you help me put this on?"

Lodiss let out a big sigh of relief, and all the color returned to her face as quickly as it had left. "Of course I can, dear, of course I can."

"I thought you were going to give it back," Michael said.

Lodiss put Tyler's necklace on him and stood back and stared at both Michael and Tyler with pride.

"I'm sorry to interrupt, Grandmother, but I've finished all my chores; I'm going to do my homework now," Sara called from just outside the door.

"All right, dear, thank you. Well, it is getting late, and you boys have a lot of work ahead of you, so you must be getting home now." Lodiss picked up the book and gave it to Michael. "I trust you will take care of Nomad? And you will need to make sure you both begin immediately, now that you have your Oltes."

Michael took the book and thanked Lodiss for all her help, while Tyler and Brandon put the chairs back. They all headed up the stairs. Lodiss handed Michael a brown bag for Nomad.

"I am not going to start talking on the way home, you know," Nomad protested from inside the bag.

"I thought I recognized you. You go to our school, right? You're in Mrs. Suzanne's class with me?" Tyler asked Sara, whose face turned red.

"Yes," she said quietly.

Tyler smiled at Sara on his way out the door. Just before it closed, he shouted, "See you tomorrow!"

CHAPTER FIVE

NOW THAT WE KNOW

"We had better go straight home, or our moms will be wondering where we are," Michael said, breaking the awkward silence.

"What type of powers do you think we have?" he asked Tyler, who was walking backward while he stared at the Mysterious Blue, lost in his own thoughts. "Well?" Michael urged.

"Well what?" Tyler asked.

"What kind of powers do you think we have?"

Tyler looked at Brandon's eager eyes, then at Michael, who was peeking into the bag he was carrying with Nomad inside. "I have no idea, but I bet there are a lot of rules. I'm sure we can't just go around using powers all the time—don't you think that people would notice if we did?"

"Well, of course there will be rules, Tyler, but I can't wait to learn them all," Michael said as they reached the bus stop and sat down on the bench to wait. Michael pulled the bag onto his lap and stuck his nose in to get another look.

"Can't you just wait till we get home? It won't look any different, you know," Tyler shot at Michael.

"How do you know? You think that a world with magic necklaces and powers can't have a book that changes? It talks—I'm sure it can do lots of stuff."

Tyler didn't answer; he just stared at the ground. The bus came right away, and the three boys stood up, ready to get on.

"This time, we should try to sit together, so we can talk without being heard," Michael said as the bus pulled up to the stop.

Unlike earlier, this bus was empty. Michael smiled at the driver as he climbed the steps of the bus.

"That's weird," Brandon said. "Usually the buses are packed on Saturday afternoon; well, at least we can all sit together."

Tyler was glad the bus was empty; he didn't much fancy risking anyone hearing their conversation. They walked to the back of the bus and took their seats. Tyler sat next to the window and stared out.

"Don't you think it's a bit strange that not one person has gotten on this bus yet?" Brandon asked Michael.

"I was thinking the same thing myself," Michael said as they both glared at Tyler.

Tyler could feel their eyes staring at him. "I don't think it's strange, I think it's nice—I was hoping nobody would get on the whole ride. This way we don't have to worry about Nomad making it home without anyone noticing he's a talking book." Tyler turned back to look out the window.

Michael and Brandon glanced at each other; they had both noticed Tyler clutching his necklace very tightly. The bus finally reached the stop in front of the park. When they got off the bus, Michael turned around and the bus had vanished. They headed toward the park, where some of their friends were still playing soccer.

"Let's go and play for a while. That way, we haven't really lied to our parents," Brandon suggested.

"Wow, you had a good idea again—that's two in one day," Michael teased as he put the bag with Nomad in it on the ground and covered it with his jacket

"We can't just leave it there! It's not very safe," Tyler shouted after them.

"Then you stay there and watch it if you like," Michael called back to him.

Tyler looked around to see if anyone was watching. He held his necklace tightly in his hand and closed his eyes. He opened his eyes, looked at the soccer game being played, and ran to join in.

"You can be on our team; Chris had to go home, so we're a man short," Dean called to Tyler as he ran onto the field. They had only been playing soccer for thirty minutes when they heard a car honk its horn at them. Michael turned and saw their mom waving to them.

"Sorry, guys," Michael said to everyone. "We've got to go home."

"No problem; I'd better get going too," Dean said, picking up the soccer ball and heading for his backpack. "See you guys later," he called as he took off home.

"It's gone! It's gone! The book—it's gone!" Michael said frantically as he dropped to the ground and started searching around.

Tyler felt his heart pounding as he began to search with Michael and Brandon. "I knew we shouldn't have left it there alone," Tyler said. Not really thinking about it, he grabbed at his necklace again, hoping that the bag with Nomad inside would just reappear or something.

"Um...it's right in front of you," Brandon said, a little confused. "I was standing here and it just sort of appeared, I think. We just didn't see it, I...I guess."

Brandon stood staring at the bag. One moment their stuff was gone—they had all seen that it wasn't there—then the next moment it was there again. Michael and Brandon found themselves once again staring at Tyler.

Tyler stuffed his necklace under his shirt. "Let's get going," he said, refusing to look at either of them.

When they reached Brandon's house, Michael warned him, "Don't forget: no matter what happens, don't tell anyone anything about what happened today!"

Brandon felt his face go red. "Don't worry—your secret is safe with me forever. After all, having friends with powers could turn out to be good thing, right?"

Tyler shot Brandon a warning glare.

"We'll see you tomorrow, Brandon," Michael said as he and Tyler continued on their way home. As they walked home, Michael looked around to make sure that there was no one nearby, and turned to Tyler. "What do you think about all of this?"

Tyler still would not look at Michael. "I hope it means that I can sleep at night," he said, with very little belief that he would.

"Did you make the book disappear?" Michael blurted out.

"No, of course not—how could I?" Tyler began to walk a bit faster.

Michael grabbed Tyler by the arm and got right in his face, forcing Tyler to look at him. "What is your problem? We just found out that we have powers—you would think you would be a little more excited. What's wrong?"

Tyler pulled his arm away from Michael's grip and turned away. "Did you ever stop to think that this could all just be another dream? We might not have any powers at all. Any moment I could wake up and realize that nothing has changed. There's no way to prove it's real, until I wake up."

All of a sudden, he felt a hard pinch on his arm. He spun around at Michael, ready to hit him. "What did you do that for? You're lucky I don't punch you for that," Tyler said as he rubbed his arm and stared at Michael, who took a step back.

"I just wanted to see if you would wake up, to see if this is all a dream or not."

Tyler smiled. "Well, I guess I'm not dreaming, then."

Michael looked in the bag for what Tyler could have sworn was the hundredth time. "Do you think that this book can really teach us how to use our powers? I mean, it looks ancient. What if there is new magic—how would the book know it? It's just a book. I sure can't wait to read it, though; I bet it's full of ancient powers, and just think of all the history we can learn about the other world. I wonder if there's anything about our grandparents in the book," Michael said, full of excitement.

Tyler shook his head. "You had better put that book inside your jacket or something before Mom sees it; you know she'll ask to have a look at it, and she'll want to know where we got it."

Michael took off his jacket, draped it over the book, and stuffed it under his arm. They arrived at their house just in time to see Mrs. Leeds checking out the front window for them. As soon as she saw them, she gave them a big smile and waved. She opened the front door, still smiling.

"Don't forget, you have karate tonight, Tyler," she beamed at him.

"Sure, Mom—we have some…uh…homework to do, so we'll go and get started before supper," Tyler said, staring at the floor.

Michael glared at Tyler. He thought they were definitely busted now: Tyler never willingly did his homework.

Mrs. Leeds put her hand on Tyler's forehead. "You feeling all right?" she asked, smirking.

"Ha, ha," Tyler laughed. "I just thought I would get it done before you started nagging me. Besides, we're going back to play soccer tomorrow—I don't want to miss it for homework."

Mrs. Leeds seemed convinced. "Okay, I'll call you when supper is ready."

"Thanks," Michael shouted as they ran upstairs to their room. Michael closed the bedroom door behind him. Tyler sat down on his bed and Michael sat on the floor, pulling Nomad out of his bag.

"You okay?" Michael asked Tyler, who looked a little uneasy.

"I'm fine—I'm not a baby," Tyler snapped.

Michael ignored Tyler's answer, got up, and moved a chair in front of the door so they would have time to hide the book if their mom was to try and come into the room. When Michael removed Nomad from the bag, a sense of calm came over the room. Tyler stared at the book, waiting for Nomad to start speaking to them as he had in the shop. Michael rubbed his hand over the book, but nothing happened.

"I don't understand—at the Mysterious Blue, Nomad began to talk as soon as Lodiss took him out. Why isn't he talking to us now?" Michael rubbed his head as he tried to think of something that could possibly make the book work. He tried asking the book to talk. "Nomad, it's us, Michael and Tyler Leeds, from the Mysterious Blue. Do you remember us?" Michael asked, but the book didn't talk or move or anything. Michael looked at the book, then at Tyler, trying everything he could think of.

Tyler slipped his hand under his shirt and fiddled with his necklace. He didn't really know what he was doing—or if he was really doing anything—but he held his necklace in his hand and closed his eyes. He opened them and looked at the curtains; they seemed to close all by themselves. Then he looked at the book and quietly whispered, "Nomad."

Michael heard him, turned, and looked again at the book. Nomad's face appeared on the front of the book once again. "You did it, Tyler—just like you did at the park, didn't you?"

Tyler looked at Michael, who could tell from the look on his face that he was right.

"You learn well, Tyler," Nomad said.

"Learn what? It was just a coincidence that it worked, that's all." Tyler looked at Michael, who also looked very impressed.

"You lack confidence in yourself. You knew somehow what to do with the necklace."

Tyler felt his face turn red; he stood up and began to walk around the room.

Michael moved closer to Nomad. "I would like to learn all I can about the necklace and our powers as soon as possible. I want to know everything: What does all of this mean? Why do we have powers? What do we need them for?" Michael questioned eagerly.

"Michael, you read the writing on the back of your necklace in the shop." Michael nodded. "Tyler, you have not yet read yours yet."

Tyler hadn't; he didn't really want to see what it said—he was sure it wouldn't say anything as good as Michael's.

"No, I haven't," Tyler grumbled.

"That's fine. You can read it whenever you're ready; just make sure you do. Now, we should get to work straight away. The necklaces you are both wearing are called "Oltes"; they are what give you your powers. Every Nytstar has his or her own Oltes. Nobody but the true owner of the Oltes should use it, or terrible things can happen. It is vital that you never take it off. Some of your powers you can already use, but the more difficult ones you will have to learn. That is why you need me. Everything you need to know is in me; if it is not written in my words, all you have to do is ask me, and I will put it there."

Michael was staring at Nomad with his mouth open slightly, taking in every word and facial expression that Nomad made.

"I will be teaching you how to use spells, or 'Drades,' as they are known by Nytstars—they can be quite complex, and very dangerous, if you don't know what you are doing. Tyler, you obviously have a lot in common with your grandfather: he too could use his powers and cast Drades very early, and without too much teaching. I wish you two would have had the chance to know your grandparents as Nytstars; you would have been very proud, and quite impressed, I'm sure."

Michael looked at Tyler, who refused to meet his eyes; instead, Tyler stared intently at the floor as though he were studying every fiber of the carpet.

"Now, as Tyler already found out, for most Drades, all you have to do is touch your Oltes and say your Drade in your head. However, you will find that it can be just as hard not to use your Drades as it can be to use them. You must be very clear with your thoughts, or the result could be far from what you intended. Now let's try something simple."

Michael's face lit up with excitement.

"I want you to think of something in your closet that you can hold in one hand. Now with your other hand, hold on to your Oltes and ask it to come to you."

Michael closed his eyes and concentrated on the first-place science fair ribbon he had won recently. In his head, he repeatedly asked the ribbon to come to his hand. He opened his eyes and stared disappointedly at his empty hand.

Tyler watched Michael try again, and again; each time he failed, disappointment replaced the excitement on his face. Tyler was used to being unable to do things; unlike Michael, he typically didn't receive top marks in school, and until now, Tyler had never known how much it would affect Michael if he failed. Tyler grasped his own Oltes, and the next time Michael tried, when he looked down at his hand, not expecting to see anything there, he gasped with excitement at the sight of the red ribbon he was now holding. Thrilled, he looked at his Oltes, which he was holding tight in his other hand.

"It worked! I can't believe it—it worked! The ribbon…Tyler…it was the ribbon!" Michael was practically jumping up and down with excitement. He couldn't believe it had worked. "What do you have in your hand, Tyler?" Michael asked, hopeful that it had worked for his brother also.

Tyler looked down at his hand and saw it was empty.

"But you did that other stuff earlier—how could you not do this?" Michael asked, dumbfounded.

"Supper is ready, boys," Mrs. Leeds shouted, just in time to save Tyler from having to answer Michael's question.

"I'll put Nomad away, Mike," Tyler offered. "You go ahead downstairs. Tell Mom I'll be right down."

Michael gave Tyler a slightly suspicious look, thanked him, and went downstairs.

"Don't bother lecturing me," Tyler shot at Nomad. "I know that you know what I did, but you don't understand: if it hadn't worked for him, he would have been devastated. I know he would have."

"You lack confidence in others as well as in yourself, I see," Nomad said to Tyler, who was trying to find a good hiding spot for him.

"I don't have a lack of confidence in Michael. I know he can do anything if he tries; he always does. I just didn't want this time to be any different."

"You didn't want him to know what it is like to fail."

Tyler found the perfect spot were his mom would never find Nomad: under their bunk bed, at the very back. "Would he have failed if I hadn't done it for him?" Tyler asked before he put Nomad under the bed.

"Yes, he would have failed."

Tyler put the book under the bed, turned around, and faced the closet. He reached for his necklace, held it in his hand, and closed his eyes.

"Tyler, your supper is getting cold," Mrs. Leeds said, poking her head around the door, which no longer had the chair in front of it. "Is everything okay?" she asked, looking concerned that Tyler was staring at his closed closet door.

"I'm fine—I was just putting something away," Tyler said as he followed his mom out of his room and down the stairs for supper, now clutching in his hand a picture of he and Michael. After they had finished supper, they didn't have any time to talk to Nomad: Tyler had karate class.

"You don't have to come, you know," Tyler said to Michael, who kept staring up the stairs to their bedroom. "I know you have some, um…reading you wanted to do."

"I have never missed one of your karate classes, have I?" Michael said, still staring up the stairs.

"No, you haven't, but I would understand."

Michael turned away from the stairs and looked at Tyler. "This is an important class for you. I'm not going to miss it for anything."

Tyler looked at Michael confusedly. "Important? What do—" But before he had the chance to finish, Mr. and Mrs. Leeds came rushing through the kitchen.

"Are you nervous? I am, and it's not me that's being graded," Mrs. Leeds said as she handed Tyler his gi. "I washed it and ironed it for you, but don't worry, I didn't wash your belt. You tell me every time I wash your gi that all your hard work and sweat is in your belt, and if I wash it, I would wash all that away." Mrs. Leeds smiled as Tyler took his gi from her and put it into his bag.

"Dad, I thought you had to work late," Tyler said when he realized that his dad was standing next to his mom trying to load a film into his camera.

"Do you really think I would miss this? It's not every day that you're graded for your black belt, now is it?" he asked, smiling big and proudly.

Tyler stared around at them all. His black belt—how could he have forgotten? This was so important, but he hadn't practiced for days; he hadn't even thought about it.

"Yeah, my black belt, that's right…um… I forgot something upstairs. I'll be right back." Tyler ran upstairs to his room, closing the door behind him.

"I forgot! How am I supposed to pass this test? I haven't practiced in days! I could tell them I'm sick—no, they would never believe me. Well, the faster I fail, the faster we can come home." Tyler took a deep breath; he felt sick to his stomach with nerves.

"Is everything all right, Ty?" his dad asked as they headed toward the car.

"I'm just a little nervous," Tyler said, and they got into the car and headed for the dojo.

Tyler stared at himself in the mirror; he was taking as long as he could in the bathroom before his test. "I need to focus, to calm down. I can do this, and I know this stuff," he said to himself. The door to the bathroom swung open.

"He's ready for you, Tyler. You had better hurry up—and take your necklace off, too," Jacob from his class said shyly.

Tyler reached his hands up to his Oltes to grab the clasp. As soon as he touched it, he pulled his hands away quickly. I can't take it off; I wonder if I could hide it under my shirt, Tyler thought to himself, holding his Oltes.

"Be invisible, just for an hour or so, please." He looked down at his chest, but his Oltes was still there. Tyler shook his head, left the bathroom, and headed for the gym to begin his test.

When he walked through the door, Tyler was shocked to see how many people were there. Everyone from his karate class was already there, warming up. Some of their parents were sitting in chairs along the side of the room, as they usually were. Today, however, it annoyed Tyler that they were there. He saw his mom and dad and Michael sitting in chairs with smiles on their faces. Even his family seemed to annoy Tyler slightly.

Tyler bowed to his sensei, then to the rest of his class. He hoped that nobody would notice his Oltes still hanging around his neck. The rest of the class sat down on the edge of the mats and watched as Tyler took his test for his black belt. Tyler's mind emptied: for the whole time he was taking his test, not once did he think of his nightmares, school, or his new powers. He was completely focused on his karate, and for a short while, he was free—free from everything.

Michael watched in amazement as Tyler moved around the mat flawlessly. "He hasn't even made one mistake. It just amazes me how he can learn all this so perfectly, yet when it comes to schoolwork, he's a blank."

When Tyler's test was over, silence lingered throughout the gym. Nobody seemed to even breathe. His sensei shook his hand and reached into his gi, pulling out a brand new black belt and handing it to Tyler. Tyler took the belt, said thank you, and turned to Michael and his parents.

"I'll just go get changed. I'll be right back," Tyler said as he started to walk back toward the changing room.

"Tyler, wait! That was great; you didn't even make one mistake. You did everything perfectly; I watched every move, just to make sure," Michael said, obviously more excited than Tyler was.

"You always do, Mike," Tyler replied.

Mrs. Leeds had a huge smile on her face as she gave Tyler a big hug, trying to hold back tears. Tyler headed to the changing room.

"I'll come with you," Michael said as he followed Tyler out of the gym.

"We'll go and wait in the car. Try not to be too long," Mr. Leeds said after giving Tyler a pat on the back to congratulate him.

"What did you do with your necklace?" Michael asked before they had even gotten into the changing room.

"I hid it in my shirt. I didn't know what else to do. I couldn't take it off; I tried."

Michael gasped. "We're not supposed to take them off! Weren't you listening?"

Tyler shot an angry look at Michael. "I didn't have much time. I—"

Before Tyler could finish, Michael interrupted. "So what did you do with it? Where is it now?" Michael pointed to Tyler's chest, where the necklace should have been, but wasn't.

"I don't know. I didn't take it off. I tried to make it invisible but it didn't work. Well, I didn't think it had worked…I mean, it was still there when I left the changing room before." Tyler felt his chest. "It's right here," he said, holding it in his hand.

He could see from Michael's face that he couldn't see it. Tyler looked down at his hand, which he could feel was holding the Oltes, but he couldn't see it either. "I know it's here—I can feel it, Mike."

Tyler got changed and they both headed out to the car to meet their parents. After celebrating his victory with Michael and his parents and a rather large helping of chocolate cake and ice cream, Tyler couldn't help but feel full of happiness; he smiled and laughed with Michael the entire ride home.

At home, Michael and Tyler went straight to their room.

"It's under the bed," Tyler said, following Michael through their bedroom door. Michael wasted no time at all; he reached under the bed, pulled out the book, and placed it carefully on a pillow on the floor. Hardly able to contain his excitement, he opened the book, reading the first page.

"You know, Tyler, you might not have any more nightmares now that you have your Oltes," Michael said hopefully to Tyler, who had been hoping that would be true since the very moment he found out that his nightmares were glimpses of the other world. "Although I was thinking that if your nightmares were showing you the other world, does that mean that the other world has terrible creatures and horrible things happen there?" Michael said.

Tyler looked out the window, avoiding answering Michael. The truth was that he didn't want to think that all the terrible things about which he had had nightmares could possibly be real; seeing them in his dreams was bad enough.

"As much as I like learning all this stuff, I have a ton of homework to do, and most of it is stuff I was supposed to do last week, so I should finish it tonight," Tyler grumbled as he stood up and gathered his stuff. He sat down on his bed and tried to focus on his math questions.

Michael nodded and continued reading the book, occasionally stopping to tell Tyler about something really exciting that he had just read. It had already been almost an hour since they had said goodnight to their mom when they finally put their books away and got ready for bed.

"So, do you think you'll be able to sleep tonight without any nightmares?" Michael asked as he pulled off his clothes and slipped into his pajamas.

Tyler brushed his hand over his necklace and hoped he would have a good sleep tonight, for the first time. "I hope so," he almost whispered, as if saying it aloud would jinx it.

It was after midnight by the time they were both in bed; the house was still and quiet.

"We can leave the light on if you want," Michael offered; he wanted Tyler to sleep just as much as Tyler did.

"No, I'm not afraid of the dark," Tyler insisted, staring into the darkness. He absentmindedly rubbed his hand over his Oltes now and then, as if to check that it was still there.

"Are you waiting for somebody?" an unfamiliar voice asked. Tyler jumped up to find himself sitting in what looked like an office. There was an oversized wooden desk in the middle of the room with a large leather chair behind it. The chair in which he was sitting was not as large or as comfortable-looking as the one behind the desk. The room was circular, with pictures of strange-looking people all over the walls.

Tyler looked around to see who had spoken. Standing on the far side of the room was a tall lady with black hair that was pulled back tightly in a bun at the back of her head. She wore big glasses that were dirty and tired-looking. Her skin was very pale, as if she hadn't been out in the sun for years. The lady was wearing a shirt that looked like a man's and was at least three sizes too big; she had a long green skirt that went all the way down to the floor, and looked like she had hemmed it with a stapler.

Tyler just stared at the lady for awhile. He looked at the chair next to him and almost fell off of his when he saw that the chair was not empty: Michael was sitting right next to him. Tyler reached out his hand and touched Michael on the shoulder.

"Are you really here? I mean, in my dream? Are you real?" he asked. Michael had never turned up in his dreams—well, at least not in a good way; he was usually being killed or eaten or something else terrible.

"Actually, you're in my dream."

"What do you mean? How are we in each other's dreams?" Tyler asked, but before Michael had the chance to answer, the lady said again, this time slightly aggravated, "Are you waiting for someone?"

Tyler just stared at Michael as he spoke. "We're not sure. We're not sure if we're in the right place or not, or how we got here, or, for that matter, even where 'here' is."

The lady looked suspiciously at the two of them, and glanced at a door that was slightly open. "I will see if he is busy. You two wait here for a moment," she said as she headed through the door.

Michael swung around in his chair to face Tyler. "I think we're here," he said excitedly.

"Where?"

"Here—you know, in the other world."

Tyler's eyes shot around the room, looking at every detail they could. The desk was covered in papers and envelopes. Books were piled on the floor, over the massive bookcases, and on top of filing cabinets. The lone window in the room was covered with dark-colored, shabby curtains; there were candles all over the room, each one burning, but only dimly. There was one light in the room and Tyler could not stop staring at it.

"Hey, Michael, does that light over there look familiar to you?" Tyler asked.

"That looks identical to that star you got from the Mysterious Blue." Michael glanced at the door through which the lady had disappeared; he slowly walked toward the star to examine it. "This is identical to the star that we have, except ours isn't a light."

Michael picked up the star to show Tyler, but the star was so hot it burnt his hands; he put it back on the shelf. "Ouch, that's pretty hot," he complained as he rubbed his hands together.

Tyler let out a little laugh at the sight of Michael blowing on his hands. "I'm going to take a wild guess that…um…we are not supposed to touch that," he snickered.

Tyler walked over to the pictures on the wall. They were all in beautiful gold and silver frames. The pictures were very old, and so were most of the people in them. There was something odd about the people in the pictures that Tyler couldn't quite figure out.

"These sure seem like odd pictures, don't they?" Michael said as he stood next to Tyler and stared at them. "They have a strange familiarity to them, as if they are all following the same purpose." Michael noticed that each picture had a little plaque beside it with the name of the people in the picture and a date. "Look at this, Tyler," Michael said quietly as he pointed to a picture; he recognized the people in it straight away as his grandparents.

Tyler stood there staring at the picture, almost lost in it; he felt possessed with anger and confusion. "Why didn't they tell us? They had plenty of time. It would have made all this so much easier if they would have told us. They didn't think about how we would feel; they could have stopped me from having nightmares years ago. They knew about my nightmares—why didn't they say something? Why? They didn't care at all about us, did they? All they cared about was their stupid Dark World and their powers. Their powers were more important to them than we were," Tyler shouted as he banged his hands on the picture of his grandparents.

Michael stood there in horror as a mixture of smashed glass and blood covered the floor at Tyler's feet. "We don't know why they didn't tell us. Maybe they had a very good reason, but we won't know now, will we? They're dead," Michael spat at Tyler.

Tyler opened his mouth to talk, but he was interrupted when the lady returned. "*Ahem.*" They both swung their heads around. "Sorry to interrupt your…whatever this is, but he will see you both now, if you're ready. Never mind the mess; I will clean it up," she said in a firm voice.

Michael shot a look of warning to Tyler as they followed her through the door. Tyler ignored Michael's look and followed with his head down. They entered another office that was just as messy as the one before. The desk in this room, however, was not covered in books, but was covered in papers and files. There were two quite comfy-looking chairs in front of the desk. The walls were covered in pictures, the same as the walls in the other room, only this room was square instead of round. Michael looked up to see how far up the pictures went, only he couldn't see the ceiling; it looked like they went all the way up to the sky.

"We have been waiting for you two for a while now. It's so good to finally meet you," said a man that neither Michael nor Tyler recognized. "Come on in—sit, sit. Megixon, could you please bring us some tea?"

"Certainly, sir." She smiled and left the room.

"Sit; don't worry, you have nothing to be afraid of here."

Michael and Tyler sat down. They were both a little unsure; they still didn't know where they were, or how they had gotten there.

"So how are you both?"

Tyler just stared at the man and waited for Michael to answer, which he did.

"We're fine, thank you; we are just a little confused as to how we got here, or where, exactly, 'here' is."

The man gave them both a suspicious look; he looked at Tyler and squinted as he leaned a little closer to him. Tyler pulled away and turned to Michael.

"Are you saying you don't know who I am?" the man asked.

"I'm sorry, sir, but we don't. I'm guessing we are in the World of Darkness, but I'm not really sure how we got here; I was hoping that you would be able to tell us that," Michael said.

"So you probably don't know very much about the Dark World. Oh my, your grandparents must have died before they had the chance to—"

Before he could finish, Tyler interrupted angrily. "I don't want to hear any excuses about why my grandparents didn't tell us about all of this."

The man behind the desk was stunned by Tyler's words. He looked at Michael for some kind of answer, but Michael just shook his head. "I am sorry…I…I didn't mean to offend you. I…just meant… Well, I'm sure that you boys will find the answers you are looking for soon enough. Anyway, we have lots to do so, we should probably stop wasting time and get started straight away. You have your Oltes, I presume?" Michael nodded. "Good, well, that's a start at least. You must have your traveler or you wouldn't be here, now would you?" the man said with a laugh.

"Excuse me—I'm sorry to interrupt, but you still haven't told us who you are," Michael said quietly.

"Oh, pardon me—how rude of me. My name is Greff; I am the holder. Now, shall we…"

"What is a holder?" Michael interrupted.

"A holder…yes, well, ahem…The holder is me, and I am the holder—the only one, see."

Michael looked at him, unsatisfied with his answer. "But what do you hold?"

Greff began to fidget in his chair. "I hold the dead. Now shall we begin?"

Michael was stunned, yet still not satisfied with the answer that Greff had given him—but he didn't ask any more questions.

"Have either of you used your Oltes yet?" Greff asked hopefully.

"Yes, Tyler has—he is really quite good—and I have tried twice. The first time, it worked, but the second, it didn't, I'm afraid. We have a book…"

Greff smiled. "You have Nomad?"

"Yes, Lodiss gave him to us at the Mysterious Blue. At the same time, she gave us our Oltes."

Megixon came back with a tray in her hands; she put it down on the desk and began to pour three cups of tea. She had also brought some strange-looking biscuits. She handed Greff a cup and he helped himself to a biscuit, then she handed a cup to Michael, and one to Tyler. Tyler shook his head.

"I don't want tea and biscuits; I want to know why we are here," Tyler spat at Greff.

"Okay, lad, calm down. You will find all that you are looking for—you just need to be patient."

Tyler jumped to his feet. "I don't want to calm down. I want you to start talking, or I'm leaving," he snapped.

"Calm down, Tyler—Greff is trying to help, that's all."

"Yeah, well, how is tea and whatever those are going to help? I want some answers!" Tyler sank back into his chair.

"Sorry, Greff. You will have to excuse my brother; he's just tired."

"I am not tired and I don't need you to make excuses for me."

An awkward silence drenched the room, until finally Greff began as though there had been no unpleasantness. "Okay, let's get started now, shall we? You need to practice using your Oltes; it is very important. You also need to learn how to use your traveler properly or you will be entering all over the place. Is your traveler a light or a box?"

Michael saw that Tyler wasn't going to offer any more help. "I'm not sure. I don't think it's a light, but on the other hand, I didn't think it was a box, either."

Tyler shook his head. "When I held it in my hands it lit up and got warm, just like what happened to Michael when he picked up the one in the other room, only yours must be a lot hotter than ours; ours didn't burn me."

Michael looked at Tyler in surprise. Tyler hadn't told him that.

"Well, it must be a light. I assumed so, I you being…well…who you are and all."

Tyler shook his head, frustrated.

"Well, you are on the right track, at least. To use your traveler, you need to make sure that you are not seen by a Lyt in the midst of your travel. You don't need to be next to your traveler, or even in the same room; when you get really good, you will be able to use your traveler from miles away. It is all in your head; you already know all you need to know. I'm sure of that. You both are special; Simon knew it—he was certain of it."

Tyler shot a nasty look at Greff. "I don't want you to tell us anything about him. You're wrong, anyway—we are not special. Even if we are Nytstars, we are still not special."

Greff stood up and stared right at Tyler. "You have no idea, do you? The powers you hold…You are not just any Nytstar. You are—"

"I don't want to hear it," Tyler spat at Greff. "My grandparents failed to tell us anything about all of this. They could have told us, but they didn't—they never even tried. I don't know if I even want to be a Nytstar at all. I do know that I don't want you to tell me I'm special. You have no idea what I go through every night; you have no idea what it's like to have everyone think you're a freak."

Michael was shocked; he had never heard Tyler talk like this before. Tyler walked over to the star, refusing to look at Michael or Greff, and reached under his pajama shirt for his Oltes.

"Don't leave yet, Tyler. We won't talk about your grandparents, I promise," Greff pleaded.

Michael walked toward him. "Stay...please, just a little while longer."

Tyler just closed his eyes lowered his head, and was gone.

"I'm sorry about my brother," Michael began. "He's just having a rough time right now. He has a lot going on with school and his nightmares. He just..."

"You don't need to worry. He will come around; he just needs some time," Greff reassured Michael. "You can go after him if you like. I will understand."

Michael looked at the star; he wanted to go after Tyler, to make sure he was okay, but something was holding him back—something was telling him to stay. "That's okay—I think I will give him some space."

Greff took a drink from his tea and sat back down behind his large desk. "Your brother is wrong, you know. You are both special; you have powers beyond that of an average Nytstar. You just need to find them. You *have* to find them; all of the Nytstars are counting on you," Greff said quietly.

"What do mean? Why would they be counting on us? Counting on us for what?" Michael asked.

"They need your help; you two are our last hope of defeating the King of Darkness. Let's not worry about that now. We have lots more to worry about; you need to learn how to use your powers, or you won't be any help to us anyway."

Michael stayed with Greff a while longer, practicing using his Oltes. Tyler had returned back to their room. He was lying in bed, pretending to be asleep, when Michael finally returned.

"Tyler, are you asleep?" he whispered. "Tyler, if you're not really asleep, I would like to talk to you." Tyler didn't move or make a sound; he just lay there. "At least he might get some sleep," Michael said to himself. He got back into bed and fell asleep right away. He was so tired, he didn't even wake up when Tyler had a nightmare and was calling out in his sleep.

CHAPTER SIX

SARA

Tyler was becoming moody and distant. Mrs. Leeds had talked to Michael on more than one occasion to try and figure out what was wrong, but Michael would lie each time.

"Honestly, Mom, I really have no idea why Tyler is being so weird lately. Maybe something is going on at school. I'll try and find out what's wrong, okay?" Mrs. Leeds seemed somewhat happy knowing that Michael would try.

Michael was partially right; there was something going on at school. Conner and Chase were doing everything they could to make Tyler miserable, and due to his already bad mood, it was all working. Usually Tyler was pretty good at ignoring them and their so-called "Gang"; he wouldn't listen to a word they said. He knew they were just bullies, and that they just wanted a re-action from him, but now they had reached a whole new level.

Their new target was Megan. She had been in Tyler's class since they were in kindergarten; she had always been nice to him, standing up for Tyler when other girls would tease him. But lately, Conner and Chase had turned on her. They would tease her in the halls as she passed by. "Oh, look, everybody, it's baby Tyler's new mommy," they would shout in a crowd of kids so that they all laughed. More than once, they had teased her so badly that she had run away, crying.

Tyler had a deep loathing for Conner and Chase; every time they bullied Megan, Tyler felt all his anger toward them growing. It was only a matter of time before he wouldn't be able to control it anymore, and then who knew what would happen? Finally, Tyler was sitting at the back of Mrs. Suzanne's class, the last class before lunch, trying to make it through the last twenty min-utes without anything going wrong. He kept his eyes down on his books, making sure they remained open. Conner was whispering to Chase; Tyler couldn't hear what they were saying, but from their giggles and their occasional looks in his direction, he knew they were talking about him. Conner showed Tyler a picture that he was drawing of Tyler in a baby carriage being pushed by Megan. He had written rude words, calling Megan nasty names all over it.

Tyler felt anger surge through his body. He stood up, and walked over to Conner, grabbed the picture out of his hands, and ripped it up. Mrs. Suzanne had been facing the blackboard; she turned around just as Tyler threw the pieces of ripped-up paper all over Conner.

"What do you think you are doing in my classroom?" she shouted in a nasty voice. "How dare you bother my students?"

Conner had a satisfied look on his face he turned to Chase, who was also smiling at the sight of Mrs. Suzanne yelling at Tyler. Tyler was trying his best to control his temper, although it was becoming almost impossible with every word that Mrs. Suzanne said. He felt like he would lose control at any moment.

"You are pushing my buttons, boy. You should be thankful that I still let you stay in my classroom. I always knew you were a troublemaker who wouldn't amount to anything. Why can't you be more like your brother?"

Tyler couldn't hold back his anger any longer. He opened his mouth to explode, but the bell rang just in time. He picked up his books and ran for the door.

"I did not say you could leave," Mrs. Suzanne shouted after him, but it was too late; he had already left the classroom and was halfway down the hall. His heart was pounding hard. He felt so angry; he wanted to just start running and not stop. There seemed to be nothing that he or anyone else could do that didn't make him angry anymore.

Tyler kept on running until he was out of the school. He didn't even stop when he heard Michael shout after him. The truth was he didn't know where he was going; he was just running. Before long, he had run off the school grounds. He looked back, but he couldn't even see the school any more, he had run so far. A short while later, he found himself in a familiar place; he looked around and saw the big red door with the brass doorknocker on it. He was on the front doorstep of the Mysterious Blue.

Tyler stood there for a while, deciding if he wanted to go inside or not. He wasn't sure why he had ended up there or who he would see. What if Lodiss isn't here? he thought to himself, not really knowing if it was Lodiss he was hoping to see. He took a deep breath and turned the handle on the door, but it was locked. He tried it again, but it didn't move. Tyler stood there, frozen, feeling quite lost. He wasn't sure why he had run there in the first place, but he knew that something must have drawn him there—of all the places to which he could have run, why there? Why the Mysterious Blue—especially if it was locked?

Tyler stared at the big brass knocker. He had to try; he couldn't just leave. He knocked on the door and waited for a while, but there was no answer. He tried again, only this time a little harder, but still nothing. Tyler couldn't help but feel angry and frustrated, but he didn't really know why, and that only seemed to make it worse. He felt tears begin to run down his face. Tyler sat down on the front step and leaned against the door. He put his face in his hands, and the thought of crying just because nobody answered the door only made him angrier. Tyler sat on the doorstep for what felt like hours; the step was cold and made his legs and his back feel numb, but he didn't care—he had no desire to go anywhere.

"What are you doing here?" Tyler heard a sweet voice ask. He lifted his head and saw Sara standing in front of him. He felt relieved yet a little embarrassed.

"I don't know; I just ran and ended up here."

Sara looked at him and couldn't help but feel sorry for him; he looked so pitiful sitting there, his eyes all swollen and his face blotchy from crying, his hair a mess from running from school. Sara reached out her hand to help him up.

"I'm not helpless, you know—I just ran, that's all," Tyler said, now feeling embarrassed.

"I…wasn't…I didn't mean anything, I just thought…" Sara stopped; she didn't know what to say.

Tyler tried not to look at her; he could see that he had upset her.

"Are you here to shop or just to be rude?" she asked.

"Neither, I just…well, I…I don't really know why I'm here."

Sara reached in her bag, pulled out her keys, and opened the door. Tyler stood on the doorstep, staring in at the shop. There were no lights on inside; he had never seen the shop in the dark before.

"Are you coming?"

Tyler looked at Sara, a little unsure.

"It's okay, my Gran went to visit her sister in London. She'll be gone for two weeks, so I'm keeping the shop closed until she gets back." Sara reached for the light switch and turned on a few lights.

Tyler took a deep breath and followed her inside, closing the door behind him. "Aren't you afraid to be here all by yourself? What if someone tries to break in or something?" Tyler asked; even he was worried for her.

"I'm a big girl; I can take care of myself. Besides, Gran has put Drades all over; nobody could break in. I'm perfectly safe." They walked through the shop to the back, through a door that Tyler hadn't noticed before, and into a kitchen. Sara threw her school bag down on the floor in the corner and pulled out a chair for Tyler.

"Have a seat. Do you want a drink?" she asked. Tyler felt a strange feeling in the pit of his stomach.

"Um…sure, thanks."

"So you don't know why you're here, but you ran all the way from school. Don't you think that's a little odd?" she asked as she handed Tyler a Coke.

"Thanks. No, I have no idea why I'm here; really, I just needed to get away."

Sara sat down at the table across from Tyler, and gazed at him. "I saw what happened in Mrs. Suzanne's class."

"You did? Well, of course you did, you are in the class, aren't you?" Tyler looked across the table at Sara, who quickly looked down and fiddled with her pop in her hand.

"Mrs. Suzanne is mean to everybody that she feels is less than perfect."

Tyler shot a disbelieving look across the table at Sara. "She isn't mean to you. You must be perfect—well, at least in her eyes," he spat nastily.

"You have no idea, do you? You think you're the only one that Mrs. Suzanne is mean to? Every time I hand in my work, she whispers to me, 'Another great job—at least you still have brains, even though you're orphaned. Too bad you live with your crazy Gran.' So you're not the only one."

Tyler felt an annoying lump well up in his throat. "I can't believe she talked that way to you. If I ever—"

Sara interrupted. "You would only make it worse."

"I'm sorry, I didn't know," he said gently.

"You can't let her win; all she wants to do is make you crack, to have a reason to watch you fall. You can't let her," Sara said firmly. "Besides, she is right, you know—my Gran is a little crazy. Are you hungry? We could order a pizza."

Tyler smiled; he didn't care what time it was, or that nobody had any idea where he was. He knew he would be in trouble when he got home, but all that he cared about at the moment was that everything felt okay. They ate pizza and talked about school, movies, and Lodiss. Tyler wanted to ask how Sara's parents had died, but he didn't want to spoil their fun.

Sara glanced at the big clock on the wall. "It's eight thirty. Did you need to call your parents to let them know where you are?"

Tyler looked at the clock. He didn't want to leave; he wished more than anything that he could just stay there with Sara. "I should probably head home. I'm sure I'll be grounded; I wouldn't doubt it if my mom has called the police or sent out a search party."

Sara laughed as she stood up to walk Tyler to the door. "If you're not grounded, you should come over again. I have lots of cool stuff in the shop I could show you."

Tyler picked up his stuff and they walked to the door. "Yeah, that sounds great," he said, and walked out the door. Sara went back inside and closed and locked the door.

Tyler walked along the street, around the corner, and to the bus stop. He was only at the bus stop for a few minutes before the bus came, just like the last time he caught the bus from that stop. The bus, except for the driver, was completely empty. Tyler went to the back of the bus. He couldn't help but think that even though he was going to be in loads of trouble when he got home, he had had a great time with Sara. Mrs. Leeds was definitely going to ground him forever: he had left school early, without calling her, he didn't even tell Michael where he was going, and he was coming home late, not to mention that Mrs. Suzanne had most likely called his house to tell Mrs. Leeds how he ripped up a paper and threw it all over another boy. Tyler didn't really care about all that at the moment; all he could think about was Sara.

He stared out the window as the bus came closer and closer to his stop by the park. He reached into his shirt to grab his Oltes. "I don't even know how you work—well, not really, anyway—I just would like it very much if I didn't get into too much trouble when I walk through the door, please," Tyler whispered quietly to himself as the bus pulled up to his stop.

Tyler stood up quickly; he hadn't been paying attention, and he had nearly missed his stop. Looking out the window, he noticed that nobody was waiting to get on the bus. He walked down the steps and onto the sidewalk. "That's funny; I didn't even ring the bell. I wonder why he stopped." He turned around to watch the bus drive away.

Tyler walked the rest of the way home, soon forgetting about the bus, and remembering all the trouble he was about to be in when he walked through the front door. Tyler walked up the path to his house, but before he reached the door handle, the door flew open, and Michael was on the other side. Tyler could see Mrs. Leeds walking toward him.

"Soccer," Michael said quietly to Tyler before he opened the door all the way.

Tyler was a little confused. Mrs. Leeds was standing right in front of him. Soon it would all be over; he wouldn't be able to hang out with Sara again, and he probably wouldn't be able to play soccer in the park either.

"Well, don't just stand there—I want to know everything," Mrs. Leeds said in a voice that was shockingly calm, and almost excited.

"Soccer," Tyler said weakly.

"I know, soccer, but tell me more—did you make the school team or not?"

Tyler shot a puzzled look to Michael, who shook his head slowly so as not to be noticed. "No, I didn't make the cut for the school team."

Mrs. Leeds smiled sympathetically. "Well, that's too bad, but there is always next year. They sure kept you there a long time, though. I hope they fed you all. I can't believe they didn't pick you; maybe I should call the school tomorrow."

Tyler shot a desperate look to Michael. "Mom, you can't do that. He'll be known as the boy who cried to his mommy for not making the soccer team. Besides, it's usually the older kids that make the team, anyway, Mom, so I wouldn't worry about it."

"Okay, then. I just hope that you're okay, Tyler."

Tyler was taken aback more than anything, but he nodded and told his mom he had homework, and went to his room. Michael followed him up shortly afterward.

"Where were you?" Michael demanded as soon as he shut the bedroom door. "Sara told me what happened in Mrs. Suzanne's class, and that you took off afterward. Where have you been all this time?"

Tyler was thankful for what Michael had told their mom so that he wasn't in trouble, but he really didn't want to tell him about Sara and the Mysterious Blue. "I was mad; I went for a run, that's all."

Michael laughed. "All this time you expect me to believe that you were running? Nice try—I know that not even you could run that long. Now I want the truth; where were you?"

Tyler thought quickly for a lie to tell Michael about where he had been. "I just went to the arcade, that's all. I had a burger and played video games for a while."

Michael wasn't sure he believed him, but he didn't want to fight. "Did you like the story I told Mom for you?"

Tyler laughed. "Yeah, it was pretty good—although you do know that if I had tried out for the soccer team, I would have made it," he joked, throwing a miniature soccer ball he was playing with at Michael. "Thanks for covering for me, Mike."

Michael smiled and threw the ball back to Tyler. "I'm going back to Greff's tonight. I would like it if you would come with me," Michael said quietly.

"I don't want to go back there tonight; I think that guy doesn't really know what he's talking about. Besides, I think Nomad would be able to tell us the same thing here, instead of going to the Dark World," Tyler said firmly.

"I know that, but we can't practice them as freely here as we can in the Dark World. What if someone here were to see us? Or if we hurt someone, even by accident? I don't think that would go over too well; besides, Greff doesn't hold anything back, and I want to know everything, no matter what," Michael said, not willing to meet Tyler's eyes.

"Well, maybe he should learn to hold things back." Tyler stormed off, back downstairs.

Michael looked at Tyler's backpack. "I know he wasn't at the arcade today. If I only knew where he was…He is definitely hiding something—but what?" Michael said to himself as he walked toward Tyler's backpack. Michael slowly picked up the backpack to have a look inside, hoping to find a clue as to where he had been.

"Put it down—there's nothing," Tyler said angrily to Michael.

Michael dropped the backpack. "I wasn't…I was just…um…I was going to look in your backpack, but I'm sorry, I was just trying to…I just want to make sure you're all right, that's all," Michael stammered.

"I assure you that I am fine. Now I have to do my homework," Tyler said as he lunged onto his bed and pulled out his books.

"Fine, you do your homework—I'll just get out Nomad and start looking through him to learn more about our other world, and our powers. There has got to be a truth power or something," Michael muttered under his breath as he reached under the bed and pulled out Nomad. Michael opened the book to the first page to begin reading where he had left off the last time, only the front page had changed. This time, the front page read:

Truth Drades

Using Drades to force the truth out of a Nytstar is most complex, They require great skill; they are often blocked by a counter Drade. One of the most common mistakes of people trying to use a truth Drade is that they don't really understand the end result. Sometimes lies are told to protect someone, or to hide something you do not need to know. So before you even try to use a truth Drade, you need to ask yourself: Do you really need to know where he was?

Michael slammed the book shut and moved to where Tyler was laying on the bed. "Did you do a counter Drade so that I couldn't find out where you really were tonight?"

Tyler looked up from his book "You can really do that?" he asked with a slight laugh.

"Don't play games with me—I know you did."

Tyler just shook his head and continued to read.

"Fine, lie to me then. After I kept you out of trouble, that's the thanks I get," Michael said before he went back to reading Nomad.

Tyler finished his homework sometime after midnight; he was so involved with it that he hadn't even noticed that Michael had gone to bed almost an hour before. Tyler put his books away and got ready for bed. He crept downstairs to see if his mom and dad were still up.

That's odd; I don't remember them coming up to say goodnight, he thought to himself as he returned to his room. Michael was sound asleep. Tyler slid into bed. He remembered what Michael had said about wanting him to go back to see Greff, but he still had no intention of joining him. Tyler lay awake for a while before drifting off into another restless sleep.

It was two thirty when Tyler sat up in bed, sweating and breathing heavily. He looked around the room before he laid his head back down. "Why can I not have just one night's sleep without all these dreams?" he whispered to himself. The room seemed to be very cold; Tyler shivered in his bed. He pulled the blankets up to his chin to keep himself warm.

It's freezing in here; did we leave the window open? he thought as he got out of bed and ran to the window to check. Tyler reached behind the navy blue curtains to pull the window closed, but it was closed already. Tyler pulled the curtains back to see for himself, but the window was definitely closed all the way, and locked.

"That's weird—it's freezing. Michael...Michael, wake up," he said quietly as he climbed onto the top bunk to shake Michael awake. Tyler reached into the top bunk and pulled back the covers; again the top bunk was empty. "He is probably still at Greff's. Well, I'm not going to get him—that's probably what he wants," Tyler said to himself.

"You think you have it figured out, then, do you? Michael is at Greff's." Tyler recognized the voice as Candor; he had been visited by him once before. Tyler turned around slowly to see Candor standing behind the door.

"What are you doing here?" Tyler asked.

"You know, the usual—trying to help you, that's all, although it seems to me that I am too late."

Tyler stared at Candor. "What do you mean, you're too late?" he asked Candor.

"Well, you and your brother have already found someone to help you, have you not? In fact, if I am not mistaken, your brother is there right now, isn't he?" Candor pointed to the star on the shelf.

"I'm not sure what you're talking about; we do not need your help," Tyler said sternly.

Candor stood up and reached for the door handle. He paused and turned around to face Tyler. "You will need my help—I guarantee you that. You will see that Greff is not what you think he is…but maybe you already know that, don't you? Or you would be there with your brother right now." Candor smiled and left the room.

Tyler stood there for a moment. He wanted to chase after Candor; he wanted to know how he would help him. Why was Greff not who they thought he was? However, he didn't go after Candor; he stood there staring at the door, hoping that maybe Candor would come back. How could he just say that and leave? What did he mean?

After a while, Tyler realized that Candor wasn't going to come back, so he got back into bed and went back to sleep. After only a short while, he felt a soft hand on his face—a warm, soft hand. Tyler sat up and rubbed his eyes. To his surprise, he saw Sara sitting on the edge of his bed, smiling at him.

"Sara, what are you doing here? In my room, I mean."

Sara just smiled as if she hadn't heard him.

"Sara, is everything okay?" Tyler asked again, but once again, Sara didn't seem to hear him; she just sat there, smiling. Tyler leaned forward to touch her, but she stood up and moved away. "Where are you going? Sara, wait," Tyler called as she walked further away from him. He tried to reach her but he couldn't. She was slipping away, further and further away. Tyler saw Candor's face appear through the window; Sara was getting closer to him.

"Sara, stop—don't go with him."

It was too late. Sara seemed to float right out the window with Candor. Tyler ran to the window after them. "SARA, NO! SARA, DON'T LEAVE— NO!" Tyler shouted. Tears were welling up in his eyes; he felt a lump in his throat.

"Tyler, what is it? Where is Sara going?" Michael asked him, trying to pull him away from the window.

Tyler didn't want to move. He tried to fight Michael off of him; he had to go after Sara. "Sara, I'm coming! I won't let him hurt you!" he shouted.

Michael shook Tyler to try to get him to wake up and move away from the window. "Tyler, there is nobody there. Look out the window. See? Nobody—you were only dreaming."

Tyler didn't think he had been dreaming. He knew that Sara was really there—he just knew it. "I have to go out. I'll be back soon," Tyler said as he hurried over to the closet and started to get dressed.

"You can't go out now! It's late—Mom and Dad would kill you if they found out," Michael argued.

"You wouldn't understand. I just need to go out," Tyler said while pulling on his sweater.

Michael looked around the room, desperately trying to find a clue as to why Tyler needed to leave so badly. "Let me come with you, then," Michael said as a last resort to help his brother.

Tyler stopped for a moment. He stared at Michael. "You don't have to, you know," Tyler shot at him.

Michael started to get dressed also. "I know I don't have to, but I want to."

Tyler was pleased that Michael was coming with him. After all, it was three thirty in the morning; he had never been out that late by himself before. He was a bit nervous about it—especially where they were going—but he didn't want Michael to know that. They both headed quietly down the stairs and out the front door. The street outside was silent; there wasn't any noise at all, not even in the distance—no cars or birds or anything. The silence seemed almost eerie. They were about to run right past the bus stop when the bus pulled up.

Michael looked at Tyler suspiciously. "Weird—I didn't know that the bus ran this late," Michael said as they stepped onto the once again empty bus. The bus driver was the same man as earlier. Tyler recognized him straight away from his tatty uniform and unkempt facial hair, but thankfully, he didn't even look at Michael and Tyler as they walked onto the bus. They walked to the very back, as they did each time; they even sat in the same seats.

"The buses don't usually run this late—I was right," Michael said. He had picked up a bus schedule from the front of the bus. "Look at this," he said, nudging Tyler and shoving the bus schedule under his nose.

Tyler stared at the schedule as he read it, then turned to Michael. "These are the times that we rode the bus already," Tyler said.

"Yes, but look: only the times that we have ridden the bus—nobody else but us. There is even tonight's run on here, and we just got on, and...wait a minute. You already rode this bus today—just once, though." Michael stared at Tyler, waiting for him to explain, but he didn't. To Tyler's relief, Michael didn't ask any more questions.

The bus stopped at the regular stop just around the corner from the Mysterious Blue. The boys got off the bus and turned around for one last look at it before it drove away, but it was too late: the bus had already gone.

"Have you noticed that the bus always shows up right when we need it?" Michael asked as he ran to catch up with Tyler, who was walking quickly to the shop.

"Maybe we are just lucky," he said. Tyler hadn't really been paying attention to Michael; he was too concerned about Sara. They reached the Mysterious Blue; Tyler started pounding on the front door.

"Have you thought about what Lodiss might say? You know, about us showing up here at this time?"

Tyler didn't turn around to look at Michael when he answered. "Lodiss isn't here."

Michael was confused. "What do you mean, Lodiss isn't here? Why are we here, then?"

Before Tyler could answer, the door swung open. Sara stood in the doorway, her mouth opened slightly in shock to see Michael and Tyler standing on the doorstep. She blushed, and tried to hide her pajamas with her housecoat. Tyler just stared at her.

"Er…we, er…well, what I mean is, Tyler, um…needed to, um…" Michael stammered, not really knowing what to say. After all, he didn't really know himself why they were standing on her doorstep at this time of the morning.

"Are you okay?" Tyler asked, not taking his eyes off of her. "I had a dream, I think, and, well, I thought you…I…I thought I saw you, I mean…"

Sara smiled. "I'm fine."

"Are you sure? Has anyone been in the shop?"

Sara gave Tyler a worried look. "Nobody can get in, remember? I told you earlier, Lodiss fixed it so no one can get in unless I let them in. I assure you, I am fine." Sara saw the look of fear on Tyler's face. She reached her hand out to touch his arm, but he pulled away. "Why don't you two come in for a while? I'll make you some hot chocolate."

Michael looked over at Tyler, who hadn't taken his eyes off of Sara the whole time, then looked at Sara, who was smiling at them. "Sure, hot chocolate would be nice. Thank you," Michael said, and they followed Sara inside the Mysterious Blue. They all sat around the kitchen table and sipped their hot chocolate.

"So what was your dream about?" Sara asked.

Michael looked at her, surprised; no one else had dared to ask Tyler about his dreams.

Tyler looked just as shocked; he glanced at Michael, who was now staring at Sara. "I, um…well, I don't usually tell people about my dreams. I don't like…They don't usually—"

"Understand?" Sara interrupted.

"Well, yes, they don't."

Sara smiled again at Tyler with a warm, understanding look. "I can only assume that the dream was about me, and something bad happened, otherwise you wouldn't be here, now would you?"

Michael opened his mouth to speak, but Tyler spoke first. "You're right. The dream was about you, but I guess it wasn't…well, terrible, I guess. You went away with Candor. You were not taken; you just went with him. You were smiling at me. You came into my bedroom, sat on my bed, and then left with him. I tried to stop you, but you couldn't hear me, I don't think."

Sara gasped; she put her hand over her mouth.

"What's wrong?"

Michael quickly looked over at Tyler; they both seemed to be thinking the same thing, only it was Michael who spoke first. "That shouldn't be all that scary to you, should it? I mean, you wouldn't know who Candor is unless you were a Ny—" Michael stopped and looked at Tyler, who pushed his hot chocolate aside to move closer to Sara.

"Are you?" he asked.

Sara looked at both of them. She seemed a little scared. "Yes," she said, staring down at the floor.

"That's not a bad thing, is it?" Tyler asked. "Why didn't you tell me sooner? I mean, it's not like I wouldn't understand. I mean, we just found out that we're Nytstars, right? If anyone knows what you're going through, it's us."

Sara looked up at them with so much hurt in her eyes that tears began to stream down her cheeks, and she turned away from Michael and Tyler.

"I don't understand," Tyler said as he put his hand on her shoulder.

Sara pulled away from him, getting up from the table. "I don't want to be a Nytstar," she shouted. Michael and Tyler jumped up from the table and followed Sara as she headed for the door. "I never wanted to be. Nobody asked me if I wanted this or not. I don't want any part of this at all; I don't want to end up like them—I won't," Sara said as she collapsed to the floor.

Tyler looked down at her. Michael bent down and asked her quietly, "End up like who?"

Sara lifted her head from her hands. "Like my parents."

Michael stroked her hair to comfort her. "What happened to your parents, Sara?" Michael asked, hoping not to upset her even more.

"They were taken by Candor," she sobbed. It suddenly made sense to Michael and Tyler why Sara had gotten upset when Tyler told her his dream.

"Taken where?" Tyler asked.

"Nobody knows. The Dreamencers looked for a long time—they looked everywhere, but nobody ever found them." Sara began to cry again.

"So that's why you live here with Lodiss," Michael added.

Sara nodded. Tyler jumped to his feet. "So my almighty grandfather, the one that so many people seem to think was so great, failed?"

Sara shot an angry look at him. "You don't understand," she spat.

"I don't need to—it's just one more time that they didn't do the right thing," Tyler snapped.

"They did do it right; it wasn't their fault what happened…it wasn't. It was Candor. He alone is responsible—well, he and the King of Darkness. They are the ones that have them somewhere, they are the ones that took them in the first place, and they are the ones that killed your grandparents." Sara stood up; a steady stream of tears had returned to her face. "It's time for you to leave. Yes, I, um…I…I think it's best," she said as she led them to the door.

"You can't just tell us that and then ask us to leave; I want to know all you know," Michael begged desperately.

Sara shook her head. "I don't think that I should be the one to tell you about that. I think you should wait and ask Lodiss when she gets back. You really should leave—I don't want to have to go through this again. I can't…I just can't." Sara was sobbing uncontrollably now. "You guys don't understand. Your grandparents are dead; you know that for sure. I have no idea if my parents are dead or alive."

"I, um…I am so sorry. I didn't think of that—I just want to know what really happened to my grandparents. I didn't mean to upset you. I'm sorry," Michael said. He put his arms around Sara, who fell into them. Michael stroked her hair, trying to comfort her.

Tyler glared at them. He felt angry, not sad as they did, and he really didn't know why. All he knew was that he wanted to get away. He didn't know where—just anywhere but there. He slipped out of the door while Michael still held Sara in his arms.

"Okay, I will tell you what you want to know. Let's go back into the kitchen," Sara said as she pulled away from Michael.

They both looked around frantically. "Tyler?" Michael shouted. "Tyler, where are you? This isn't funny."

Sara opened the door to see if she could see him walking or running away from the shop. Tyler was sitting on the step.

"I wanted to leave, but I couldn't," he said, staring at a small crack in the stone.

"You know, it's okay to be sad, or even angry, with your grandparents," Sara said as she wiped the tears off her face, which were quickly replaced by new ones.

"I'm not sad or anything—it's just that they didn't tell us themselves. They had lots of time before they died. It seems as if they didn't want to tell us or something."

Michael came through the door. He saw Tyler and shot him a look to let him know he was mad that Tyler left without telling him. "I see you didn't get very far this time," Michael said, just as they both looked up at the sound of a bus. Michael looked at his watch. "We have to leave now, or we'll miss the bus," he said hastily, pulling Tyler to his feet.

"We'll talk tomorrow, okay?" Sara reassured them.

The boys ran down the path and around the corner. They reached the bus stop just in time. The bus pulled up and opened its doors; they got on and went to their seats at the back. They didn't speak for the entire bus ride home. They sneaked quietly into the house and up the stairs. They both hopped into bed, and fell asleep almost the moment their heads hit the pillow; for the first time in what felt like forever, Tyler didn't wake up for three whole hours.

"Tyler…Tyler, I'm sorry to wake you. You need to get up for school," Mrs. Leeds said as she gently shook him. She had waited as long as she could; she really hated to wake him up when he was finally sleeping what seemed to be a nightmare-free sleep.

"What time is it?" Tyler asked, rubbing his eyes from the light that was shining directly onto his face.

"It's late—you only have fifteen minutes before you need to leave for school. I'm sorry, I didn't want to wake you; you looked so peaceful sleeping. Were you having good dreams?" Mrs. Leeds asked as she was leaving the room.

"I don't remember having any dreams," Tyler lied.

When Tyler finally headed downstairs for breakfast, Michael was already sitting at the table. He had finished his breakfast, and now had his head buried in a rather thick book.

"Good morning, sleepyhead—how was your sleep?" he asked Tyler without taking his eyes away from the book.

Tyler didn't even look in his direction when he grunted something that sounded like "Okay."

"You know, I had the best sleep. It was like I was a rock or something last night—best sleep I've had in ages," Mr. Leeds said as he picked up his lunch bag, kissed Mrs. Leeds on the cheek, shouted goodbye, and headed out the door.

"You had better hurry up or you're going to be late for school, boys," Mrs. Leeds said firmly.

"Mom, I won't be home for supper tonight. I have to go over to Brandon's house to work on a school project. Hey, Tyler, why don't you come too? We could use your help," Michael said, smiling.

"No, thank you. I have my own homework to do, thanks," Tyler said rudely, but he felt Michael kick him under the table, and Michael gave him a look that he recognized all too well as the "Go along with me" look. "Oh, fine, I'll come and help you—after all, it's not your fault that you're not as smart as me," Tyler laughed.

Mrs. Leeds smiled at them both. "That's fine, boys; your dad is working late, and I have a meeting. Okay, good—well, I have to run and so do you." She kissed them both and headed off to work. Michael and Tyler grabbed their backpacks and started their walk to pick up Brandon on their way to school.

"So I hope you don't really want me to help you and Brandon do school-work today," Tyler said as they stopped outside Brandon's house.

"Of course not. I thought we could go and visit with Sara—you know, pick up where we left off last night."

Tyler was relieved but a little disappointed that he would have to talk all about his grandparents.

"Hey, guys, what's with the serious faces?" Brandon asked as he ran up the path to meet them.

"Hey, buddy," Michael said, forcing a smile. "We were just talking about..." Michael looked at Tyler. "Can I tell him?"

Tyler turned his head away from Michael and shrugged his shoulders. "Whatever—if you don't tell him now, you'll only tell him later anyway."

The three of them walked to school as Michael told Brandon everything. Brandon listened in amazement; he hung on every word that Michael said, nodding at all the right times.

"How come all the cool stuff happened when I wasn't there? Next time you go out in the middle of the night on an adventure, please stop by and bring me along with you, okay?" Brandon said, still staring at Michael in excitement.

Tyler shot a nasty look at Brandon. He didn't think it was much of an adventure, talking about his dead grandparents and Sara's missing parents.

"Tyler! Tyler, wait up!"

Tyler looked around and saw Megan running toward him. He smiled; for the first time that morning, he felt happy.

"Good morning," Megan said happily to all of them.

"Good morning," Michael and Brandon said at the exact same time. Tyler smiled shyly but also said, "Good morning."

"I stopped for a hot chocolate and they had a 'buy one, get one free' thing, so I thought you might like one. I know you like hot chocolate and, well, I just thought...well...here," she said, smiling almost uncontrollably at Tyler and handing him the hot chocolate.

Tyler was going so red in the face, he almost looked like a cherry. "I, um...I...sure, I...thank you," Tyler stammered.

Michael and Brandon giggled. Tyler shot them a warning glare, which they ignored completely.

"Thank you for what you did yesterday in Mrs. Suzanne's class. That Conner is such a jerk."

"Well, you know we can't all be heroes like Tyler here, now can we?" Brandon laughed.

Tyler turned to him, and before anyone knew what he was doing, he flipped Brandon into the air and onto the floor. Brandon stared up at Tyler, not laughing anymore, and groaned, "Sorry." Tyler shot another warning look at Michael, who put his hands up jokingly. Tyler was even more embarrassed; he looked at Megan, who was still smiling at him.

"So you're a hero now?" she teased.

"No," spat Tyler.

"I was just kidding, Tyler. I didn't mean anything..."

"Yeah, don't flip her now, Ty," Michael said timidly, but laughing still.

"So, did you get all your homework done?" Tyler asked Megan.

"No, I was busy last night. I had a class, and I didn't get the chance to finish it all. How about you?" Megan asked, turning her eyes away from Tyler.

"Of course not. You know me—do I ever get it all done on time?"

"What class were you at last night?" Michael asked.

Megan looked embarrassed. "I joined a…um…a karate class," she said quietly.

Tyler looked at her, surprised. "You did? That's cool—which club did you join?" he questioned.

"I joined the same class that you go to. I hope you're not mad. I wasn't trying to follow you or anything—my dad thought it would be a good idea because of Conner and Chase. He says a girl needs to know how to defend herself. I hope it will eventually help me to teach them a lesson."

Tyler smiled. "Why would I be mad? I think it's a great idea."

Megan's face lit up. "Great! Then how would you feel about maybe giving me extra lessons after school?"

Tyler looked at Michael for help. Michael nodded. "Um, sure," he said weakly.

"Great, thank you. How about—"

But before she could finish, Sara walked up to them. "Hey, guys, how's it going?" she asked, smiling at Tyler, who was looking at Michael and Brandon as they waved goodbye and started to walk away.

"I'm fine, Sara. How about you?"

Sara smiled. "Better now, thanks to you."

Tyler blushed again. "Sara, this is Megan, Megan, Sara." Tyler introduced them to each other as they reached the edge of the school field just in time. The bell rang and they broke into a jog and headed for their lockers. Tyler said goodbye to Sara and he and Megan walked to class together.

All the way through Mr. Blain's very dull, very long lecture on fractions and how they will be a part of everyone's daily life forever, Tyler gazed out the window. Images of Sara talking about her missing parents the night before were drifting through his mind; he could see Sara crying in Michael's arms. He remembered how important it had seemed at the time to be mad about his grandparents, but Sara had been right: at least he knew they were dead. Sara had no idea. Suddenly a mass of guilt came over him. How could he have been so selfish, so immature, and so stupid? Sara was suffering way more than he was. He had all the time he needed to find out why his grandparents didn't tell him the truth; Sara might not have much time, if any at all—nobody knew for sure.

"How about tonight?"

Tyler turned around quickly. Megan was leaning in as close as she could without it looking too noticeable. "How about tonight?" she repeated.

"Tonight for what?" Tyler whispered.

"You know, the extra karate class you promised me." Megan was smiling sweetly.

"Sure," Tyler said, just before Mr. Blain looked their way.

"*Ahem*…I hope I am not interrupting you two," he said, loudly enough for the whole class to hear. Megan's face went red, and Tyler turned to face the window again, neither one of them answering Mr. Blain. "I will take that as a no, then, shall I?" he said, and returned to his lecture.

After their math class, they had English: the one class that Tyler truly hated. When Tyler finally reached the English classroom after taking the long way around the school, he was almost the last one there; only Sara had yet to arrive. Megan was sitting in the back of the class. Tyler spotted two empty seats at her table, and he went to join her.

"Why aren't you sitting with all your friends like you usually do?" he asked, noticing that all the people with whom she usually sat were sitting elsewhere today. Megan was quite popular; she was usually surrounded by lots of friends, but today she was sitting alone.

"It turns out that they may not have truly been my friends—well, not right now, anyway," Megan said, ignoring the giggling going on in front of them.

"Do you mind if we sit here?" Sara asked.

"Sure, why not?" Megan said, moving her bag off the seat next to her.

"Thanks." Sara smiled.

"What is going on over here? Tyler, one girl isn't enough to defend you? You need two?" Conner laughed.

"Just ignore him." Megan whispered.

"Did you have a good sleep last night? Or did you have scary-wary dreams?" Chase said loudly.

"Shut up," Tyler spat at them both.

"Tyler Leeds, causing trouble so early today, are we? Maybe you would like to tell me what the problem is. Stand up, then—let's hear it," Mrs. Suzanne said nastily.

Tyler would have loved to tell her that the problem was her, that she was always the problem; in fact, the mere thought of her—with her long, bleached-blonde hair and her constant show of black clothing—was his problem. Not to mention her arrogance, her "I'm better than everyone" attitude—that was his problem. Yet instead, he stood up in front of the entire class and weakly stated that his "problem," as Mrs. Suzanne put it, was that Conner smelled like he hadn't bathed in years. The sound of laughter echoed through the class, bouncing off the walls. Mrs. Suzanne glared nastily at Tyler before yelling at him to get out. Conner's face was so red that it looked like, given the chance, it would have exploded.

Tyler left the room once again, walking outside into the sunlight to sit under the tree where he usually sat when told, as he often was, to leave someone's class—only this time he didn't reach the tree.

"Where do you think you are going, Mr. Leeds?" said a voice that Tyler knew all too well. He turned around. Mr. Young, the school principal, had a disapproving look on his face as he walked over to Tyler. "Were you sent out of Mrs. Suzanne's class again, Tyler?" he asked sternly.

Tyler wasn't scared of Mr. Young like most of the other kids at school were; he thought he was way nicer than Mrs. Suzanne. "Yes, sir," Tyler answered honestly.

"Why this time? Oh, let me guess, it wasn't your fault, right? It was all somebody else's fault." Mr. Young led Tyler back into the school to his office. "You know, someday you will have to grow up. You cannot be thrown out of class all the time; you will never pass English if you are never in class long enough to learn any thing."

Tyler was furious. It wasn't his fault that Mrs. Suzanne always blamed him for everything; it wasn't his fault that Conner and Chase were complete jerks.

"You need to smarten up, Tyler; you are very close to being suspended."

Tyler didn't really care. A few days home from school would be great: no Conner, no Chase, and, best of all, no Mrs. Suzanne.

"I think you should go and apologize to Mrs. Suzanne, and I don't want to hear anything more about you being thrown out of Mrs. Suzanne's class. Do you understand me?" Tyler nodded his head. "Now go back to Mrs. Suzanne's class. No more problems—do I make myself clear?" Tyler nodded once more, left the room, and walked slowly back to class.

For the rest of the class, Mrs. Suzanne didn't talk to Tyler at all. She pretended she didn't hear Conner when he made comments to Tyler, Sara, and Megan, and she shot dirty looks at Tyler every chance she got. Tyler was so pleased when the bell rang for the next class that he didn't even care that Conner was yelling "Baby Tyler wet his diapie" across the class. In fact, Tyler didn't pay much attention to any of Conner and Chase's comments for the rest of the day. After school, Tyler met Michael outside; he was standing with Brandon and Sara.

"So, I'm glad that you remembered to ask Sara if it was okay for us to come over tonight," Michael teased.

"Oh, I forgot...sorry, I had a—"

Before Tyler could finish, Megan walked over to them and reminded Tyler about their karate lesson after school.

"I forgot...sorry, I, um...I already have to, um...I promised Michael and Brandon I would do something with them. I'm sorry," Tyler stammered, now wishing he had paid more attention when people were talking to him.

The smile on Megan's face faded. She glanced around at all of them. "Um...that's, uh...sure, no problem...Maybe tomorrow?" she said quietly. "Well, I had better go, then. See you tomorrow." Megan walked away quickly.

Tyler watched her leave, feeling guilty; he wanted to go after her, but his feet wouldn't move. He felt like he was stuck to the ground. All he could do was hope that she wasn't mad. He would help her tomorrow, he promised himself.

"If you have plans, Tyler, you can come over tomorrow," Sara said.

"No, let's go...it's fine. This is more important."

Brandon smiled at Tyler. "Too many women, hey?" he laughed. Tyler spun around quickly. Brandon moved out of the way. "Sorry," he said.

They all reached the bus stop just in time, as usual. When they got to the Mysterious Blue, they went straight to the kitchen. Sara handed them each a pop.

"Let's not waste any time," Michael insisted. "Last night, you told us that your parents were missing in the dark world—how long ago did that happen?"

Sara took a deep breath. "Two years ago, they were working for the Dreamencers. They were on duty, guarding something, and all I know is whatever it was they were guarding was almost lost. If it hadn't been for your grandparents, Candor would have taken it, and according to Lodiss, that would have been the end of the Dark World as we—well, as I—know it."

Michael glanced at Tyler; he was waiting for him to get mad, but he didn't. "So Lodiss must know what it was that Candor tried to take, then. I wonder why it's a secret. What could possibly change the Dark World forever? You don't have any idea what it could be?" Michael asked hopefully.

"Well, I did think that it could be a weapon, but there isn't a weapon big enough to kill all the Nytstars that don't support the King of Darkness."

Tyler walked over to the counter and put his empty pop can down. "Well, it has to be something important, doesn't it? Maybe we could check with Nomad—maybe he knows what it is that Candor wants," Tyler said as he sat back down at the table. He was still somewhat distant. "Wait a minute—you said if it weren't for our grandparents, Candor would have gotten it. Do you mean it's still hidden somewhere? Then Candor could still come after it."

Sara gasped. "I have never thought about that before. You're right, though. Nothing much has changed in the world of darkness, other than people are being more cautious of what they say and some Nytstars have disappeared—but that's all."

Michael reached into his backpack and pulled out a notebook. He began writing things down that he wanted to ask Nomad.

"Your grandfather hid whatever it was somewhere else. We have to find it; maybe that would help us find my parents."

Tyler shook his head. "We can't go searching all over the Dark World for something if we don't even know what we're looking for."

Michael stopped writing. "You're right, Tyler. We can't go looking for—well, who knows what—and so we need to figure out what it is we are looking for first."

Tyler stared at the table. He still didn't know very much about his powers; how were they supposed to go after the great lord of the night?

"You didn't finish telling us what happened to our grandparents," Michael urged.

"Candor—he killed them. They were protecting you two when they died. Somehow Candor found out that you both were Nytstars and that Tyler had the mark, so he tried to kill you both. Your grandparents made themselves take your form just before Candor cast his Drade, so they were killed instead of you."

"So why didn't Candor get us after he saw that it wasn't us that were dead?" Tyler snapped.

"He didn't know—not until just recently, anyway. I don't know how he found out; neither does Lodiss. But that doesn't matter—he must know now.

That's why he visited you that night, and that's why he wanted to get you to join his army."

Tyler looked at Michael. He felt angry, sad, and scared all at the same time. He didn't know what to say, so he just stared at Michael, hoping he would say something.

"So he either wants us on his side, or wants us dead," Michael said. He could feel Tyler's eyes on him, but he didn't want to look at him. Brandon just sat back; he didn't really have anything to say, so he just tried to be as unnoticeable as possible.

"So we need to find out what it is that Candor is looking for—that's our first step—and until we do that, we can't really do anything else," Michael said, taking out his notebook again. "Sara, I think we should look around here first; this is really our best link to the Dark World." Sara nodded. "Tyler, you need to pay extra attention to your dreams. Try to remember as much as you can about them; there could be clues in them. I'll search through Nomad; if there is anything in that book, I'll find it. The next chance we get, we should go and visit Greff—maybe he could help us." Michael took the role of the organizer; nobody seemed to mind.

"Shall we begin to search the shop?" Sara asked, sounding somewhat excited, as she looked around at all of them for an answer. They all nodded, then followed Sara out of the kitchen to begin their big search.

CHAPTER SEVEN

THE BIG SEARCH

They stood in the middle of the main level of the Mysteriousx Blue.

"We should start at the top and work our way down," Michael said. "We should split up: Brandon, you come with me; Tyler, you go with Sara. Look at everything and anything that looks suspicious. We should, um…"

"Put it in front of the shelf on the floor. That way, after we have all looked at it, we can put it back where it goes. Lodiss will never know," Sara said.

Michael smiled at her; he was impressed. "Okay, good luck," Michael said to them all as they went up the spiral staircase once again. Michael and Brandon headed off to the rear left side of the room.

"How about we start on the right side?" Tyler suggested, and he headed for a shelf. The shelf was covered in what seemed like hundreds of tiny statues of animals. All of a sudden, Tyler felt like he was trapped; he couldn't see a way out of all of this, searching for who knows what to help find two people who knows where. He stared at every statue blankly. They all looked so normal.

Sara was looking at a shelf filled with books. She took each book off the shelf, read the back of it, and flipped through the pages, just in case there was anything on the inside. Book after book, shelf after shelf, little statue after little statue…and nothing. Neither one of them took anything off the shelf on the top floor. The same happened on the main floor.

"This is hopeless—I don't know what is suspicious and what isn't," Brandon moaned.

"I know, but we have to keep looking. I'm sure we'll know once we find something." They moved down to the basement.

"What time is it?" Brandon asked. "I'm getting hungry."

Tyler was becoming irritated with Brandon; he began to walk away, but he stopped when Michael said that it was seven thirty.

"Should we tackle this floor tomorrow?" Brandon asked Michael hopefully.

"Why don't you guys call your parents and ask if you can stay here for the night? It is Friday."

"My mom would never let me stay at a girl's house overnight, especially when there are no adults in the house," Brandon said quickly. Tyler shot him a look of disgust; Brandon pretended not to notice.

"We could say we're sleeping at each other's houses," Tyler suggested.

"What if our moms talk? They always do," Michael said. "No, it has to be better than that." He walked up and down a few steps, thinking. He scratched his head as he muttered under his breath. The others were also trying to think, but they couldn't help staring at Michael. They silently watched as he paced the floor; they all jumped when he shouted, "Aha!" They looked at each other, and then returned their stares to Michael as he explained his plan. "We will all tell our parents that we're staying at, let's say, Tad's house. Yeah, I'm sure that he wouldn't mind; I'll call him and let him know. Then we'll have our moms talk to Tad's mom."

Michael pointed to Sara and gave the others a sneaky smile. They were impressed; Tyler gave Michael a pat on the back. "You are brilliant, absolutely brilliant. As soon as Mom talks to Sara—I mean, Tad's mom—she won't have any trouble with us sleeping over." Brandon also gave Michael his praise for his great plan.

"We should go home first so we can pack some stuff, and I can grab Nomad," Michael said.

They said goodbye to Sara and ran to the bus stop. Once they got home, they threw some stuff into a bag; Michael wrapped Nomad up in a sweater and shoved him into his bag. They phoned Sara at the shop so she could talk to their mom; just as Michael had predicted, their mom said it was fine. They rushed out of the house and met Brandon at his house; his mom had also spoken to Sara and was fine with the sleepover.

Once they were back at the Mysterious Blue, they put their stuff in the living room. They had been so quick getting their stuff it seemed as if they hadn't even left at all. They ordered pizza for supper and just hung out until it arrived. They had decided to wait until they all had full stomachs before they went back to work searching in the basement.

They were still searching at midnight, and they had only looked through about half of the things in the basement. "I don't think we're going to find anything here; we've been searching for ages," Tyler grumbled.

"We can't just give up. We have to keep looking; there has to be something here. A lot of this stuff Lodiss brought back from the Dark World; I'm sure there must be something here," Sara pleaded desperately.

"Wait—I found something!" Tyler shouted. They all ran over to where he was standing, holding something shiny.

"What is it?" Michael asked.

Tyler looked worriedly at Sara. He slowly opened his hand, showing the old, yet still shiny, necklace he had found. Sara looked terrified. "It can't be…you don't think that it's…well…that it's my…my…father's?" Sara stammered.

Tyler stared at Sara as he clenched the Oltes tightly in his hand.

"It might not be. It may not even be an Oltes—it could just be an old necklace," Sara said.

Tyler opened his hand once again. "It is," he whispered, "trust me. Watch this," he said as he slowly closed his eyes and whispered something so quietly that nobody could hear what he had said.

"What are you doing, Tyler?" Michael asked.

Sara gasped; she was staring at the Oltes, which was no longer black: now it had a face in it. The face was familiar to Sara. His eyes were dark brown and filled with despair. His nose looked swollen; most likely, it had been broken. There were scratches and cuts all over his face; some looked like they were fresh, and some looked as though they had been there awhile. He looked lost. Tyler knew the face was Sara's dad, even though he had never met him before, and although his face was battered and bruised, the resemblance was uncanny. The face in the necklace had the same big, brown, lonely eyes as Sara.

"Daddy, is that really you? Where are you?" Sara asked the face in the Oltes, but the man couldn't hear her; he was unaware that he was being watched. "Daddy, where are you?" Sara screamed.

Tyler looked to Michael for help, but Michael just stared at Tyler and Sara. He didn't know what to do. If the person in the Oltes was really Sara's dad, it still didn't mean that he was alive—it could be a picture stored in there.

"He's real, I'm sure of it. I don't know why, or how I know he is alive— I just know he is." Sara stared at the Oltes, hoping, wishing that he would look back and see her, or even jump right out of the Oltes, and hold her tightly in his arms. But he didn't; he just kept looking around, lost, with no idea that there were people so close, staring at him, watching his every move.

"What do we do? Michael, what's the plan? Now that we know he is alive, we need to go find him. We have to go and…well, we…go, and…We need to go find him," Sara said, jumping up and down, overcome with excitement.

"We can't just go off somewhere. We still have no idea what Candor was looking for, or where he is. I don't think it's a very good idea to just go off on some kind of wild hunt; we could get hurt—or worse. Besides, neither Tyler nor I really know how to use our powers very well. If all those Dreamencers went looking for them, why would we have any better luck than they did?" Michael was sure he was right. Even though he knew that Tyler and Sara probably wouldn't listen to him without a fight, he knew he was right; he knew they needed more.

"We know that he's alive; that's all we need to know, isn't it?" Sara spat at Michael.

Tyler didn't speak; he just sat there looking at the Oltes in his hand.

"I am not saying that we won't help you—just that we need more to go on, that's all. We need to know more," Michael said firmly. He wanted to tell her that they would find him, and her mom, and that everything would be okay, but he knew he couldn't promise that, and the last thing he wanted to do was lie to her.

Sara fell to the floor, crying. She buried her head in her hands and sobbed. "I just miss them so much. I want them back—I need them back. I miss them," she cried.

Michael knelt down on the floor next to her and wrapped his arms around her again; she fell into him and cried as Michael tried to console her. Tyler stared at them. His heart sank at the sight of Sara and Michael. He would do anything to help her; he didn't care that they didn't know where to look. He would look anywhere.

"We need to help her, Michael; we have to do whatever we can," Tyler said as he got up and walked over to the spot where he had found the Oltes, continuing to look. Brandon looked at Sara and Michael, who were still sitting in each other's arms, and decided to join Tyler and start to look again.

"We will help you," Michael whispered into Sara's ear.

Sara sobbed, "Thank you," as she wiped her eyes. "I know they are still alive—I just know it."

Michael nodded. He took Nomad out of his backpack and sat back on the floor next to Sara. He stared at the front of the book, where Nomad's face appeared. "I need some answers, Nomad; I don't want you to lie to me, either," Michael said sternly.

"I will do my best to tell you what I know, Michael, but you need to understand: some knowledge can be dangerous. The answers you are all looking for are very dangerous. You all need to be careful; do you understand me?" Nomad spoke loudly, loudly enough that Tyler and Brandon heard him, and they came to join Michael and Sara on the floor. They all sat so quietly they could hear themselves breathing. "You are all wanting to search for Sara's parents, am I right?" Tyler looked at Michael, then they both nodded. "They were taken by Candor. I don't know where they are. There are strong Drades surrounding them, so no spells, nor any amount of power, can penetrate and get to them. Their Oltes were taken from them, so they have no powers of their own."

"We have one of the Oltes; we found it here in the shop tonight. It's Sara's dad's," Tyler interrupted.

"Then you have made the first step to finding them. You will need to take the Oltes with you when you go looking for them; otherwise, you will never stand a chance of getting them away from Candor without their powers. Yours alone will not be strong enough to take on Candor."

Michael scratched his head, the way he always did when he was thinking hard. "Nomad, how do you know for sure that he is in the World of Darkness? Maybe he is hiding them here, in our world. It would be the least obvious place, wouldn't it?"

"You are right, Michael—it would be the least obvious place. But Candor, just like the King of Darkness, and most of the Nytstars, is of true descent."

Michael just stared at Nomad. "You mean their whole families are Nytstars?"

"As far back as they go. There are more and more Nytstars now that are not of true descent, just like you both—"

"So what does that have to do with Candor not hiding them in our world?" Tyler interrupted. Michael glared at Tyler, who shrugged his shoulders.

"True Nytstars can't take anything from our world—not even other Nytstars—"

"That's why Candor didn't take me that night when I saw him downstairs in our living room: he couldn't. He said that, too, but I didn't know what he meant," Tyler interrupted once again.

"That's right; even the King of Darkness cannot cross into the Lyt world and take things. Once you find Sara's parents, you need to get them back to the Lyt world as soon as possible. This is the only place you are all safe."

"Do you have any idea where my mom's Oltes might be?" Sara asked Nomad. She had stopped crying, but she was still trembling—now with excitement instead of sadness. She knew they were closer to finding her parents; she was closer to finding them than she had been.

"I'm afraid I don't. I am sorry."

Sara forced a smile.

"That's okay…so we just keep looking," Michael said as he reached for her hand.

"I think that's enough for tonight. Let's move into the living room with our sleeping bags and stuff," Sara suggested.

Michael glanced at Tyler, who was blushing slightly. "Sure, we'll grab our stuff," Michael said as they all headed to the doorway where the pile of sleeping bags, pillows, and backpacks lay.

When they were all in their pajamas and had their sleeping bags laid out, Sara came downstairs with her stuff. Tyler glanced at her, then turned away quickly. Sara was wearing army-print PJ bottoms with a dark army green tank top. Her hair was tied up loosely in a half-ponytail. She was wearing pink bunny slippers that looked like they were on the wrong girl's feet. "Don't laugh at my slippers, all right? They were a gift from Lodiss. She thinks that every girl should have a pair of pink bunny slippers," Sara said, giggling. She looked around at the three of them; they were all staring at her with their mouths slightly opened. "What's the problem with you three?" Sara asked, laying her sleeping bag down next to Tyler's.

"Um…nothing. Why?" Tyler asked, looking around at Michael and Brandon for help.

Michael smiled. "I was just thinking that Tyler sure would look cute in pink bunny slippers," he laughed. Tyler punched him in the arm.

"So, are you going to give everyone karate lessons, or only Megan?" Brandon asked Tyler from a safe distance where he thought he wouldn't get hurt.

"Shut up," Tyler spat at him.

"I was just wondering if you were offering them to anyone, or only pretty girls," Brandon added, laughing. Tyler flew from his sleeping bag, and before Brandon knew what had happened, he was pinned down by Tyler, finding it a little hard to breathe. "I...I was...ugh..."

Michael sat back and laughed.

"Should we stop them?" Sara asked. "They might hurt each other."

Michael shook his head. "They won't hurt each other, not to worry. Tyler might hurt Brandon, but that's about it."

Tyler let go of Brandon, who coughed until he caught his breath. "I was just kidding, jeez."

Tyler smiled at Brandon. "Well, next time you won't, then, will you?" He laughed, then returned to his sleeping bag.

Sara looked at both of them, still a little shocked. They both seemed to have gotten over it quite fast.

"They do it all the time," Michael said calmly.

"Oh, that's great," Sara said, somewhat relieved.

"So, where do we go from here? I mean, it's not like we can just head over to the Dark World and start putting up 'lost parents' posters, or put their faces on milk cartons, now can we?" Michael joked.

"We should start by finding out what they were protecting. That might give us a clue as to where they are," Tyler said.

"They were protecting you," Sara said quietly, staring at the floor.

"What?" Tyler shouted. "Who—or why?"

Sara refused to look at either one of them; she knew they would be mad.

"They were protecting us? And you knew? All this time, you knew and you didn't tell us? You kept it from us? Why? Why wouldn't you tell us? We are trying to help you!" Tyler said angrily.

"I am sorry, really I am. Lodiss told me not to tell you no matter what. She said that it would be too dangerous for you to know."

"What? Why would it be dangerous? I don't understand. I don't see why we needed protection in the first place. Protection from what? Why are we so delicate?" Tyler demanded.

"You're not delicate; you were being protected so that Candor couldn't steal your powers."

Tyler stared blankly at the floor. "Why doesn't anyone tell us the truth? Everyone treats us like babies all the time. You said our grandparents died protecting us; then why were your parents protecting us too? You were the one person that I thought I could trust, and now...you...damn it."

Tyler's head was filling with all sorts of angry thoughts. He got up and left the room. He didn't care that he was in his pajamas; he was going to go home, pack some things, and go to the Dark World. Michael and the others shouted after him to come back, but none of them stopped yelling at each other long enough to go after him. Out on the street, he stared up at the moon, then walked around the corner to the bus stop. Within moments, the bus arrived. He got on the empty bus, headed for the back, and stared out the window until the bus arrived at his stop. Once he reached his house, he snuck quietly through the door, up the stairs, and into his room. He mindlessly threw a few items in a bag and stood in front of the star on his bookshelf. So many thoughts were rushing through his head: thoughts of Sara, her parents, Candor, and Michael. He shook his head, trying to clear all the voices in his head telling him to stay.

Tyler held his Oltes tightly in his hand. He closed his eyes, took a deep breath, and thought as hard as he could about the Dark World. His body suddenly felt empty; he felt like he was floating, all the while looking at his body, watching his own body float without being in it. He felt lost, and then he was spinning, spinning so fast he was out of control—he couldn't stop. Slowly, his body came back to him, and the spinning stopped. Now he was cold, so cold he was shivering uncontrollably, and then he suddenly stopped. He opened his eyes and all he could see was black. There were no sounds—nothing.

Tyler closed his eyes tightly. He wasn't scared; he somehow felt nothing. When he opened his eyes again, he was sitting in a huge chair in a dimly lit room. There were candles all over, but the room was so big that there could have been a thousand candles and the room still wouldn't look bright. There were three other chairs in the room, each a little bigger than the chair in which Tyler was sitting. Tyler's chair was very soft. It was red and silver, and there were markings on it that Tyler had never seen before. The other chairs were also red and silver, but the markings looked different. Tyler ran his hand over the chair, feeling every inch. The walls were bare. There was no wallpaper or paint on them; they were just bare stone, and they looked cold, even though the room felt warm. The candles were all light and in holders that were mounted onto the walls.

Tyler stood up from the chair. He was very dizzy; he fell backward and slumped back into the chair. His head bobbed from side to side as he continued to look around the room for some clue as to where he was. In the far corner of the room, he saw what looked like a globe—a globe unlike any other Tyler had ever seen. This globe had planets around it, which didn't look to be attached to anything; they were just circling, perfectly suspended, around the globe. Tyler tried once more to stand up, even though he felt dizzy and his body seemed to want more than anything to sit back down in the chair. He forced himself to walk toward the globe. Tyler stared in amazement: the globe wasn't of earth—it was of the Dark World. He slid his hand between the globe and one of the planets to see where it was attached. He wasn't at all surprised to find that there was no string or anything. They were not attached; they were just floating.

Tyler began walking away from the globe, back to the chair, when he heard voices coming from another room. He couldn't make out what they were saying. He didn't really care; his body ached and his head was pounding. All he wanted to do was sit in the chair and close his eyes. The voices became louder and louder. Tyler realized that the voices were right outside the door. Usually, he would have looked for somewhere to hide or something, but not this time. Tyler couldn't even stand up now; his body felt like it was stuck to the chair. He tried to lift his arms, but they didn't move. The door to the room opened.

"Well, look who has finally come to join us," a familiar voice said from the doorway. Tyler couldn't see who it was, but he knew from the gruff-sounding voice of one of them that it was Candor. Tyler tried to turn around, but he couldn't move. "So, Tyler, tell me—how are you?" Candor walked to the back of Tyler's chair. Tyler could feel that Candor's hand was very close to him, but he didn't answer; he didn't even try to talk. "You are probably feeling a little drained. That won't pass, I'm afraid—not for a while, at least."

Something was wrong. Tyler felt weak; the last time he had come to the Dark World he hadn't felt this way at all. This time was different—but why? Candor finally walked in front of the chair so Tyler could see him. He was wearing the same black robe with the hood covering his face in the same way. He seemed even taller than before as he towered over Tyler, who remained weak and stuck to the chair.

"Your friends will soon start looking for you, I assume, seeing as you didn't tell them that you were leaving. You are so predictable: you have decided to join me, yes?" Candor asked.

Tyler wanted to stand up and shout, "No! No way will I never join you; I will fight against you until I win." Yet even if he could have stood up, or had enough strength to even talk, he wasn't sure why, exactly, he wouldn't join him. Nobody had told him yet why Candor so bad; he had no idea what he was fighting against. What had Candor done? If he really had taken Sara's parents…well, who was to say that they were the good ones? Why were they fighting against each other? Tyler thought to himself as Candor stared at him so intensely Tyler had the feeling that he was reading his mind.

"Have you made your decision yet? Is the great Tyler Leeds going to fight on the same side as I, Candor? Together, you and I would have more powers than any other two Nytstars. We could rule the Dark World. All you have to do is join me, Tyler; you will have everything you have ever dreamed of. You will be great—we will be great."

Tyler stared at Candor as he stood in front of him, his face still covered by the hood of his robe. Tyler still could not move. There was so much that he wanted to ask Candor, if he could only speak. Tyler tried everything he could to make a sound. His head was pounding, his body felt hot, and he could feel the sweat all over his body. He struggled and strained; finally, he opened his mouth—but nothing came out. He wasn't going to give up. He tried again and again, and finally, just when he thought he was going to fade away, he spoke. He wasn't sure what he had said—his head was pounding so hard, he couldn't hear his own words—but Candor seemed to like what he had heard.

Tyler watched Candor walk out of the room. He watched the door carefully; moments later, Candor returned. He walked back into the room, straight toward Tyler, clutching something in his hand. Tyler squinted his eyes, trying to see what it was.

"So, if I return to you your Oltes, do I have your word that you will not use it?" Candor asked sternly. Tyler couldn't understand why he would be worried that he would use his Oltes: he was just Tyler, and this was Candor. Tyler felt his head nod forward. Candor lifted his large hands and put Tyler's Oltes back around his neck. Instantly, Tyler felt his body returning back to normal: his toes tingled a little painfully, then the tingling went from his toes up his legs, through his back, up into his arms, and then filled his head. His whole body was tingling painfully—then it stopped.

Tyler blinked his eyes and stood up. Candor stood inches in front of him; Tyler so badly wanted to reach out his hand to touch him, just to make sure he was real. He fought off his temptation by reaching for his Oltes, but he didn't want Candor to think he was going to use it, so he quickly put his hand back by his side. "Why am I here?" Tyler asked.

Candor pointed to the chair for Tyler to sit back down. Tyler sat down; he was so eager to ask Candor all his questions. "You are here because you wanted to come; you came here all by yourself."

Tyler didn't know how he could have gone there, especially when he didn't know where "there" was. "Okay, then why did you remove my Oltes and do...well, whatever it was that you did to me?"

"I removed your Oltes so that you couldn't use it against me. I had no idea why you came; I needed to protect myself."

Tyler shook his head. "Protect yourself against what?"

"Against you," Candor answered.

"Why would *you* need to protect yourself against *me*?" Tyler asked, staring at Candor in disbelief.

"Tyler, it is time that I tell you the truth: the truth about who you really are, the truth that nobody else seems to want to tell you."

A shiver of excitement and relief ran through Tyler's body. Finally, he thought to himself, finally I will know the truth. Tyler sat straight up. He stared at Candor; he was going to listen to every word that he said, better than he had listened to anything else. He could hardly contain his excitement.

"Tyler, that mark on your foot—that Triss—was not supposed to be there. However, there it is, clearly." Tyler's shoe and sock slid off his foot, landing gently on the floor of their own accord. Tyler, startled, just stared at his now bare foot. "That Triss and the role of King were passed to your ancestors over a century ago, when Alaford Leedsonath saved Dramess and his infant son from a horrible beast sent by another king, Remade. Dramess owed him his life, and the life of his infant son. He repaid him by giving him the kingdom mark: a Triss. With that Triss, he passed on his kingdom.

"Did you know that your grandfather was a king?—and a very powerful king, at that. Almost all Nytstars followed your grandfather. He was one of the most powerful Nytstars in centuries; everybody respected him and his ways. Well, almost everybody—you see, your grandfather did some things that not all the Nytstars agreed with. Some felt that he was a little too trusting of other people—that is, others that were not Nytstars. There have always been Nytstars that believed that only pure Nytstars were to be allowed in the Dark World and that we shouldn't mix with Lyts. When your grandparents' children were born without powers, that just made matters worse. Another king, Eljord, formed a group that did not follow your grandfather; in fact, they tried to fight against him. They wanted things back to the way they were before your grandfather took over as King, and jeopardized the sanctity of our world. More and more Nytstars were marrying Lyts, therefore risking total exposure of our world. People were scared, and who can blame them? What would happen if the Lyt world were to find out about us? Everything we have would be destroyed—EVERYTHING!" Candor yelled.

Tyler didn't even jump at Candor's thunderous voice; he was entranced by Candor's words, his eyes wide, his mouth slightly open, just listening. Candor turned away from Tyler for just a minute, cleared his throat, then continued. "When that Triss was passed on to you that made you the new King, as soon as your grandfather's time as King was over, you were to replace him. You—and only you—are the new King of the Dark World."

"But what about the King of Darkness that you told me about that time that you were in my living room? Isn't he the King?" Tyler asked, dumbfounded.

"Yes, he is the King of Darkness. He rules over those who didn't follow your grandfather, the ones that are fighting against—well, you, now."

Tyler took a deep breath. He didn't want to have people fighting against him in a fight that he didn't even really understand. He had no opinion on any of that yet; he felt he didn't really know enough to have an opinion.

"You have more powers than you know, Tyler. You are still so young. That's why I want to help you: you need someone to show you everything, to teach and guide you."

Tyler looked at Candor suspiciously. Why does he want to help me so much? Isn't he working for Eljord? Tyler thought to himself.

"Why?" he finally asked Candor quietly. "Why do you want to help me? What is in it for you?"

"I want to see the Dark World back to the way it was. I want you to join forces with Eljord and lead your people and his back together as one. We have enough enemies without fighting each other; we would be much stronger as one world instead of two. You, Tyler, are the only one who can make that possible."

"Why is my brother Michael not the one with the mark? After all, he is older and smarter; he should be the one who is King, not me."

"You were born with the mark; nobody put it there. You were chosen for whatever reason. It was you who was chosen."

"Where are Sara's parents? Why were they taken?"

Candor shifted in his chair. When he answered, his voice seemed angry. "They were protecting you. Eljord was trying to take you so that he could destroy you; he was trying to stop you from becoming King. Once he had your Oltes, he was going to kill you."

Tyler gasped. He couldn't believe what he was hearing. He couldn't help but think that maybe his grandfather had done some terrible things; why else would Eljord be trying to kill him? Maybe Eljord believed that he would do things the same as his grandfather. Maybe his grandfather had been wrong; maybe the two worlds should not mix.

"Did Eljord kill my grandparents?"

"Your grandparents were killed by a horrible monster they were trying to capture," Candor replied in somewhat of a whisper.

Tyler stared down at the floor. "So where are Sara's parents?" Tyler asked again.

"I don't know. I had nothing to do with their disappearance; I wish I could help you."

"Who were you talking to outside the door?" Tyler had suddenly remembered hearing more than one voice before.

"Just one of the servants," Candor answered—a little too quickly, Tyler thought. He wasn't sure which story to believe.

"I need to discuss this with my brother. I will return in a few days and we can talk then," Tyler said as he jumped to his feet.

"I am not sure if that is a good idea," Candor said as he stood up in front of Tyler, towering over him.

"Why not?" Tyler asked, not one bit intimidated by Candor's size anymore.

"I don't think your brother is very pleased that you are a king and that he is—well, nothing of great importance, really. He is just another Nytstar."

Tyler was worried that Candor might be right. What if Michael was angry that he wasn't King? After all, he was the oldest; why was it Tyler that had the mark? "What should I do? It's not like I can stay here for days at a time; my parents are sure to get worried and start looking for me." Tyler hadn't thought much until now about whether his parents had any idea about any of this. He had just assumed they didn't—but really, how could they not? At least his mom should know that her own father had this whole other life. He was sure they couldn't have kept his life a secret all this time.

Candor stood up. "I have no idea. Your grandfather's personal life is of no interest to me. You see, when two different worlds intertwine, there are bound to be tangles. I assure you, you will not be missed in your world—no one will even know you are gone."

"That's impossible! My parents will notice if I am not there...Michael...my teachers," Tyler shouted, feeling a bit insulted.

"We don't know how it works or why, but time can stay still in the Lyt world while still moving in our world." Tyler stared at Candor; he couldn't believe his ears. "Well, then, it's settled: you shall stay here for a while. I will show you around and answer any more questions you may have."

Tyler ignored the nagging feeling he had that there was still more that Candor was not telling him. He also knew he should be confiding all this to Michael. However, blinded by curiosity and confusion, Tyler stood up and nodded to Candor, accepting his invitation to stay in the World of Darkness.

CHAPTER EIGHT

MEETING THE DRAGON

Something had come over Tyler; he was not himself. He seemed to have more trust in Candor right now than he did in Michael; he hadn't even given Michael the chance to tell him how he felt. Tyler spent the night in the castle with Candor. He spent most of the night tossing and turning. He dreamt that he saw Michael and Sara laughing at him, teasing that he would never make a good king, that he was still just a baby. He woke up feeling lost. He didn't know who to believe, and he needed to learn more about Candor and the World of Darkness; he wasn't going home until he did.

"We shall begin after you have had breakfast, so eat up," Candor said as he took Tyler into a very extravagant dining room. The dining room was bigger than Tyler's entire house in the Lyt world. Each wall was lined with ornate candleholders that were mounted high on the walls, with thick orange candles resting in each one, their flames lighting the room as brightly as the morning sunshine. Each candleholder looked like a wrought iron sword, the blade stretching all the way down to the magnificent marble tile floor. The ceiling was so high that Tyler could barely make out the splendid battle scene painting that covered every inch of it. After straining to examine as much of the detailed painting as he could, he was quite shocked to see that there were no paintings on the walls; there was, however, a large cloth banner hanging on the back wall. Tyler was drawn to the banner, almost mesmerized. He ran his hand gently over the banner. His fingers caressed the delicate and obviously expensive fabrics. The banner was a deep blue, almost black; there was a brilliant sword in the middle, circled by maroon-colored stars with the letter L in their centers. The sword had a jeweled L on the handle.

Tyler was finally distracted by the large table, which would easily have seated thirty or more, in the center of the room. It was completely covered with an enormous feast. There was every kind of breakfast food you could imagine on the table. Tyler's mouth watered at the sight of all the food. He eyed all the food, then stared at Candor. "Who else is joining us for breakfast?" he asked; surely all this food wasn't just for them.

"What do you mean, joining 'us'?" Candor asked. "This table is set for you, not us."

Tyler's mouth dropped open. "What? That's ridiculous—there is no way I can eat all this myself. You have to eat with me; look at all this food," Tyler insisted.

"You have to understand, Tyler, that you are a king while you are in the Dark World, and that is how you will be treated. As King, you will be waited on hand and foot. People will do what you ask them to because you are a king, a ruler—people listen to you, serve you, protect you, and honor you, Tyler, because they have to. That is how things work," Candor said as he turned around to walk through the door into the kitchen.

"So let me get this straight: as King, I get anything I want, right?" Tyler asked, smiling, yet still a little nervous.

"That's correct," Candor replied.

"Then I wish for you to join me for breakfast."

Candor turned around and bowed slightly, and sat down at the table with Tyler. Tyler was excited; he hadn't thought about all the privileges that went along with being King, having everything you wanted at your fingertips. "Is this my castle?" Tyler asked between bites of bacon.

"Yes, this is your castle, and everything in it is yours, including the servants."

"What about you? I am sure you are not one of the servants, so why are you here?" Tyler asked.

"No, I am not one of your servants, but there has been no king in this castle since your grandparents died. Eljord sent me here to look after it, so that's what I did, but now that you are here, I will be leaving and returning to Eljord."

"So if Eljord is fighting against me, then—"

Candor interrupted. "Eljord is not fighting against you—not yet. He was fighting against your grandfather; that doesn't mean he will be fighting against you. That all depends on how you decide to run things," Candor said sternly.

"Why haven't you taken off your robes yet? I haven't seen your face before."

"I do not take off my robes in the presence of others. We should hurry up—we have a lot to do today."

Tyler quickly ate the rest of his breakfast, and they both left the table.

"We shall begin with a tour around the castle. After all, this is your home—you should know about it. You wouldn't want to get lost, now."

Tyler couldn't quite understand why Candor was being so nice to him. Why would he want to help him now, and for that matter, why was he able to walk so freely around his castle? Nobody seemed to fear him or distrust him.

After all, Candor worked for Eljord, and even if Eljord wasn't fighting against him right now, he had fought against his grandfather. Why was everyone in the castle accepting of Candor? Where did their loyalty lie? Tyler couldn't help but feel a little uneasy. He kept looking over his shoulder, almost expecting to see someone or something about to sneak up and attack him from behind. If only Michael was here, Tyler thought to himself.

Tyler followed Candor out of the dining room. "We shall begin in your sleep chambers, which are located in the main tower," Candor said as he glided through Tyler's castle as though he had walked the halls hundreds of times before.

"But I slept there last night; it's just a bedroom," Tyler moaned. The last place he wanted to see right after breakfast was the bedroom.

"We shall begin in your sleep quarters, in the main tower," Candor repeated.

Tyler shrugged and followed Candor toward a large spiral staircase at the foot of the main tower. Tyler remained unimpressed by the grand décor of the circular hallways through which they passed as he and Candor climbed the stairs all the way to the top. He didn't even ask about anyone in the portraits lining the walls, or the banners that hung with strange symbols. They finally reached the top of the staircase. Unlike the other rooms in the tower, Tyler's sleep chambers took up the entire floor. Candor opened the large and heavy-looking double doors and entered the room.

"I got it, sleep chambers at the top of the tower; what's next?" Tyler grumbled.

"You cannot walk around dressed like that; you will need to change your attire," Candor said.

"Well, I didn't bring my King clothes with me, so this will have to do."

Candor ignored Tyler and glanced around the room. "There will be appropriate attire in your dressing quarters, through that door." Candor pointed toward a small door on the far side of the room. Tyler looked at Candor's hooded figure and hoped that the clothes he was about to put on would not be the same. "You must dress as the King—you are Tyler."

Tyler walked through the door, leaving Candor alone in his sleep chambers. Tyler stared around in amazement: the dressing quarters looked like a clothing store, with more clothes than Tyler would likely own in his whole life in the Lyt world. He could hardly imagine needing all of them. He ran his hand along the clothes lining the wall closest to him. He allowed the soft, luxurious fabric to caress his fingers, until he quickly pulled his hand away as if the fabric had suddenly burnt him—it was the thought that his grandfather must have worn the clothes he was touching that had burnt into his thoughts. Tyler no longer felt comfortable in the dressing quarters. He grabbed the first outfit he touched, and after fumbling awkwardly with ties and wrapped bits of fabric, he emerged back into the room feeling somewhat exposed and uncomfortable.

"Now you look like a king," Candor stammered, a little nervously.

"What's wrong? Did I not put it on right? I wasn't sure whether this went this way or not," Tyler said, fiddling with a tie around his arm. "It does feel strange, like I'm dressed up for Halloween or something, and I don't think I feel comfortable wearing my grandfather's clothes," Tyler ended in a near whisper. Tyler tugged at the long black robes that hung almost to the floor. He realized that the clothes seemed to fit perfectly, yet his grandfather was significantly bigger than he was; there was no way these were his clothes.

"Those were to be worn only by you; they were not your grandfather's," Candor stated.

Tyler, now relieved, couldn't help but feel like a king in his new clothes. The black pants were freshly pressed, along with the shirt, straight and jet black. Tyler wasn't sure how he had known how to tie the red band that crossed over his chest, with the crest placed neatly over his heart, and wrapped around his waist, yet somehow he had managed it flawlessly. There was a pouch inside his shirt to hold his Oltes while it remained hanging around his neck, yet Tyler hung his proudly on the outside of his shirt.

"Halloween?" Candor questioned.

"Yeah, you know, like 'trick or treat', costumes, candy?" From the look on Candor's face, however, Tyler realized they didn't have Halloween in the Dark World. "Never mind, it doesn't matter. Well, did I put it on okay? This isn't PJs or something, right? It all kind of looked the same to me." Tyler noticed, however, that Candor seemed to be distracted, almost nervous; he wasn't even listening.

"Are you ready to go?" Tyler asked, but Candor didn't answer. Tyler asked again, but still Candor said nothing. Tyler walked toward Candor and reached out toward him to grab his arm. As soon as he ever so slightly touched Candor, Candor disappeared, then just as quickly reappeared right behind Tyler. A deafening, deep sort of scream filled the room; Tyler covered his ears with his hands and dropped to his knees as pain surged through his body.

"Let us continue."

Tyler opened his eyes and looked up to see Candor's dark figure standing over him. "What the hell was that?" Tyler yelled, his ears ringing as he stumbled trying to stand up.

"What was what?" Candor replied.

"What do you mean, 'what'? That sound—how could you not have heard it? I think the whole Dark World heard it."

"There was no sound, Tyler, I assure you. Now shall we continue?" Candor turned and walked out of the room. Tyler ran and caught up with him on the stairs but decided not to mention the noise again. "This is your private tower; this floor is your trophy floor. Everything your grandparents and every other king that ever ruled this kingdom ever won, earned, or anything else, is displayed in these rooms."

Tyler was quite interested. "Shall we go in?" Tyler asked while he tugged on what was apparently a locked door.

"The door will not open. None of them will while I am in the tower—they are for castle blood only. If you like, I will wait downstairs," Candor offered.

"No, it's okay. I can look in there later—they're only trophies."

"They are important to your kingdom. They must have been important to your grandfather, or he wouldn't have put them in those rooms. You should have at least a quick look," Candor persisted.

"I will look later; I want to see the rest of the castle."

Candor turned and carried on down the stairs. "This floor is for your armor and weapons, but these rooms, as with the rest of the tower, will not open—perfect for hiding your secrets," Candor almost whispered.

Tyler followed Candor through the rest of the castle, from hallway to hallway, room after room: libraries, drawing rooms, sitting rooms, a grand ballroom, and more bedrooms than Tyler could ever keep track of. Tyler was getting bored and was sure he still couldn't make it around the castle without getting himself lost. Finally, they came to the last hallway, which Tyler was sure they had not yet ventured down.

"These rooms are your passageways to the other world—the Lyt world. Each room can be set up to go wherever you want to go." They entered the first room; it was quite small compared to the others. This room was empty; the walls were all black, with a row of candles around the room that lit themselves as the two walked in. Tyler was amazed by the candles. He stared around the room. He couldn't help but wonder what Michael and Sara were up to. Had they even noticed that he was gone? Did they even care? Were they looking for him?

"As you can see, these rooms are not like the others: they are always empty, except for the candles. When you come into the room, all the candles will light, just as they did for us; then you must close the door and use the transport star. Well, you know how to do the rest—otherwise, you wouldn't have been able to get here, would you? Well, let's go back to the kitchen. We will have the cook make some lunch; it is almost past lunchtime." Candor walked out of the room. Tyler took one last look around, then followed him. Tyler was quite thankful that the tour of the castle was finally over; it had taken hours.

After he had finished his lunch, Tyler wanted nothing more than to go back to his sleeping chambers. He needed to think; he wanted to clear his head and decide what to do next. Should he contact Michael, tell him everything? Or trust Candor? Really, Candor so far had not given Tyler any reason not to trust him, and thanks to Candor, Tyler was actually in the Dark World, in his own castle, of which he was King.

As Candor entered the room, all Tyler's thoughts of Michael seemed to slip away. He was overwhelmed by the desire to know more. "Are you finally going to show me around the Dark World? You know, other than my castle?" Tyler asked as he followed Candor out of the dining room.

"Yes, sir. I believe it is time that you are shown around—after all, who better to give you the grand tour of the Dark World than I?"

The sound of Candor's voice sent a chill down Tyler's spine. He was suddenly reminded of the first time he had met Candor, that night in his house. "Remind me again why I should trust you. I mean, suddenly it all seems a little strange to me. The first time we met, you were not this helpful. In fact, I thought you had taken my brother. I thought you were going to kill me. Everyone has warned me about you: they all say that you are the one who took Sara's parents when they were protecting me, and they were protecting me from you. You were working for Eljord; you were trying to get rid of me so there would only be one King. Eljord would be the only King, and he would...well...he would make things back to the way they were before my grandfather."

"You don't trust very easily, do you? Why is that?" Candor said calmly.

"Answer me! Why are you helping me now? Are you the one who has Sara's parents? Were they protecting me from you?"

Candor turned around and stepped closer to Tyler. He was so close that Tyler could feel his breath, yet he still could not see his face. "Like I told you before, Eljord sent me to help you so that you would have the opportunity to rule things the way you wish to rule things; he wants to give you a chance. No, I do not know where Sara's parents are." Candor turned away from Tyler and continued to walk away from the dining room. "Are you coming?" he called back to Tyler, who stood in the same spot, frozen, torn—who was right? Who was actually telling him the truth?

"Yes, I'm coming," Tyler said, and followed Candor once again. They walked through the front doors of the castle. Tyler turned to look at his new castle from the outside for the first time. He could hardly believe his eyes. The castle looked like it was out of a fairy tale. It wasn't the enormous doors, the twenty windows he counted on the bottom floor alone, or even the fact that twenty-four hours ago, the only place he called home was a three bedroom, two bathroom family home that he lived in with his parents and brother, and now he stood in front of his very own four-story, too-many-rooms-to-count castle that had Tyler standing frozen on the steps with his mouth slightly open and his eyes looking like at any moment they would fall completely out of his head. It was the fact that he was standing outside in the Dark World for the first time ever, and it didn't seem much different than the Lyt world that he knew. Well, except for the creatures that he had never seen before or the tree that had just bowed to him or the rosebush that said, "Pleased to meet you, Your Majesty."

"Wow," Tyler said, staring at the rosebush, "I, um...I mean...uh, pleased to meet you too." Then, to Tyler's amazement, all the trees and bushes bowed to him. An odd creature that at first looked to be a very small dog ran up to Tyler, but when it got closer, Tyler could see that the creature's skeleton was on the outside of his body. The creature looked almost inside out; you could see its fur waving under its bones.

"What is that?" Tyler said, jumping back in surprise.

"That is a Darp. They are quite harmless, I assure you. They are often kept as pets; there are a few that run around the grounds," Candor said, ignoring the Darp, which was now licking his shoe. "As far as you can see are the castle grounds. You are safe here; not just anybody can get onto the grounds."

Tyler thought it was strange that Candor would say that; obviously, anybody could get in, or he wouldn't have been able to get in.

"Your grandfather took very good care of the grounds, all the people that work here, and all the creatures."

"How do you know?" Tyler asked suspiciously.

"Everybody knew what kind of a man your grandfather was. Shall we?" Candor said.

Tyler nodded; they walked slowly around the grounds Candor pointed out all the different types of trees and plants. Tyler gazed at the size of them: they all seemed at least twice the size of the plants that he was used to. There were so many different types, yet Candor knew the names of them all. He also knew where everything was and how many of everything his grandfather had had. Tyler thought that odd, as his grandfather seemed to be Candor's nemesis.

Just as they were going over a hill, Tyler heard a loud roar, then smoke and flames began rising above another hill in the distance. Candor turned quietly to lead Tyler back in the opposite direction; however, Tyler didn't follow. Instead, he walked closer to the edge of the hill. When he was close enough, he lay down on the top of the hill and looked over the edge. His mouth dropped open when he saw, on the other side of the hill, a very large white dragon. It looked just like the dragon he had seen before in his dreams. "Wow," Tyler whispered to himself. He slowly walked down the hill to get a closer look. He soon noticed that, just like in his dream, the field he was standing in was perfect—the grass was perfect, the flowers were perfect—only this time he wasn't scared. He felt the need to get closer to the dragon.

The dragon had not yet seen him, so Tyler walked as quietly as he could, closer and closer. Excitement filled his body; his heart was pounding faster and faster as he walked closer to the dragon. Finally, he was so close that all he had to do was reach out his hand—but the dragon was gone. It was as if it had simply disappeared. But really, how could something that big just disappear? he thought to himself. Then, realizing that if this was exactly like his dream, he would see the dragon again, Tyler turned around—and he was right.

The dragon came flying toward him. Just like in his dream, he looked around for something to protect himself, but there was nothing. Tyler ducked just in time as the dragon flew right over him, barely missing his now trembling body, but the dragon was almost right in front of him, its enormous mouth open so wide Tyler was sure it could have swallowed him whole. He could see its gigantic yellow and black teeth. Smoke was now coming from the inside of the dragon's mouth; Tyler tried to crawl away from the heat, but he just couldn't escape it. His whole body was getting weaker; the harder he struggled to get away, the weaker he became. The smoke was so thick it was almost impossible to breathe. Tyler's body became hotter and hotter, and flames seemed to dance out of the dragon's mouth. The heat was too intense. Now overcome with heat exhaustion, Tyler closed his eyes. He saw Michael and Sara; they looked to be standing over his burned and lifeless body, and then everything went black. Tyler was sure that he was dead. His body now felt like ice, but he wasn't shivering. In fact, he felt nothing; no pain—nothing.

It was three days before Tyler regained consciousness; he had been closer to death than he would ever know. The dragon had burned most of his body. When he finally opened his eyes, all he could see were bandages; his entire body was covered in them, and he hurt all over. He was lying in a rather large four poster bed, which he quickly realized was in his room in his castle.

"Well, I guess it wasn't a dream, then, if I am lying here," Tyler said to himself—or so he thought, until he heard a familiar voice.

"No, it wasn't a dream; you were almost killed by that dragon. You are very lucky to be alive. You should be more careful. What are you doing here, anyway? Why did you leave the Mysterious Blue?" Michael asked Tyler as he stared at his bandage-covered body.

Tyler looked around the room. "Well, it's nice to see you too. Oh, yeah, and I'm fine—thank you for asking."

"I'm sorry, but you left without saying a word. We searched all over for you, and then we find you here, in a castle, lying in a bed, covered in bandages, and all anyone will tell us is that you were attacked by a dragon. Who saved you?"

Before Tyler could answer, the door swung open. He hoped that it was Candor, but to his disappointment, it was a nurse. "How are you feeling, Your Majesty?" she asked as she put a tray down on the table at the side of the bed. Michael swung around and glanced at the nurse, then at Tyler.

"I hurt all over, but my Oltes—did you take of my Oltes?" Tyler tried to reach his neck, but his arm was too burnt; the slight movement sent pain rushing through his arm into his back. He let out a screech of pain.

"Don't try to move, Your Majesty. Yes, you still have your Oltes; we didn't take it off or anything. We checked that it wasn't completely melted into your skin, but it was just branded to your chest. You were lucky. There are medics searching as we speak for all the things we need to fix you up again. I am sure you will be all better very soon."

"What about his skin? Most of his body is burnt; it will take a significant amount of reconstructive surgery and skin grafts to fix him so he is somewhat the same as he was before," Michael said angrily.

"Your Majesty, as soon as they find all the ingredients, I will make the serum that will heal your skin. It will be painful, but it won't take longer than twenty-four hours for your skin to regroup. Like I said, you will be all better very soon," the nurse said with a nervous glance at the clock and a half-smile at Tyler, but ignoring Michael. She acted as if Tyler were the only one in the room. The nurse gave Tyler something to drink. "This will make you unable to feel pain. Let me know if there is anything else that you need, Your Majesty," the nurse said as she bowed to Tyler and left the room.

Michael whipped his head around and stared at Tyler. "What was that all about?" Michael asked.

"She's a nurse, Mike; I don't think she meant to be rude or anything. She's just doing her job, that's all."

"I wasn't talking about her being rude. I meant her calling you 'Your Majesty'," Michael snapped. Tyler turned around and looked out the many windows that lined the back wall. Michael knew that he was hiding something. "Tyler, you need to start talking. I am your brother; you can trust me, if nobody else. We need to be able to trust each other. Whatever it is, we are both in all of this together."

"Lodiss told us that the mark meant I was a king, remember? This is my castle," Tyler said quietly, waiting for Michael to blow up at any moment.

Michael, however, didn't get mad; instead, he started to laugh. "You, a king?"

Tyler didn't expect him to laugh; it made him mad. He could have handled it if he had been mad or jealous, but laughing? "What is so funny?"

Michael looked at Tyler and started laughing again. "Well, I just can't believe that you're a king, that's all. I'm sorry. How do you know that this is your castle?"

"Candor told me," Tyler said quietly. He knew that Michael would think he was crazy to listen to Candor, but he hadn't met him or even talked to him.

"Candor told you? You've been talking to Candor? Well, what else did he say? Did he tell you where Sara's parents are?"

"No, he didn't. I haven't talked to him too much," Tyler lied.

"Well, do we have any proof? I mean, it's not to say that I don't want you to be King or this to be your castle—I just think we should find out for sure, that's all. I mean, let's face it: it's not like we can trust Candor, now can we?"

Tyler was wishing already that he hadn't told Michael. "This castle used to belong to our grandfather. After his death, the castle and the role of King were passed down to the next Nytstar with the mark of Dramess—that would be me. If you don't believe me, go and see for yourself. It's all in a document in the safe."

Michael had stopped laughing; he now just stared at Tyler in disbelief.

"Well, King or no King, you still shouldn't go running off without telling anyone. Your brother was really worried about you," Sara spoke up.

"Nice of you to stop by. I would get up, but as you can see, I'm a little tied up right now," Tyler snapped.

"Ha, ha—quite the comedian, aren't you? Did you not think we would be worried? You should be a little bit more considerate, Tyler—or should I curtsy and call you 'Your Majesty'?"

"If you're both just going to mock me, you can leave anytime. Besides, neither of you seem too worried about me now that I'm in pain, you know."

"No, you're not. The nurse just gave you a drink to make sure you can't feel pain. You're just fine," Michael grumbled.

Tyler was furious but exhausted; he wanted to continue to argue with Michael and Sara, but he was beginning to feel quite strange. He closed his eyes and tried to go back to sleep, but it wasn't long before Michael noticed that Tyler had begun to twitch and shake slightly.

"What's wrong? If you're faking it, Tyler, I will make sure you're in pain," Michael snapped. Tyler didn't answer; his body was now shaking quite violently.

"Nurse! Nurse!" Sara yelled as Michael tried to calm Tyler down. Tyler's eyes rolled back in his head; he was sweating profusely. He began to cough and blood sprayed out of his mouth. "Nurse!" Sara screamed.

The nurse came running into the room, pushing Michael aside. "Your Majesty, Your Majesty," she stammered as she fumbled with a small red vial. Her trembling hands finally removed the lid; she tilted Tyler's head back and poured the thick liquid down his throat. Almost instantly, Tyler's body began to relax. His eyes returned to normal and then closed. Any small bit of unburned skin was now extremely pale; his body went limp. Michael and Sara stood frozen, staring at each other in disbelief.

"Your brother needs to rest," the nurse said, trying to urge them out of the room. "You should go home. You can come back tomorrow. I will tell him you said goodbye."

"I'm not leaving him here on his own," Michael snapped.

"You must. Can't you see you are upsetting him? You both being here is making his condition worse. He is in good hands here; I will take care of him."

"No. I will not leave him."

"You must let him rest—I insist."

Michael turned to Sara, his eyes full of desperation. "I can't leave him here like this! Look at him: this happened because he was here by himself, because I wasn't here to protect him."

Tyler's body began to twitch again. Sara grabbed Michael's arm. "Michael, I think we should go. The nurse will take of him; he'll be fine," Sara said softly, stroking his arm. Michael stared at Tyler's shaking body and reluctantly agreed. He and Sara left the room without saying a word to the nurse.

It was quite a while before Tyler was awoken again by the door opening.

"Was your brother angry with you for being here?" Candor asked as he stood at the foot of Tyler's bed.

"He'll get over it," Tyler said as he opened his eyes. He was quite happy to see Candor. "Thank you," Tyler said, smiling.

"Thank you for what?" Candor asked.

"For saving me from the dragon."

"You are certain it was I that saved you?" Candor asked as he sat down in a chair.

"I just know that it was you—thank you. Where did you go? I was hoping that you could have met Michael."

Candor looked at Tyler's bandages. "Does it hurt much?"

"No, the nurse gave me a serum so that I can't feel any pain; I just can't move, either."

"You need to learn how to control that dragon. I will teach you as soon as you are well. There are many creatures here; you are going to need to learn about all of them."

Tyler wasn't too eager to go back to the dragon again, so he gave Candor a smile and didn't say anything more about it.

Four days later, Tyler was still lying in bed, covered in bandages. Michael and Sara had returned each day. Tyler would pretend to be asleep when they came; he didn't feel much like fighting with them. Most of the time, while pretending to be asleep, he would actually drift off to sleep; when he awoke, his bandages would be drenched in blood and sweat.

"There is a cure for dragon burns, not to worry," the nurse explained to Tyler. "It is very complex, but don't worry, Your Majesty, don't worry. I have almost all the ingredients, and the gatherers are searching right now for the rest. As soon as they return, I shall finish the cure. I expect them back soon…yes, soon, very soon…they will be back very soon," the nurse rambled, all the while avoiding meeting Tyler's eyes. The nurse was still giving him the serum to stop the convulsion episodes in the meantime.

"What will we do if they don't return? Does his brother know that you are with him?" Tyler heard the nurse asking Candor just outside his door.

"They will return, and no, Michael has no idea that I am here, and that is the way I want it stay. Do you understand me? Michael must not know that I have been here the whole time, or that Tyler has had anything to do with me. Not yet; it is too soon."

Tyler didn't know why it was such a big secret. Michael did know a little and was not too happy about it, but Tyler didn't care. He wasn't going to tell Michael about Candor; he didn't want Candor to leave yet. When his door opened, he closed his eyes and pretended to be asleep.

"There is still no change," the nurse whispered. "If they don't come back soon, it might be too late."

Too late? Too late for what? Tyler wondered. After all, he felt okay—really sleepy, but other than that, he felt fine.

"Damn it, what is taking them so long? They know there is a time limit on this. If he doesn't get that cure by midnight tomorrow, it will be too late." Candor had sadness in his voice for the first time.

The nurse finished checking Tyler's vital signs, then left the room. Candor sat next to Tyler's bed without moving or speaking; he just sat there, waiting. Tyler fell asleep after a while. He slept until suppertime the next day. When he opened his eyes, he saw that Candor was still sitting next to his bed.

"Have you been here this whole time?" he asked.

"Yes."

"Why don't you go down to the kitchen for something to eat, or go and rest for a while? Its not like there is much going on here," Tyler suggested.

"I am staying right here until you are better," Candor said sternly.

"You know, if my grandfather could see you now, I'm sure he would change his mind about you."

"I don't think so."

"Why not? You have stayed with me this whole time, you saved my life…I'm sure he would see all that."

"If your grandfather was still here, none of this would have happened." Candor looked around the room, trying not to be obvious, looking at the clock for the tenth time in the last ten minutes. "How are you feeling?" Candor shot at Tyler.

"I'm fine—just a bit tired, that's all, like I told you ten minutes ago. What is up with you and the clock today?"

"Nothing; I just want to make sure you're okay, that's all."

"Do you think they will be back before midnight?" Tyler asked Candor, who stared at him.

"Why by midnight?"

"I heard you talking to the nurse; I was pretending to be asleep. What is going to happen at midnight? Am I going to die?"

Candor just stared at him. There was a long pause before Candor finally took a deep breath. "Yes," Candor stated, and they both fell silent.

Tyler was shocked; he didn't know what to say. He couldn't believe this was happening. He couldn't just die—not now. He had just learned he was a king in another world. He wanted to explore the new world; he wanted to know what it was like to be King. He couldn't help but envision himself as King, sitting on a throne, ruling his kingdom. Besides, he didn't really feel all that badly; he wasn't in pain, although he couldn't really feel anything. Tyler tried to wiggle his toes, but became a little worried when he couldn't move them. He tried to wiggle his fingers, but again, nothing. He knew he needed to tell Candor, but when he tried to open his mouth to speak, nothing happened. It was as if his mouth had been frozen shut. He tried again and again, but the effort only exhausted him.

Overcome by exhaustion, Tyler's body once again went limp and he drifted off to sleep. His body temperature began to rise; some feeling seemed to be returning, as he could now feel his body burning. Sweat was drenching his whole body, soaking his bandages. His breathing was starting to get heavy, and he was falling in and out of consciousness. The nurse came into the room every couple of minutes with ice and cold cloths, trying as best she could to cool him down.

"Don't you think his family should be here? What if he doesn't make it? I'm sure they would all like the chance to say their goodbyes," the nurse told Candor.

"How am I supposed to do that? Don't you think that if I show up in their house and tell them to come with me, they're going to think that I'm trying to kidnap them or something?"

"I suppose you're right," she said sadly. "There is not much time left. Tyler isn't looking so good; his body temperature is too high, I...um..." The nurse couldn't finish her sentence; she broke down into tears.

"Michael...Mike...M..." Tyler stammered.

Candor looked up at Tyler, then at the clock. "It's eleven forty-five—where the hell are they? They should have been here by now," Candor shouted as he stood up and began to pace the room. Candor watched the clock as the minutes seemed to rush away.

Tyler had slipped away into a deep sleep. The nurse tried to wake him up, but nothing happened. "Your Majesty...Your Majesty, wake up. Wake up, Your Majesty...Come on, Your Majesty—please wake up!" the nurse shouted hysterically, shaking Tyler. "He is not waking up, Candor. He is not waking up—what do I do? We have to do something."

Candor looked up at the clock. "It's eleven fifty-nine. It's too late."

"No, it's not too late, Candor. You can't just give up. Candor, we need to do something. Your Majesty, wake up!"

"Leave him alone! What's going on?" Michael said as he burst through the door and saw the nurse shaking Tyler, trying to wake him up. Candor had disappeared just in time.

"I'm sorry, it's too late—"

"We've got it, nurse," a short, strange-looking man frantically shouted as he ran into the room holding onto a small pouch. "Sorry it took so long—we tried, but the ingredients...they are not easy...The mountains...they—"

"Give me that. You are too late—he's dead."

"No! No, you give him that medicine! It's not too late—you have to try. Give him the medicine!" Michael shouted as he snatched the pouch from the man and shoved it at the nurse.

"Michael, it's too late..."

"No! Now give him the medicine."

The nurse took the pouch and ran out of the room. Michael held his breath, tears streaming down his face. He did not take his eyes off Tyler's lifeless body. The nurse rushed back into the room with a small bottle full of a shiny black serum and gave Tyler the medicine. Nothing happened.

"What now?" Michael asked, shaking and pale, still shocked. He wasn't going to believe that his brother was dead.

"We wait," sobbed the nurse. "But Michael, you need to understand: he might not make it. It was too late; he was already dead when we gave him the medicine."

Michael didn't say a word; he simply sat down in the chair in which Candor was sitting mere moments before. Michael sat by Tyler's side all through the night. In the morning, the nurse came back into the room. She checked Tyler over.

"There is no change. I'm sorry, Michael."

"I am not leaving his side. I know my brother, and he wouldn't give up so easily."

Sara arrived a little while later. When Michael told her what was going on, she burst into tears. "What if he…"

"Don't even think like that. He will wake up. He will; he has to." Michael fell to the floor in tears. "Tyler, why did you go near that dragon? Why? What were you doing here in the first place? You should have waited for me; you know I would have come here with you."

The nurse came back into the room; she couldn't look at Michael as she pulled the bedsheet over Tyler's face.

"What are you doing?" Michael yelled as he jumped up and pulled the sheet back down. "I am sorry, Michael, but it is too late. You need to say goodbye to your brother. We have to move him; we can't just leave his body here," the nurse sobbed.

"Don't touch him! Don't you dare touch him! He is not dead—you wait! Get out…GET OUT!" Michael yelled. The nurse ran back out of the room. Michael looked at Sara, then dropped back to the floor. "I will kill that dragon, Tyler, I swear to you."

Michael sat on the floor for hours, crying. Sara was sitting by Tyler's side, holding onto his ice-cold hand. "Michael," she whispered. "Michael—his hand…Michael, his hand, it's…it's…it's warming up," she shouted excitedly.

Michael jumped up from the floor and grabbed Tyler's other hand. It was warming up. He smiled at Sara. "Come on, Tyler. I still need you—we have to finish helping Sara. You have a castle, remember, and a kingdom to rule. What about Mom and Dad; what will I tell them? You have to wake up, Tyler. Please wake up," Michael pleaded.

Sara wept at Michael's words. Tears streamed down her face, landing gently on the exposed fingers of Tyler's cold, lifeless hand, which she still held tightly.

"C…Ca…C…"

Michael whipped his head around in disbelief. "He's…he…Nurse! Nurse, he's alive—nurse!" Michael shouted.

The nurse came running into the room. "What's happened?" she panted.

"He's alive! His hands—I'm sure they are warming up. And he tried to speak," Michael told her.

The nurse checked for a pulse. "He has a pulse; it's really weak, but it's there. Oh, thank goodness, he has a pulse." The nurse checked Tyler's heart rate and gave him a little more of the shiny black medicine. She checked his pulse again, then more medicine, then checked his pulse once more, while Michael and Sara looked on, anxiously awaiting a sign—anything just to know that Tyler would make it.

Then, finally, the nurse smiled. "He's going to be okay," she told Michael as she slowly pulled back some of the bandages from his face. Michael and Sara watched in amazement as the burns on his face slowly faded away right before their eyes.

"Candor," Tyler said as he slowly opened his eyes. He looked around the room. "Where is he? Where is Candor?"

Michael stared at him. "Is he the one who did this to you? I'll kill him," Michael said angrily.

Tyler just lay there; he couldn't remember why he was there. "What happened?"

Sara looked at Michael. "You died," she said quietly as she kept her eyes fixed on the ground.

"What? Why? How? Am I still...?"

Michael smiled. "You were attacked by a dragon, but you are fine now, and no, you're not dead anymore."

The nurse carefully removed the rest of Tyler's bandages. Tyler slowly regained the feeling in his body; he could move again without the pain. He was going to be okay.

Tyler was told to stay in bed for three days, but after the first day, he was so tired of lying down that he got up and went for a walk around the castle.

"I thought you were supposed to be resting," Candor said when he found Tyler standing in the main doorway to the castle.

"I was bored. I can't lay in bed for that long; I was going crazy. Besides, it's not like I'm running around fighting dragons or anything."

"You're eager to get back to normal, I see."

Tyler stared at Candor in both annoyance and disbelief. "*Normal?* What do you mean, 'normal'? Am I not a Nytstar anymore? Am I no longer a king of another world, a world that is a secret from all people who are not Nytstars—the only world I have ever known? Normal? There is no more normal." Tyler stared out into the grounds. "I don't think you should be here anymore, if it has to be a secret from Michael."

"That's fine, Your Majesty—I will leave right away. Well, good luck." Candor turned to walk away.

"Wait—that's it? You're not going to try and stay?"

"What do you want, Your Majesty? If you want me to leave, then I will leave. If you want me to stay, I will stay. However, either way, Michael is not to know—not yet. He wouldn't understand."

"Understand what?"

"We still have a lot to do, so you need to decide: Should I go?"

"I don't know. I don't want to lie to Michael, but...um...Oh, you had better stay, I think."

"Well, we shall start right away. You need to put on a traveling cloak. I don't think your nurse would be too happy if you were to catch a chill, now would she?" A cloak appeared instantly in Candor's hand; he handed it to Tyler, who hastily put it on.

"Okay, where are we going today?" Tyler asked.

"Outside—outside the castle grounds, I mean—into town."

Tyler stared at Candor, full of excitement. He was finally going to see the other world: all of it.

CHAPTER NINE

KING

All of it? Tyler thought to himself. Was he really ready for all of it? As exciting as it seemed, it was also a scary thought. This was another world; everything was going to be different, and he was going to be different from everyone else. Tyler looked around as if seeing this world for the first time all over again—and it was just as magical as before. Tyler took a deep breath and tried to prepare himself—for what, he had no idea.

"Shall we?" Candor asked, leading the way through the gates and off the castle grounds.

Tyler was excited he walked alongside Candor. They walked up and down streets that were filled with people. Tyler looked around at all the different shops. "Well, what are you waiting for?" Candor asked, pointing toward a shop.

"Can we go in?"

"Well, you can go in, but what do you think would happen if I walked into a shop?"

Tyler just stared at Candor. "I don't know, really."

"I don't think that it would be good, considering that most people supported your grandfather—remember? They aren't going to be too happy to see one of your grandfather's nemeses, and I am sure everyone feels I am responsible for what happened to you."

"You're right. Sorry, I didn't think about that."

"I will be outside waiting for you."

"What am I supposed to do in there?"

"Greff is the holder; I think he may be able to help you find something you are looking for," Candor said as they stopped outside a rather small-looking shop with a sign over the front that was almost as big as the shop itself.

"'The Holding Shop'—and what do I need here?" Tyler asked. But as he turned around, he couldn't see Candor anywhere. "Candor? Candor, where did you go?" Tyler whispered. When there was no answer, he walked slowly into the shop. The shop was exactly as he remembered it from his dreams, when he and Michael had visited.

"Your Majesty, I am so pleased to see that you are okay. Now, what can I do for you today?"

Tyler stared at the pictures on the wall. How could this place help me? Why would Candor bring me here? Tyler thought to himself as he stood there in front of Greff. He noticed that Greff didn't seem to remember him.

"Don't you remember me?"

Greff just stared at him. "Of course I do, Your Majesty—you are the King." He sort of smiled weakly; he didn't really know what to say.

"I was here just a short while ago, with my brother, Michael."

Greff squinted and leaned a little closer to Tyler. "Oh, yes, I remember. You were a little, um...well, out of sorts that day, if I remember correctly."

Tyler smiled. "Yeah, I was. I, um...I was..."

"Oh, I'm sorry, Your Majesty. I didn't mean to be rude, sir—I am very sorry." Greff bowed down to Tyler.

Tyler was quite embarrassed "Get up, get up. It's okay, Greff—it's fine. You're right: I was out of sorts that day. Well, actually, I was just rude. I am the one who should be sorry; I think I was quite rude to you." Tyler reached out his hand to help Greff up.

Greff smiled. "Well, Your Majesty, what can I do for you today? What brings you here to the Holding Shop?"

Tyler wanted to tell him that he really had no idea why he was there, that Candor had brought him there to find some answers, but he couldn't. Greff probably wouldn't believe him anyway. "I am not too sure, really; I...um...well, I thought I would learn things about the Dark World—you know, get involved with the people, find out what they do," Tyler lied.

"That's a great idea. You are going to make a fine king, and you're just like your grandfather, if I may say so. You are very young, though. Well, what would you like to know? You can ask me anything, anything at all."

Tyler looked up at the pictures on the wall.

"Let me guess: you want to know what I hold. Am I right?"

Tyler smiled. "Is it that obvious?"

"Well, you are new at all of this, so why not start at the beginning? And yes, it is that obvious." Greff was very nervous. He didn't want to upset his new king.

"So why are all these pictures here? Who are they all? There are so many."

"These pictures are memories; I hold the memories of all the Nytstars that ever lived."

Tyler thought for a while. "You mean to say that they are all pictures of dead Nytstars?"

"Well, basically, yes, but they are much more: you see, each picture holds within it the person's memories. Let me show you." Greff reached for the closest picture on the wall. It was a picture of an old lady. The lady looked to be about eighty years old. She had silver hair and her face was covered in wrinkles. She was wearing a brown flowered dress with an orange cardigan overtop. The lady looked to be smiling at something in her hand. Next to the picture was a plaque with two dates on it, which, Greff explained, were her birth date and her death date.

"They all have them next to their pictures. Sometimes there is a person whose death date is unknown, so I can't write the date on the plaque, but it will show up on there all by itself."

"How? Who writes it on there?"

"Nobody writes on the plaques except me," Greff insisted. "The dates will just always be there. Now do you want to see this?"

Tyler nodded; he wasn't sure what he was about to see, but he hoped it would help him figure out why he was there. Greff opened the back of the picture; Tyler gasped as he jumped back in surprise. There in the back of the picture was the old lady. She was about the size of Tyler's hand, but she seemed to be very much alive. Tyler looked at Greff. "This is Jibe. Watch; you are about to see her memories." The old lady seemed to look straight at Tyler, who leaned in for a closer look at her.

"Hello, my name is Jibe. Who are you?"

Tyler quickly looked at Greff, who smiled and nodded, encouraging Tyler to answer. "Hi, um...I...um...I am Tyler. Pleased to meet you."

"Pleased to meet you too, Tyler. Do you want to know how I died, or how I lived?" Tyler was shocked; he had no idea. He was thankful that Greff spoke.

"Hello, Jibe, how are you?"

Jibe smiled. "I'm still dead, Greff, but I can't complain."

"Jibe, this is Tyler. He is the new King."

Jibe looked Tyler up and down, inspecting him. "Well, he is a little young, don't you think?"

Tyler felt insulted; what did she know? She had only just met him. Besides, he wasn't that young, he thought to himself: she was just a little old.

"This is the King's first time ever seeing a dead plate; I thought you wouldn't mind showing him yours."

Jibe smiled at Greff in a smug sort of way. "Well, I do have very interesting memories," she said, keeping her eyes on Tyler. "Okay, I will show him."

Tyler stood there and watched and listened as Jibe told stories of the things she had done, and of her family. She talked about how life changed when there was a different king, and how her husband had served for the dark army for years, and—as she put it—never was known for his greatness. It was like watching a movie with commentary. Tyler could see the things happening that

Jibe was talking about—just in miniature. Tyler wondered what would happen if he reached in and touched one of the people. Would he actually feel anything, or would his hand glide right through as if he were touching ghosts?

Tyler was almost asleep two hours later, when she was finally finished.

"…and that's how I died. It was peaceful, at least. I didn't suffer; I was thankful for that—"

"Thank you, Jibe," Greff interrupted. "Thank you—that was wonderful." Greff seemed as glad as Tyler was to close the picture and put it back on the wall. "So, that is impressive, right?" Greff asked Tyler.

Tyler nodded. He was still unsure why he was here. Why would Candor send him to see a bunch of dead people in pictures? Then it hit him.

"So everyone that dies, every Nytstar—if they have died, you would have their picture here?"

"That's right: every Nytstar that has ever died is somewhere in here."

Tyler smiled. "So if I was trying to find out whether someone had died or not, I would just have to look for their picture, right?"

"That's right. Are you looking for someone, Your Majesty?"

Tyler thought for a minute; he couldn't even remember their names. "I think it would have been two years ago, but I don't know the exact date or anything."

Greff scratched his head, scrunching his face up tightly. He walked behind the dusty, untidy counter that looked like it hadn't been cleaned in years, pulled out a giant gray book, and dropped it onto the counter, which sent dust flying into the air. Tyler coughed and waved the dust out of his face. Greff opened to the back of the book. "Same name, Your Majesty?" Greff stammered.

"I don't know. Well, last names…Yes, you're right, Greff—they would have the same last names, wouldn't they? As long as they both died together, we would see two of the same last names in the last two years. May I help you look, Greff?"

Greff looked at Tyler, then quickly looked at the book and pulled it a little closer toward him. "I am the only one who looks in the book; nobody is supposed to but me. That is why I am the holder." Greff bowed at Tyler and kept looking in the book.

"Oh. I'm sorry, Greff—I didn't mean to intrude. I just wanted to help."

"There are no names the same, Your Majesty. I am sorry; I did look in the last two years: no same names." Greff closed the book with a loud bang and put it back under the counter. "I am sorry I was not more helpful to you, Your Majesty. Now I have work to do." Greff bowed once more to Tyler and walked through the door leading to the back of the shop.

Tyler walked out of the shop back onto the street, looking around for Candor.

"Are you him?" a small voice asked from behind Tyler.

Tyler whipped around. He was surprised to see a small fairy-like creature that was glowing a brilliant blue. It seemed to be a young boy with wings that came from his back and spread out twice his size. He was quite a beautiful creature.

"Who am I supposed to be?" Tyler asked as he stared in amazement at the tiny flying creature.

"You are the new King. You're not very big, though—I thought you would be big and strong."

Tyler felt insulted. Who was this little fairy to say that he wasn't very big? The fairy was only as big as Tyler's hand. "I'm big enough," he spat back.

"Are you strong?" the fairy asked.

Tyler was starting to get annoyed; he started to walk away from the fairy, ignoring his question. He had only taken two steps when the fairy appeared right in front of him again.

"Are you strong?" he repeated.

"I think I'm strong enough. Who are you?"

The fairy smiled and stuck out his little chest proudly. "My name is Keadon. I am the prince of the fairies; one day I will also be a king, just like you. I will be strong then, too."

Tyler smiled at Keadon. "Well, it was nice to meet you, Keadon, but I really need to go. I am looking for—" Tyler stopped; he didn't want to say he was looking for Candor.

"Candor is hiding behind that shop over there," Keadon said, pointing to what looked like a plant shop. It had a picture of a bush on its sign and markings that Tyler didn't recognize.

"What makes you think I am looking for Candor?" Tyler asked, trying not to look too obvious.

"I saw you come here together when I was flying around. I was waiting to see if you were okay; I knew you got hurt by the dragon. You're not very good with dragons, are you?"

Tyler shook his head. "No...no, I'm not very good with dragons. Are you?"

Keadon flew around Tyler's head. "I am great with dragons—especially the really big ones! They don't scare me; I can ride them and everything. I once rode this dragon that was as big as your castle! It was red and black and—"

"Keadon, I hope you are not bothering the King." Another little fairy had appeared—only this was a girl fairy. She had long, glowing purple hair that reached all the way down to her tiny feet. Her wings were large, just like Keadon's; she was very beautiful and spoke in a soft, soothing voice.

"No, Mom, I wasn't bothering him—I was telling him how good I am with dragons," Keadon announced proudly.

"Telling tales again?" The girl fairy bowed at Tyler and both fairies flew away.

Tyler stared after them in amazement. He noticed that one of Keadon's wings was injured; it almost looked like it had been burnt on the edge.

"It is time for you to go home, I think," Candor whispered.

Tyler jumped. "Don't sneak up on me like that! Why do we have to go back to the castle already? I have only been in one shop; I thought you were going to show me around."

Candor started to hurry Tyler back to the castle.

"Candor, what is going on? What is the hurry? Is someone after us? Are we being followed?" Tyler tried to see what was going on behind them, but he couldn't see anything.

"No, we are not being followed—why would we be? It's just time to go, that's all. And we are not going back to the castle. You need to go back home, to the Lyt world."

Tyler stopped walking. "What? Why do I have to go home already? I don't want to go yet; I want to stay here. I have a lot to learn, you said so yourself. I need to learn how to handle the dragon and the other creatures. You said you—"

"This is not the time to act like a little boy. You are a king, and you are acting like a child. You need to go back to the Lyt world, and you need to go now."

Tyler opened his mouth to yell at Candor—how dare he speak to him like that? After all, it was he, Tyler, that was King, not Candor, so it was up to him when he wanted to go home, and he was not ready yet. But before he could say anything to Candor, Tyler felt a push from behind. He fell, but he didn't hit the ground: he just kept falling and falling. He reached his hands out in front of him just in time; he hit the ground with a thud.

Tyler jumped to his feet and spun around to shout at Candor, "What did you do that—" but stopped short when Sara threw her arms around his neck and sobbed on his shoulder.

"I was so worried about you, Tyler. I'm glad you're back—are you okay?"

Tyler knew he should have been happy to see her, and he should have been happy to be back home, but he wasn't. He pulled away from Sara and turned around. "I'm fine," he moaned, just as the door opened and Brandon walked in the room.

"There you are; I though you did another runner. Well, I'm going back to bed, if we're going to have another exciting day again tomorrow looking for the pretty necklace. Goodnight again." Brandon yawned and left the room.

"What? The necklace? What is he talking about?"

"You're back—I was wondering when you would come home. How are you feeling?" Michael asked as he came into the kitchen.

"Yep, I'm back. What is Brandon talking about? What necklace?" Tyler asked.

"We were looking for the Oltes, remember? We were looking for them before we went to bed earlier."

Tyler was confused; how could Michael have forgotten that he had been in the Dark World? And the dragon? Then Tyler's heart sank. Was it all just another dream? Had he not gone to the Dark World? Could he really just have dreamt it all?

"I thought your buddy Candor would have told you everything by now. I thought, you being King and all, you would be an expert." Michael jumped at Tyler and gave him a hug. Tyler pulled away from Michael and stared at him. Michael laughed. "I'm just kidding, Ty. I'm glad you're back."

Tyler moved to a chair at the table. Sara handed him a soda. "Thanks," he nodded. "So, what—it's the same day here?" Tyler asked Michael as he opened his soda.

"When we go into the Dark World, time here doesn't change. I was surprised too when I realized it, and I only went to the Dark World for a little bit. When I got back, Brandon just rolled over in his sleeping bag. It sure will make things easier. I checked with Nomad just to make sure. That explains how Mom didn't know about our grandparents. I don't think we should tell Mom any of this, at least for now—Mom, Dad, or anyone else, for that matter. Besides, it's not like anyone would believe us anyway."

Tyler was furious. "Well, it seems like you have everything figured out then. I'm going to bed." Tyler left the kitchen and crawled into his sleeping bag. His head hurt. He was so confused; he just needed time to think, to figure out what he was going to do next. How was it that Michael was so sure of everything? Was he trying to make Tyler look bad? Was he that jealous that Tyler was King instead of him? Tyler rolled over and closed his eyes. He could hear Michael and Sara talking in the kitchen; he lay as quiet and still as he could to listen to what they were saying.

"I just think you should take it easy on him, Michael, that's all. He has just gone through a lot, with the dragon, and finding out he is a king—that's a lot for a kid to take in. I mean, he died, remember? He actually died and then was brought back to life—how often has that ever happened?"

Kid? Who is she calling a kid? Tyler thought to himself.

"Sara, you don't know him like I do. Something is different, I can just tell…"

"Well, of course he is different, Mike—just give him some time."

Michael and Sara chatted long into the night. Tyler tossed and turned for a while until he finally fell asleep.

"He is not much for a new king; he is just a boy. I don't think he is very powerful, my lord: it should be easy to persuade him to join us—uh…I, uh…I mean, to join *you*, my lord."

Tyler opened his eyes and looked around, trying to see where the voices were coming from, but it was pitch black. He wanted to know to whom the voices belonged, but he wasn't so sure he wanted whoever they were to know he was listening to them, so he just lay as still as he could.

"I think you underestimate him. Our new King has more powers than he knows. He is even more powerful than both of his grandparents put together—I can feel it. I can feel the greatness of his powers."

"My lord, he is still so young. He does not know our world—he does not know how we run things—I mean…um…I mean, um, how *you* run things, my lord."

"Foolish servant, you think just because he is young, he will do as I say? Just because he is young, he will join me to rule our world?"

"I…um…I thought, my lord, that he would."

"You are foolish, servant. Our new King is also foolish: he lies there pretending he is asleep while he listens to us speaking."

Tyler gasped, but before he could move or say anything, he felt a hard blow to his whole body. He couldn't move; it was as if he were glued to the floor. He opened his mouth to yell, but nothing happened. He could see a hooded figure walking around him. The more he tried to move, the more tightly he seemed to be pushed into the floor.

"So you are the new King? I can't say I am pleased to meet you, Your Majesty—though that depends on what your plans are. You can join me and we can rule together, or you can be foolish like your grandfather and rule against me." The hooded figure bent down next to Tyler and whispered in his ear. "I assure you, Your Majesty, if you rule against me, you will not rule for long." And with that, the hooded figure was gone.

Tyler sat up in his sleeping bag and looked around the room. Michael, Sara, and Brandon were still asleep in their sleeping bags. The sun was starting to rise outside; the light was slowly starting to creep through the gaps in the curtains. Tyler slipped out of his sleeping bag and quickly got dressed. He folded up his things as quietly as he could and packed them back in his bag. Brandon started to fidget in his sleeping bag, so Tyler, who wasn't in the mood—for not only Brandon, but anybody—so early in the morning, slipped out of the room, into the Mysterious Blue.

He wandered around, looking at the things on the shelves, occasionally picking something up to take a closer look. His head was filled with a million thoughts, yet he didn't know with whom to talk about them. He would usually talk to Michael about everything, but not now—not since he went to the Dark World. Maybe it was because he went without Michael, or because Michael knew that he had been with Candor. Maybe Michael was jealous that it was Tyler who was King instead of him, but that wasn't Tyler's fault: he hadn't asked for the Triss to be on his foot—he hadn't asked to be King. Besides, had Michael forgotten that being King hadn't come without a price? After all, it was Tyler who had had nightmares all his life and had never slept through the night.

Maybe he could talk to Candor; he had at least answered all the questions Tyler had asked him. But how could he be sure he had told him the truth? After all, he was told that Candor was against his grandparents; what if he wasn't telling the truth? What if he was trying to hurt Tyler? Although, if he was trying to hurt Tyler, why didn't he just do it when Tyler was in the Dark World by himself? And why did he save Tyler from the dragon? And from what—or from whom—was Candor trying to save Tyler when he pushed him back to the Lyt world? Tyler didn't want to be at the Mysterious Blue anymore; he didn't even want to be in the Lyt world anymore. He needed to tell

Candor about his visit from the King of Darkness. He needed to find out why Candor had made him leave the Dark World so quickly.

"There you are, Tyler. How are you feeling this morning?" Sara asked as she walked into the aisle of the shop in which Tyler was standing.

"I'm fine—you?" Tyler answered, picking up a box that was on the shelf in front of him.

"I'm good…I was worried that you had run off again." Tyler shot a look at Sara; she knew right away that she had said the wrong thing. "Oh, Tyler, I'm sorry. I didn't mean to—"

"What? You think I run away every time something happens that I don't like? You think I'm a coward?"

Sara put her hand on Tyler's, but he pulled it away. "No, I don't think you're a coward, Tyler—that's not what I meant."

"Whatever. Look, I couldn't sleep—I thought I would just look around for a bit, that's all." Tyler looked down at the box he was holding. It felt quite heavy. He tried to open it, but it wouldn't open. The box was deep blue with black markings all around it that almost looked like feathers. On the top was a silver sword with a black handle; there was a small silver star on the top of the handle. Covering the sword was a deep black shield with a strange bird with huge wings; the bird was a deep, almost glowing blue. Tyler shook the box gently. There was definitely something inside. He tried again to open it, but still the box remained tightly closed.

"It won't open here," Sara said quietly.

Tyler looked up at her; he had almost forgotten that she was standing there. "Why not? What is it?"

"I don't know; all I know is that it won't open here. Lodiss laughs when people try to open it. It has been bought a few times but it is always returned. It's the same as a lot of things in this shop: you cannot have it if it is not meant to be yours."

"You sound just like Lodiss, saying stuff like that," Michael laughed as he joined them. He took the box from Tyler and shook it. "Great box—weird, but hey, so is…well, everything lately. You guys hungry? I'm starving—what do you say we have breakfast?"

"How much is it?" Tyler asked, taking the box back from Michael.

"I'm not sure. You take it—I will ask Lodiss when she gets back."

Tyler put the box back on the shelf and started to walk away. "Tyler, don't be such a jerk. Just take the box—we can pay Lodiss when she comes back," Michael shouted.

"Really, Tyler, Lodiss won't mind—especially for you." Sara followed Tyler out of the room and handed him the box. "Just take it," she said, shoving the box at Tyler and walking into the kitchen.

Michael walked past Tyler, following Sara; he turned around and stared at Tyler. "Seriously, Tyler—she was just trying to be nice to you." Michael walked into the kitchen, leaving Tyler standing there, holding the box. Tyler put the box in his bag and joined the others in the kitchen. They all sat eating their breakfasts quietly.

"Thank you."

Everyone looked up at Tyler.

"For the box, I mean. Thank you."

Sara looked at Tyler, who quickly looked down at his bowl of cereal. "You're welcome," she said, smiling.

CHAPTER TEN

THE NYTHAWK

By Sunday night, they had not made much progress in their search to find out what happened to Sara's parents. Tyler had been waiting since Sara had given him the box from the Mysterious Blue to talk to Nomad without Michael around, and finally, after supper Sunday night, when Michael had gone out with their dad, Tyler stayed home to do his homework—well, at least that's what he had told his parents. As soon as they left, Tyler went up to his room. He locked the door and pulled Nomad out from the bag under the bed.

"Tyler, how nice to see you. I was wondering when you would ask me about that box you have," the book said.

"How did you know, Nomad? That's right—you know everything. You just don't feel you should tell me anything," Tyler spat back at Nomad.

"Tyler—or do you prefer 'Your Majesty'? You did not ask me about your castle. Now do you want to take out your anger and frustration on me, or would you like me to tell you about that box?"

Tyler took the box off his dresser and stared at it. He tried again to open it.

"It won't open here, Tyler—and you wouldn't want it to, either."

Tyler sat down in front of Nomad and put the box on the floor. "Why wouldn't I want it to open here?"

"The box of Treptropsis contains an egg."

But before Nomad could continue, there was a knock on the door. "Tyler? Tyler, why is the door locked?" Michael shouted through the door as he knocked loudly.

"Just a second," Tyler snapped as he quickly put Nomad back in the bag and pushed him under the bed. "I was doing my homework. I need to get it done; it's due tomorrow."

Michael lay in his bed, reading a book, while Tyler tried to write the poem he had to read to the whole of Mrs. Suzanne's class first thing the next morning. He was dreading it. He knew that whatever poem he wrote, it would not be good enough for Mrs. Suzanne: nothing Tyler did ever was. Michael and Tyler said goodnight to their parents, and Michael went straight to sleep without saying anything to Tyler. Tyler sat staring at the same blank piece of paper at which he had been staring for the last hour or two. He tapped his pen on the desk and scratched his head, but nothing seemed to help: not a word came into his head. If only I could explain to Mrs. Suzanne that I am a king in another world and I am not going to waste my time writing poems, Tyler laughed to himself—but he turned around so fast he nearly fell off his chair when he realized he wasn't the only one laughing.

Standing right behind Tyler, wearing the same kind of robe as Candor usually wore, hiding his face the same way, was Eljord—the King of Darkness. "Tyler, you are still afraid to use your powers. Tut, tut...how do you ever expect to rule? A little king, afraid to use his powers." Eljord laughed again; his laugh sent shivers down Tyler's spine.

"I am not afraid to use my powers," Tyler exclaimed.

"My mistake, Your Majesty—I didn't realize you don't know how to use your powers. Then I do not need to worry; you will have to join me. I am glad. The Nytstars will be glad they do not have to fight again; no one will need to die this time." Eljord walked over to the bed where Michael was sleeping and stroked his hand across his head.

Tyler jumped up and pushed Eljord's hand away from Michael. "Don't touch him," Tyler warned.

Eljord grabbed Tyler around the neck with one hand and lifted him up in the air. "I am Eljord, the King of Darkness, and you are a mere boy. Do not think you stand a chance against me. You are not even able to stand up against your teacher, who is a nothing but a Lyt." Tyler struggled to get loose from Eljord's grip, but the more he struggled, the tighter his grip became. Eljord reached out with his other hand and once again touched Michael's head. "I should kill him right now, right here, for you to watch—then maybe you would know how to deal with worthless nothings. But I will wait; I think in time you will do that for me. Yes, when you finally realize that it is in the Dark World, ruling with me, that you belong, not here with your bigger and smarter brother, the one who doesn't believe in you—the one who will be your downfall." And with that, Eljord was gone.

Tyler fell to the floor with a bang. He sat up in his chair; it had been a dream. Tyler checked to see if Michael was in bed: he was, and fast asleep, just as Tyler knew he would be. Tyler went back to his desk to turn the light off. He looked down at the paper, which now said the words "Kill the Lyt." Tyler scrunched up the paper and threw it away, then crawled into bed. He tossed and turned, waking every hour or so from nightmare after nightmare of watching himself standing over Michael's dead and lifeless body. When his alarm clock went off in the morning, he wasn't sure whether to be happy that the nightmares would be done for the day or to be worried that soon he would have to stand in front of Mrs. Suzanne and the rest of the class and make a fool of himself.

Tyler couldn't help but think on the walk to school how he would love to use his powers to get rid of Mrs. Suzanne—or even to turn her into an animal or something. Michael waved at Brandon as he came running over to join them.

"Hey, how are my two favorite Nytstars doing this morning?" he asked joyfully.

Tyler grabbed Brandon's arm and pulled him in closely. "Are you crazy or just stupid? Do you think that going around announcing that to everyone is the best way to keep a secret?"

"Lay off him, Tyler. Nobody heard, and besides, even if someone did hear, it's not like anyone will know what he is talking about." Michael and Brandon walked a little faster, leaving Tyler trailing behind.

"I see His Highness is in a great mood again today," Brandon whispered to Michael.

"As usual, lately," Michael replied.

As they reached the school, Tyler saw Megan walking by herself and jogged to catch up to her. "Hey," he said quietly.

Megan smiled. "Did you finish your poem for Mrs. Suzanne, Tyler?"

"No. I tried, but so far, I have nothing. I was thinking of skipping first period—I don't feel like starting off my week with humiliation."

"Too late," Megan whispered, just as Mrs. Suzanne walked up to them.

"Oh, good, you did show up today, Tyler; I didn't expect you to. Well, what a surprise for me. I trust you didn't do your poem?"

Tyler stumbled for words, but nothing came out.

"From the look of pure blankness—or dumbness—on your face, I see that I am right. Well, who can expect much from nothing, I always say."

"You cannot speak to Tyler that way," Megan protested.

"I just did," Mrs. Suzanne spat as she glared at them both and walked away with her nose held high.

"You shouldn't have done that; now you'll be a target for her too."

Megan laughed. "I already was."

Tyler started to smile, but stopped when he saw Michael and Sara whispering together and laughing. Tyler stormed away, leaving Megan standing alone.

Tyler was the first one in the room for Mrs. Suzanne's class, so he quickly pulled out a pen and a piece of paper. Still angry about Mrs. Suzanne's comments and knowing there were more to come as soon as she walked through the door, he wrote his poem. As soon as everyone was in their seats and Mrs. Suzanne was standing at the front of the class, looking as smug as ever, she started.

"Okay, let's not waste any time. I am sure everyone is as eager as I am to listen to Tyler's...um...'poem,' or lack thereof, so let's hear it. Up to the front so we can all watch," she said, smirking. Tyler stood up and walked slowly to the front of the class. He stood there for a minute, looking at everyone, until he saw Megan and Sara. He felt his anger boil again; he thought of Michael and Sara laughing outside and couldn't help but think they were laughing at him. "Well, Tyler, your poem?" Mrs. Suzanne chuckled. Tyler stared hard at Mrs. Suzanne in an almost frightening way and recited his poem.

> *I close my eyes and disappear*
> *With courage to replace my constant fear*
> *The wicked*
> *The nag*
> *The one I dread*
> *I pierce her heart*
> *Lay cold*
> *Lay dead*

Tyler stood there staring at Mrs. Suzanne; the whole class was silent.

"Sit down," Mrs. Suzanne stated flatly.

"Did you like it? My poem, I mean—did you like it?" Tyler asked, feeling quite pleased with himself.

"I said sit down."

Tyler walked back to his desk, smiling back at Mrs. Suzanne. He knew he wouldn't get a good grade on his poem, but he didn't care: the look on his teacher's face was well worth it. He couldn't help but wonder if she knew it was meant for her. If she knew, he wanted so badly for her to feel just a little of how she made him feel. For the first time in Mrs. Suzanne's class, she didn't speak to or mention Tyler for the rest of the lesson. Tyler knew he had made her feel something.

"That was a great poem, Tyler—chilling. It gave me goose bumps," Megan teased as they walked out of the classroom together into the hall toward their next class.

"Thanks. I'm glad someone liked it; I don't think Mrs. Suzanne did," Tyler joked.

"I liked your poem too," Conner laughed as he and Chase moved toward Tyler, forcing him to back into a locker. "Only we would like it better if it was you who 'lay cold lay dead'—and I want to be the one to do it." Conner stared at Tyler for a moment, then walked away with Chase, as always, right behind him. Tyler looked around at the crowd of kids that had gathered to watch; they all snickered, whispered, and carried on their way. Tyler just shook his head and went to his next class.

The rest of the morning seemed to drag on. Tyler's head was bobbing and his eyes were just about to close when the lunch bell rang. Tyler grabbed his lunch from his locker and headed outside.

"Tyler," Megan shouted as she ran to catch up. "Hey, Tyler, do you mind if I eat with you?"

"Sure, if you want to."

They sat together under a tree at the very back of the school field. "Tyler, you look really tired again. You can take a nap if you want; I'll wake you when the bell goes."

"I'm fine. I'm not a baby—I don't need a nap."

"I didn't mean that—I just meant that you could, uh…I mean, if you wanted to…"

"It's fine. I'm fine."

"You two look cozy," Brandon teased as he sat down next to Megan. "Where's Michael?" he asked, biting his sandwich.

"How would I know?" Tyler snapped.

Brandon looked at him, confused. "Well, you guys are always together…you know, your brother? Your best friend? I don't know what your problem is, Tyler. You are being a right pain. You're acting like a baby. King of the Babies!" Brandon laughed.

Tyler jumped on Brandon and started punching him. Megan was trying to pull him off when Michael came running up to them and pulled Tyler off of Brandon, who jumped to his feet. "What is wrong with you?" Brandon yelled. Sara tried to stop Brandon's nose from bleeding.

"Tyler, have you lost your mind? You need help—you are out of control," Michael shouted as he pushed Tyler. Tyler just froze; they were all watching him.

"You know, Brandon did antagonize him," Megan stated crossly. Everyone just looked at her.

"You have lost it, Tyler—totally lost it," Michael shouted as he pushed Tyler one last time and walked away with Brandon and Sara.

"Don't worry about them; they'll calm down. You guys will be laughing about it soon," Megan said as she put her arm around Tyler, trying to comfort him.

"Look, Megan, I have to go. I'm sorry—I just…I have to go."

"It's fine, go. I have some homework to do. I'll see you later."

Megan was surprised to see Tyler at school after lunch, but not as surprised as Sara. "I thought you would have been long gone by now," Sara said to Tyler as she passed him in the hall.

"I told you, I don't run away every time things go wrong."

"That's what you think? Just that something went wrong? What part went wrong—getting caught beating up a *friend*?"

Tyler shot a nasty look at Sara. "A friend wouldn't have talked to me like he did."

"Yes, a friend would have. You've changed, Tyler: you are angry all the time lately. He was being a friend, that's all."

Tyler laughed. "Well, I don't need him to be my friend. I don't need anyone to be my friend." Tyler stormed off to his class, leaving Sara standing there, close to tears.

"Maybe you guys shouldn't be so hard on him. I mean, Brandon was pretty rude to him, and you three gang up on Tyler. You're no better than Conner and Chase right now," Megan said to Sara before she too went to her class.

After school, Tyler went to his locker quickly so he could head home without Michael and Brandon. He was relieved to get home and see the note from his mom saying she and his dad would both be home late and there was pizza money in the cookie jar. Tyler went up to his bedroom and reached under the bed to pull out Nomad, but the book wasn't there. "Michael must have it," Tyler said to himself. He took the box of Treptropsis out from his dresser drawer and stared at it. "What kind of egg is in here? It can't still be any good—I mean, it could have been in here for ages."

"What could have been in where for ages?" Michael said suspiciously as he came into the room and threw his bag on his bed.

"Nothing," Tyler said.

"Whatever. I just thought you might need my help, that's all."

"Your help? No, I don't need your help—thanks," Tyler snapped.

"Fine. Why don't you go to your precious castle and finish your mood there? Because we are getting really sick of it here."

Tyler held on tight to the Treptropsis, looked Michael in the eye, and disappeared.

Michael was furious. "He left, I can't believe it—again, he just left." Michael paced the room. He wanted to follow Tyler, but he wasn't sure whether he wanted to follow him to finish their conversation or to see what he was up to. Sara, Michael thought to himself, and he ran to the phone.

Tyler walked through the castle, opening every door. "Candor! Candor, where are you?" he shouted into each room. He turned around to go down another hallway.

"Tyler," Candor said calmly from behind him.

Tyler turned around quickly. "Where were you? I was calling you."

"I do not wait here for you to return, Tyler. I am not your servant."

"I know you're not. I was just looking for you, that's all."

"Your Majesty, I am ever so pleased to see you. I have had your room made up for you. Is there anything I can get for you, Your Majesty?" asked a woman who Tyler had never met before. She was wearing a very old-fashioned-looking dress that went all the way down to the floor; it was deep purple and had a black apron over top that tied in the back. Her dark brown, gray-streaked hair was tied tightly in a bun on her head. Her skin was pale, which was probably due to the fact that the Dark World was...well, just that: dark. She looked like she was pretty once but had worked hard for such a long time that you could see it in her face.

Tyler stared at her for a moment. "I don't...um...no, I'm fine, thank you." The woman bowed slightly to Tyler and started to walk away. "Wait! I'm sorry—I don't even know your name."

The woman stared at Tyler. "I'm sorry, Your Majesty?" the woman said.

"Your name—or do I just call you ma'am?"

The woman looked at Candor with a confused and somewhat timid look. "Her name is Laydin; she is the castle keeper," Candor said flatly. "Now why were you calling me?"

Tyler looked around, but Laydin was gone. "I have some questions I was hoping you could answer for me, and…well, I just…"

"Wanted to be here in your castle with people who will not judge you or antagonize you?" Candor finished Tyler's sentence as if he had just read his mind.

"I wanted to know about this." Tyler shoved the Treptropsis at Candor. He was annoyed and embarrassed that Candor knew what he was thinking.

"Where did you get this?" Candor asked as Tyler handed him the box.

"It was at the Mysterious Blue."

"You mean to tell me it was just sitting there on a shelf?"

"Well, yeah, it was. I was just looking around the shop and it was just that: sitting there on a shelf. Nomad told me it won't just open for anyone, and Sara told me that it had been returned a bunch of times."

Candor paced the floor, mumbling. "I knew that old woman was trouble. She has no idea—what if someone did open it? She is putting us all at risk. I have told Eljord we need to get rid—" But he didn't finish; he stopped and turned to Tyler, who just stood there.

"What do you mean, 'get rid'? You can't be talking about Lodiss—you can't!" Tyler shouted.

"Calm down; you are acting like a little boy having a temper tantrum. Now that we know where you got it, do you know what it is?"

Tyler took the box back and held it gently. "I know it has an egg in it, but I'm sure it can't be any good—I think it would be rotten by now. I mean, who knows how old it is? That's why I came to you."

"I see. Well, you are right about one thing: it does have an egg inside. However, the egg will not be rotten. It will not awaken until it is where it is supposed to be. You will also need to take care of it before you can open it."

"How do I take care of it?"

"Really, Tyler, you need to think for yourself. You depend on Michael to do all the thinking."

"It is just a box—it doesn't need food or water! Oh, I see, I should put it on a leash and take the box for a walk!" Tyler spat back at Candor.

Candor turned and started to walk away. "I am not going to get into a childish quarrel with you. I have things to do." And with that, he was gone.

"Wait! You cannot talk to me like that—I am not a child." Tyler shouted after him. Tyler was angry; he looked down at the box, threw it on the floor, and stormed off toward the main tower, not really thinking about where he was going. He climbed the staircase in the tower to the trophy floor. Tyler tried to open one of the doors, but it wouldn't open. Glancing around the stairwell, Tyler remembered what Candor had told him about how the doors would not open if someone without the castle's blood was in the tower, but as far as he could see, he was alone: there was no one else in the tower. Tyler walked around the hallway to try another door, but just like the last door, this one also would not open.

"Typical," Tyler snapped. "The Drade isn't working right. I'm sure somehow it's my fault." Grumbling, Tyler left the tower and headed for his dressing quarters. He changed into his king's robes and hung his sword at his side. He took a moment to look at himself in the mirror; he couldn't help but feel somewhat important.

When Tyler left the room, he saw Laydin walking down the hall. He ran to catch up with her. "Laydin, hi."

Laydin bowed to Tyler again. "What can I do for you, Your Majesty? I put the box in your room. I checked it—you know, to make sure it was okay. I hope you don't mind."

"Thank you, Laydin. I must have dropped it. Anyway, do you know when Candor will be back?"

"Candor is here when he is meant to be here, and he isn't when he isn't," Laydin replied.

"Great," Tyler snapped. "Laydin, were you or Candor in the main tower a moment ago?"

Laydin hesitated and began to fidget. "No, Your Majesty—nobody was in the main tower. Candor left the castle and I only go there to clean, Your Majesty, but I make sure you are not there—I would not want to interrupt you."

Tyler forced a smile. "The Drade isn't working, then."

"The Drade is working, I assure you. You are very powerful; a simple Drade is no match for you. I almost forgot, Your Majesty: there is someone here to see you. He is in the entry room."

"Who is it?" Tyler asked, surprised.

"Your brother, Your Majesty," Laydin replied, and again disappeared.

Tyler wasn't sure he wanted Michael to be there. He had come to get away from the other world, including Michael. A little hesitant, Tyler went to the entry room; he stood outside the door for a moment, took a deep breath, and opened it

"Michael, what are you doing here?" Tyler walked in the room, not very surprised to see Sara standing next to Michael. "Here to gang up on me again, I see—well, what did I do now?"

"Nothing. You didn't do anything. We just wanted to help—well, we wanted your help," Michael said quietly.

"What? You wanted my help? Why? Doing what?"

"Well, we were looking for Sara's parents, right? She got a sign—at least, I think it was a sign."

Sara handed Tyler a patch of grass with the soil still on it. Tyler held it in his hand and looked, unimpressed, at both Sara and Michael. "Grass? That's your clue—grass?"

"It was on my pillow. I found it when I got home."

"So maybe you came to the Dark World and it was on your shoe or something," Tyler joked as he handed the grass back to Sara.

"First of all, Tyler, we haven't been here in a while. Second of all, I have yet to see grass like this here. This grass grows on hills and moors mainly in Europe: it needs the damp conditions."

"So it doesn't sound to me like you need my help. You seem to have it figured out."

Michael started to walk to the door. "So, are you going to show us around? It's not every day you get a new castle."

Tyler smiled and led the way out of the entry room. He showed them through every room in the castle, trying to remember some of the interesting things Candor had told him about it. "This is the main tower," Tyler recited. "As you know, my room is at the top. There's an entire floor dedicated to trophies and weapons. The tower is protected by a Drade, and you cannot get into the rooms if there is anyone in the tower who is not of the castle's blood."

"Oh, well, I can wait if you guys want to go in," Sara offered.

"No need—the Drade doesn't work. The rooms won't open; I tried already, earlier. Besides, I'm getting hungry. Let's go down to the dining room; I will have the cooks make us something to eat."

"The cooks? You have your own cooks now, too? Must be nice," Michael said as he followed Tyler through the stairwell.

"Mike, this is your castle too, remember? So they are also your cooks. Don't start on that again," Tyler snapped.

"It was a joke, Tyler. Chill out."

"Are you sure it was a joke, or was it—"

"What do you mean, 'the Drade doesn't work'?" Sara interrupted.

"What?"

"You said the door wouldn't open."

"Yeah, so what? Maybe the Drade wore off or something," Tyler said, beginning to get annoyed. Sara gave Michael a look; they both seemed to know something that Tyler didn't. "What, you don't I'm the real King or something?"

"Tyler, we didn't say that."

"You didn't have to. I can tell from the look you just gave each other."

"Tyler, how did you know about the Drade?" Sara asked, ignoring Tyler's comment.

"Um…well…Laydin told me. Yeah, when she showed me around the castle."

"The thing is, though, Tyler, Drades don't wear off: they need to be removed, and it is very difficult. There has to be a reason the doors wouldn't open."

"Well, maybe Laydin wasn't completely out of the tower yet. It doesn't mean I'm not the King. There could have been another maid in one of the rooms."

"The rooms are not cleaned directly by the maids; they are not able to enter them. They use a Clenzis Drade in the rooms—I am surprised Laydin didn't tell you that. I'm going to leave the tower. Try again," Sara said, already running down the stairs.

"Well, go ahead, Your Majesty," Michael mocked.

Tyler glared at him and grabbed the door handle to the trophy room. He tried a few times, but still it wouldn't open. Michael snickered behind Tyler. "Here, then—you try it," Tyler snapped.

Michael gripped the door handle. He tried gently at first, but when nothing happened, he tried harder and harder. He tried wiggling it, but nothing happened: the door just would not open. "Well, at least we know you weren't adopted, Ty." Tyler shot Michael an angry look, but couldn't help but laugh at Michael's red face. "I wonder what types of trophies are in there, anyway," Michael said.

"I don't know. He didn't say."

"He? He who? You said that Laydin showed you around. Who are you talking about?"

"Michael, relax—I meant she." Tyler turned away from Michael quickly and ran down the stairs. "It didn't work. We both tried, but we couldn't open it."

"Are you sure there was no one else in the tower?" Sara questioned.

"No, there was no one else in the tower—I am positive. You know, the Drade could have messed up or something when our grandparents died and the castle changed hands. I'm sure Nomad could tell Michael all about it," Tyler said as he began walking away from them.

"Where are you going now?" Michael called after him.

"I told you, I'm hungry. Are you two coming?" Tyler shouted over his shoulder. Michael and Sara gave each other a quick, concerned look, then followed Tyler to the dining room, where Laydin served them dinner.

"I think we should go to your library, Tyler. There may be some books or maps or something to find out where this grass came from."

The library—sure, that's a good idea, Tyler thought to himself; he wasn't thinking of the grass, however: he was thinking of the box of Treptropsis. He was hoping he would be able to find a book telling him about the box. They finished eating and went to the library; just like every room in the castle, it was lit with candles: the walls were lined with hundreds of them, all in glass cases so as not to damage the books. The room was round and seemed to just keep going up; there were hundreds and hundreds of books on every shelf. There were three large, dark wooden desks in the center of the room. Large burgundy leather chairs were placed over a rug by a huge stone fireplace that burned along the curved wall at the back of the room.

"Wow, Tyler, this place is great. There are more books here than any library I have ever seen," Sara said with a smile as she looked around, trying to see everything. Her eyes were big with delight.

"Yeah, Tyler, there are a lot of books here. Are you going to read them all?" Michael joked. Tyler shot Michael a dirty look. Michael and Sara began looking through book after book. Michael noticed Tyler sitting down at one of the desks, looking at a book. "Did you find something?" Michael asked.

"Um…no…no, I didn't," Tyler stammered.

Michael walked over to the desk where Tyler was sitting to see what book he was looking at, but before he could see it, Tyler shut the book and put it in one of the drawers of the desk. "What, was that a book for kings only?"

"Wow, that was almost funny," Tyler snapped.

Michael reached for the drawer where Tyler had just put the book. He opened the drawer with not too much resistance from Tyler; much to Michael's surprise, the drawer was empty. "Where is it?" Michael snapped.

"Where is what?"

"Don't act dumb—that book you were looking at, Tyler. Why are you hiding it?"

"I am not hiding anything…"

"Guys, I found something," Sara shouted. Michael walked over to Sara and sat down next to her on the floor, looking over her shoulder at the open book on her lap. Sara turned to Tyler. "Are you going to come and look? This is it, I think: this is the grass." Tyler joined them on the floor, but he really wasn't interested in the book, or the grass.

"This is it—you're right, Sara," Michael said. "It's mainly found in England; I thought so." Michael flipped through the pages in the book; he did it so fast that Tyler didn't get a chance to read any of it.

"So you have grass on your pillow. It doesn't mean anything; it's just grass," Tyler said.

"Are you serious? It has to mean something. How would the grass get on her pillow? We are not in England," Michael shouted as he punched Tyler in the arm.

Tyler got up from the floor. "I thought you were here for my help, not to get yourself into a fight."

Sara jumped up. "Look, I don't want either of your help—I will do this on my own. I'm sick of all of your fighting." Sara walked out of the library. Michael shot Tyler an angry look and followed her.

Tyler didn't go after them; he went back to the desk where he had been sitting before Michael had interrupted him. He opened the same drawer that Michael had opened just moments before, which had been empty—only this time, there was the book that Tyler had put in it. Tyler just laughed to himself. He didn't care if Sara and Michael were mad at him; he was quite pleased with himself for using his powers to hide the book. Tyler had been using his powers more and more; he was getting quite good at them. He put the book on the desk and started to flip through it until he found exactly what he was looking for: a picture of the Treptropsis. Finally, he was going to find out what type of egg was inside. Tyler read through the pages as quickly as he could, stopping often to reread a sentence or a paragraph. He couldn't believe the words. Could what he was reading really be true? "No, there's no way—not even here." Tyler continued to read for hours. Finally, when his head hurt and his eyes burned, he closed his eyes, held onto his Oltes, and summoned the Treptropsis.

After a few moments, he opened his eyes. He was a little shocked and proud of himself to see the Treptropsis sitting on the desk in front of him. With no doubt it would work this time, and his eyes open, he held onto his Oltes once again and summoned a bag. Just as the Treptropsis had done, there was the bag, sitting on the desk in front of him. Tyler put the Treptropsis into the bag, threw the bag over his shoulder, and left the library.

"Good evening, Your Majesty. May I have the kitchen prepare a snack for you and your guests?" Laydin asked when she met Tyler in the hall.

"They…um…they had to go, and I'm not hungry, but thanks anyway." Tyler was a little mad that he and Michael were not on the best of terms right now; Tyler knew his brains would have been helpful with the Treptropsis. I could go back first; I could ask Michael to help me, he thought to himself, but then he remembered what Candor had said: how he shouldn't depend on Michael, how he needed to think for himself. "I don't need Michael. I don't need anyone," he grumbled to himself, and he headed for the front door of the castle. He pulled the very large and very heavy door open, took a deep breath, and walked through.

Once outside, he felt a cool breeze blow through his already messy hair. He pulled his robes tightly around him and walked around the castle grounds. Trees bowed and said good evening as he rounded the castle to the back. There seemed to be a wall of trees surrounding most of the grounds. These trees bowed to Tyler as the others had done.

Tyler nodded back at them. "Is there nowhere I can go to be alone?"

"Your Majesty, you are alone. You don't have to worry about us: we are just trees." Tyler turned to see a tree, larger than all the others (it looked to be the oldest tree from the look of its bark), that was talking to him. "We will listen to you and talk to you, Your Majesty; however, your words are like our branches, you see: they grow for you and only you. We will not share your words, or anything we see you do, with anyone. There is nothing that can keep a secret like a tree, Your Majesty." Tyler smiled. He suddenly felt relieved. He sat down under the big tree and pulled the book and the Treptropsis out of the bag. He started to flip through the pages he had just read moments ago in the library until he found the page he wanted.

Laying the Treptropsis gently down on the grass in front of him, Tyler held onto his Oltes with one hand and placed his other hand, which was trembling slightly with both excitement and fear, on the top of the Treptropsis. He looked down at the words in the book. Slowly and clearly, he began to recite them.

The light will shine up from the ground
Your song will be the only sound
Lifelong companions, you and I
We will sail across the darkest sky

We will go to battles side by side
And grow together with courage and pride
I am your master, I do command
For you to emerge and come to my hand
Together, united, we both shall stand
I ask of you to at last be born
To your king your loyalty is sworn

Tyler held his breath as he waited for something to happen. Within moments, just as the words in the book had said, a blue light shot up from the around the Treptropsis. The box started to get very hot. Tyler pulled his hand away quickly, but the light disappeared as suddenly as it had appeared. Tyler took a deep breath and returned his hand to the Treptropsis. Once again, the blue light shot up from the ground around the box. An eerie silence fell suddenly over the grounds. Tyler kept his hand on the box as it got hotter and hotter, all the while excited and nervous about what was going to come out of the Treptropsis. The silence was broken when a high-pitched, yet peaceful, bird-like song seemed to emerge from the box. As the top slowly started to open, the song got louder and louder, until the lid was all the way off and slid to the ground. Tyler kept his hand on the lid and peered into the box. "The egg," Tyler gasped he reached into the box and carefully picked up the large, jet black egg. It was almost weightless; it too was very warm. "What now?" Tyler asked himself. Yet it wasn't he who answered.

"Wow, is that what I think it is?" a small yet familiar voice replied.

Tyler spun around quickly, but nobody was there. He turned back to the egg and jumped, startled to see Keadon the fairy prince hovering right beside the egg in Tyler's hand. "What do you think it is?"

Keadon puffed out his tiny chest as he replied. "That is a Treptropsis. They carry eggs, Nythawk eggs. They are very rare. They don't open for just anyone, you know; you must be very powerful. Some Treptropsis can be owned by many Nytstars and never open. Your grandfather never had one; you must be even more powerful than he was."

Tyler stared at Keadon; he was quite impressed. "How do you know all that?"

"I know lots of stuff. I'm very smart and brave; my mom says that when I am the King of the Fairies, I will be the bravest ever," Keadon said proudly.

Tyler smiled. "Do you know how long it will take for the egg to hatch?"

"That depends on how powerful you are. You need to use your powers to connect with your Nythawk; it will sense your powers and—"

But before Keadon could finish, they both heard a cracking noise. Tyler and Keadon stared down at the egg. They watched as cracks quickly appeared all over it. Tyler gently placed the egg on the ground. They both stared in amazement as they watched a tiny bird emerge from the egg. The bird was so small it could fit right in the palm of Tyler's hand. Its feathers were shiny and black with a purple tint; its eyes were a deep blue, and the infant Nythawk struggled to keep them open. Tyler held out his hand toward the bird; he watched excitedly as the bird staggered toward it, squeaking and squawking just as any baby bird would. It reached Tyler's hand, lay down, and fell asleep.

"Aw...it's so cute," Tyler said as he examined the bird closely.

"Yep, but I would be careful if I were you. I wouldn't get too close," Keadon warned.

"What? It's so tiny. It can't hurt me; it's barely big enough to stand up on its own." Tyler was a little surprised that Keadon would say that, until, right before their eyes, the bird began to grow, all the while singing its sweet song. The bird doubled in size in seconds, and as the bird grew, its song got louder. It didn't take long before the bird was too big for Tyler to hold in his hand, so he put it back on the ground in front of him.

"I told you I wouldn't get too close," Keadon teased.

"How...um, how big do they get?" Tyler asked.

"Very big—almost the same size as Candor's dragon you were playing with."

"What?" Tyler spat.

"You know, Candor's big white dragon you were playing with until I saved you."

Tyler was confused; what was Keadon talking about? He didn't save him, Candor did, and the dragon was his grandfathers, not Candor's. "How do you know it's Candor's dragon? And what do you mean, you saved me?"

"I told you before, I know lots of things, and I mean that I saved you. It was me that pulled you away from the dragon, of course," Keadon stated proudly.

Tyler looked at Keadon's injured wing. "Is that how your wing got hurt?" he asked quietly.

"Yeah—it's great, isn't it? I will be able to tell the story forever of how I, Keadon the Fairy Prince, saved Tyler the great Nytstar King from Candor's deadly white dragon. It's brilliant."

Before Tyler had the chance to say anything, the Nythawk's song was getting so loud, they couldn't hear each other. The bird was now enormous. It towered above Tyler and Keadon, and just as Keadon had said, it was almost as big as the dragon. Suddenly, the singing stopped. The bird spread its gigantic, shiny, black and purple wings and flapped them; its whole body shook as it ruffled its feathers.

"Wow...I can't believe it. It's beautiful," Tyler said, his eyes wide and mouth open in amazement.

"It's a he," Keadon announced.

"How do you know?"

"Well, the boys are black and purple and the girls are black and pink and not as big. Traydome, that's his name."

"How do you know that?" Tyler asked again.

"It's on his necklace."

"Traydome," Tyler repeated as he reached out to touch his feathers, but Keadon lifted Tyler up onto the Nythawk's back.

"Let's fly," he shouted excitedly, and before Tyler had the chance to say anything, they were off. Traydome jumped right into the air with a loud squawk, flapping his enormous wings hard. They flew higher and higher. Tyler held tightly to the bird.

"This is great!" Keadon shouted as he floated around Tyler's head. Tyler nodded, not loosening his grip.

Traydome spoke for the first time. "Master, finally we are united. How I have longed for this, for the chance to fly with you, to spread my wings."

"I have never heard them speak before; too bad I can't understand them," Keadon said, sounding disappointed.

"What do you mean you can't understand him? He is speaking clearly."

"They only speak to their masters; all everyone else will ever hear is squawking," Keadon said. "Anyway, it's been fun, Tyler, but I'd better get home—you know moms. See you later." Tyler waved goodbye to his new friend as he flew away.

Traydome flew around for just a little while longer before landing back within the castle grounds. "I must go and hunt. I need to get stronger, master, but I will always be at your side when you need me. I need to stay out of sight as much as I can; it is safer." Tyler nodded and petted his feathers and watched as he flew off until he couldn't see the gigantic Nythawk anymore.

"What next?" Tyler said as he picked up the open box, stuffed it and the book back into the bag, and headed back inside the castle. He went apprehensively to the entry room. He didn't want to leave; he wanted to stay, to ride Traydome, to hang out with Keadon, his new friend, but he knew he had to return to the Lyt world. He had to help Michael and Sara find Sara's parents; he was their best hope so far.

CHAPTER ELEVEN

THE FOREST

Michael hung up the phone and ran into the bedroom. "Sara!" he panted. "Something is wrong—I can feel it."

Tyler just looked at him blankly. "What are you talking about? Look, if you're going to start in on me, saying I did something to Sara, well, you're wrong."

"No, I didn't mean you. Look, forget our fight, okay? It's just something is wrong with Sara."

Tyler felt a little anger starting to boil again, but he did his best to ignore it. "What do you mean, you can feel it? Are you and Sara that close?"

Michael shot an angry look at Tyler. "I am not doing this with you now. Sara and I are just friends, that's all—and if you would stop being such a jerk all the time, you would be a part of that! Now I'm going to find her. Are you coming?"

"I don't care if you're just friends or not. It really doesn't make a difference to me."

"Fine. I'm going on my own then," Michael said as he turned to leave.

"Wait—I'll come with you," Tyler said, and followed Michael out of the house.

They ran to the bus stop. Only a moment passed, and there, again, was the empty bus.

"We'll check at the Mysterious Blue first. She said she was going straight home. I was going to call her to see if—"

"Okay, so maybe she's in the shower or something and didn't hear the phone," Tyler interrupted. Michael just shrugged. They returned to silence. Michael stared out the window. Tyler rested his head against the seat and shut his eyes.

"Michael!" Tyler opened his eyes. "Michael, did you hear that?"

"Hear what?"

"I just heard Sara shout your name! You have to have heard it—it was loud."

"I didn't hear anything."

The bus stopped at their stop; they both jumped off and ran to the Mysterious Blue. Michael opened the door and went straight inside.

"Sara? Sara, are you here?" he called as he ran through to the back of the shop into the kitchen. Sara wasn't anywhere to be found. Michael ran up the back stairs to Sara's room. "Tyler, you need to see this," Michael shouted.

Tyler came running upstairs and stopped, stunned, at the door. Sara's room was total chaos: There were things thrown everywhere. Her bed was turned upside down. Dresser drawers were pulled out and dumped. Things were floating around the room in midair: clothes, shoes, books—all floating.

"What's going on?" Michael asked Tyler.

"How would I know?" Tyler spat, but as soon as he stepped into the room, everything fell to the ground. Michael stared at Tyler with suspicion. "I didn't do anything! You can't think I would have—"

"No, I'm sorry. I didn't—or I don't—think you did anything. It just surprised me, I guess, that's all," Michael said. Tyler walked around the room, looking at everything. He sat down on the floor next to a picture whose frame had smashed. "Those are her parents," Michael said quietly, not looking at Tyler.

The woman in the picture looked just like Sara. She was wearing a red robe with a matching hat and her hair was tied back. The man was a large man, quite a bit taller than the woman. He was wearing a black suit and had short black hair. They both looked very well kempt.

Tyler ran his fingers across the broken picture and the glass sliced his finger, drawing blood. As soon as the blood dripped, the room went ice cold. The windows iced over; it was so cold that Michael and Tyler could see their breath. Then the picture became so hot, it turned to ashes. Tyler stood up; he looked around the room frantically. "Where is her star?" he asked Michael as he picked up a pile on the floor, looking for it.

"It's usually on the dresser, but I already looked: it's gone."

Tyler closed his eyes just for a moment. He saw a glimpse of a black cloak, then he heard it again. "Michael!" Tyler opened his eyes and looked at Michael. "Eljord," he stated, and turned and walked out of Sara's bedroom and down the stairs.

"Wait, what do you mean?" Michael shouted, running after Tyler.

"Eljord has her. We need to go—now." Tyler grabbed his Oltes with one hand and Michael's arm with the other. And they were gone.

"Where are we?"

"In the Dark World."

"Well, I guessed that, but where in the Dark World are we?"

"I don't know, but I know where we need to go. We need to find Eljord's kingdom: we find Eljord, we find Sara."

"Oh, it's that simple, is it?"

Tyler spun around to face Michael. "Do you have a better idea? Eljord is the only one who would take Sara. I know he took her. We need to figure out where we are."

"I think we are in the Slome forest," Michael stated.

"How do you know?"

"Well, the Slome forest has daywood trees. See these trees right here? They are daywood trees. The inside of the trunk of a daywood tree is light, like daylight. When the trees are cut down, the light beams higher than the forest, then goes out. I read it in Nomad."

Tyler smiled. "Okay, so where now?"

"Well, I'm not sure where Eljord's kingdom is, but I do know that to get out of the forest, we need to go…um…that way," Michael said as he looked around, then pointed in the direction they needed to go. "If we get out of the Slome forest, we should be able to see for miles; it will be easier to see where we are."

"What do you mean, 'if we get out of the forest'?" Tyler asked, sounding a little nervous.

"Well, there are creatures in the forest—creatures that are not too friendly, I don't think, from what I have read."

"Great. Could I have found a better place to enter the Dark World?" Tyler groaned.

"Tyler, I don't think it was you that brought us here."

"What? Of course it was me. I obviously wasn't trying to bring us *here*, but I don't think now is the time to be judging."

"That's not what I meant. I think that someone intercepted us and sent us here, and I would guess that if you're right, it was Eljord. He obviously doesn't want us to follow him." Michael sat down on a tree stump and dropped his head to his knees.

"Great—so now we're lost in a forest in another world that's full of dangerous creatures that we have never heard of," Tyler said as he began his usual pacing.

"It's too bad you don't have some of the fancy swords that were all around your castle. They might have helped," Michael teased as they headed in the direction Michael had figured may be the right way. "I've been practicing summoning things, but I have only managed to get it to work on paper clips so far."

Tyler held out his hand and concentrated on his dressing quarters. He envisioned the clothes hanging there that he had worn when he and Candor had first left the castle grounds and gone into town. The clothes, including the sword, appeared on the ground in front of Tyler. Without breaking his concentration, he searched for Michael's room in the castle, soon realizing that he had no idea which room was Michael's.

"Wow, these are great. Thanks, Tyler."

Startled, Tyler opened his eyes to see Michael holding clothes and a sword that looked similar to the ones Tyler had summoned for himself. "I didn't find them yet…well, I didn't think I had."

"Well, you must have, 'cause I know I didn't."

Tyler began to change into his clothes and Michael did the same. "Wow, you look just like a real king," Michael said as he fumbled with his sash.

"Here, let me help you. It goes around like this," Tyler explained as he tied Michael's sash, then his own.

"Thanks," Michael said as he took the sword from Tyler and held onto it awkwardly.

"You need to hold it with a firm grip or you will drop it and cut your foot off—like this." Tyler helped Michael adjust his grip on his sword. Michael tried swinging his sword, only his didn't glide weightlessly as Tyler's had: Michael's seemed heavy and awkward, rubbing the ground and coming dangerously close to Tyler's feet.

"Watch out!" Tyler said as he swung his sword right in front of Michael, who jumped back, startled. There were creatures coming from every direction. Tyler swung his sword again and again; each time he killed one, there seemed to be two more in its place.

"What are these things?" Tyler yelled.

"It's a Gremmit, and there is only one—well, one real one: the source. Each time you kill one that isn't the source Gremmit, they multiply, but if you don't hit them—the non-real ones, I mean—then they will attack you."

"How do you know which is the real one?" Tyler was frantically swinging at the creatures. They were about three feet tall and moved very quickly in any and every direction. They had skinny, rough-looking bodies almost entirely covered in mud and dirt. Tyler could see their veins running through their bodies, and when they bled, their blood was black. They had little sporadic patches of wiry hair all over their bodies and large, yellow, fang-like teeth, but no eyes or nose: just two very large ears that pointed down. The Gremmit made a terrible gurgling, snarling type of noise.

"The largest one is the real one. You need to cut its head off, but don't injure it in any other way, or it won't die—it will multiply."

"Great—that should be easy. Are you helping at all?" Tyler asked just before he spotted the largest one, and with one quick slice of his sword, off flew its head.

"I was just about to help, but you did it already," Michael lied. As they watched, the body of the source Gremmit shriveled up to nothing and all the others did the same.

"Any more surprises?" Tyler asked as he wiped the blood off his sword with his shirt.

"Oh, I think there may be a few," Michael stammered, still a bit in shock.

"Do you feel that?" Tyler asked as he bent down to touch the ground. Michael stared at Tyler. He felt it too: the ground was shaking.

"Run!" Michael shouted as he grabbed Tyler by the arm, and they both began to run. The tree roots were rising up from the ground. They tried to jump over them as they ran, but a thick, long root rose up from the ground, wrapping around Michael's leg and pulling him hard to the ground with a loud thud. The root began pulling him backward across the ground, toward the trunk of the tree. "Tyler!" Michael shouted. Tyler looked back, horrified. "Tyler, help!"

Tyler ran back to Michael, pulled out his sword, and cut the root from Michael's leg. "Thanks—now we have to get out of this patch of pullusroots."

Tyler pulled Michael up and they kept on running, stumbling on roots as they rose higher and higher. Tyler swung his sword, slicing the branches out of their way; the ground was shaking so much that they struggled to stay upright. Then, as quickly as it had begun, it stopped. The ground once again was still and the roots were where they should be: beneath the ground.

"We're through the patch of pullusroots," Michael said as he wiped the blood off his leg.

"Did I cut you?"

"Just a little, but hey—it's better than being pulled into a tree. If they pull you in, that's where you stay: you can never get out. You become the tree."

"Well, this is one place in the Dark World I will not be revisiting," Tyler joked.

The forest was thick with trees and plants; it was dark in the forest because the candles that lit the Dark World were above the trees. Tyler used his powers to conjure lanterns for both he and Michael. "Here, take this," he said as he handed one to Michael.

"Thanks."

The lanterns lit up the path as they walked. They were in the thickest part of the forest; there was not much space between each tree.

"Wait!" Michael whispered. They both stopped and stood breathless and still, listening: there was something moving closer. Tyler pointed to the lanterns and the lights in both of them went out. They could hear something darting quickly through the trees.

"Michael! Michael, help!"

"Sara," Tyler gasped. "Michael, it's Sara."

Michael looked around the darkness, listening carefully; he could just barely hear a hissing, snarling noise.

"Michael, come on, it's Sara."

"No," Michael whispered back, "that's not Sara."

"What? Of course it's Sara—who else would be calling you?"

"Michael! Help me, Michael!" the voice called out again, whoever it was still darting through the trees around them. Tyler waved his hand over his lantern and the light came back on.

"Aaah!" Tyler gasped. Right in front of his face was a very ugly, foul-looking creature, with eyes so black they were like balls of coal. Its nose was just two holes in its head; the mouth was narrow; there was blood and dirt all in its teeth, which were green and jagged. The creature's breath smelled like death. It was wearing a long, brown, tattered robe that covered its whole body. It stood face to face with Tyler. It opened its mouth, ready to attack, but suddenly dropped to its knees and fell dead to the ground.

Tyler looked up to see Michael standing right behind the creature, his sword in the creature's back. "That was not Sara," he said, pulling his sword out of the dead creature.

"I'm surprised," Tyler said as he relit Michael's lantern.

"Let's keep going. We are close to the edge of the forest; the trees seem to be clearing a little. I hate to think of what other creatures are in the Slome forest."

"What was that creature?" Tyler asked.

"That was a Mimake. They can make any sound they want you to hear. They do it to lure you to them; it's how they hunt."

"Well, let's hope there aren't any more Mimakes—or anything else, for that matter."

"So, do you have a plan, Tyler?"

"A plan? Well, no, not really."

"Great—so we're just going to walk up to Eljord's kingdom, knock on the door, and say, 'Excuse me, may we please have our friend back?'"

"Well, what about you? Do you have a plan? You're the smart one, remember?"

"You're the powerful king! I thought you could use your powers—AAAHH!"

Tyler stopped quickly. Michael had been walking in front; the path just suddenly stopped, with no warning. Michael hadn't seen it, the forest being so dark, so he had just stepped right into a lake. Tyler knelt down at the edge of the lake, peering in. "Michael! Michael!" Tyler shouted, but the lake was still: there were no ripples in the water, no bubbles, nothing—the lake looked like a large, deep, blue sheet of ice. Tyler dipped his hand in the water; it was ice cold. He set his sword and lantern down at the edge of the lake, took off his robe, and jumped in after Michael. He swam around but couldn't see Michael anywhere.

Suddenly, something grabbed his leg and started pulling him further and further under the water. Tyler started struggling, trying to get free. He needed to go back to the surface to get some air. He couldn't breathe; he was starting to panic. He couldn't get free from whatever was holding onto his leg. He opened his mouth, trying to gasp for breath, but his mouth filled with water. He coughed, but still there was only water—no air. Tyler's body just went limp; no longer fighting, he was pulled further under the water.

Tyler gasped for air the moment he was no longer submerged in water. "Tyler, are you okay?" Michael asked as he patted Tyler on the back while he choked and coughed.

"Where are we?"

"We are underneath the lake."

Tyler looked up to see that they were just that: under the lake. He could see the water just floating above them like a cloud. He reached up and touched the water. "How is that possible?" he asked Michael.

"How is any of this possible, Tyler?"

"Okay, so what do we do? Shall we go back up to the top or try and cross under here?" Tyler summoned their swords and lanterns to them under the lake. He lit the lanterns and looked around. The ground was moist and covered with rocks and moss. They could see what looked like fish swimming above them in the lake. "I'm sure this lake is too big to swim across, not to mention dangerous; we have no idea what is swimming in there, and I don't think I want to find out the hard way."

"Then we need to try crossing under it. We'll just walk under to the other side, then swim back to the top."

Tyler nodded at Michael, then followed as Michael led the way. "Watch your step this time, Mike," Tyler joked as they walked along under the lake.

"Look at the markings along the wall." Tyler held his lantern up to the wall. "This looks like a map, Tyler. Look, this is the Slome forest." Michael ran his hand over the wall; it was as smooth as glass and felt damp. "This is where we saw the Gremmit...there's the pullusroot...the Mimake...and the lake. Okay, so all we have to do is—"

Both of the lanterns suddenly went out. "What happened?" Michael asked.

"I don't know; they just went out." Tyler relit the lanterns. They both saw what looked like two small eyes shining in the distance—then the lanterns went out again. This time, Tyler relit them straight away. They saw the same two eyes, but this time, they were closer. Again the lanterns went out. Tyler again relit them, only this time, it wasn't just eyes they saw: it was what looked like a little old man, only he was unnaturally wrinkly. They could barely see his eyes through all the wrinkles on his forehead, but the little yellow and black dots they could see were bright. He had white hair that went all the way down to his feet, which were also wrinkled, as skin gets when submerged in water for too long. His legs were so short, they were almost covered by his stomach, and his arms were just as short as his legs. He looked like he had enough wrinkly skin on him for a ten-foot giant. The man wasn't wearing clothes—just a dirty, ripped old cloth around his waist.

"Who are you? Why are you down here?" the very strange-looking man grunted at Michael and Tyler, who stood there staring at him.

"I, um...I am Tyler, and this is my brother, Michael," Tyler said as he held out his hand for the old man to shake.

"What are you doing down here?" the old man repeated.

"My brother fell into the lake, and I jumped in after him. We didn't know it would lead us down here."

"You didn't know that the top of the lake would lead you to the bottom?" the old man grunted at them.

"Well, we didn't know the bottom of the lake would be like this, sir," Tyler said apologetically.

"Well, it is! You need to go—now!" the old man shouted.

"Now, wait a minute. All we need to do is cross under the lake. We mean you no harm, sir. I assure you, we will cross quickly."

"No! You cannot cross under my lake! Go now! And try not to get eaten by my lake creatures—or get eaten! Makes no difference to me!"

Michael stepped in front of Tyler, closer to the old man. "Just wait a minute—do you know who this is?" he asked the old man, pointing to Tyler. "This is Tyler Leeds; he is King of the Dark World."

The old man grunted again, only this time, it sounded more like a laugh. "You are not very big for a king, are you?"

Tyler just glared at him. "I am big enough."

"If you say so. So why are the King and his brother in the Slome forest? Don't you know it's not safe in here?"

"Well, we do now, but we didn't come here on purpose. We are trying to find Eljord; he has taken our friend," Michael started to tell the man before Tyler tapped his arm quite hard.

"Ow—what was that for?" Michael whined.

"You shouldn't go blabbing that to just anyone," Tyler warned.

"Your brother is right, you know. You should always watch where you're walking, and who you are talking to. But Eljord is not someone to mess with. If he has taken your friend, I suggest…well, that you get a new friend. You boys hungry?" The old man gestured for them to follow him. Tyler jumped in front of him.

"I will not just let him have my friend—I will save her! I am not afraid of Eljord!" Tyler shouted angrily.

"Well, you should be: Eljord is a very powerful Nytstar. It will take more than a couple of kids to get your friend back. The Dreamencers tried before, but they failed. He killed many innocent Nytstars and tried to take over the whole Dark World. Some of the most powerful Nytstars were killed, or disappeared and were never seen again. Now, I am hungry—you are welcome to join me if you wish. It will not be a meal fit for a king, but it will have to do."

Tyler glared back at Michael, who just shrugged. "Thank you, sir—I am hungry, now that you mention it," Michael said as he followed the old man. Tyler followed behind them both.

"My name is Irrid," the old man said as they walked through a tunnel into a cave that sort of looked like a house. All the furniture was made of rocks; there was a table with large boulders around it for chairs, and a bed in a corner that was made out of dirt and moss. The floor was just dirt with a patch of moss that looked like a rug. Irrid pointed to the table for the boys to sit down. "I will make us some soup." Irrid lit a fire by pointing his finger at some very wet-looking branches. All of a sudden, a large black pot appeared out of nowhere and was in midair just above the fire. Within minutes, there was a wonderful smell that filled the cave. Tyler's and Michael's stomachs both rumbled; it had been a while since they had eaten. Irrid pointed to the table and three bowls appeared, full to the top with soup, and a plate in the middle of the table was mounted with bread. Beside each bowl was a spoon and a large cup filled with a red liquid. Michael picked up his spoon right away, but Tyler glanced at Irrid, who seemed to know exactly what Tyler was thinking. "It is not poisoned; I would never kill a king, especially one who has come to fight Eljord—no matter how foolish I think that may be."

Michael began to eat the soup. "It's good, Irrid—thank you. I apologize for my brother. Tyler, eat the soup. It's fine." Tyler shot Michael an angry look and began to eat the soup.

"Tyler, you are wise to be cautious. Eljord is a very powerful Nytstar; he would go to great lengths to stop you, but he himself will not kill you."

Tyler looked up from his soup. "Why not?"

"Anyone that kills a king becomes forever cursed."

"So that's why he wants me to join him, because he won't kill me?"

"Eljord has tried for hundreds of years to control the entire Dark World. He wants to be the only king; that way, he can ensure that only true Nytstars live in the Dark World. Already I have said too much. I do not wish to make an enemy of Eljord again. If he were to find out I have helped you, there is no telling what he would do this time."

"What do you mean, 'this time'?" Tyler asked.

Irrid was beginning to fidget nervously. "I have said too much again. You must not pay too much attention to an old fool. Now, I am going to pack you a satchel to take with you tomorrow and I will show you how to get out of the Slome forest, but for tonight, you rest here. I had two boys myself once, but that was a long time ago. No more—no more."

Tyler looked at Michael with uncertainty. Michael smiled back at him and thanked Irrid. Irrid pointed at an empty corner of the cave and two more beds appeared, just like Irrid's, of dirt and moss. "Now you boys need to get some rest. Something tells me you have a long day ahead of you tomorrow."

Michael and Tyler finished their soup and bread, and lay down on their beds for the night. They were both so exhausted from their journey so far through the forest that they fell asleep almost instantly.

"Michael! Michael, help me! Michael, where are you? I need you, Michael—please, help me!" Tyler sat up and opened his eyes. "Michael, help me!" Tyler hopped out of the bed, found his lantern, and looked around the cave. He expected to find a Mimake, but there was nothing there. "Michael, help me!" Tyler heard again, only this time, he realized he was hearing the voice inside his head. Sara's voice was as clear as if she were standing in the room next to him. Yet she was calling Michael, not Tyler. Why wasn't Michael hearing her? Tyler tried to go back to sleep, but he couldn't help but feel angry or annoyed—he wasn't really sure why.

"You boys better get up; you will want to get going soon. You have a difficult day ahead of you," Irrid said as he began to set the table for breakfast. Michael and Tyler got out of bed, gathered their swords and lanterns, and sat at the table. Irrid pointed at the beds and they disappeared. He then pointed at the plates he had put on the table and they became instantly full of a steaming hot breakfast. They all ate quickly; Irrid hurried them along. They had barely scooped up their last mouthfuls of food before the plates disappeared from under them.

"Thank you so much for everything, Irrid. How can we ever repay you?" Michael asked as they were leaving Irrid's cave, heading back toward the map where they had first met.

"There is no need, no need at all. Just make sure you stay safe, and find that friend of yours quickly and get as far away from Eljord as you can. Good—here is the map." Irrid seemed very uneasy; he was fidgety and kept looking over his shoulder. When he spoke, he whispered as if he were worried that someone else would hear him. "See? Here is the lake. When you surface, you should be right around here," Irrid said as he pointed to the map, continuing to look over his shoulder. "Then you are going to have to move quickly to pass through the firefield. The field is short, but every time you step, the ground bursts into flames, so whatever you do, keep moving. This section of the forest is quite thick, and for the most part harmless. Just keep your eyes open for spurrets; they are little creatures that scurry along the ground and nip at everything that moves. Their bites hurt something fierce and will leave a mark, but that's it. One last section here—"

Irrid stopped quickly and looked over his shoulder. This time, so did Michael and Tyler; they had heard something too. "What was that?" Michael asked.

"You need to go now. Hurry, swim up to the top—don't look back."

"But this last section of the forest, Irrid...there seems to be a giant hole. How do we—"

Irrid was pushing them along. "You will need to figure that out. You go now; there is no time—I can't hold it off for long. Go!"

"Hold what off? We can't just leave you here." Tyler drew his sword, but Irrid just pushed him aside.

"Go! Don't be foolish—you are too important for this. Go now!"

"Come on, Tyler, let's go," Michael urged as he tried to pull Tyler along with him.

"Go!" Irrid yelled, just as a loud roaring noise shook the lake. Drops of water began to fall from the lake just above their heads. Michael jumped up; as soon as his outstretched arm reached the water, it seemed to pull him into it, and he began to swim up to the surface of the lake. Tyler looked behind him one last time to see a horrible-looking creature come out of the shadows. Like a giant pig, the creature ran on four legs and was extremely fat. It had a snout like a pig but was covered in wiry hair that was gray and stuck out all over its body. The creature had blood and drool dripping from its mouth as it snarled; its teeth were large and yellow and had what looked like its breakfast stuck in them. Tyler wanted to stay and help Irrid, especially when he saw more of the same creatures coming from the darkness, but Irrid turned quickly to Tyler and pointed his finger at him. At that moment, the creature pounced on Irrid. Tyler felt himself being lifted up to the water.

"Irrid—no!" Tyler shouted, but all he got was a mouthful of water. His body was thrust through the water and within moments, he joined Michael on the bank at the edge of the lake. As soon as Tyler caught his breath, he held his sword tightly in his hand and dove back into the lake. He tried to swim down to the very bottom again to reach Irrid, but all he could see at the bottom of the lake was just that: the bottom of the lake, not as it had just been, but how the bottom of a lake should be—just rocks, dirt, moss, and water, all the way to the bottom. Tyler couldn't hold his breath much longer, so he swam back up to the top.

"Was he okay?" Michael asked.

"He was gone—all of it was gone," Tyler explained.

"I'm sure he's fine," Michael tried to reassure Tyler.

"Yeah—let's get going. Irrid said we need to do this quick," Tyler moaned as they both walked on toward the firefield.

"Well, this is it," Michael stated as they reached the field. "It doesn't look too big; you can see the other side, at least."

"It's not the size I'm worried about—it's the flames," Tyler sighed as he picked up a tree branch from the ground and threw it into the field. Instantly, it burst into flames.

"Well, we'd better run quickly then, hadn't we?" Michael joked. They both took a deep breath. "Race you?" Michael nudged Tyler and set off running.

"Hey, cheater," Tyler shouted as he ran after him. With each step they took, fire burst out under their feet. They ran as fast as they could to the other side, not stopping once. Michael dropped his lantern. "Leave it," Tyler shouted as he caught up to Michael and began to pass him. Michael had slowed down but didn't stop to pick it up; when he saw Tyler starting to pass him, he began to run faster, and he just made it to the other side first.

"Ha! I won," Michael said as they both sat down and pulled off their shoes, which were smoking and almost melted right through. The skin on their calves and ankles was singed and sore.

"Only just," Tyler shot back. "At least I didn't drop my lantern."

"Okay, now we just have to make it through this thick patch and try not to get nibbled alive by spurrets," Michael joked. They got back on their slightly tender feet and set off again, swords drawn, ready for the spurrets—well, at least they thought they were, until a few paces in, when they heard a terrible squeaking sound like hundreds of rats. They came from every direction. They also looked like rats, just bigger; they were green and brown, almost blending in with the ground. The spurrets jumped slightly, nipping painfully at Michael's and Tyler's ankles.

"Irrid was right: they do hurt something fierce," Michael complained as a spurret sank its tiny, sharp teeth into his ankle, then another, and another. Tyler, who was being bitten just the same, swung his sword at as many as he could, slicing each one he could reach. Michael followed, doing the same, and they both began to swing their swords while running, stepping on the spurrets with each step. They could feel the tiny bones crushing under their feet, and could hear the squirting of their blood and guts bursting out of their sides. By the time they realized there were no more spurrets to be seen, their ankles were bleeding quite badly. They sat down on a fallen tree. Michael got the flasks of water out of the satchel Irrid had prepared for them and poured water on his and Tyler's cuts.

"That stings," Tyler complained.

"I know. But I have to clean them." Michael reached for a handful of weeds that were next to the fallen tree. "These will help. They're dogwood: they will help take the sting away and make sure the wounds are clean," he said as he wiped the blood from Tyler's wounds with the weed, tore off the sleeve of his shirt, and wrapped his ankles up. "That will stop the bleeding. Spurrets are not poisonous, but we don't want to bleed all over, either; that will attract animals or creatures or whatever else is lurking around." Michael did the same to his own ankles. They both rested for a while and ate some of the sandwiches Irrid had packed.

"So…any ideas, Ty? You know, to get over the giant gorge?" Michael asked.

Tyler thought for a while.

"We could build a bridge. All we need are trees, and…well, there are a lot of those here, it being a forest and all," Michael said between bites.

"We could fly over," Tyler suggested.

Michael stared at him. "Oh, great idea. There may just be one little problem: we can't fly."

"No, we can't, but my Nythawk can."

Michael looked up in the sky as he heard a loud squawk. "How…when…?" Michael stammered in disbelief. The Nythawk soared through the air gracefully, flapping his enormous wings. As soon as he spotted Tyler on the ground, waving fiercely, Traydome came closer and closer, finally landing on the ground right beside Tyler. Michael had stumbled backward, trying to get out of the way of the giant bird.

"Michael, this is Traydome. Traydome, this is my brother, Michael." Traydome bowed his head and stepped toward Michael. Michael smiled and mumbled hi, but stepped back. "Don't be afraid, Mike—Traydome won't hurt you."

"I'm not afraid. I just didn't want to startle him, that's all," Michael lied. Tyler stroked Traydome's beak while his head was still bowed. Michael moved a little closer, his hand shaking as he reached out and stroked Traydome's beak with Tyler.

"Traydome, do you think you can fly us both over this gorge?"

"I believe I can."

Michael stared at Tyler, waiting for him to translate the bird's squawking. "He thinks he can fly us both over," Tyler explained.

"He thinks he can, or he definitely can? I don't want to find out halfway across that he can't!"

Tyler shot an angry look at Michael. "Do you have a better idea? Traydome is our only hope here."

"I didn't mean to be rude, Tyler—relax. I just want to make sure we're not going to…you know, fall to our deaths down into a giant gorge, that's all."

"Let's pack up. We need to keep moving; we're almost out of the forest, and we still don't know where to find Eljord," Tyler said as he started packing up their satchel. Traydome held their satchels in his talons and Tyler climbed onto his back. Michael grabbed onto a handful of Traydome's feathers to pull himself onto his back and Traydome let out a deafening squawk and flapped his wings.

"I'm sorry, I'm sorry!" Michael shouted. Tyler grabbed Michael's hand and pulled him onto Traydome's back.

"I do need my feathers," Traydome said to Tyler, who laughed quietly. With a giant leap, Traydome took off. He flapped his giant wings and they flew high above the gorge. Michael held closely to Tyler and kept his eyes shut tightly. Tyler, however, looked around excitedly; he wanted to see as much as he could.

"Traydome, are you able to go higher?"

"What? Higher? Why?" Michael asked.

"Then we might able to see where Eljord's kingdom is."

"Just a little higher; I am not full-grown yet."

Tyler looked as far as he could see in every direction. "There—Michael, look over there. Do you see it? It looks like a brick wall."

Michael opened his eyes but held more tightly to Tyler. "Yeah, you're right, Tyler. That must be it; that must be Eljord's kingdom."

Traydome started to fly lower and lower. "I need to land, Tyler. I am sorry."

Tyler patted Traydome. "You did great, Traydome—thank you."

"Thank you for making it all the way across," Michael said, sighing with relief as both feet safely touched the ground.

"I will return when you need me, Tyler," Traydome said. The giant Nythawk bowed his head, then with a leap, he took to the skies. Tyler watched him fly away until he could no longer see him.

"Let's get going." Tyler urged.

"Hold on—what, did you just forget to tell me you got a new pet?"

Tyler spun around. "Traydome is not my pet! And I didn't tell you because he just hatched; we just got each other."

"Fine, whatever. Why shouldn't you get a giant Nythawk and a castle—oh, yeah, and get to be King? After all, you were the one that had nightmares," Michael mumbled under his breath. Tyler heard him but pretended not to, and set off a little ahead of Michael through the last patch of the forest. Michael followed behind, and they both walked without speaking to one another. It seemed peaceful in the last section of the forest: there were birds chirping and the wind was blowing through the branches of the trees, and there were no creatures or anything. The trees were thinning; they were so close to the edge of the forest that they could see beyond the forest through the trees.

"Who was that?" Michael gasped as a hooded figure glided past the clearing in the trees.

"Candor," Tyler whispered.

Michael stared at him. "Candor? Why would Candor be here?"

"Your guess is as good as mine," Tyler shot back at Michael.

"No, Tyler, I think your guess is better than mine. I think Candor is here for you."

"For me? Why would Candor be here in the forest for me? It may not even be Candor."

Michael grabbed Tyler's arm. "Don't think you can hide everything from me; I am not weak. I'm your brother, not just any Nytstar, and I am here with you."

Tyler pulled his arm from Michael. "I think it is I who am here with you, if I'm not mistaken—here with you to find your girlfriend."

"Sara is not my girlfriend, she is just a friend—a friend who I really like, who I would like to be my girlfriend, but I would never do that to you."

"Why are you telling me this? I don't want to hear it. I just want people to leave me alone. I'm tired; all I want to do is sleep, that's all. I want to go to bed and sleep for hours and hours, a long, dreamless sleep. I don't want to be afraid anymore."

"Tyler, stop talking," Michael interrupted.

"What? I have had enough of you, bossing me around, thinking just because you're older and more popular—"

"No, that's not what I mean, I—"

"You think that here in the Dark World, you're better than me, just like in the Lyt world? It is cold in someone's shadow, isn't it? Now—"

Michael turned and pushed Tyler to the ground. Tyler whipped his legs around Michael's ankles and pulled him to the ground beside him, then jumped on top of him, pinning him to the ground so he couldn't move. Tyler raised his fist; Michael closed his eyes. "The forest—there is a Triss."

"What?" Tyler spat, still holding his fist ready to punch at any time.

"A Triss, remember, is like a charm."

"I know what a Triss is, I'm not stupid. I know you think I am; you think I'm weird, too. I bet you wish I wouldn't hang around all the time."

"There is a truth Triss in this part of the forest. Don't speak as much as you may want to."

Tyler got off of Michael. They both silently picked up their things and walked through the last patch of the forest without a word. When they were out of the forest, they kept walking for a little while. They made sure they were well out of reach of the truth Triss before either one spoke. Neither of them wanted to talk about what they had said in the forest; they didn't look at each other.

"Where do we go from here?" Tyler asked, staring at the ground.

"I don't know. If I had Nomad, I know he would be able to tell us the way."

"Of course; why didn't we think of that before?"

"I did, but this is not our chosen path, to go looking for Eljord. We—well, you, I should say—are supposed to defend the Dark World against him, not hunt him."

"I'm not hunting him—we're looking for Sara, remember? The friend he took? So do you want Nomad or not?"

Michael thought for a moment. "He will not be happy with us. You know that, right?"

Tyler spun around. "Since when do I worry about people being happy with me?" he spat.

"Okay, good point. It would help to know where we are going."

Tyler held his Oltes and summoned Nomad; the book appeared instantly out of thin air into Tyler's open hand.

"Here you go," Tyler said, handing the book to Michael.

"You do not want to hear what I have to say," Nomad said.

"No, not really."

"So you don't think you are being foolish?"

"No, I don't! But I do think that if you're not going to tell us how to find Eljord, I will send you back."

"Summoning doesn't work that way; you need to do your lessons, Tyler. You need to spend the time to read my pages as your brother has."

"I don't need you to tell me what to do. I may not be able to send you back, but I can leave you here," Tyler snapped.

"Okay, Tyler, take it easy—that's not going to get us anywhere. Nomad, we need to find Eljord's kingdom."

"Oh, I see...and you plan to just walk into his kingdom and ask for your friend? Then what—you think he will politely comply?"

Tyler rolled his eyes in annoyance, but before he had the chance to respond, they all heard a tiny sneeze.

"What was that?" Michael asked, startled. The sneeze had come from Tyler's satchel, which was still lying on the ground. Michael and Tyler both looked at the satchel curiously; then came a second sneeze, and a third. The satchel toppled over; there was something inside, struggling to get out. Tyler walked over to the satchel. He reached out his hand to open it, all the while leaning back so as not to get too close. As soon as he opened the satchel wide enough, out jumped Keadon.

"Thanks, Tyler—it's hot and muggy in there," Keadon said happily as he spread his wings and flapped around Tyler's head.

"What are you doing here?" Tyler asked.

"I caught a ride on Traydome. I knew you would need my help! You're Michael, right? Tyler's brother?" Keadon asked as he flew around Michael's head. "You're a Nytstar too, aren't you? I'm Keadon. I am the Fairy Prince, and the future Fairy King!" Keadon said, puffing his chest out with importance.

"Well, I am pleased to meet you, Keadon!" Michael said with a bow.

"Keadon, how did you know we were even in the Dark World?" Tyler asked.

"I could sense you were here. I heard people talking around town; everyone is talking about it."

"Talking about what, Keadon?"

"About how Eljord took something from you and you have gone looking for him to take it back. I don't care what they say; I think you should go take it back. Who does Eljord think he is? He can't go pushing everyone around, taking whatever he wants just because he is a king. You're a king, and you don't go around taking whatever you want."

"You are both foolish, foolish boys. You are going to get yourselves killed, and everyone that is involved with you," Nomad shouted at them. "You have no idea the struggles we all suffered in the past. Tyler, your grandfather was a very powerful Nytstar, and he was not able to defeat Eljord—and he had the Dreamencers with him! You have your brother, who hasn't even mastered a simple summoning so far, you have the Fairy Prince, who is just a little boy still, and you have an ageless book—that is it! I know you are powerful, Tyler, but not even you are that powerful."

"So what do you suggest? Should we just give up? Let Eljord win again? If no one ever stands up to him, he will continue to push everybody around forever."

"Tyler, Eljord is not just a schoolyard bully; he could be the most powerful Nytstar in the Dark World! We have yet to see anyone as powerful as he is."

Tyler was fuming; he knew there was some truth to what Nomad was saying, but he couldn't just sit back and let him take Sara.

"You are right about one thing, book: you have yet to see any *one* as powerful as he is, but there are more than one of us here, and together we are powerful," Keadon buzzed.

"Just a bunch of kids—that's all you are: a bunch of kids! Now be warned, you do not stand a chance against Eljord—be warned!"

"Tyler, your book is a goody-goody!"

"Tell me about it," Tyler groaned.

"We need to get some things cleared up here," Michael stated firmly and authoritatively. "Tyler, does Keadon need to go back home? He's just little; I don't want him to get hurt—or get in the way, for that matter."

Keadon folded his arms across his tiny chest and glared at Michael.

"I don't know. Keadon, do you need to go home?" Tyler asked through mocking giggles.

"No! I won't get hurt, and I won't slow you down, either!" Keadon shot back.

"I think he is fine to stay, Mike."

"Fine then, he stays. Now, Nomad: if you are going to help us find our way to Eljord's kingdom, then you can stay, but you will go in my satchel until we need you. We need to sit down and come up with a plan," Michael said. He closed his eyes very tightly, grabbed onto his Oltes, and seemed to be pushing or something. Tyler looked at him curiously. A minute or two (and one very red face) later, a flower and a bucket appeared in Michael's hand.

"What are those for?" Keadon asked.

"Well, they're not what I was trying to summon, obviously; I wanted a pen and paper." Tyler and Keadon looked at each other, then at Michael, until they couldn't hold it anymore: they both fell to the floor, laughing uncontrollably. "You know, it's not that funny." But Tyler and Keadon paused only for a second, then continued to laugh.

Michael was getting annoyed. "Yeah, maybe it is that funny—I mean, that you can actually do something that I can't. Really hysterical, or maybe just amazing." Tyler and Keadon stopped laughing instantly and Tyler glared at Michael.

CHAPTER TWELVE

THE PLAN

Michael sat down on the floor. "Let's get to work." He motioned to Tyler and Keadon to sit down with him. "First thing we need to do is figure out where Eljord's kingdom is."

"You guys don't even know where you are going?" Keadon laughed. "Boy, was I right; you two need me more than I thought," he teased.

"You know where it is?" Michael asked.

"Yeah, I know where Eljord's kingdom is."

Michael and Tyler both smiled at Keadon. "Okay, so let's map out the way to Eljord's kingdom so we know exactly where we're going," Michael said. "We're going to have to find out everything we can about his kingdom. I'm sure we won't just be able to walk right up, knock on the door, and enter. We three alone don't stand much of a chance against Eljord; even if we do make it to his kingdom, he probably has an army waiting for us."

Tyler glared at Michael. "If you're giving up, fine, but I'm not," Tyler spat.

"I never said I was giving up; I was just pointing out the obvious. What kind of chance do two kids and a fairy kid have against a king and his army?" Michael said as he pulled Nomad out of his satchel.

"Michael is right, Tyler. I think you three should return home; you have no idea the dangers you face if you continue on this journey. This is not your destiny; this is not what you, a great Nytstar king, are supposed to do," Nomad shouted at Tyler.

"So you think a great Nytstar king is supposed to sit back and do nothing when his enemy takes things from him? You think a great Nytstar king should be a coward?"

"You are just as stubborn as your grandfather was, and just as foolish. You are fighting a battle that is not yours to fight, Tyler!"

"I did not start this battle, Nomad; Eljord did when he took Sara. I cannot just leave her with him to be his prisoner for the rest of her life—or worse. A good king protects his people; a good king fights for his people; a good king does not just leave them to save himself!"

Michael stared at Tyler as if he were seeing him for the first time. "You're right, Tyler. Nomad, Tyler is right; we have to do this if we have any hope of helping the Dark World be one again. We need to stand up to those who are preventing peace," Michael said firmly.

"Michael, I know you sense the trouble that is brewing. People are beginning to take sides, old rivalries are resurfacing, tensions are rising all over the Dark World; you feel it, don't you?" Nomad asked.

"Yes, I feel it, but I also feel like we are doing the right thing, no matter how dangerous and crazy it may be."

"Michael, we're wasting time. Keadon, can you tell Michael the way to Eljord's kingdom? We need to find Sara."

"We are still quite far away. Tyler, I would suggest you call Traydome; however, the closer we can get before Eljord knows we are near, the better. Besides, once Traydome is with you, it will be easier for Eljord or Candor to have their dragons attack us."

"What dragons?" Tyler asked.

"The white dragon you met used to be Candor's dragon—that is, until your grandfather had to take control of it. Candor used it to kill people that got in Eljord's way."

"So Candor is on Eljord's side?" Tyler whispered. Michael shot Tyler a look of both concern and anger. "Do you think Eljord knows where we are right now?" Tyler asked.

"I don't think so; there's no way for him to know everything that's going on all over the Dark World," Michael said. "He will be able to sense when we're close to him, but we aren't close enough yet. There are limits to a Nytstar's powers; even the most powerful of Nytstars can't do everything. I'm sure he will have allies of his watching for us to warn him."

"Wow, Mike, you sure know a lot about this stuff."

"Thanks, Tyler. That's what happens when you read: you learn stuff," Michael joked.

Michael and Keadon worked on the map to Eljord's kingdom while Tyler leaned against a tree, sharpening their swords. "You know, Tyler, I don't see why you didn't bring the Dreamencers with you," Keadon said as Michael finished writing the directions down.

"What do you mean?" Tyler asked.

"The Dreamencers—you know, your army. Why didn't you bring them with you to rescue Sara?"

"Well, I didn't know. I don't know where they are or who they are or anything."

"Well, why didn't you ask Nomad? That's what your book is for, isn't it? To find out what you need to know about the Dark World?"

Tyler hadn't even thought about the Dreamencers. He didn't really know anything about them except what Lodiss had said in the Mysterious Blue. "I haven't asked Nomad very much of anything, really."

"I'm sure he wasn't going to offer any help without being asked for it, either. Well, that's why you have me now, right?" Keadon smiled proudly.

"There are not many Dreamencers left, especially ones that are willing to fight again," Michael said, looking up from his paper. "Many died the last time the Dark World was divided; I don't think they would be too eager to go up against Eljord again."

"Well, we can try, right? Tyler, maybe we can use Traydome to go back to the village and get a message to anyone willing to help. I'm sure there will be some Dreamencers who do not want to see Eljord rule the entire Dark World."

Tyler closed his eyes. "Traydome…come, Traydome," he said quietly. Michael and Keadon both watched the sky as Tyler wrote a note on one of the pieces of paper he had summoned.

Dreamencers,

I am sure you all know by now that Eljord is once again trying to divide our world. As your new King, I will not let this happen!

We will fight against him and win!

We will have peace in our world!

To do this, I need your help. I know you were all loyal to my grandfather; I hope you will be as loyal to me, and I, in return, will remain loyal to you. Eljord has taken a fellow Nytstar—a friend of mine. My brother, Keadon the Fairy Prince, and I are going to Eljord's kingdom to rescue her. I am asking for help from anyone willing.

Your King,
Tyler Leeds

Tyler folded the paper just in time, as Traydome came into view.

"He's here, Tyler," Keadon said excitedly.

As the giant Nythawk landed just in front of Tyler, Michael stepped back nervously. Tyler walked up to him and rubbed his beak. "I need you to take this to the village, Traydome, and quickly. Give it to…" Tyler stopped and turned to Keadon. "Who do we give it to?"

Keadon thought for a minute. "Give it to my mom; she will know what to do."

Tyler nodded at Traydome. "I will fly fast, Tyler, and deliver your message." And with that, Traydome leapt into the air and was gone.

"I just thought of something: How will he know who your mom is?" Tyler asked.

"Tyler, everyone knows who my mom is; it's hard to miss the Fairy Queen."

"Okay, let's get going. We have a lot of ground to cover before nightfall. I, for one, want to reach the caves before it gets dark," Michael began. "Well, I mean dark*er*. You know, it truly is amazing: all the candles—they never burn out. They dim and brighten back up but never burn out or get blown out by the wind or rain. Did you know—"

"Michael, I'm glad you learned all there is to know about the Dark World and all, but I'm not in the mood for a lesson right now. But I would like to know where we're going so it's not all a surprise like the forest," Tyler said.

"Whatever, Ty—just thought you might like to know something about the world in which you're a king," Michael said mockingly. "We are going to the mountains; that's where the caves are. We'll be safe there to sleep for the night."

"Well, how far are the mountains?"

"I don't know exactly, but you can't see them until you're there, so just make sure you watch where you're going or you will run right into them."

"How do you not see mountains?"

"You can see them once you get there, but not until then. They are Trissed, I guess—magic mountains."

"I shouldn't be surprised by anything here anymore," Tyler said as he walked carefully, a little more slowly so he could follow behind Keadon. They followed the map through a large green field. At the end of the field, they came to a small, run-down shack. The roof was collapsing and missing most of its shingles, windows were smashed, and the door was being held on by only one hinge. There was a decrepit brick wall surrounding the house, but the gate was missing.

"Who do you think lives there?" Michael asked. Both Tyler and Michael looked at Keadon, assuming he knew.

"I don't know; it doesn't look like anyone lives there at all."

"I hope nobody lives there, but I don't want to find out either," Michael whispered.

"Aww, does the wittle house scare you?" Tyler teased.

"It's not the house that scares me; it's what could be in the house that I'm worried about."

As they were passing the house quietly, all of a sudden, it disappeared.

"Where did it go? The house—it just disappeared!" They all stopped. Keadon hovered right next to Tyler; they stood staring at the empty space where the house had been just seconds before.

"How does a whole house disappear?" Tyler said as he started walking closer toward where the house used to be. His hands were stretched out in front of him, feeling the air around him for the house.

"I don't think you should go over there, Tyler," Michael warned.

"It's just a house, Mike." Tyler moved closer and closer until he was standing right in the middle of the house—or at least he would have been, if the house was still there. He bent down, feeling the ground.

"Tyler, let's go!" Michael shouted.

But suddenly, the house reappeared. There it was, right where it had been before—only now, it was right where Tyler had been standing. "Tyler!" Michael shouted as he dropped his lantern and satchel. He hopped over the wall and ran toward the house with Keadon right behind him.

They stopped in front of the door. "Tyler?" Michael whispered. But there was no answer. Michael slowly opened the door. "Tyler, where are you?" Keadon flew inside the house. Michael looked around, took a deep breath, and followed him in.

"Tyler! Tyler!" Keadon shouted. Inside, the house was as old and run-down as the outside. A dirty, ripped-up couch sat up against one wall. In front of the couch was a coffee table with a leg missing, and the top had been smashed. Broken glass covered the floor in front of the windows. What few bits of glass had not been broken were so filthy you couldn't see out of them. There was a thick, musky smell in the house, and dust covered everything. The floor was as dirty as the rest of the house; there was mud and garbage all over.

"It doesn't look like anyone has lived here for ages," Keadon said.

"Then who made the house vanish?" Michael said as he walked over to the spot where Tyler had been standing before the house reappeared. The floor creaked; Michael and Keadon both jumped around to see Tyler standing in a doorway. There was something different about him. He had a vacant look on his face. He just stood there; he didn't speak or even seem to recognize Michael or Keadon. "Tyler, there you are! You okay?" Michael asked worriedly, stepping closer to Tyler.

"Wait!" Keadon shouted.

Michael stopped and turned to Keadon. "What?"

"That's not Tyler."

"What? Tyler, come on, let's go," Michael stammered.

Keadon flew in front of Michael. "That's not Tyler; if it was, he would have said something to us by now."

Michael stared at Tyler, who still just stood there.

"Tom, let's go back outside," Keadon said to Michael.

"Hi, Tom," Tyler said, waving at Michael, still with a vacant look and a monotone voice that sounded somewhat like Tyler.

Michael turned to Keadon. "It's a Mimake."

"I thought so. What do we do? I don't want to hurt it. I am not sure—is it Tyler's body?"

"No, it's not Tyler's body. Mimakes can take the form of whatever it is you want to see; that's how they hunt you. There may be more than one of them."

"So where is Tyler then?" Keadon asked as he looked around the room.

"I don't know…I wish I hadn't left my sword outside, though," Michael moaned.

"Just use your Oltes. Summon it, Michael—you have to."

"But I can't; I'm not that good with my powers yet."

"Well, now is the time to get good," Keadon said as the couch started to move. Michael closed his eyes, held onto his Oltes, and tried to summon his sword, but nothing happened. The couch Keadon was watching was changing shape. "Michael…your sword?" Michael tried again, but still nothing happened. The couch was beginning to look like a man wearing a robe that covered his whole body, with a hood covering his head. Keadon drew a tiny sword and held it out at the hooded figure. "Michael, you can do it—you have to."

Michael tried for the third time to summon his sword. To his surprise, this time, it worked: his sword appeared in his hand. Michael looked down at his sword. "What do we do now?" Michael asked nervously.

"We look for Tyler, and if the Mimakes attack, we…um…well, we attack back." Keadon flew around the house looking for Tyler. "Tyler, it's me, Keadon. Where are you?" Keadon flew into a room that would have been the kitchen. Most of the cupboards were missing doors and the shelves were either missing or broken. The sink was covered in grime and dirt. There were bugs coming out of holes in the floors and walls.

"Keadon, is that you? I mean, really you?" a voice said from behind the door.

Keadon flew to the other side of the door, into a bedroom; there in the room was Tyler, with his sword drawn. "Tyler, are you okay?"

Tyler looked Keadon up and down to make sure it was really him. "Keadon, thank goodness it's you. Is Michael in the house with you?"

"Yeah, he's in the other room, but there are Mimakes in there," Keadon said.

"There are Mimakes all over the house; I have seen four or five that looked like you and Michael. We need to get Mike and get out quick. I have killed two Mimakes already, but it's not easy to kill something that looks and sounds like your brother. I'm stuck; I need you to pull my sword out of my foot."

"What? How did you get your sword stuck in your foot?" Keadon shrieked.

"I was fighting one of the Mimakes and two more came and joined in. Two of them grabbed me from behind and I dropped my sword. The other picked it up and tried to stab me with it, but that's when you guys came in the house; the one with my sword stabbed it through my foot, then they left the room."

Keadon looked down at Tyler's foot, which was pinned to the floor with the sword, and shuddered. "What do I do, just pull it out? That's going to hurt, Tyler!"

"I know it's going to hurt, but it hurts right now too, and it's going to hurt a lot worse if those Mimakes come back, so just pull it out—and quick."

Keadon looked at Tyler, then at his foot again. He flew over to the sword and grabbed the handle with both hands. Tyler flinched from the pain. "I can't do it, Tyler." Keadon let go of the sword.

"Come on, Keadon, you can do it. Just pull it."

Keadon once again grabbed the handle of the sword and pulled; it moved ever so slightly.

"That's it—keep pulling!" Tyler shouted through clenched teeth. Keadon's wings were flickering so fast, you could barely see them. Then, finally, the sword slowly came out. Blood spilled from Tyler's foot; his shoe and sock began to turn red, along with the floor around them. "Thank you, Keadon," Tyler said as he ripped the sleeve off his shirt and wrapped it around his foot. "Okay, let's go," he said as he led Keadon back through the door into the room where Michael was—only now, there was more than one Michael standing in the room. "Michael?" Tyler shouted.

"I'm Michael," each Michael said at the same time. "It's me, Tyler," one of them said, but then three more of them repeated the same thing. They were all moving around; it was hard to tell which one was the real Michael. When Tyler and Keadon thought they knew which was the real one, they moved again. Then they started to move closer to Tyler and Keadon. Tyler and Keadon drew their swords again, ready to fight off the Mimakes.

"Michael, you need to let us know which one is the real you," Tyler shouted.

"I am your brother, Tyler! I am the real Michael." "No, I am the real Michael!" they all began. One of the Michaels leaped toward Tyler. "It's me!" it shouted. Tyler stepped back, but it was a Mimake, and it clawed at Tyler, leaving scratches on his arm. Keadon stabbed the Mimake in the shoulder and it screeched and moved back. Mimakes started to come at Tyler and Keadon from every direction; there were so many of them, Tyler had no choice but to start swinging his sword. As he did, the Mimakes began to draw back. "Tyler, it's me. It's Michael." Tyler looked unsure. There was only one Michael coming toward him this time; it had to be Michael, he thought—until one more Mimake leaped forward. "Tyler, it's me! It's Michael!" Tyler swung his sword at both of them, slashing them both on the arm.

"Ow! You cut me!" Michael shouted as he held the cut on his arm.

"Michael, it is you! Sorry about that."

"It's okay—let's get out of here."

Tyler pushed Michael and Keadon toward the front door and followed them out, making sure the Mimakes that were left didn't follow them. Once they were all safely out of the house, Tyler faced the house, held his Oltes, and pointed toward the door. Boards appeared across the door, sealing it tightly. He did the same to the windows and a large hole in the side of the house. There was no way for anything to get in or out; they still walked away quickly, however, just in case. They walked for a while, as Keadon flew beside them, to make sure they were safely away from the house.

"I need to stop for a bit," Tyler said as he stumbled on his injured foot. He sat down on the ground and unwrapped the bloody shirt from around his foot.

"What happened?" Michael asked, staring at all the blood.

"One of the Mimakes stabbed my sword through my foot. It's okay; I just need to rest it a minute."

Michael sat down beside Tyler and pulled his foot toward him to have a closer look. "That's not okay, Tyler—you need to go to the hospital."

Tyler looked at Michael, shook his head, and pulled his foot away. "I don't think there's a hospital around here. Anyway, we don't have time for that."

Keadon flew over to Tyler's foot and put his hand over the cut. He closed his eyes and mumbled some words that neither Tyler nor Michael understood. Tyler felt his foot getting warm and the cut began to heal right before their eyes. Tyler stared at Keadon in amazement. Once Keadon removed his hand, there was just a mark on Tyler's foot where the cut had been.

"How did you do that?" Tyler stammered.

"You're not the only one with powers," Keadon laughed as he flew over to Michael and did the same thing to the cut on his arm. Michael felt his arm get warm as the cut disappeared, leaving only a mark in its place.

"Thanks," Michael said as he stared at his arm.

After a few minutes' rest, they picked up their stuff and were on their way again to the mountains. The air was pleasant; a warm breeze blew as they walked. Michael was just a little in front of the other two when he suddenly crashed hard into something and fell backward to the ground. Tyler and Keadon stopped quickly so they didn't crash into Michael and whatever it was he had hit, but they couldn't see anything right in front of them. There was nothing but open field, the same as they had just traveled through; but Michael had definitely run into something, and he was lying unconscious on the ground. Tyler dropped his things. He reached his hands out in front of him, feeling for whatever Michael had run into. Tyler took a few slow steps forward, and instantly, an enormous mountain appeared right in front of him—right where, just a second before, there had been nothing but open field. Tyler stepped back and the mountain disappeared, showing the field once again. Tyler moved forward and ran his hand along the side of the mountain. "Keadon you need to come see this."

Keadon flew closer; he too saw the mountain appear out of nowhere. "Wow…I've heard about these mountains, but I've never seen them. I've always wanted to, but my mom wouldn't let me; she said it was too dangerous." Keadon flew down to Michael, who was slowly coming around.

"Wait—what do you mean, 'too dangerous'? 'Because you may fly into them' kind of too dangerous, or because there is dangerous stuff in them?"

"I'm not sure, really—maybe both."

Tyler shook his head. "I hope she meant the latter of the two." He knelt down next to Michael. "How's your head?" Tyler asked as Michael began to open his eyes.

"I found the mountains," Michael stammered.

"That you did," Tyler laughed. He held his hand out to Michael and helped him sit up. "That's going to leave a mark," Tyler teased. "Do you think you're okay to keep going?"

Michael rubbed his head. "I will be…just give me a minute."

Tyler stood up and walked along beside the mountain, feeling the rock and looking for a place that they would be able to climb. The side into which Michael had walked was just a flat rock that went as high up as they could see; it was definitely too flat to climb. A little further around the mountain, it began to slope enough so they should be able to climb up. Tyler went back to get Michael and Keadon. "I found a place where we can get onto the mountain; it's just a little way around."

Michael stood up slowly, with Tyler's help. He stumbled a little. "Are you going to be able to climb?" Keadon asked.

"I can climb; I'm fine." Michael stood for a minute and regained his balance. "See? I'm okay."

They walked around the mountain until they reached the slope Tyler had just found. "I'm going to go up first and check it out. You two wait here. Keadon, keep an eye on Mike, please."

Michael glared at Tyler. "I am fine, Tyler. I don't need to be babysat."

"I won't be long—just watch him," Tyler repeated, ignoring Michael.

"Tyler, that's just a waste of time; let's just climb it together. It's just a mountain. We both have to do it eventually, anyway, so what's the point of you doing it twice?"

"Tyler, Michael's right. It would save so much time if we all just went one time together," Keadon agreed.

Tyler looked at Michael. "Fine, but stay right behind me and be careful; neither of us have climbed before. We can wait for a bit until you feel better."

"I'm fine, for the millionth time. I just banged my head, that's all," Michael snapped.

"He seems okay; his face looks a little funny, though," Keadon laughed.

"It's always looked funny," Tyler joked. Michael just rolled his eyes at them both as Tyler led the way around the side of the mountain. He summoned ropes for Michael and himself. "There seem to be trees and large rocks all the way to the top, so at least we can anchor ourselves a little. Keadon, fly close by, but keep an eye out. Let me know if Michael needs help behind me."

"Tyler, I don't need help! You may be King, but in case you forgot, I am the older brother; I'm supposed to be the one protecting you. Now, are you going to lead the way, Your Majesty?" Michael mocked.

"Just try to keep up, big brother—oh, and try not to hit your head," Tyler said as he threw one end of his rope around a large rock and grabbed hold of the other end. He gave the rope a hard tug, making sure it was secure, then he pulled himself up and began to climb. Michael copied Tyler and climbed behind him.

They had climbed quite high and the wind had started to get colder the higher up the mountain they got. There were a few low clouds surrounding them, making it difficult to see clearly. Michael tossed his rope around another rock and grabbed the other end. He began to pull himself up, but the rock slipped loose and fell off the mountain, plummeting toward the ground. Michael didn't have time to re-anchor himself; he too began to fall.

"Tyler!" Keadon yelled.

Tyler turned around quickly. He could just see Michael's legs as he slipped through the clouds. Without a second thought, Tyler let go of his rope, pushing himself hard off the side of the mountain. He fell fast toward Michael with his arms outstretched, reaching him in no time. He grabbed hold of Michael with one hand and his dagger in his other hand; he stabbed it as hard as he could into the side of the mountain. Tyler hung on to his dagger and Michael as tightly as he could. "Michael, can you reach that branch there?"

"I think so." Michael reached as far as he could, but the branch was too far. "I can't reach it." Michael began to panic.

"Hey, whatcha doing?" Keadon teased.

"Not much—just hanging out," Tyler laughed.

"So do you need a hand? Or a rope, maybe?" Keadon laughed as he tied a rope around a branch and handed it to Michael.

"Thanks," Michael said as he grabbed the rope. Slowly, he let go of Tyler's arm and pulled himself up. They continued the climb; Michael carefully checked each rock and branch before he pulled himself up with them. It wasn't until they had all made it safely to the top that Michael was finally able to breathe again. He looked at Tyler, a little annoyed that their fall hadn't even seemed to faze him, but also thankful that he wasn't being a jerk about it. "Wow, it sure is amazing up here," Michael said as he stared around. And it was: the view was unbelievable; they could see for miles. The only problem was that they could see mountains for miles.

"We can make it to the caves, I think, before it gets too dark, but we will have to hurry," Michael said as he started walking. Tyler and Keadon followed Michael; the path was rough and uneven and seemed to get rougher the further they walked. "We need to climb up a little; this path is going to dead end at the cliff. We need to move to the next mountain. If we climb up a ways, there will be a bridge made out of the mountain, connecting the two together," Michael explained. The three of them trudged on cautiously as loose rocks slipped out from under their feet and disappeared over the edge of the mountain. The sounds of the large ones echoed, a chilling reminder to watch their step throughout the mountains.

"Over there, I see it! I see the bridge—it's not too far!" Keadon shouted.

"Does it look safe?" Michael asked.

Keadon flew on a little to have a better look. "I think it will hold you both; you're not that big."

"Ha, ha—funny," Michael sighed.

"Um, Mike? I don't think he's kidding," Tyler said as he pointed toward a rather long, rickety-looking, swinging bridge. As they got closer, they could see that some of the wood had broken and most likely fallen down into the seemingly bottomless crevice. "Great—that sure looks sturdy," Tyler joked.

"There is no way that will hold us," Michael stammered as they both stood frozen in front of the bridge, staring at the other side, which looked impossible to reach.

"Let's go," Keadon said as he hovered above the bridge.

Tyler took a deep breath. "Okay, let's do this," he said, stepping onto the bridge.

"You can't be serious, Tyler; we will never make it across. There is no way. That bridge will not hold; forget it. No way."

"Relax, Michael—it will hold. We just need to move quickly. Let's go." Tyler continued along the bridge with Keadon flying by his side. Michael was terrified; he could barely walk, he was shaking so badly, but he knew there was no other way. Slowly, he followed Tyler, trembling a little more with each step. He felt like he was going to be sick. Michael stopped to lean over the side to throw up, but he stumbled from fear as he looked over the edge.

Tyler had turned around just in time. "Michael…easy," Tyler said, holding him up. "Hold onto me and don't look down. We're halfway across already." Tyler stepped forward, but the wood broke under his foot. He pushed Michael back a step as he slipped through the hole. He grabbed onto the bridge and Michael grabbed his arm.

"Keadon, help me pull him up!"

Tyler's hand began to slip. "I can't hold on." Tyler let go of the bridge, but Michael grabbed the back of his shirt with Keadon and they pulled him up. They both could just barely step over the hole in the bridge, and they crossed as quickly as they could to the other side.

"We made it—just barely, but we made it," Michael gasped as he flopped down on the ground to catch his breath.

"I think one of my first jobs as King will be to have that bridge fixed," Tyler laughed as he sat down next to Michael. "Let's rest for a minute, but then we should keep moving. Keadon, come over here. Sit down and rest your wings for a bit."

Keadon spun around quickly. He darted back and forth as if he were looking for something.

"What are you doing?" Tyler asked.

"I think…" Keadon darted again. "I think someone or something is coming."

Tyler and Michael jumped up and looked around. "I don't see anything," Michael said.

"I don't see anything, either; I feel it. Something is coming."

"Do you have any idea what?" Michael asked.

"No—I don't know whether it is something good or bad. I just know something is coming."

"I think we should get going; we need to get to the caves." Michael urged Tyler and Keadon along the path toward the caves, continuously asking Keadon if whatever it was he felt coming was getting closer.

"I don't know exactly where whatever-it-is is," Keadon snapped.

"Okay, sorry—I'll try to stop asking."

It was getting darker and darker. The wind picked up a little more; the temperature started to drop as the path led them higher up the mountain. "The caves are right there," Michael said, pointing to a very small crack in the side of the mountain just a little further along the path.

"That's it? That's the caves? It's just a hole," Tyler groaned.

"Well, what do you think a cave is, Ty? It's a hole in a mountain," Michael joked.

"I know that," Tyler snapped, giving Michael a little nudge.

"Well, what did you expect?"

"I don't know…I just thought it would be bigger, maybe."

"Well, that's just the entrance. You don't want the entrance to be too big; it makes it easier to block once we are inside," Keadon stated.

They hurried along, eager to get into the caves and rest. When they reached the entrance to the caves, Tyler moved in front of Michael and Keadon to go through the entrance first.

"Wait, Tyler. Maybe I should go first," Keadon said, flying in front of Tyler.

"No, I will go first to make sure it's safe," Tyler insisted.

Keadon smiled and moved out of the way. "After you, oh brave one," Keadon snickered.

Tyler shot him an annoyed look and walked toward the entrance. Even though there didn't look to be anything there, Tyler walked right into an invisible wall with a loud thud. "What the heck?" Tyler moaned, rubbing his head.

"You knew that was there, didn't you?" Michael asked Keadon, giggling.

"I sure did," Keadon laughed.

"Ha, ha—laugh it up," Tyler snapped, still rubbing his head.

Keadon moved in front of the entrance. "Ode Onaysa Brodane," he said loudly and clearly. Michael and Tyler stood back and watched as Keadon repeated the words three more times, then flew through the entrance into the cave. "Are you two coming or staying out there to greet the company?"

Michael quickly looked around, expecting to see something terrible right behind him. Even though there was nothing, he very quickly followed Tyler into the cave.

"Wow, this place looks cool," Tyler said, looking around. The cave was enormous. There were well-burnt candles all along the walls; their wax trails went all the way down to cave floor. They were quite dim, leaving the caves not very well-lit. There were numerous tunnels leading to more caves, each as amazing as the first. One of the caves had a small lake in the middle of it, with a narrow ledge running all the way around the edge.

"I don't want to know what could be swimming in there," Michael commented with a shudder.

"You don't feel like going for a swim, then?" Keadon teased.

"You first."

"Aw, I didn't bring a towel; I'll have to pass," Keadon laughed.

Tyler walked over to the lake and knelt down, staring into the water. "Irrid," whispered, dipping his fingers in the icy water. Michael solemnly turned around and left the lake, returning back to the first cave with Keadon flying by his side.

"Who is Irrid?" Keadon asked Michael as they sat down on the hard ground. Michael told Keadon all about their stay with Irrid in the bottom of the lake in the forest, and how Irrid bravely faced the monster so he and Tyler could escape to safety.

Tyler finally came to join them in the cave, where Keadon and Michael had made a small fire to help them stay warm. Tyler pointed to a space on the hard rock floor; one large bed appeared, and one small bed for Keadon. "You two need to get some sleep. We're going to have a hard day tomorrow," Tyler said as he walked closer to the entrance and drew his sword. He sat down on a large rock.

"You can't just not sleep at all, Tyler; you need to get some rest too," Michael warned.

"I'm going to keep watch. It's not safe for us all to sleep at the same time; anything could find us here."

"What about all the other entrances?" Michael pointed to the many openings to the other caves.

Tyler stood up and began to walk around the cave. "I will watch them too; don't worry. Get some rest."

Michael stared at Tyler. He knew why Tyler didn't want to go to sleep. He knew Tyler didn't want to have nightmares, but he also did think it was a good idea for one of them to keep watch. "All right, but only for half the night—then we switch and I'll keep watch."

"What about me? When is it my turn to keep watch?" Keadon shouted. Michael and Tyler looked at each other, then at Keadon. "What—you two think I'm too small, right?"

"Well, what are you going to do if some big creature or something comes into the cave?" Michael asked.

"I'M NOT GOING TO GET SCARED AND SCREAM, LIKE YOU!" Keadon shouted. Tyler laughed; Michael didn't.

"Fine—we will each take a turn keeping watch, okay? But I am going first, so go to sleep," Tyler warned them both. So they did; Michael and Keadon lay down on the beds that Tyler had made appear, and it wasn't long before they were asleep. Tyler walked around the cave for a while with his sword drawn. After about an hour or so, he sat down on the large rock by the entrance. He tried to keep his eyes open, staring at all the tunnels, but his eyes became heavy; his head began to bob, jolting awake each time, until finally, Tyler's head leaned up against the hard wall of the mountain. He couldn't resist any longer: he was overcome by slumber and he fell asleep.

A cold hand rested upon Tyler's cheek. Startled, he opened his eyes—and there, right in front of him, was Candor. "Where have you been?" Tyler demanded. "All this time, you couldn't even try to contact me, to give me a clue as to where Eljord's kingdom is?" Candor just stared at Tyler without saying a word. "Answer me; you are supposed to be on my side! You are supposed to help me!" Still Candor said nothing. Tyler was getting furious; he stood up and stepped closer to Candor, but Candor stepped back. "What is wrong with you?" Tyler yelled. Candor drew a sword from under his cloak and stabbed it through Tyler's heart.

Tyler gasped, opened his eyes, and sat up. He grabbed his chest, just to make sure; he looked around the cave, almost expecting to see Candor standing there, when he knew it was only a dream. "It's always just a dream." Tyler stood up and walked across the cave. He kicked a rock angrily. "Even here, I can't sleep. Even here—this is the one place I thought I would be able to sleep," Tyler mumbled to himself as he walked past the tunnels, checking to make sure they were all still safe. Tyler sat back down on the rock and stared through the entrance of the cave.

"Tyler!" a voice within the cave whispered. "Tyler, you are too weak." Tyler ignored the voice; he thought it was just in his head or another dream. "Tyler, you are too late. You cannot save your friend, Tyler—you are too weak." Tyler put his hands over his ears. There was a loud bang and Tyler was knocked off the rock onto the hard floor. He turned over onto his back; at that same moment, Eljord sprang on top of him, pinning him down. "Again we meet, Tyler—or do you prefer 'Your Majesty'?" Eljord laughed. Tyler tried to fight him off, but it was no use: Eljord was too strong. "You are too late, and you are going to get yourselves killed. Go home while you still can; return to the Lyt world."

"No—I'm not afraid of you. We will get Sara back. You can't control the Dark World anymore; we will keep the peace. You will not win this time," Tyler said as he continued to struggle.

Eljord laughed. "You little children don't stand a chance against me." Eljord slammed Tyler hard into the ground; his head hit so hard that he fell unconscious.

"Tyler! Tyler, wake up." Tyler opened his eyes and saw Michael standing above him. Tyler was lying on the ground. He sat up; his head throbbed so much he couldn't see straight. "Why didn't you wake me up if you were so tired?"

"What? I, um…I'm not…I mean, I wasn't sleeping—I don't think I was. I just fell asleep. I didn't mean to fall asleep."

"Hey, sleeping beauty—did you keep watch at all?" Keadon laughed.

"Why didn't you wake one of us? We were supposed to take turns keeping watch," Michael snapped.

Tyler just stared around the cave, his head throbbing. He stood up, held onto his Oltes, and pointed at an empty space on the floor, and a table full of food appeared. "Eat—we all need our strength," Tyler said as he sat down at the table and began to eat breakfast. Michael and Keadon looked at each other, a bit confused. They knew something was wrong with Tyler; they knew something must have happened the night before.

"So, how was your night?" Michael asked Tyler nervously while helping himself to a second plateful.

"Fine," Tyler said, standing up and walking away from the table. "They're here," Tyler whispered, spinning around to Michael and Keadon.

"Who?"

"I don't know who they are; I guess whoever it was that Keadon felt coming," Tyler said, moving to the back of the cave with Keadon and Michael.

"What do we do?" Michael asked.

"I don't know. Maybe they're not coming for us; maybe they are just passing through the mountains too," Tyler said none too convincingly.

"I didn't say they were bad," Keadon reminded them.

"Yeah, but you didn't say they were good either."

"I can fly out there and look around to see how close they are."

"No!" Tyler snapped.

"Why not? I'm the only one that can go out there without being seen," Keadon said, getting right in Tyler's face.

"I don't care—I am not risking that."

"That's not up to you; you are not the boss of me! If I want to go out there, I will," Keadon said, flying toward the entrance.

Tyler grabbed him. "I will not let you go out there! It's too dangerous!" But Keadon was no longer in Tyler's hand; he had disappeared. "Grrr!" Tyler yelled with clenched fists. "I'm going after him! Stay here!" Tyler yelled at Michael.

"Tyler, let him go!" Michael yelled, standing in front of Tyler. "It's not up to you to protect everyone. Keadon will be fine. Let him do this. He's small; no one will see him. He will be safe." Tyler angrily walked back to the table and pointed forcefully at it; with a bang, it disappeared in a cloud of smoke. "Tyler, you need to control your temper. I'm worried; you could be dangerous. You don't know enough about your powers…neither of us does."

"Just because you don't know how to use your powers, don't take it out on me!"

Michael stared at Tyler. "Here you go again, being a jerk. It's not my fault if you had a nightmare last night." Tyler opened his mouth to yell back at Michael, but at that moment, Keadon came back through the entrance—but he wasn't alone.

"Keadon, are you okay?" Tyler asked as he drew his sword.

"I'm fine—I told you I would be. Tyler—or, sorry, I should say 'Your Majesty'—this is your army," Keadon said proudly.

"What do you mean, 'my army'?" Tyler stared at the strange-looking group behind Keadon.

"These are the Dreamencers—well, what's left of them. They came to fight Eljord with you."

The Dreamencers all bowed to Tyler. Tyler just stared at them in disbelief. There were ten altogether, each very different. A tall, very skinny man with a large head that looked too big for his body, small, dark green eyes, a rather large, round nose, and straw-like hair stepped forward. "I am Lelx," he said, bowing to Tyler, then stepping back.

"I am Vedin." He looked just like any normal man did. He was tall and well kempt, with brown hair and brown eyes; he wore a jacket and pants that looked a bit too small.

A fairy that looked a lot like Keadon flew forward, only this fairy was a girl. She flew right up to Tyler, fluttering around his head. "My name is Flain," she said sweetly. Tyler smiled at her; she was very beautiful. Keadon was staring at her in an admiring sort of way.

"Grundun," grumbled a very old-looking man who walked with a cane. He was missing most of his teeth; the few that remained looked as if they wouldn't be there for long. He wore very thick glasses that were bent so badly, they barely covered both eyes. Tyler wasn't sure why Grundun had come; he was obviously too old. He probably wouldn't make it the rest of the way through the mountains, let alone in a fight against Eljord.

A hooded figure stepped forward and ever so slightly bowed to Tyler, but didn't say a word. The cave went icy cold: so cold they could see their breath. The hooded figure stepped back, still without saying a word, and the temperature returned to normal. Tyler instantly thought that the hooded figure was Candor. Tyler moved toward the hooded figure and pulled the hood off, but instead of a face, there was nothing; whoever it was disappeared, and the robe fell in a pile on the floor.

"Shadow!" Keadon whispered, with a stunned yet excited look on his face. He turned his head slowly toward Tyler. "That is—or was, I mean—Shadow." Tyler just looked at Keadon and shrugged his shoulders. "Shadow: a very, very powerful Nytstar! Shadow is a legend!" Keadon's face lit up.

"Oh—well, will Shadow come back?" Tyler asked, but as he turned back to the group, his question was already answered: Shadow was back in the same place as before. Tyler stared at Shadow for a while; he was very intrigued. Then the one member of the group who didn't seem to belong at all stepped forward. Michael's, Tyler's, and Keadon's jaws dropped to the floor.

"Hello, boys," said the most beautiful voice any of them had ever heard.

"Uh...help—um...I mean, hello," all three stumbled to say at the same time.

"My name is Willow," a beautiful girl giggled. The girl was tall, with long, flowing blond hair. Her skin was so perfect, she could have been a doll. Her eyes were a brilliant shade of blue, with long eyelashes. She was beautiful. She was wearing a little sundress and sandals; she looked like she was going to the beach, not to fight Eljord. She looked too perfect to fight anyone. Flain the fairy shot Willow a mean look, then shot the boys, who were still staring at her, the same look.

"If you kids are quite finished…? I am not taking orders from little kids; I am only here today out of respect for your grandfather, so if you think you can boss me around, you are wrong!" stated a tall, broad-shouldered man with a long black coat on, which was most likely hiding his sword He had a black hat on, his long black hair tied back in a ponytail. He had very heavy-looking boots on that were also black. His face looked a little old and tired, yet still strong.

Tyler quickly snapped out of staring at Willow and turned very defensive. "Hey, I am not a little kid! I am the new King—you cannot talk to me like that," Tyler snapped.

"Are you going to have a temper tantrum?" the man replied. "I am not here to babysit you!"

Tyler was furious; who did this guy think he was, talking to him like that? "What is your name?" Tyler asked.

"No manners, either. Your grandfather would be very disappointed," the man grunted.

Tyler was about to jump toward the man angrily, but Michael and Keadon pulled him back. "I am sorry, sir; my name is Michael. May I ask your name?" Michael asked politely.

"My name is Dronand." The man nodded at Michael.

Tyler, now more furious, pushed Michael aside and moved in front of Dronand. "I am not scared or intimidated by you. You don't know me and I don't wish to know you—in fact, I don't think you belong here with us!"

"Tyler, we need all the help we can get. You can't turn people away who are willing to fight with us just because you don't get along," Michael stated firmly.

"I am not going to fight with someone who cannot see me for who I am."

"I do see you for who you are; the problem is that you don't see yourself for who you are. You seem to think you are this great savior; you think you are invincible. You seem to forget that you are just a kid—and yeah, maybe the new King, but just that: the *new* king. You have no idea what this world has gone through. You think you are going to walk up to Eljord's kingdom and demand that he release your friend, and he will graciously comply? No—thirteen of us will go to Eljord's kingdom, but we will be lucky if five of us return, and those who die will do so saving you."

"Not saving me, saving Sara—and saving the Dark World from Eljord's constant bullying."

Dronand laughed at Tyler's words. "You talk of Eljord like he is a playground bully. He is more powerful than you could even begin to understand. He could end the Dark World right now if he chose to."

"He wouldn't do that," Tyler insisted.

"You think you know him?" Dronand asked tauntingly.

"I know he is a bully, and I believe that just like any bully, bullying makes him happy, so if he were to 'end the Dark World', he wouldn't have anyone to bully anymore. I also think that fear makes him stronger; I think it fuels him somehow. I also know that everyone has a weakness, no matter how evil you may be." When Tyler had finished, he noticed that everyone was just staring at him. "What?" he snapped.

"Well, I just didn't know you had put so much thought into this, that's all," Michael said weakly.

"Why? Because you didn't think I had that much thought at all?" Tyler snapped, and walked away from the group. Michael turned to walk after him, but Dronand grabbed his arm.

"Leave him; he just needs to calm down." Michael looked closely at Dronand; he didn't see him as a threat like Tyler did. Michael was intrigued. He felt like he could learn so much from Dronand. He had so many questions to ask that he knew Dronand could answer, but he also knew he couldn't talk to him right now: Tyler would be furious. The rest of the group was now sitting on the floor, chatting amongst themselves. With only three people left to meet, Tyler and Michael both had the same idea: to get going as soon as possible.

"So, you three, what are your names?"

One of them stood up, nodded at Tyler, and opened his mouth to speak, but it wasn't words that came out—it was a strange noise, like a cross between a wolf snarling and a bear growling. Tyler stared at him for a moment; somehow he seemed to know what the man was saying. He was a very hairy creature who walked on two legs like a man but looked more like a wolf. He was covered from head to toe in what looked like fur. He had black eyes like a wolf, yet they were shaped like those of a human; so were his nose, ears, and mouth. The man pointed toward the two men left and they stood next to him. They also nodded at Tyler; when they opened their mouths to speak, they made the same sound as the last man, and just as with the last man, Tyler understood what they said. All three had told Tyler what their names were: the first was named Moven, the second Danned, and the third Weven. They were three brothers; the last of their kind, they told Tyler. Eljord and his army had come to their village to try and have all the village men join his army to fight against Tyler's grandfather; when they refused, the army killed everyone in the village, including the women and children. Tears filled Moven's eyes as he spoke.

"How come you three were not killed?" Tyler asked.

Moven spoke again, telling Tyler how he and his brothers were just boys at the time. They had snuck away from the village to swim in the lake in the Slome forest; they had been forbidden to swim there: their mom said it wasn't safe. They had come home and found the entire village dead. Tyler looked at the brothers sympathetically.

Dronand grabbed Tyler's arm. "Why did it look like you understood what they were saying?" Dronand demanded.

Tyler pulled his arm away and shot Dronand a nasty look. "They were speaking clearly."

"There is only one person who can understand Wovbes other than Wovbes themselves, and that is Eljord. That is why he wanted them to join him." Dronand looked suspiciously at Tyler. Moven stepped between Tyler and Dronand and let out a loud, snarling roar toward Dronand. Tyler smiled; he knew Moven had just warned Dronand to back off, but Dronand had no idea what he had said.

"We are very grateful that you all are here, whatever your reasoning is to fight with us against Eljord. We are not far from his kingdom now, as I am sure you all know. I trust you all have brought with you whatever weapons you require?" The group all nodded at Michael. "We are greatly outnumbered, so as little fighting as possible would work in our favor. I believe if we can move quickly into Eljord's kingdom undetected, find Sara, and leave the same way, we may stand a chance."

"I am going into Eljord's kingdom alone; the rest of you are to keep watch and only enter if needed. I don't want to be to blame if any of you are injured or worse," Tyler stated firmly.

The entire group expressed their disagreement. "We are here to fight for you; to defend you, Your Majesty," Willow said softly. "You cannot go into his kingdom alone. Don't be foolish, child," Dronand spat.

Tyler's whole body tensed up. "I believe the King is the highest in command, and if I am not mistaken, the King would be me." Tyler turned his back on Dronand. Moven snarled at Tyler, and Tyler shook his head.

"Why is it that you can understand them?" Michael asked Tyler quietly.

"I have no idea," Tyler replied, somewhat annoyed.

"We will not let you go in alone. You need us; that's why we are here. You were the one who sent for us," Flain the fairy said as she flew in front of Tyler.

"She is right, you know," Keadon smiled.

Tyler turned to face the group. He was taken aback by the army in front of him: his army. Sure, they were not much, and they looked like an army of misfits, but they were on his side. He had only really ever had Michael on his side before; now he had a small army, he thought to himself. "Okay—Flain, Keadon, you two can come inside with me; you will be less likely to be seen and can hide better than anyone else."

"I beg to differ, Your Majesty." Shadow stepped forward and disappeared instantly, then reappeared on the other side of the cave as quickly as he had disappeared.

Tyler was impressed. "Okay, you can come too." Tyler nodded toward Shadow.

"If you think I'm waiting outside for you, you're wrong! I will not take orders from you, Tyler; I want to help Sara just as much as you do!" Michael shouted.

"If not more," Tyler said under his breath.

"What was that?" Michael snapped.

"It's too dangerous, Michael. I can't be worried about you the whole time."

"I am the older brother, remember? It's my job to protect you, not the other way around! I am going into that kingdom, whether you like it or not." Michael stormed away from Tyler, picked up his sword and satchel, and stood by the entrance to the cave.

"Fine, big brother," Tyler said mockingly. Moven growled something; Tyler nodded somewhat hesitantly. "Okay—Flain, Keadon, Moven, Shadow, Michael, and I will go into Eljord's kingdom to rescue Sara. That leaves Dronand, Willow, Grundun, Lelx, Vedin, Danned, and Weven to keep watch on the outside."

"Tyler, be warned: Eljord has before committed regicide; I have no doubt that he will again if he feels he must," Grundun warned.

"Thank you—I will keep it in mind," Tyler said as he gathered his things.

"We must move on. I feel danger approaching. I don't want to just waylay; we need to prepare a counter-ambush. It is his army of Nytelves; they are just entering the mountains. We need to move out of the caves or we will be cornered," Grundun explained.

"This is it: we have our plan—let's put it into action," Tyler shouted. The army turned to Tyler and bowed, each member raising their weapon high.

"For Tyler, we fight—for peace, we win!" they all shouted.

Tyler filled with excitement and fear. This was it: this was his time to shine.

CHAPTER THIRTEEN

REACHING ELJORD

The army of only thirteen, four of whom were just children, began their final trek through the mountains, knowing they would soon run into an army of Nytelves. They all had their weapons drawn and ready. Grundun walked just behind Tyler, his cane supporting his every step. Each time he stumbled, Moven and Michael tried to help him, but Grundun did not want their help.

"Get off of me! I can walk on my own. I have been coming through these mountains since before you were born," he would snarl at them both. All of a sudden, Grundun stopped and raised his cane into the air.

Tyler looked around. He wasn't sure: was that a sign? But everyone had disappeared and left him and Michael standing there alone. "What the heck is going on? Where did they all go?" Michael asked.

"I don't know," Tyler said, but no sooner were the words out of his mouth than he heard Moven trying to whisper.

"What is he saying?"

"We need to hide," Tyler told Michael. They both moved quickly to where Moven was hiding behind a boulder. Moven explained to Tyler that Grundun's signal meant that they needed to take cover; the enemy was almost upon them. Tyler repeated the explanation to Michael. "Can you feel that?" Tyler whispered.

Michael was as still as he could be and placed his hand on the ground and held his breath. He turned and looked nervously at Tyler and nodded. The ground was vibrating. It felt like a mini earthquake. Rocks began falling all around them: just small rocks at first, but they got bigger and bigger the more the ground shook. "What's happening?" Michael asked worriedly, but Tyler didn't need to answer; the answer came charging over the hill, riding on the backs of giant spiders.

"The elf, the spiders…I've seen them before. They were in our house. I had no idea he had anything to do with Eljord."

Tyler's army jumped out from their hiding places, their swords drawn. Vedin slashed three spiders' legs with one quick swipe of his sword; the spiders fell to the ground, a thick black blood oozing out of their wounds. The Nytelves that were riding the three spiders fell also. The elves jumped to their feet and started swinging their clubs around wildly, not aiming at anyone in particular. Tyler jumped at one of the elves with his sword drawn and joined in the battle—his army of thirteen against the army of at least a hundred Nytelves. Tyler's sword hit the elf's club so hard he stumbled back; the elf just laughed for a moment—that was, until Tyler quickly jumped toward him, stabbing him with a dagger. The elf fell dead to the ground. Tyler stared at the elf he had just killed for a moment, stunned by the noise of the battle all around him: the deafening clanking of swords and clubs colliding, elves and giant spiders falling dead.

"Tyler, watch yourself!" Moven warned as he sliced an elf that was just about to strike Tyler with his club. "They are slow, but they are not stupid. They attack those who are slower than they are. You need to keep moving; it confuses them. They are extremely lazy, too."

Tyler nodded and moved toward another elf. He slashed the spider's legs first, and then the elf as it fell to the ground. Michael stayed close to Dronand, who was killing elf after elf with no trouble at all. Keadon and Flain flew high above the battle to try and get an idea of how many elves there were. "There are too many to count, Tyler! They are coming from every direction!" Keadon shouted.

"Keadon, keep watch up there and let me know if any of our army gets hurt."

"Yes, Your Majesty," Keadon said proudly.

Tyler looked around for Michael to make sure he was okay. He saw Michael and Dronand together working as a team. Tyler stared a little longer than he should have; he felt the hard, sharp blade of a dagger slice his arm. He grasped it tightly, dropping his sword. Blood came rushing out of the wound. Shadow leaped over toward Tyler, killing the elf that had attacked him.

Keadon flew to Grundun. "Grundun, Tyler's been hurt—hurry!"

Grundun ran toward Shadow and Tyler. "It's not too deep; the elf wasn't close enough," Grundun reassured Tyler.

"I'm fine," Tyler grunted. "I just need to wrap it up to stop the bleeding." Grundun pulled Tyler's hand off his wound; blood spilled down his arm onto the ground. Grundun put his fingers into the open wound. Tyler screamed in pain as Grundun slowly pulled his fingers out; the wound healed. Tyler stared at his arm, then looked back to Grundun, but he was gone, back to the battle.

"Tyler, Shadow, Lelx is in trouble!" Keadon shouted. "Over there—he's surrounded by twenty or so elves!"

Tyler ran, following Keadon, but Shadow was no longer beside him. Tyler reached the group of elves and saw that Shadow was already there, trying to fight the elves off of Lelx. Danned, Moven and Weven were working together, fighting the elves that were coming up one side of the mountain, while Willow, Vedin, and Grundun were fighting the elves on the other side. Michael and Dromand had slain almost all of the elves that were left on the top. All the spiders had been killed and the ground was now covered in their thick black blood. The sound of the swords and clubs echoed through the mountains, until finally, the last elf fell dead.

"All right—we did it! We did it!" Michael shouted excitedly. Willow and the others joined in the excitement, until Michael stopped and stared over toward Tyler and Shadow, who were crouched down at a heap on the ground. The army ran over to them and stood around silently, staring at Lelx's lifeless body.

"He's dead," Tyler whispered. Tyler looked at Grundun. "What are you waiting for? Quickly—you need to help him!" Tyler yelled, but Grundun just stood there and shook his head. "Why are you just standing there? Fix him like you fixed my arm, Grundun—please!"

"I cannot save him, Your Majesty."

Tyler jumped to his feet. "As King, I command you, Grundun, to save him. Save Lelx now!" Tyler shouted as tears streamed down his face.

Grundun stood firm. "There is no way to restore life. I am sorry, Your Majesty," Grundun said sadly.

"Yes, yes you can! The nurse gave me something when I was attacked by the dragon; I was dead and it restored life in me."

"This is not the same. I don't know why that worked for you—it shouldn't have. I can only assume that you were not completely dead, but Lelx is," Grundun said as he rolled Lelx's body over. Tyler gasped at the sight of Lelx's bloody wounds. "I'm sorry, Tyler, but the club smashed through his chest, completely crushing his heart. He is gone." Grundun got up and walked away.

"You okay?" Michael asked, bending down next to Tyler. Tyler just nodded. He couldn't help but feel like it was his fault, like he should have done something; after all they were his army—he was the King.

"There was nothing you could have done, Tyler. There was nothing any of us could have done," Moven said with his hand on Tyler's shoulder.

"That's what happens in battle. We need to keep going," Dronand said roughly as he picked up Lelx's sword, stashing it in his holster.

Tyler jumped up angrily and stepped in front of Dronand. "How dare you? One of our army has just died. Show some respect," Tyler snapped.

"Lelx died in battle. He was a Dreamencer. He died honorably; he would have wanted that."

Tyler shook his head, but before he could say anything, Moven pulled him away from Dronand. "I know you are upset; you feel that as King, it is your job to protect everyone, and because we are here for you, to find your friend, if anyone were to die, it should be you. Am I right?" Tyler nodded, choking back his tears. "Well, you are wrong. Every one of us is here because we are Dreamencers; we are your army. Every one of us here, including Dronand, would give our lives to save yours. You are King: your life is more important than ours. That's just the way it is, Tyler; that's the way it always has been and always will be. Don't say anything—just take a moment, and when you are ready, we will move on with you." Moven walked away from Tyler.

Dronand stormed toward Moven. "I know you can understand me. Do you really think you can be his friend? Do you think he will actually bring peace to our world? You are nothing but a fool, just like your kid King!" Moven growled fiercely at Dronand.

"Tyler, I don't mean to interrupt, but I just thought maybe Flain and I could fly on a bit to make sure everything is clear," Keadon suggested.

"Keadon, are you okay? You didn't get hurt or anything, did you?"

Keadon just laughed. "Not me, Tyler—I am way too fast for those lazy elves, and too small. They can't gang up on me; they would end up killing themselves."

"We should try that next time. We do need to move on; just make sure you fly high enough…"

"Tyler, I will be careful—and I will keep a really close eye on Flain, too." Keadon winked and flew off toward Flain, filling her in on the plan, and off they went.

"Okay, everyone, gather a club or two to take with you, just in case, and let's move on," Tyler instructed. Shadow appeared again and stood over Lelx's body. His robe waved over Lelx's body and it disappeared. Tyler took one last look at the place of his first battle, somehow knowing it wouldn't be his last.

Grundun, clutching his walking stick, walked in front with Tyler, trying to sense any sign of danger. "Our path through the mountains is clear and short, Your Majesty," Grundun assured. Tyler thanked him; he was relieved to almost be out of the mountains. "You know, our powers are not limitless or without consequences, most of which we come to discover through our own suffering."

Tyler was getting annoyed with the constant advice everyone was giving him; he was relieved to see that they were finally at the edge of the mountains. They only needed to climb down a little bit from where they were.

"This isn't going to be any easy climb, Tyler," Michael warned.

"I know, but this is the only way down, Mike. If you're afraid, why don't you get your buddy Dronand to carry you on his back?" Tyler snapped.

"I wasn't thinking of myself; I was worried about Grundun. He has a hard enough time walking with his cane; how is he going to climb down the side of a mountain?" Tyler looked next to him, where Grundun had just been standing, but he wasn't there.

"Are you lot not coming down?" they heard Grundun shout from below; he was so far down they couldn't even see him.

"He will be able to manage it, I guess," Michael said, quite impressed.

One by one, they all climbed down the mountain. Moven, Weven, and Danned raced each other down playfully, as most brothers would. Michael glanced at Tyler; before they found out they were Nytstars, they too used to be as close, and would have had just as much fun.

Tyler was relieved when his feet reached the ground; everyone had made it down safely.

"Tyler, we flew to the edge of Eljord's kingdom; it is clear," Keadon reported proudly.

"Well done, Keadon—you are sure it is clear?"

"I'm positive, Your Majesty. We are close—very close; just a small meadow to cross and we are there."

"That seems easy enough. Let's keep going. We should split up into our groups now so that once we have crossed the meadow, we will be ready," Tyler instructed. Dronand mumbled something under his breath, but Moven must have heard: he shot a nasty warning growl his way. Tyler, Michael, Moven, Shadow, Keadon, and Flain led the army to the edge of the meadow, where they could just see the giant wall surrounding Eljord's kingdom.

"Finally," Michael sighed.

"It's only going to get worse from here," Tyler warned.

Moven moved toward Tyler. "Wait!" he snarled, and picked up a rather large boulder and threw it into the meadow. The grass suddenly rose up like hundreds of giant snakes, wrapping all around the boulder tightly, pulling the giant boulder into the ground. Just before it was completely out of sight, the boulder burst into thousands of tiny pieces. "Oh, good—I was really hoping this wasn't just a normal meadow," Tyler moaned.

"Normal, here?" Willow laughed.

"Sorry, Tyler, we didn't know. We were flying high, just like you said," Keadon stammered.

"It's okay, Keadon. I told you to fly high, remember? You were following my orders," Tyler reassured him.

"Amazing!" Michael gasped. "Octigrass—this stuff is deadly, yet fascinating. Together, it is strong enough to crush anything, yet one single blade by itself is useless," Michael explained.

"That's great—really interesting—but there seems to be a whole lot of it here," Tyler snapped. "Well, we'll just have to take the long way around, that's all. Let's go."

"Tyler, it's not that simple. It grows where it has to. The further we walk, the bigger the meadow will become. We have to go over it, but high over it: the grass can reach ten feet or more into the air."

"Great. Well, what now?"

Tyler heard Sara's voice in his head again. "Michael, please leave me. Turn back; he will kill you both. It's a trap." Tyler ignored it; instead, he called out to Traydome. They all heard the bird squawking; they looked up and saw the giant Nythawk gliding through the air. "I will go on Traydome; he can carry Sara and I back. Keadon, you and Flain can fly with us. Everyone else, wait here."

"Don't be foolish, Tyler. You will be dead as soon as you get over the wall," Dronand snapped.

"What other options are there? Can you fly?" Tyler argued.

"Stop trying to be the hero, Tyler. Dronand is right: you can't do it by yourself," Michael added.

Tyler hopped onto Traydome without listening to anyone and they flew off.

"Tyler!" Michael yelled after him. Moven, Danned, and Weven roared so loudly that everyone covered their ears. They looked into the sky to see a flock of enormous flying creatures. Michael was amazed; he had read all about them in a book he had borrowed from Sara. "Flying Rhiorecs," Michael whispered to himself. They looked like skinny rhinoceroses with wings: so skinny you could see their ribs through their thick, leathery skin. Their horns were a lot larger than a rhinoceros's and they were a deep blood red. Their eyes were black and glazed over. As they landed, the ground shook under their enormous weight. Moven stepped up the biggest one, which was in the front, and bowed to it. He rubbed its horn and stared into its eyes; it seemed as if Moven and the creature were silently communicating. The creature nodded occasionally and looked around at the group that was standing on the edge of the meadow, then nodded once more. Moven climbed onto the creature and said something; the only problem was that other than his brothers and Tyler, no one could understand him. Danned and Weven did as Moven had done: they each climbed on the back of a creature. Moven then said something to the others, but nobody moved, so he motioned to them to do the same.

"I think he wants us to ride on them too," Michael said.

"I think so—I just hope they are safe, that's all," Willow said, sounding a little nervous.

"I just hope it is not a trap. There is something about those three I do not trust—especially Moven," Dronand snapped as they took off after Tyler.

There was an excruciatingly earsplitting screech in the sky that startled the creatures and their riders so much that Michael, Grundun, and Willow almost fell off.

"Dragons, there!" Dronand shouted.

Michael turned to catch sight of about thirty very fierce-looking dragons. The dragons were enormous. They had spikes on their tails and backs; they were mostly brown with some white patches, except for one: there was one all-white dragon. Michael recognized it right away as the one that had attacked Tyler. Without thinking, Michael thrust himself forward on the Rhiorecs he was riding, which began to glide quickly toward the white dragon. Michael took out his sword and held it as tightly as he could. They soared closer and closer; he could feel the heat of the dragon's flames, but he didn't care. All he could think about was when he saw his brother's lifeless body after he had been attacked by the white dragon; now he wanted to avenge his brother and kill the dragon.

"Michael, you are going to get yourself killed!" Dronand shouted, but Michael just flew on. Flying quickly behind the white dragon, he stabbed at his tail, but missed. The dragon let out a roar, which seemed to make all the other dragons start attacking the Rhiorecs and their riders. Michael flew back around and stabbed his sword again at the dragon's tail, only this time, he didn't miss. "Gotcha!" Michael shouted. The dragon squealed and swung its tail, hitting Michael's Rhiorecs. They lost their balance a bit, but steadied up again. There was a loud screech as one of the Rhiorecs that wasn't carrying anyone fell from the sky in a ball of flames; another dragon swooped down, caught it in its enormous mouth, and ate it.

Moven flew alongside one of the dragons and a large spear appeared in his hand. He stabbed it through the dragon's side; the dragon screeched in pain and fell to the ground, dead. Weven held a bow, shooting arrow after arrow through one dragon after the next: he alone killed ten. Danned used the club he had brought from the battle with the elves and killed five dragons. Willow flew past Michael after a dragon that had tried to knock Michael away from the white dragon but had missed. She pulled out two daggers from a holster at her waist and jumped from the Rhiorces onto the dragon. She stabbed it in the head four or five times with each dagger and jumped back onto the Rhiorces again as the dragon plummeted to the ground below, where it was crushed by the meadow of octigrass. Michael still flew around after the white dragon, stabbing it sporadically with his sword.

"Grundun, look out!" Willow shouted, but it was too late: a dragon's flames engulfed him and his Rhiorecs, and they fell toward the ground. A dragon swooped down to try and eat them, but Danned threw an axe and Weven shot arrows at it, and the dragon, the Rhiorecs, and Grundun all fell to the octigrass, dead. All the Rhiorecs that did not have riders, along with Grundun and the one he had been riding, were dead, as well as all but four dragons. Michael flew higher after the white dragon, but suddenly, the dragon dove toward the ground. Michael followed; they were flying fast. The white dragon blew so many flames that thick smoke lined the ground. Everyone tried to see what was going on, but the smoke was too thick. Suddenly, the white dragon flew up again, but Michael was nowhere to be seen, and neither was his Rhiorecs.

"Michael!" Tyler yelled. Everyone turned to see Tyler on Traydome.

"He took off after the dragon, Tyler…we were all killing dragons…we didn't—" Willow began, but stopped when she noticed the white dragon begin to fall to the ground right in front of Traydome, who moved and clenched Michael tightly in his claws just in time to stop him from falling with the dragon. Dronand flew beneath him so Michael could get on the back of his Rhiorecs.

"I told you I would kill that dragon for you, Tyler, didn't I?" Michael shouted proudly.

"I can't believe you did it." They all landed at the other side of the meadow and met up with Keadon and Flain. "Wait a minute—where's Grundun?" Tyler asked.

"He didn't make it, Tyler; he was killed by a dragon. I'm sorry," Moven said empathetically.

Tyler looked back at the meadow quickly, then toward the wall to Eljord's kingdom. "This is it. Michael, Keadon, Flain, Shadow, and I are going to get Sara. The rest of you stay here. We will be as quick as we can; if there is trouble or we need your help, Keadon will fly out to you," Tyler stated.

"I think we all should stay together; we are stronger together," Dronand snapped.

"We are also easier to spot together."

"The six of you are just as easy to spot as eleven, and are more likely to be killed," Dronand argued.

"Maybe Dronand is right, Tyler—the more of us there are, the stronger we will be if we have to fight something again," Michael said, trying not to sound argumentative.

"Fine," Tyler said through clenched teeth. They were all surprised that Tyler had agreed, but no one said a word.

"We need to get over the wall, but I believe there is a Drade protecting it from intruders," Michael explained.

"Well, of course there is—that's obvious. We need to disarm the Drade," Dronand said, sounding annoyed. All the Dreamencers touched the wall; they began to mutter strange words very quietly. Then they tossed eleven ropes over the wall. "Climb quickly," Dronand shouted at Tyler and Michael. "Now!" he said, and they both obeyed. They climbed up the wall and down the other side; they were surprised to see Shadow standing there, but other than that, nobody. The rest of the army came over the wall as quickly as Michael and Tyler had. As soon as the last ones were over, there was a zapping noise and a flash and the ropes disappeared.

"Why is there nobody here, no army, nothing to defend Eljord?" Tyler didn't like it; something was not right.

"He knows we're here; don't you worry about that," Dronand hissed; he almost seemed excited by it. The kingdom was dark. There were stone statues all around, statues of all kinds of strange creatures of all sizes. Some were quite grotesque.

Tyler felt an uneasy presence around him, like he was being watched. "The statues!" Tyler whispered to Keadon.

Keadon flew up to the closest statue and hovered around it. "They're just statues, Tyler," he said, tapping the top of one of them.

Tyler nodded uneasily. "Go back, Michael! Go back! It's a trap! Leave me and go back!" Tyler heard Sara's voice again, only this time, it was stronger, louder; he knew they were close. He shut his eyes and tried to reach Sara. "Sara, we are here to help you. We are not leaving without you, Sara." Tyler waited to hear a response, but there was none. He tried again and again, but nothing. "We need to find where Eljord is holding Sara," Tyler began, but he was interrupted by Keadon.

"Flain and I will search the buildings."

"No, we are all going to stay together, remember?" Tyler said, shooting a nasty look at Dronand.

"I know, but we can go in and out of the buildings quite easily and without being seen—unlike the rest of you!"

Tyler agreed.

"You two kids cannot go wandering around Eljord's kingdom alone!" Dronand snapped.

"I will go with them," Shadow stated. Keadon smiled proudly.

"Stay out of sight and be careful," Tyler said, and the three left quickly, not giving Dronand a chance to argue.

"They'll be okay," Michael reassured Tyler.

Moven growled a deep, quiet growl and moved in front of Tyler as if he were protecting him, but there was nothing around. "What is it?" Tyler whispered, but Moven didn't answer. Instead, he let out another growl, the same as before. This time, Danned and Weven came and stood around Tyler also. Tyler and the others had no idea what was going on. Tyler asked Moven again, but just as before, he did not answer.

"Tyler, what is going on?" Michael asked, very worried.

"I don't know," Tyler answered.

Dronand realized something was wrong; he motioned to Vedin and Willow to stand and protect Michael with him. They all stood frozen for a while, but nothing happened.

"Moven, we don't have time for this," Tyler said as he tried to step out from behind his three guards, but he was pushed back by Weven with a snarl. The statues were gone—all of them. They had just vanished. When, exactly, no one had noticed; they had all been preoccupied with Keadon going looking for Sara. Moven's growls got louder and louder. Tyler's heart was beating so hard, his chest hurt; he was sure everyone could hear the thuds. Lightning flashed and lit up the deep black sky just enough to reveal that all the statues had reappeared and were now surrounding them like an army of stone. The sky turned black; once more, they were gone. Moven, Weven, and Danned moved in closer, shielding every inch of Tyler. Lightning flashed again. The sky, as before, was lit; the statues, this time with their weapons drawn, were stone, but no longer still. They attacked the group with swords and spears of stone.

"Move! Let me fight!" Tyler yelled, trying to push his way out of his barricade.

Dronand, Willow, and Vedin remained strong around Michael, who, just like Tyler, was trying to push his way through to join in on the fight. "Let us fight—we can help!" Michael yelled.

Tyler's army were able to defend themselves, but no matter how many times they stabbed the statues, nothing happened to them. Michael realized they would have to find a Drade that would stop them. He pulled Nomad out of his satchel. "Nomad, we need your help," Michael pleaded.

"Finally—I wondered how long it would take you to realize that I am useful, that not everything can be fought with fighting, that knowledge is power—"

"Nomad, we need your help fast!"

"Yes, yes—sorry."

"Nomad, the Dreamencers are fighting statues, stone statues, inside Eljord's kingdom. They won't let Tyler and I fight, but they don't stand a chance; nothing affects the statues."

"That's because they are made of stone, Michael. You cannot injure or kill stone: it is not living, therefore it cannot die."

"That part I got; what I can't figure out is what we can do to them."

The statues were pushing the army closer to the wall. Tyler was still yelling to be let free. Tyler had used his Oltes; he was now holding a shield and a club, eager to join in. "As your King, I order you to let me fight," Tyler commanded.

"I disobey!" Moven finally responded.

"I am your King!" Tyler yelled once more. Now he was extremely angry; how dare Moven disobey him?

"ALLINDRAY VONARDE BAXIRE!" Michael yelled. Nothing happened. He tried again, only this time he held onto his Oltes tightly with one hand. "ALLINDRAY VONARDE BAXIRE!" His voice was so loud, it thundered over all the fighting. Each statue once again became frozen, as statues should be. Michael moved slowly out from behind his barricade. "YAQET ODIE," Michael said, walking with one arm outstretched toward the statues, which began to slide slowly back into place.

Tyler furiously pushed his way out from behind Moven and his brothers. "What do you think you are doing? I commanded you to move to let me fight! Why did you disobey me?" Tyler yelled.

"Tyler, they were not statues! Well, they are now, but they were not always statues," Michael interrupted. "They were people or creatures that came into Eljord's kingdom without an invitation, so to speak."

"What?" Tyler snapped.

"The statues—Eljord turns trespassers into statues, forever cursed to defend the kingdom."

Tyler stared at Moven. "You knew this?" Moven nodded without saying a word. He pointed to three of the frozen statues. "My brother, Yagger; my sisters, Pide and Qeat." Moven turned away; Tyler saw him wiping tears from his cheek.

"Thank you, Moven."

"I am a Dreamencer; it is my duty to protect you," Moven said flatly. Weven, Danned, and Moven took one last look at their brother and sisters.

"Tyler, I think we found her!" Keadon was flying toward them excitedly, followed by Flain.

"Where?" Tyler asked.

"Follow me!" Keadon led the way around the edge of the kingdom. They all stayed close together. It was hard to see where they were going; they just followed the little bit of light from Keadon's and Flain's wings, who kept looking back so often that Tyler was beginning to think they were being followed.

"Michael, go back! Go back—he sees you, Michael, he sees you!" Tyler heard Sara's now screaming warnings. He could almost feel her pain as she spoke. They were close; he could feel it. Tyler looked behind him again after seeing a worried look on Flain's face.

"Candor?" Tyler whispered. Tyler was sure it was Candor he had seen. But why was he here? Why was he not helping Tyler? Tyler slowed down slightly, trying to fall to the back of the group. He had to see if it in fact was Candor.

"What are you doing?" Michael asked Tyler as he stopped walking.

"Nothing—I'll catch up. I just need to take a breath," Tyler lied.

"Look, Tyler, I know there's something wrong between us right now, but I'm still your big brother and I know you're up to something. Now what is it?"

Tyler was annoyed. So what if Michael was his big brother? It was Tyler who was King, not Michael. "Get lost, big brother—I don't need you to protect me," Tyler snapped.

Michael furiously left Tyler behind.

"Candor! Candor, I know it's you. Stop hiding from me." Candor moved slowly into sight; Tyler felt somewhat pleased to see him. "Why are you hiding? We could use your help! You know this place better than anyone. Do you know where Eljord has Sara?" Tyler asked.

"Tyler, Eljord does not wish to hurt you. He will give Sara to you; there is no need for all this fighting. You and Eljord together could rule the entire Dark World. Dronand is afraid of that. He wants you thrown, Tyler, he wants you dead: that is why he has led you this way. He is going to use you to kill Eljord. Regicide, Tyler—you lose your soul, your very being. Dronand is a coward; that is why he is using you. He will not commit regicide; he is afraid to be devoured by demons. You are his sacrifice, Tyler."

Tyler stared at Candor. He knew Dronand was no good; he had known all along, and Michael had sided with him. Tyler knew Michael was jealous, but was he jealous enough to go along with Dronand and sacrifice his own brother to be consumed by demons? Then Michael would be King, and he and Dronand could rule together. Tyler filled with rage; he felt betrayed.

"Come with me, Tyler. We will go and get Sara from Eljord and then we will deal with Dronand together," Candor said, holding out his hand toward Tyler. Tyler slowly reached for Candor's hand.

"Tyler, no!" Moven pushed Tyler aside and growled and snapped at Candor. "Do not trust him, Tyler—he is filling your head with lies, and your heart with anger! Dronand is a Dreamencer: he is loyal to you, Tyler. He may not always be nice, but he is loyal to you," Moven said, holding his stare on Candor. Moven rocked back and forth on the spot like a wolf ready to pounce on his prey.

Candor laughed sinisterly. "You understand him, don't you? You are more powerful than I imagined! Eljord must have foreseen." Moven snarled and snapped at Candor, moving closer to him. "Call off your pet, Tyler. You can trust me," Candor insisted, but Tyler didn't say a word. Moven had not taken his eyes off Candor; he stared him down. He was not about to let Candor come anywhere near Tyler, and somehow, Tyler knew that.

"I have to find the others first, then I will find you, Candor. Go wait with Eljord and we will all come to you," Tyler said calmly.

"I do not take orders from you, Tyler. I believe I have told you that before. Eljord will not take too kindly to you showing up unannounced with an army by your side. That is why I am here. I knew you would come after Sara. Now come with me. Together, just you and I—we will go to Eljord."

"How exactly did you find out that Eljord had taken Sara? And I wouldn't mind knowing how you know how he would feel."

Candor shifted a little; he suddenly seemed nervous. "I have never lied about my contact with Eljord. I told you the first time we spoke, if you remember."

"You told me he sent you to get me, to come and join the dark army."

"You do remember—that's good."

Tyler shook his head. "No, you lied to me. Eljord doesn't want me to join the dark army; he wants my sovereignty."

Candor knew Tyler's trust in him was fading. Without saying a word, Candor disappeared. Moven waited for a moment, just to make sure Candor was really gone, before he turned to Tyler. "You cannot trust Candor, Tyler. He is not your friend. He is not trying to help you, Tyler; if you put your trust in Candor, we are all in danger," Moven warned. Tyler was once again left confused and feeling alone. "We must get back to the others," Moven urged, leading the way to where they were hiding.

"How are we supposed to protect you if you run off like an unsupervised child?" Dronand snapped at Tyler when they returned. Tyler just ignored him and looked anywhere he could so as not to meet anyone's eyes. "Well, where were you? I think we have the right to know—I mean, we are here risking our lives for you…the least you could do is try to stay alive, at least until we find your friend!" Dronand continued.

"I don't believe that Tyler needs to answer to you!" Keadon jumped in before Tyler even had the chance. "In fact, I don't believe you should speak to him that way. He is our King. He may be young, but he is as brave and noble as any king should be, and I, for one, am honored to be here with him. You are either with us or against us!" Tyler smiled at Keadon, who was fluttering around Dronand angrily.

"How dare you? I am here, aren't I? You think it makes Tyler brave and noble to risk our lives to go looking for his little friend? Is it noble to fraternize with the enemy?" Dronand shot nastily at Keadon.

"How much further, Keadon?" Tyler asked, interrupting the two.

Keadon stuck his nose in the air and puffed out his chest as he turned away from Dronand. "We found an entrance to Eljord's castle at the back. It's just a servants' entrance door. It was locked, but there were only two or three guards; Shadow took care of them already. He's there waiting for us, so we should hurry up."

They crept quietly around to the back of the castle. It was now so late that the grounds were pitch black; the kingdom looked deserted.

"Don't you think there should be more guards?" Tyler whispered to Moven.

"Eljord would not have expected anyone to get past the statues. The words Michael spoke are from the beginning of the Dark World; those words have not been heard by any Nytstar alive today, not even Eljord himself."

"Candor knew we would get past the statues, I'm sure of it—or he would have come to me earlier."

Shadow opened the door to the castle and they all slipped inside.

"We can't all go wandering around the castle; we will be seen. I will go; you all need to hide. Keadon, where is she?"

"Tyler, we have to—" Dronand began.

"You will do as I say!" Tyler warned.

"I will come with you," Keadon insisted. Tyler nodded, and with Keadon leading the way, they were gone.

Michael did not like being ordered to stay behind by Tyler. He wanted to find Sara; he wanted to be the hero for once. "I am not just going to sit here and wait. I'm going with them," he said, and followed them quickly, before anyone could try and stop him.

"I told you to wait there," Tyler whispered.

"I didn't listen," Michael answered. Tyler just shook his head and they continued silently down the corridor. It was dark in the castle. Candles were placed along the walls very much like in Tyler's castle, but these were black, and the flames were such a deep red that they almost looked like glowing black flames. There was an evil presence throughout the castle that sent chills down their spines; all three felt cold. There were so many doors lining the walls; Tyler was curious to know what was on the other side of them—that was, until he heard a loud pounding noise coming from behind the door right next to him.

Michael jumped. "What is that?"

"I don't know, and I don't think I want to know, either," Tyler said as he quickly moved away from the door.

"Eljord! Eljord, someone is in the castle without permission!" a piercing voice shrieked. Tyler spun around to see a little old woman standing behind him. The woman was only about three feet tall and very round; she wore a dress that was so long, she had to hold it up so she didn't trip over it. Her hair was almost all gone; the bits she had left looked like scraggly silver straw. She jumped around with excitement as she shouted, "Eljord!" Tyler held out his hand toward the old woman and she suddenly froze.

"Hurry—we need to hide. There is no way Eljord didn't hear that woman," Tyler said as they all quickly ran through the closest door. Closing the door quietly behind them, they all held their breath, waiting to hear Eljord come running down the corridor.

"Who are we hiding from?" said a low, sinister voice from behind them. They spun around quickly. The room was dark; they could just make out a shadowy figure in the corner. It was Eljord. Michael and Keadon gasped, stepping slowly backward, ready to run through the door, but Tyler stepped forward.

"We are here for Sara," Tyler said firmly. "We are not leaving without her."

Eljord laughed. "Who said anything about leaving? You and your friends, along with your little army in my kitchen, are not going anywhere." Eljord stepped into the faint light. "I have been waiting for you. I was impressed by your journey; I did not think you would make it out of the Slome forest, let alone all the way here, and you managed to scrounge up the remaining Dreamencers for me. For that, I must thank you, for that will be one less thing for me to do once I am rid of you."

"Candor said you don't want to harm me; you want me to join you so we can rule together."

"Candor lied!" Eljord yelled. "He does that; he can't help it. You see, he wants your kingdom: he will do or say anything he must to get it. But you can't blame him; I mean, you must understand how he feels...or maybe your brother will understand. Michael? You know how it feels to be in the shadow of a great king, to be number two, not quite good enough, not quite brave enough, not quite...enough."

"You are wrong, Eljord. Michael is nothing like Candor. Michael is not number two to anybody; he is braver than I am, he is better than I am at most things. He should be the King. I know that."

"Your army knows that too, I believe. Oh, well—they don't matter, anyway. They will be dead soon...you all will," Eljord laughed.

Tyler knew he had to do something; he wasn't just going to stand there and let Eljord kill them—not now, not after all they had gone through to get there. "You may be right; the Dreamencers don't think I should be King. They have been quite open about how they feel, but who can blame them? They don't know me, they don't know how powerful I am. Maybe they are jealous. Maybe they don't like taking orders from a kid. I do know that they'd better get used to it; I plan on giving a lot of orders." Tyler stepped closer to Eljord, not showing any fear. "Well, there is only one way to deal with those who don't obey. After all, I am King: my word is law whether they like it or not. They have no right to question me or to judge me...but anyway, you don't want to hear all this—you were saying you wanted to kill us?"

Eljord smiled at Tyler. "Let's not be too hasty; maybe you have some potential. I am not sure with you, Tyler. I think you need to prove yourself. I do believe you may have a dark side...oh, yes, it is there. You feel it too, don't you? You feel your anger taking over, consuming you."

"You leave Tyler alone! He does not have a dark side—he is good on both sides. He is a better king than you will ever be," Keadon yelled.

"Do you really believe that, Keadon?" Tyler said. "Well, of course you do—you are a good little fairy; how could you not try at least to see the good in everyone? However, I think you were wrong this time. I just needed you for a while…you know a lot about the Dark World, things that others didn't know or wouldn't tell me—but you? You told me everything I wanted to know; you did everything I told you to."

"Tyler, I am your friend! I thought you were mine," Keadon sobbed.

"I don't have any friends—not in this world or the Lyt world. The difference is, however, that in the Lyt world I am weird and different; nobody wants to be my friend. In this world, I am King; everyone wants to be my friend, but I don't want friends. I don't need friends," Tyler snapped.

"Tyler, you're not making any sense. What is wrong with you?" Michael stammered.

"What's wrong with me? Michael, you are blind. You are so busy worrying about Sara, you can't see what's going on in front of your face."

"Now this is fun, Michael—did you know your brother had another side? Well, you must have; I mean, he has snapped more than once, he's been keeping secrets from you…he's changed, hasn't he?" Eljord stood behind Tyler, resting his hand on his shoulder. Michael stared at his brother, but Tyler refused to meet his eyes. He glanced at Keadon, who turned away quickly, sobbing into his hands. "Tyler, I believe you and I have a few things in common," Eljord sneered.

"Tyler has nothing in common with you! You are evil!" Keadon yelled, drawing his sword and flying toward Eljord, but Tyler threw his hand out toward Keadon and struck him down with a powerful force. Keadon fell to the ground.

"Tyler, what did you do?" Michael yelled. Tyler just stared at Keadon lying on the floor. "Tyler, you are more messed up than I thought—Keadon is your friend."

"Michael, I am so tired of you thinking you know me. Yes, I said you are brave, and yes, it should be you who is King, but you forget, it isn't you: it's me. I am King. I am the powerful one now. You may be smarter than me, but you are not the one in control!" Tyler yelled, pushing Michael toward the door. "Go—take your fairy with you!" Tyler said, picking Keadon up from the ground and throwing him to Michael.

Michael gasped, catching Keadon's limp, lifeless body in his hands. "You have lost your mind," Michael snapped.

"Michael, maybe you're not so smart after all. I only needed all of you because I didn't know the way here. Think about it: it wasn't me who drew the map, it wasn't me who knew how to get past all the creatures and through the mountains. I wouldn't have had a chance on my own. Besides, why would I care if your girlfriend is saved or not? Remember, you want her for yourself, so really, why should I save her?"

Michael punched Tyler in the face. Tyler stumbled backward, blood pouring from his nose; he wiped it on his sleeve and pushed Michael back. "You want me to do to you what I did to Keadon?" Tyler yelled.

"You used us? All of us? I am your brother, Tyler!"

"So maybe you should have thought about that when you tried to push me around. You are jealous; you want to be King. You and Dronand want to rule my kingdom."

"I don't know you at all. Maybe Eljord is right, Tyler—you have turned evil. You are not my brother anymore," Michael yelled. Carrying Keadon in his hands, he ran out the door, down the corridor, and back to the room where the others were waiting. "We need to go now!" Michael shouted, running for the door.

"What? Where are Keadon and Tyler? We cannot just leave them here!" Willow said.

"Now! We need to go now, before we are all dead!" Michael said, opening the door. He ran back outside and didn't stop. Clutching Keadon, he kept running as fast as he could until he reached the kingdom wall. He sobbed, staring at Keadon.

"What is going on, Michael? We just left Keadon and your brother alone with Eljord?" Dronand snapped. Michael shook his head. "What?" Dronand demanded.

Michael held up Keadon's body in his hands. "Tyler did it—he…he used us, all of us, to get here. He has joined Eljord," Michael said, sobbing.

"I knew it! I knew that boy was no good!" Dronand spat. Moven growled, but nobody could understand what he was saying.

"I can't believe it; what a coward! He lied to us all—this time, he got Grundun and Lelx killed, and now he killed Keadon, too?" Vedin snapped, pacing the floor.

"Listen to yourselves! Michael, you either don't know your brother very well or you just don't trust him," Keadon said, jumping to his feet.

They all turned and stared at him. "But I saw Tyler kill you…I held your body…you were cold, you had no pulse."

Keadon flew around excitedly. "You brother is brilliant, did you know that? He just saved both of our lives. He set us free so we can get Sara and get away from here."

"Did you know all along what he was doing? Did you know he was going to be stupid and try and trick Eljord?"

"How dare you? Your brother just saved your life! How dare you call him stupid?"

"He should have told me what he was going to do."

"When? When could he have told you?" Keadon snapped.

"Well, when he told you."

"He didn't tell me what he was going to do. I just knew he was trying to get us out of there. I just trusted him, that's all."

"We need to get Sara now," Shadow snapped. "Keadon, you and I will go."

"I am coming with you!" Michael said, standing up.

"No," Keadon snapped.

"I am coming!"

"We go now!" Shadow repeated. Shadow, Keadon, and Michael once again headed toward the castle. "Sara is in a locked room in the east tower. There are no guards on the roof, so that's where we go: to the roof," Shadow whispered.

"How am I supposed to get on the roof?" Michael asked.

"You're the smart one, remember? Figure it out," Keadon snapped angrily. They reached the east tower quickly. There was a thick, black, steaming substance all around the bottom of the tower.

"Don't step in that or you will lose your foot; it's a tar moat to stop anyone from climbing the tower," Shadow warned.

"Great, so now I have to jump and fly. This should be easy," Michael said, frustrated. There was a loud squawk in the sky. Traydome flew down, scooped Michael up in his claws, and flew him up to the roof, then flew off again. Keadon flew to the roof; Shadow was already there, waiting for them.

"There is a chimney over here; we should fit down," Shadow said.

Michael held his Oltes, closed his eyes, and smiled happily when a rope appeared in his hand. "Well done—finally," Keadon hissed. Michael tied the rope around the base of the chimney so he could safely climb down.

"I'll go first to check it out. Wait here," Shadow warned, disappearing. Michael and Keadon stood there in silence, waiting for Shadow to return, neither one wanting to talk about what had just happened.

CHAPTER FOURTEEN

GEOFFREY

Michael climbed down the chimney quickly. "Sara!" he gasped as he scrambled out of the fireplace. He ran across the room, grabbed Sara, and held her tightly. "Are you okay? Are you hurt?" Michael asked, still hugging her tightly.

"I'm fine, Michael, really."

"Did he hurt you?"

Sara pulled away from Michael and stared at the floor. "He showed me my parents—they're dead," she sobbed, falling to the floor. "He killed them both—I saw their lifeless bodies. They were covered in blood. He said they were trying to stop him from finding Tyler; they knew Tyler would join him. My parents told him Tyler was evil; your grandfather knew, so he ordered them to keep Tyler away from Eljord, even if they had to kill Tyler to do it," Sara cried.

Michael sat down and held Sara again, stroking her hair to comfort her as she wept. "My grandfather would never have ordered them to kill Tyler. Eljord must be lying," Michael said.

"That's it?" Keadon snapped. "What about Tyler? What about the fact that there is no way Tyler is evil? No way at all! Your grandfather knew he was powerful; he knew Tyler was even more powerful than he was. That's why he wanted your parents to protect Tyler from Eljord, until they could teach Tyler about his powers. He had to know how to control them first. Tyler has been seeing the Dark World since he was a baby. He has had nightmares since he was born; nightmares that led him here to the Dark World. Eljord has tried to lure Tyler here for years. He wants Tyler to join him; he knows that Tyler is the only Nytstar powerful enough to kill him. Tyler is not evil!" Keadon yelled. Sara and Michael both stared at Keadon.

"We can't stay here and discuss this; we need to go, and quickly. I don't know how much time we have before Eljord figures out that Tyler is deceiving him," Shadow said, pulling Michael and Sara up and urging them toward the chimney. Once they were all on the roof, Traydome returned. He grasped them in his claws and took off. Michael explained to Sara what had happened back in the castle: how Tyler had pretended to kill Keadon so they could escape, and all the things they had both said to each other.

Sara reached out her hand to Michael, who held it tightly. "Tyler is strong, Michael. I'm sure he'll be fine. Are you sure he was pretending, though? You said yourself that he has changed," Sara said.

"I don't know. Keadon is sure it was all just an act to save us, but I do know that some of what he was saying was true; I just don't know how much. He has been secretly meeting with Candor, and he kept his Nythawk a secret…who knows what else he's hiding?"

Keadon and Shadow returned to the Dreamencers on the ground. "We got Sara—Traydome is flying them out of the kingdom," Keadon explained.

"And Tyler?" Dronand questioned.

"He is still inside the castle," Shadow said.

"Michael left Eljord's kingdom without Tyler?" Willow shouted.

"I am sure Tyler knows what he is doing. We should follow Michael and Sara to make sure they make it back to Tyler's castle safely," Dronand said, watching the Nythawk fly overhead.

"I am not going without Tyler. That's who we fight for, remember? For Tyler, we fight; for peace, we win! Or have you forgotten?" Keadon shouted.

"Keadon, you are not a Dreamencer; you are the Fairy Prince," Flain warned.

"I am Tyler's friend, and I will not leave him behind!"

"Our mission was to rescue Sara, and that is done. Now we just need to make sure she gets home," Dronand stated.

Moven, Weven, and Danned all growled and snarled at Dronand. Keadon couldn't understand them, but he knew they were not leaving without Tyler, either.

"We split up now: Dronand, Willow, Vedin, and Flain, you four follow Michael and Sara home. We will get Tyler."

"Shadow, what makes you think we will take orders from you?" Dronand demanded.

"You don't have to—if you want to be the one to rescue Tyler, go ahead," Shadow snapped. Dronand just nodded, and the four of them set off to take Michael and Sara home.

"That was too easy to rescue Sara; why would Eljord go through all the trouble to get her here and then just let us walk in and take her?" Keadon flew nervously around.

"It wasn't Sara he wanted; he knew Tyler would come for her. He didn't care what happened to her; she is of no use to him," Shadow explained.

"So what now? Do we go after Tyler?"

Shadow shook his head. "No, *we* don't; *I* am going into the castle. You four are going to stay here in case he comes out," Shadow said, then disappeared. Keadon flew around nervously. Shadow appeared in the castle, moving along the corridors in the dark shadows so as not to be seen.

"They are not going to fight us. How can they? What hope would they have of winning anyway? Their strengths rely solely on me and they know that."

"Tyler, killing your little fairy friend doesn't prove to me that you are totally on my side. I feel your anger—you're hurt, but I sense something more. Why do you lie to me?"

Tyler glared at Eljord. "Lie to you? About what? You think after all you have done to my brother and I that I'm just going to come and join you without any hesitation? How do I know you are not lying to me? Everyone else seems to. You killed my grandparents, remember? You have started war after war in this world—why would I trust you?"

Eljord laughed. "You are too kind, really. But I cannot take credit for every war that has broken out in our world; you deserve credit for the last one."

"Me? Why? What did I do to start a war? I was only a baby during the last war; I knew nothing about this world all."

"Tyler, you were the reason the last war started: you and your mark, the mark you should not have had. You should not be King."

"I didn't choose this! I had no say in any of it! What I want to know is what happened to start all the fighting in the beginning."

"Tyler, as long as there is good in a world, there will always be evil—the question is, which is which? Our world was made up solely of pure Nytstars a long time ago—that is, until a foolish king entered the Lyt world, which was forbidden. We did not cross into their world, but this king, Dramess, was greedy: he wanted more followers; he wanted to be the most powerful of all the kings. He went to the Lyt world to try and bring Lyts to our world because he couldn't convince any more Nytstars to join him, but he fell in love with a Lyt and she had his son, the first mixed ever. When word got around that the first mixed was born, people became worried; they didn't want to contaminate our world. They didn't want to share our world with Lyts. This son was the beginning of the end. Olbive, another king at the time, convinced many Nytstars that they had to kill the boy and any other Lyts in our world to keep the Dark World pure, so war began between the two kingdoms. Dramess hid his wife and son, but all the other Lyts were killed. When Dramess's son was found, Olbive sent his dragon to kill him, but your grandfather's ancestor saved him and killed the dragon. Dramess was so thankful, he gave him the Triss and his kingdom, then Dramess and his family disappeared. They were never seen again. Some say they left the Dark World completely and lived as Lyts in their world."

"So why didn't all of the fighting end there? If all the Lyts were killed, the Dark World would have been pure again."

"There were Lyts that had been hidden. It was too late: the Dark World had already been divided. Kingdoms fought other kingdoms for their power; each king wanted to rule the whole Dark World himself."

"That's not really my fault," Tyler snapped.

"The last war began because when your grandfather didn't have a son, his kingdom should have fallen: only sons can take the power of King and keep the kingdom alive. If you had not had the mark, his kingdom would be no more. Instead, the kingdom is now ruled for the first time ever by a non-pure Nytstar. As soon as the Dark World learned of your mark, your life was in danger. You should have been killed in the beginning. Many tried. Candor came very close more than once, but you were heavily guarded by some of the most powerful Nytstars. Your grandfather, as had his father before him, and so on, tried to bring peace between the two worlds. They developed decrees that they expected everyone in the Dark World to follow. However, that just created more tension. Before the Lyts came to our world, we didn't need rules; we never fought amongst ourselves. We only fought to protect our world from outsiders. Nytstars and creatures all turned against each other; our world is now divided so many ways that war is constant. Peace is no more, and death is certain for all Nytstars who try to fight me. You see, I am the last King— the last true King! You are impure; your kingdom is weak."

"I had no say in who my parents are. I am a King; I have the mark. I will not give up my kingdom to anyone—not even you."

Eljord walked around the room as if he were looking for something. "Why is it that your little army follows you everywhere? Shadow, do come out and play in the light," Eljord snapped. Tyler looked around, surprised.

"Eljord, you know you will not commit regicide; you will be consumed by demons," Shadow warned.

"I am already consumed by demons, Shadow," Eljord laughed.

"Let Tyler go, Eljord. Our world does not need another war. Our people do not need to die just because of your greed, Eljord."

"What makes you think I am holding Tyler here? Tyler is free to go if he wishes." Eljord moved aside, leaving a clear path to the door. Tyler just stared at the door, frozen; no matter how much he tried to move, he couldn't. Part of him wanted to run as fast as he could out of the door and far away from Eljord and his kingdom, but another part of him wanted to stay: he wanted to know more.

"Let's go, Tyler." Shadow urged. Tyler still didn't move. "Tyler, it's time to go—come on." Shadow pulled on Tyler's arm.

"Is it all true, Shadow? What Eljord's been saying?" Tyler asked.

Shadow nodded. "Yes, it is true, but it doesn't change anything. You are still King—pure or mixed, you have the mark: you are King."

"Yes, he is a king—that we know, but what we don't know is how he will rule. Tyler, will you follow your grandfather and trick Nytstars into thinking you are doing the right thing for them when really you are only trying to do what is right for you, or will you be honest about your own selfishness and greed?"

"What do you mean? How did my grandfather trick Nytstars? And trick them into doing what?"

"Shadow, do you mean to tell me nobody has told Tyler the truth about his grandfather?"

"Tyler, do not listen to his lies—let's go!" Shadow yelled.

"Wait—Eljord didn't lie to me before...why would he lie now? How did my grandfather trick Nytstars?" Tyler demanded.

Eljord smiled. "Your grandfather told his followers that he would keep our world pure—that he would keep peace in our world and unite the kingdoms in the Dark World once and for all."

"He couldn't help it if you didn't cooperate. That is not tricking; he tried and he failed."

Eljord snickered. "I wouldn't cooperate because I knew the truth. I knew all about the Lyts that he allowed in his kingdom: Lyts who had been hidden since Dramess. I knew your grandmother was not a pure Nytstar. I knew, and soon, so did others. It was a secret that had to be told. Didn't you ever wonder why your mother was not a Nytstar? Didn't you realize that she doesn't know anything about our world? Your grandfather tried to hide it; he didn't want the same fate as Dramess."

"But Lyts are no threat to our world! They have no powers; they cannot enter our world unless they are brought here. Why do you fear them?"

"I do not fear them! I do not fear anything!" Eljord shouted; now he was getting angry. "Lyts are not welcome in our world!"

"Why haven't you killed me?"

Shadow moved in front of Tyler in case Eljord took Tyler's question as an invitation.

"Do you want me to kill you?"

"You said I should have been killed in the beginning, so I was curious as to why you have spent your time telling me all this instead of just killing me as soon as I walked into the room."

"You were busy putting on a show for me, pretending quite convincingly that you killed your fairy friend—well, at least your brother believed it, so much so that he even ran back to the others you brought with you telling them all you had turned evil. They all believed it, too. Well, until the Triss wore off Keadon; he had a hard time convincing them you were saving them. I do believe Michael may need a little more convincing, however—once you find them, that is. He and Sara ran off together with a few others from your army. Not very loyal, are they?"

"They didn't run off! They took Sara somewhere safe! They are loyal; they are finishing what they came to do," Shadow argued.

"Your brother doesn't trust you, does he? He is jealous, I assume; he is the oldest, after all. He doubts your intentions, perhaps? Maybe he believes you are not good enough to be King. Candor seems to think so. He is not the only one, is he? You see it too."

Tyler felt the recurring anger inside him. "I don't want to talk about Michael! Tell me why you haven't killed me yet!" Tyler snapped.

"Tyler, don't be foolish. I am taking you back," Shadow said, grabbing Tyler tightly and pulling him out of the room.

"Let go! Let me go!" Tyler yelled, struggling in Shadow's tight grip. "I order you to let me go! I am your King; you must obey!" Shadow didn't listen to Tyler; instead, he disappeared with Tyler out of the castle.

"Oh, Tyler, thank goodness," Keadon said excitedly when Tyler and Shadow appeared in front of him. "I was just about to come in after you. Shadow, what took so long?"

"Let me go!" Tyler shouted again.

Keadon stared at them, confused. "What is going on?"

"Shadow is disobeying his King. You will be punished, Shadow," Tyler growled at him.

"Do with me as you wish, Your Majesty, but I will not let you fall for Eljord's manipulation. He just wants you to fill with anger and hate, as he is; that is what turns people evil."

"I am no longer your concern. We have rescued Sara; now you may all return home. Your services are no longer required." They both stared at Tyler as if seeing him for the first time. "You are dismissed!"

"Tyler, you are not yourself right now. Return with us and rest. You are just tired; it has been a long journey," Keadon suggested timidly.

"Do not tell me what to do!" Tyler snapped, hitting Keadon with a Triss, making him fly backward and fall to the ground. Keadon flew at Tyler with his sword and cut him on the arm. "You attacked your King! You will be punished!" Tyler yelled, holding his Oltes. He tied Keadon up with a Trissed rope; Keadon's sword fell to the ground. Keadon glared at Tyler. "You will remain a prisoner of the Dreamencers until I tell them otherwise. Shadow, return to my kingdom and lock him up!" Tyler ordered. Shadow stood still, staring at Tyler. "Do you need to be imprisoned also? I AM KING!" Tyler bellowed.

Moven growled. "Tyler, what do you plan to do—lock up everyone who tries to help you?"

"No, only those who disobey me. Are you next?" Tyler snapped. Moven snarled and pounced. Tyler thought he was going to attack him until he saw that Moven had pounced at Eljord. "Moven!" Tyler shouted, but it was too late: Eljord had turned him into a statue, the same as his brother and two sisters. "Release him, Eljord," Tyler commanded.

"He was going to attack you," Eljord said flatly.

"He wasn't going to attack me; he was going to attack you."

"Well, then I was merely defending myself. Besides, there is no way to reverse the Triss." Tyler stared at Moven's statue. "I can only command them to attack, to defend my kingdom. Sorry. Now, I wanted to show you something before you were whisked away. Would you like to see it?"

"What is it?" Tyler was curious.

"Well, why don't you come and see?" Eljord turned and walked away.

Tyler looked at Shadow and Keadon. "Take him away!" Tyler snapped, and walked away, following Eljord.

"I see your army's failing quickly. They don't respect you, Tyler. They fight for you to honor your grandfather. That will not last forever; they will eventually turn against you. From the looks of your arm, they already are." Tyler ran his fingers across his cut from Keadon's sword. He pushed down hard on it, making the blood spill out faster, sending a sharp pain down to his fingers. "You enjoy the pain, don't you? Tell me, which do you prefer: to feel the pain or to cause the pain?" Eljord asked snidely. Tyler didn't answer; he just followed in silence. "You must know about Sara's parents, correct? Well, of course you do—that is why you rushed to save her."

"You have them, don't you?"

"No, I do not. They were caught trying to kill you, and your grandfather killed them." Tyler stopped suddenly; Eljord turned around and smiled. "You thought your grandfather was too good to kill, didn't you?"

"I just don't believe he would kill them. They were Dreamencers; they were guarding me."

"They, just like most Nytstars, Dreamencers or not, wanted to kill you, Tyler. Most still do."

Tyler felt uneasy. He felt like he was being hunted by the entire Dark World. "What do you want to show me?" Tyler snapped impatiently.

"Right over here…you will see." Eljord led Tyler toward a small wooded area. The woods didn't look to be very big, yet they were extremely thick with trees. Eljord walked calmly straight into the woods. Tyler hesitated at the edge, looking around nervously. He suddenly wished he hadn't sent the others away; he had a bad feeling about entering the woods with Eljord. "Are you coming?" Eljord shouted back to Tyler. Tyler took a deep breath and slowly followed, catching up to Eljord, ignoring his own inner warnings not to. "What do you think of my woods, Tyler? The lost woods are an amazing place, really—one of my favorite creations, I have to admit. I think you can appreciate it from the outside. The lost woods look small, so small they can barely be called woods at all, but once you see the inside, they are gigantic. The lost woods are always underestimated; no one sees their potential. Remind you of anyone?"

Tyler just stared at Eljord uneasily. He knew Eljord didn't bring him into the woods for a metaphorical visit. "Why are they called the lost woods?"

"Once you are in the lost woods, you will be just that: lost forever. There is no way out; I am the only one who can leave the woods."

Tyler looked around at the trees. "There has to be a way out. Why would you create woods you can't get out of?"

Eljord shook his head. "Tyler, Tyler, Tyler—think about that for a minute. I know Michael has the brains, but I didn't think he had yours as well. The lost woods are where I take people I wish to disappear, people I want to make disappear but not kill—not yet, at least. I mean, if they die here in the woods, well, that's just left up to chance. What do you think? Do you like it? Well, you will eventually. You see, Tyler, it has been fun today. I have given you lots to think about; in fact, I think if I decide to return for you, you will have found the evil inside of you, if you haven't already."

"You can't just leave me here! I thought you and I were going to—"

"Going to what? Rule together? Did you not listen to a word I said? You are mixed; everyone wanted—or wants, I should say—you dead. I am no exception to that. I think you have potential to become a truly wicked king. I think we would be great together: we would rule the Dark World the way it should be ruled. There is no end to what we could do—why stop at the Dark World? We could do what no other Nytstar has done before: together, you and I could rule the Lyt world also. You being mixed and all, it makes sense. But we don't know the extent of your powers. You can't control them, and I know you are not completely evil yet, so this is the best place for you. If you are not evil now, you soon will be." Eljord turned his back on Tyler and began to walk away.

"Wait—you're mad! They'll come looking for me; they'll know you have done something to me."

"The army you sent away, the army that didn't want to fight for you in the first place? You did have friends that may have helped you; however, one is a prisoner until you free him, and the other is a statue. What makes you think that they would save you even if they knew you needed saving? Tyler, let's face it: they all think you have left your kingdom to join me. You are now truly alone," Eljord laughed.

Tyler started to panic. He drew his sword and swung at Eljord. Eljord drew a large, black-bladed sword. Their blades clanked together as they fought, moving around quickly, swinging their swords harder and harder. Tyler spun around, trying to move out of the way of Eljord's sword and trying to stab Eljord with his own, but he was blocked again. Eljord leaped high into the air and landed behind Tyler, slicing his side with the black blade. "Aagh!" Tyler yelled in pain as he spun around, stabbing his dagger into Eljord's chest. Eljord fell to the ground with a thud. Tyler's dagger got burning hot, singeing the skin on his hand. "Ouch!" Tyler looked at his hand; there was a perfect imprint of the dagger burned into it. Tyler stared at Eljord lying on the ground. He wasn't sure if he was dead or not; his cloak covered his whole body. Tyler stepped back. He became worried; he couldn't help but think about what Shadow had said.

"Regicide!" he whispered to himself, looking around frantically, expecting to see demons coming from every direction to consume him for his crime. He looked back at Eljord's body, but it was gone; it had disappeared. Now Tyler was left there, alone in the lost woods. The woods suddenly looked a lot thicker than they had a moment ago. Fully grown trees seemed to just appear out of nowhere; all the trees were in full bloom, which gave the feel of a roof closing the woods in.

"Eljord!" Tyler shouted. "Moven! Anyone! Hello!" But nobody answered. The woods were so quiet. There was not a sound: no birds or insects or animals—nothing, nothing but deafening silence. "There has to be a way out of here; I just need to try and remember the way in. The woods are not that big. I could see almost the whole way around them when we were walking toward them. I just need to think, that's all," Tyler said to himself. He walked forward a few steps, then turned around. "I should mark this spot; then I'll know where I have been in case I get lost. Then all I have to do is pick another direction to walk in. Really, the forest can't go on forever...it has to end somewhere," Tyler said, flicking his hand out quickly. A bright yellow, paint-like substance flew out of his hand, spraying the ground and the trees. Tyler turned and began to walk through the trees. All the trees seemed to look the same, every rock identical, each patch of moss or grass as green as the next. It was becoming quite clear why no one could ever find their way out of the lost woods.

Tyler whipped his head around quickly at the sound of a twig snapping behind him. He looked but didn't see anything. "Hello?" he whispered, but there was no answer. Tyler kept walking, just a little faster now, the panic and fear inside of him leading the way. A little bit further, and the same sound of a twig snapping echoed throughout the woods. Tyler froze. He knew he was being followed; he just wasn't sure by what. He looked all around, through all the gaps in the trees; as far as he could see, there was nothing there. Tyler started walking again, as quietly as he could. He had one hand on his sword, just in case, and the other was moving branches out of his way. He had the lingering feeling he was being followed. He tried to convince himself that it was an animal that snapped the twigs, but he knew it wasn't. He felt eyes staring at him; he could almost feel their breath on his neck...then he heard a loud crunch like someone stepping on a pile of dead leaves. Tyler spun around quickly and fell over, startled.

"Who...who are you?" Tyler asked the man who was standing over him. There was something familiar about his dark brown eyes and scratched face. "Wait a minute—I know who you are—or who you were. I mean, I thought you were dead. I mean, if you are who I think you are...that is...you're Sara's dad?" The man stared at Tyler hesitantly, looking him over, as if he weren't sure if he was really there or not. "I'm Tyler—Tyler Leeds."

The man reached his hand out to Tyler to help him up. "I know who you are. I'm just surprised to see you alive, and here, of all places. My name is Geoffrey...sorry, I'm sure you knew that already, didn't you?"

"Um...no—sorry, I didn't, but I'm pleased to meet you."

Geoffrey looked surprised to hear that Tyler didn't know his name. "I thought your grandfather would have told you all about me. We are very good friends. Oh, well—never mind."

"My grandfather...he...well, he didn't have time to tell me anything, really—not anything," Tyler said with some bitterness.

"What do you mean, 'he didn't have time'?"

Tyler realized that Geoffrey was missing before his grandfather had died; he probably didn't know anything that had been going on. "Oh, I'm sorry to have to be the one to tell you this, but my grandfather—he died."

Geoffrey's face fell. His eyes welled with tears, and he swayed back a little, then sat down, putting his head in his hands. "Was it Eljord?" he sobbed.

"I think it was, but I really don't know—sorry." Tyler looked at Geoffrey as he wept uncontrollably for a man for whom Tyler felt nothing but resentment.

"Oh, wait—I am sorry, I didn't realize…um…" Geoffrey scrambled to his feet and bowed to Tyler.

"Don't, please don't. You don't have to do that, sir. I am not what you think I am," Tyler said.

"You are King Tyler. I hope your grandfather at least had time to tell you that much before he died."

Tyler shook his head. "I know—well, at least I've been told the story by others—but I can't be King; not me."

"Well you definitely can't be King from in here, that's for sure."

Tyler couldn't help but feel a little relieved. "Well, that's good, then. I mean, we can never get out of the lost woods, so it looks like I won't have to worry about being King anyway." Michael was next in line for the throne, so the Dark World would be just fine—better than fine, he thought. Michael would make a great king.

"You are special, Tyler; that's why it was you born with the mark." Geoffrey was extremely excited; he could barely contain himself.

"I don't mean to be rude, but so what? What does being special—which I am aware is just another word for weird, odd, strange, unusual—" Tyler began.

"No, no—you have got it all wrong, Tyler. I do wish your grandfather could have been the one to tell you all this. I'm not sure I'm the right person for it. Maybe it can wait…first, we need to find you something to eat. You must be starving." Geoffrey smiled and turned to walk in the other direction, waving for Tyler to follow him.

"Wait a minute, Geoffrey! You can't just say something like that and leave it. Besides, who else is going to tell me—unless there are others hiding in here…"

"No, Your Majesty, unfortunately, I am the only one left. There were two others with me, Axril and Mottao, but they didn't make it. Axril went mad; he couldn't take being in here. He had been walking in the same direction, chopping down the trees in front of him, which only reappeared behind him, for ten years when I came. He eventually died of exhaustion. And Mottao, poor thing…he fell from a tree trying to leap—or fly, maybe—out of the woods. He came in after me; he had been caught trying to steal from Eljord. Believe me, we tried everything we could think of to get out. After all, we have nothing but time to think of a way out. Digging the tunnel was my least favorite: all that hard work, just to bury ourselves."

Tyler felt sick to his stomach at the thought of being there in the lost woods for so long, slowly going mad, until he died. "So Eljord never comes back for anyone? Well, I know that he isn't always truthful—I mean, he told me you were dead, and that my grandfather had killed you and your wife."

"Well, he was a little right about that; that's why I am here. You see, your grandfather staged our deaths, Elaina and I—that's my wife. Our duty was to protect you and your brother; we had done so since your mother first became pregnant with Michael. We made sure nothing ever happened to either of you. We knew that once Eljord found out about you, he would want you dead. We guarded you for as long as we could, but Eljord was getting too close, and so were many other Nytstars who felt the same as Eljord. Our deaths were staged as part of a plan to hide you both, only Eljord found out the truth, and somehow I ended up here. Elaina went into hiding; I don't know where. Do you know?"

"I don't know about anyone else, sir. Sorry, but I thought you were both dead. We were looking for you both, though—Michael, Sara, and I. We found this," Tyler said, handing Geoffrey his Oltes. Tyler had kept it in his pocket since he had found it back in the Mysterious Blue.

"You found it! Oh, thank goodness—I had hoped someone would. I couldn't risk Eljord trying to take it from me. I can only hope that Elaina is safe. I have been unable to sense her without my Oltes. It has been too long now; she is brilliant at hiding. No one ever saw her when she was guarding you and your brother. She used to guard you at home, and I, when you were out— that's what your Grandfather insisted upon. I bet you never knew she was in your home, did you?"

Tyler was surprised that he had never seen either of them, especially in his house. He couldn't help wonder where she would have hidden. "No, I didn't...can she turn invisible or something?"

Geoffrey shook his head with a smile. "Nope—she can't make herself invisible, thank goodness: we would never find her then. Let's go hunt; we are going to need to eat first. We need our strength."

"For what?"

Geoffrey smiled at Tyler. "To get out of the woods."

"But there is no way out of the lost woods, unless Eljord comes back for you. I don't think he is coming back anytime soon. Besides, if there's a way out that you know of, why didn't you get out sooner?" Tyler followed Geoffrey as he headed through the woods, slowly and quietly, looking for something they could eat.

"I couldn't. I don't posses nearly enough power to get out of the lost woods, and apparently Eljord doesn't realize that I am still alive to help you use your powers, which is good for us. That will make this easier. I saw some rabbits around here not too long ago; they will do. Have you ever been hunting before?"

"No, I prefer the grocery store—I used to, anyway."

"Tyler, you have a very long life ahead of you. Trust me, these woods are no match for you. Shhh," Geoffrey said, waving his hand, signaling to Tyler to stop. Tyler looked over Geoffrey's shoulder and saw a very large rabbit eating a leaf. Geoffrey suddenly had a bow and arrow. He aimed at the rabbit; slowly, he drew back the arrow and fired, striking the rabbit dead. Tyler was quite impressed, yet was surprised to see another rabbit hop over next to the dead one. Geoffrey pulled back the arrow again, striking the second rabbit dead; then another rabbit came, and another and another. Before they knew it, they were surrounded by rabbits, very large rabbits—at least four times the size of normal rabbits—and they didn't look too friendly.

"Is this what usually happens when you hunt?" Tyler joked.

Geoffrey laughed slightly as he shot arrows as quickly as he could. Tyler summoned his own bow and arrow and shot at the rabbits just as Geoffrey was—only when Tyler shot an arrow, it wasn't one arrow that hit the rabbit: one arrow hit each rabbit, and they all fell dead. Tyler looked around, expecting to see lots of people all around with bows and arrows, but there was nobody there.

"How…um, what…who…?" Tyler stumbled.

Geoffrey was beaming from ear to ear. "I told you this would be easy! Your powers are stronger in the woods because the woods are full of Drades. Your powers just use the Drades like fuel."

"Why? How can my powers do that and yours don't?"

"Tyler, your powers are unlike anyone else's. I can only assume that Eljord could not have known; otherwise, he wouldn't have put you in here."

Tyler groaned. "You know, I am getting really tired of people going on about how powerful I'm supposed to be. If I'm that powerful, why am I here? Why is it that so many of my friends are now dead? Why is it that I don't feel powerful? You know what…forget it. What do we do with all these rabbits?"

"Tyler, I can't tell you how you should feel—"

"I said forget it. I didn't mean to say anything. What about the rabbits?"

Geoffrey looked worriedly at Tyler. "We can cook one or two, but the rest we need to dispose of so they don't attract other creatures." Geoffrey pointed at the rabbits and all but two disappeared. Then he built a fire and summoned a large pan, and they cooked the rabbits. They sat around the fire and Tyler told Geoffrey all about how they ended up at the Mysterious Blue and met Lodiss. When he started to tell Geoffrey about meeting Sara, and how he, Michael, and Brandon had spent the night at the Mysterious Blue, he was a little embarrassed and worried that Geoffrey would be angry with Sara, but he wasn't; he seemed to be impressed with his daughter. "That's my girl; she knew you would be able to help. Tyler, tell me about her…I have missed her so much."

Tyler smiled with relief. He told Geoffrey how they had all become friends, and hung out together, and had some of the same classes at school; he started to tell him how Eljord had taken her and brought her to his kingdom, but stopped.

"Go on, Tyler—did something happen to her?" Geoffrey asked, panicked.

"No, no—she's fine. That's how I came here, to Eljord's kingdom," Tyler continued, but as he told Geoffrey about their journey, he couldn't help but be overwhelmed with anger. He clenched his fists.

Geoffrey watched fearfully as the water in the pot boiled over and the fire flared, igniting the trees close by. "Tyler…Tyler, you need to control your energy." Tyler didn't seem aware of the fire that was slowly engulfing everything around him; the flames danced angrily, then suddenly, they were gone, and Tyler fell to his knees, exhausted. "Tyler, are you okay?" Geoffrey asked, frantically laying Tyler down on the ground and folding his coat as a pillow for Tyler to rest upon. "You are going to have to try and control your emotions, especially in here. I'm not sure what got you so angry, but I suggest you put it out of your mind. Eljord may have seen the fire. That may be good: he will think you are turning already, that you are on your way to finding the evil inside you."

Tyler sat up. "I am not evil!" Tyler snapped.

"I know you're not. If you were, I would be dead by now, burnt to a crisp, and so would the trees." Tyler looked at the trees, which had been engulfed in flames just moments before, but there was no sign of that now. The fire was small once again, burning under the pot with the two rabbits cooking.

"Let's eat!" Geoffrey said—quite nonchalantly, considering what had just happened—as he placed each rabbit on a plate and handed one to Tyler. Tyler stared at the rabbit on his plate. Even though it had been skinned and properly prepared, it still looked like a rabbit. Tyler hesitantly ate it; he hadn't realized how hungry he had been.

"Well, what do you think? They are pretty tasty, right?"

"Not bad—not as good as a burger, though," Tyler joked.

Geoffrey handed Tyler a flask of water. "Drink up. The sky will be black soon, then we can abscond unseen."

"Abscond how? Which way is the way out?"

"I don't know which way is the way out, but you will know. We should just keep moving until you sense it."

"That's it? That's the plan? We walk around until I sense the way out? That's great. We don't have a chance; sensing things is not really my area of expertise."

Geoffrey smiled. "Well, unless you can fly hundreds of feet above the trees for miles and miles, then we have no other option."

Tyler shrugged, somewhat frustrated, until he realized he could fly—well, at least be flown. "Traydome!"

Geoffrey just looked at Tyler; he didn't know who Traydome was.

"Traydome is my Nythawk. He can fly us both out of here."

"You have a Nythawk? A real Nythawk? That's great! Is he full grown?"

"I don't know…I guess so. He's really big."

"That's great! Do you think you can reach him from here?"

"I can try. He won't fit down here, though; he's too big. We will have to climb the trees. Are they safe to climb?"

"Yes, as long as you don't fall out." Geoffrey was ecstatic; finally, after all this time, he was going to leave the lost woods. He could barely contain himself; he was going to see Sara again. Geoffrey jumped around excitedly.

"Once we're out of the lost woods, I'm going to have Traydome put me down by the statues. I need to find a way to free Moven; I can't leave him there."

Geoffrey's excitement quickly came to an end. "Moven, the Dreamencer?"

"Yes—Eljord turned him into a statue when he was trying to protect me. He wouldn't leave me behind and I am not going to leave him behind. Traydome will take you to Sara; Moven and I will follow."

"Tyler, how do you plan on saving him? There is no way to unfreeze the statues; the Drade is irreversible."

"How do you know that for sure? Maybe there just hasn't been a Nytstar powerful enough to do it until now!" Tyler snapped angrily.

"You could be right…I'm not really sure. It's a very old Drade. I don't know anyone who knows how to use it other than Eljord, so I think if there was anyone who could reverse it, unfortunately, it would be him."

Tyler shook his head. "I don't believe that. You said yourself that nobody knows the extent of my powers, so maybe I can help him. Maybe I'm his only chance. I can't just go and leave him without trying."

The sky was starting to go black. Tyler began trying to reach Traydome as Geoffrey paced nervously. He knew Tyler wasn't going without attempting to save Moven; he also knew he couldn't leave without Tyler. But this was his chance! He had been in the lost woods for years; he was finally going to be free, to see Sara. How could he risk it all to fulfill his duty to his King?

"I reached Traydome; he is on his way. We need to climb the trees so he can pick us up. He will fly as far out as he needs to to make sure we are free and clear of all Drades of the lost woods, then he will fly me back to Moven, and you to Sara," Tyler stated, and began to climb the tree closest to him.

"I am going with you. I cannot let you go alone; I have a duty to protect you. I will fulfill my orders."

"Your orders do not apply anymore. My grandfather gave you those orders and he is dead. As your new King, I revoke them. Your orders now are to go and reunite with your daughter!" Tyler said firmly.

"I cannot just leave you behind. I am a Dreamencer; that would be dishonorable."

Tyler stopped climbing and looked at Geoffrey as if trying to read his thoughts. "Then you are no longer a Dreamencer. I relieve you of your duties."

"You cannot do that—please! Being a Dreamencer is my life; it's all I know."

"Well, now you need to get to know Sara."

"Dreamencer or not, I cannot leave you behind. What do you think Sara would think of me if I did?"

Tyler continued to climb up the tree. "Fine—if you must come, come, but I don't want to have your death on my hands. What would Sara think of *me* then?"

Geoffrey smiled and nodded at Tyler, and they both climbed to the top of the trees and watched as Traydome glided silently towards them. "Wow…he is truly magnificent. Look at the size of his wingspan. I have never seen anything so spectacular." Tyler beamed with pride at Geoffrey's words. "I can't believe it survived in the Treptropsis for all those hundreds of years. All my life I have studied creatures; I have seen many of different kinds, but this one…this one is above the rest. Have you ridden him very much so far? How high have you flown? What is his gliding distance?"

"Geoffrey, I don't really know. I haven't had much chance to get to know him yet," Tyler sighed. Geoffrey was somewhat disappointed, but he didn't have the chance to ask anything else as Traydome came closer. "Here we go; he will grasp us in his claws, so be ready," Tyler shouted over the sound of the wind through Traydome's enormous wings. Tyler and Geoffrey braced themselves as Traydome flew toward them with his claws open and ready. He swooped down. Tyler and Geoffrey closed their eyes; they were ready. They could feel Traydome's breath on their backs, but they didn't feel his claws grab them. Tyler opened his eyes and looked up to the sky, and saw Traydome passing overhead. "What happened?"

"I am sorry, Tyler, I can't get close enough. I will try again." Traydome circled around and tried again; again, Tyler and Geoffrey braced themselves, ready to be picked up in Traydome's claws. Traydome swooped down, closer this time; they felt his breath on their backs as they had before…and just as before, he still wasn't close enough. He circled around again.

"It's okay, Traydome—just keep trying."

Traydome tried again and again. The trees were all different heights, making it hard to get close enough to reach Tyler and Geoffrey without crashing into the surrounding trees.

"Is there a group of trees that would make it easier for Traydome to fly closer?" Tyler asked Geoffrey.

"It doesn't look like it. They all look the same," Geoffrey said as he looked through a tiny telescope.

"Traydome, you are so close—I know you can do it!" Tyler yelled. The words were barely out of his mouth when Traydome picked him up in one of his enormous claws. Tyler sighed in relief; he looked over to Traydome's other claw and saw Geoffrey waving excitedly at him. Tyler smiled back at him. He didn't feel totally free yet; he knew they had one last mission to complete before he could go home, yet the thought of going home left him feeling more uneasy than going to try and save Moven. Traydome flew exceptionally high; Tyler felt a little dizzy from looking down at the trees, which were so far below them that they looked like little dots. Once they were high enough to be sure they would not be pulled back down to the lost woods, Traydome began to fly away from them. The wind was blowing through Tyler's shaggy hair. His eyes were closed so he could feel the wind on his face, and a sense of total peace and contentment swept over his body. He didn't want to stop flying; he didn't want to ever stop. Right there, high above everything and everyone, was blissful.

"Tyler, I think we have flown far enough away to be sure we are free of all Drades from the woods. I believe it is now safe for us to land," Geoffrey said, snapping Tyler out of his daydream.

"Oh, right—good. Traydome, you can take us down now." Both Tyler and Geoffrey stared toward the ground in anticipation, waiting to see if they were out of the woods.

"You did it, Traydome! You rescued us from the woods! Thank you— thank you so much!" Geoffrey shouted excitedly as the ground came into view and there was not a tree in sight.

Traydome opened his giant claws when they were close enough to the ground for Tyler and Geoffrey to drop safely, then landed beside them, pulling his enormous wings into his sides and sitting up proudly. Tyler rubbed his chest, praising him. "Well done, Traydome—you are the best. That was a wicked ride. Now we have to go back to Eljord's kingdom to rescue Moven."

"Tyler, that is foolish; you are going to get yourself killed. You're safe now; let me take you back to your castle. You can have a good night's sleep and think about it in the morning. Missions like these are what your Dreamencers are for; they will go rescue Moven."

"I don't have the Dreamencers anymore; they will not fight for me ever again—that I am sure of. No, this is for me to do on my own. That's just the way it is now."

"Well, you have one Dreamencer by your side, whether you want him or not, so let's go. We can figure out how to do the impossible on the way," Geoffrey said as he walked back toward Traydome's claw and braced himself to be picked up.

"What are you doing?" Tyler asked, staring at Geoffrey.

"I am ready to go."

"Wouldn't you prefer to ride on his back? That's usually how I ride him. In his claws was just the easiest way to get out of the woods."

"Oh, good—that will be more comfortable."

Tyler pulled himself up onto Traydome's back and Geoffrey followed. "Okay, Traydome—back to Eljord's kingdom, but don't fly anywhere near the lost woods. We don't want to get pulled back in," Tyler said as Traydome leaped back up into the air.

CHAPTER FIFTEEN

DOING THE IMPOSSIBLE

They flew back toward Eljord's kingdom; it seemed to take twice as long, and with the wind being a little cooler now, Tyler held close to Traydome to keep warm. Geoffrey, however, had his arms stretched out like wings; he excitedly looked down toward the ground, then back up, high into the sky. Finally, Traydome began to descend. Tyler looked down at the wall that surrounded Eljord's castle. Once again, Tyler felt that the fear of not knowing what may wait on the other side of that wall was taking over; he could almost see Eljord waiting for him to cross the wall, then killing him, along with Geoffrey and Traydome. But maybe Eljord had no idea that he had escaped from the lost woods; after all, nobody had ever done it before. And maybe Eljord, like Geoffrey had said, didn't know how powerful Tyler was, so he would have no reason to know he could escape. After all, Eljord didn't know that Tyler had Traydome.

Tyler was feeling a little more optimistic; maybe all he would have to do would be to figure out a way to reverse the Drade on Moven. But maybe he shouldn't just release Moven; how could he walk away and leave all the others as statues? If he actually figured out how to reverse the Drade on Moven, he would have to reverse it on all of the statues, which might be a bit harder to do without being noticed.

"Tyler, are you getting down, or did you change your mind?"

Tyler sat up quickly and realized that they were on the ground and Geoffrey had already dismounted Traydome. "Yeah, I'm coming...sorry." Tyler slipped slowly off Traydome and patted him thankfully. "Don't go too far, in case we need to make a quick getaway."

"I will remain here, waiting for you."

Tyler smiled and nodded; having Traydome close by made him feel a bit safer. "Okay, I think I remember…let me try," Geoffrey said, walking up to the wall. He placed his hands on it, muttering under his breath. Tyler moved closer, trying to hear what he was saying, but before he could, two ropes appeared over the wall. Tyler, remembering from last time, jumped onto one of the ropes and climbed as quickly as he could over the wall and down the other side. Geoffrey followed a moment later. "You are quick—either that, or I'm getting old."

Tyler stared, frozen on the spot. "Don't move," he whispered to Geoffrey. "The statues—I forgot: they're all going to start moving and attack us. Last time, Michael said some words and they refroze again, but I don't remember what the words were."

"You forgot we would be attacked by a rather large army of statues? How does one forget that?"

Tyler turned angrily to Geoffrey. "I just didn't think about it, that's all—it wasn't my first concern," he snapped.

"Well, it should have been! But that is just one of your problems, isn't it? You don't think about things before you do them!"

Tyler turned around, full of rage. "Dronand, how dare you talk to me like—"

But he stopped, stunned, surprised, and relieved to see Dronand, Michael, Sara, Shadow, Flain, Keadon, Willow, Vedin, Weven, and Danned all standing there, their swords drawn, ready to fight. Tyler drew his sword and stepped back Geoffrey, however, didn't draw a sword; instead, he stepped from behind Tyler and stared in amazement, with tears in his eyes, at Sara.

"Daddy?" Sara shouted excitedly, dropping her sword and running into his arms. "I thought you were dead! I saw the pictures of you and Mom…your bodies…Eljord said—"

"I will tell you all about it later. I have waited for so long to see you. But you should not be here! It is not safe for you here!" Geoffrey said, not so convincingly.

"Why are you here?" Tyler shot at her. "In fact, why are you all here?"

"We are here to defend our king!" Keadon said firmly.

"You obviously need our help!" Dronand said nastily.

Tyler ignored him and turned toward Weven and Danned. "You know I am not leaving without him!"

"He would not think ill of you if you did," Weven replied, without meeting Tyler's eyes.

"Tyler, you don't even know how to stop the statues from attacking you. How did you hope to save Moven?" Michael asked, which, from the look on his face, seemed to irritate Tyler.

"I don't know; I just knew I wasn't going to leave him here."

"I hate to break up the reunion, but we are not alone!" Willow gasped as the statues began moving toward them, weapons ready. Sara picked up her sword. The army, united again, stood fierce, ready to face the statues again.

Michael moved to the front of the group, guarded by Dronand, Weven, Danned, and Tyler. "ASSINDRAY VONARDE BAXIRE!" Michael yelled loudly and clearly, and the statues all froze. Holding his hand out in front of him, he walked toward the statues. "YAQET ODIE!" And they all moved back to their places.

Tyler smiled, impressed with Michael. "So if you know how to freeze them again and move them back to their places, how do we reverse the Drade?" Tyler asked hopefully. But all his hope faded quickly; from the look on Michael's face, he knew the answer.

"I'm sorry, Tyler. There is no way to reverse the Drade. I have looked and looked, but Nomad and I were both unable to find any clue that it's even possible, let alone the way to do it."

"So why did you all even bother coming back then?" Tyler snapped.

"We knew when Weven and Danned came back without you and Moven that something had happened. Shadow and Keadon told us you had gone off with Eljord and they explained what had happened to Moven. I knew you wouldn't leave here without trying to help him. That's why we came back for you; to bring you home."

Tyler turned away from Michael. "I don't need rescuing. Just because you and your book don't know how to save Moven, it doesn't mean he can't be saved." Tyler started walking away. He walked toward a statue that he recognized right away as Moven.

"Why did you have to jump at Eljord? He wasn't going to kill me; he wasn't even going to hurt me. Stupid plan, really, if you ask me: the lost woods didn't hold me very long. He should have turned me into a statue," he whispered to Moven's statue. Tyler sat down, leaning against the statue, trying to think. Maybe he could take Moven back to his castle as a statue for now, until he could figure out a way to reverse the Drade. There had to be some way; someone must know how. "That's it! Someone does know how to reverse it!" Tyler jumped to his feet excitedly. "There is someone that has to know how to reverse it!" They all looked at Tyler. "Eljord knows how! He was aiming that Drade at me, not Moven, but Moven knew that. That's why he jumped in front of me: to protect me from becoming a statue."

"Then why didn't Eljord turn you into one once Moven was out of the way?" Dronand questioned nastily.

"Because he couldn't. It is a very powerful Drade; it drains you, leaving you weak for while—I am not sure how long, exactly. He would definitely have been too weak to use the Drade on Tyler after just having used it on Moven, and then to protect himself against Weven and Danned. I think taking Tyler to the woods was a last-minute idea," Michael explained.

"There is no way Eljord would have planned to take me into the lost woods. He was desperate; he needed to do something fast so I didn't turn on him. He had to have known there was a chance I could have been found by Geoffrey, and he couldn't be sure I wouldn't be able to escape. He only took me there because he panicked. His plan was to turn me into a statue; he knew he was the only one who could reverse the Drade, so he could keep me here as long as he wanted to—as long as it took him to figure out how to bring out the evil he is so sure is inside me." Tyler felt Dronand's burning stare on his back; he knew Dronand agreed with Eljord.

"Well, I am slightly impressed to see you are able to think for yourself, Tyler. I honestly thought you would need your brother to figure that out for you." Everyone turned quickly to see Eljord standing arrogantly, surrounded by a small army of soldiers. The soldiers were dressed in brilliant silver and black armor that covered every inch of them, holding shields that looked very thick and heavy and were decorated with dragon crests in the centers. Their swords had thick silver blades with black dragon-hide handles. "You were wrong about one thing though: I didn't panic. When your pet got in the way I was more annoyed, really. I never liked pets; they are unruly and somewhat of a nuisance."

Tyler, Weven and Danned all moved toward Eljord, but his army stepped in front of him in unison. "Down, boys!" Eljord taunted. "You need to train your pets and your brother, from the looks of it, Michael—or are you too busy with your girlfriend? Although now that she has her daddy back, she won't have time to be naughty with you, will she?"

"Don't you talk about Sara like that!" Tyler snapped at Eljord.

"Why are you defending her, Tyler? She is Michael's, not yours—or maybe Michael is too afraid and he needs his little brother to do it for him."

"I am not afraid of you," Michael said, not very convincingly.

"I see…well, I apologize. I thought you were a coward; I thought that was why you hide behind Tyler, and only say how you really feel when he is too busy saving your life to hear you."

Michael blushed, trying not to meet Tyler's eyes. "You're wrong…I don't say anything, I—"

"Not so brave now, are you? Oh, well, never mind. I guess that is why you, being the oldest brother, who should have been first in line for the throne, are not the King. Kings have to be brave and honorable, and you are neither, are you? It is not the honorable thing to kiss the girl your brother loves, is it? Oh, forgive me—I said too much. You haven't told him yet, have you?" Tyler was filling with anger toward both Eljord and Michael. "You can't blame her, really, Tyler; she was easily convinced. Isn't that right, Michael? It wasn't that hard to convince her that Tyler was turning evil. I mean, when you told her all about how he didn't save Grundun and Lelx, and how he tried to kill Keadon, of course she wouldn't want anything to do with Tyler. It really is sad how many kingdoms fall because of love. Well, you made it easy for me, and for that, I thank you." Eljord's sinister smile burned into Tyler's anger; he turned to look at Michael. Tyler was sure from the look on his face that there was some truth in Eljord's words.

"Tyler, this is not the time to throw a tantrum over a silly little girl! You can all play nice for now!" Dronand snapped, but his words only fueled Tyler's anger.

"What makes you so sure you know how I feel about Sara and Michael? I don't care what they do together! And I don't care how either of them feels about me!" Tyler snapped.

Eljord smiled at the obvious conflict. "Grindor, I want all the statues destroyed!" Eljord ordered the soldier closest to him. The soldier grunted and nodded.

"You can't do that!" Tyler shouted, moving in front of the statue of Moven.

"Start with that one," Eljord said, ignoring Tyler and pointing to the statue he was protecting.

"No!" Tyler yelled, pointing his open hand toward Eljord, who had turned his back on Tyler. A flick of light came out of Tyler's fist and a force knocked Eljord to the ground.

Eljord slowly lifted himself back to his feet and turned to face Tyler. "Only a coward would attack from behind!" Eljord stated, but the words had barely left his mouth when Tyler hit him again in the chest with the same force. Again Eljord fell to the ground.

"Was that more to your liking?" Tyler hissed.

"No, wait!" Eljord commanded to his soldiers, who were ready to attack Tyler. Tyler's army all drew their swords, ready to fight. Tyler hit Eljord again before he had the chance to try and stand up. Eljord lay still on the ground. Tyler took a few steps closer, but was suddenly hit with a force, throwing him backward into Moven's statue.

"Fool!" Eljord shouted. Michael stepped in front of Eljord with his sword drawn and raised it to swing at him, but was thrown back into the kingdom wall and zapped by the Drade of the wall. Sara and Flain ran to Michael's side. "You see? Even here, she runs straight to Michael, yet you still think she will love you."

"No, I don't!" Tyler snapped. "You are wrong!"

"You are second again, Tyler, even here in the Dark World. You are a king, and you are still second to him, just as in the Lyt world!" Eljord hit Tyler a second time.

Shadow suddenly disappeared, then reappeared, striking at one of the soldiers, which started the battle between the two armies. Tyler got to his feet quickly. Drawing his sword, he ran at Eljord. Eljord drew his own sword; the two Kings, again in battle, swung vehemently. The sound of swords striking each other was deafening. Blood was being spilled on both sides, but the soldiers were falling dead all around, as Tyler's army seemed to be undefeatable.

"Rise, all who have fallen into the darkness of defeat: all of the diminished souls who reside within the depths of darkness and dwell in the evil of the Dark World!" Eljord roared. The ground began to tremble. An earsplitting noise forced everyone to cover their ears. Smoke erupted from the ground, along with creatures that were almost totally decomposed, their rotting flesh hanging off them, revealing their skeletons. They were covered in dirt and some kind of slimy substance, most likely the remains of their own rancid flesh. Insects were escaping out of their mouths and eye sockets; some of the creatures' eyes were hanging down past their cheeks. They were very stiff as they moved, groaning, a rattling, gargling kind of moan that sent chills down the spine of anything alive.

"Your time has come to protect your King! My dead army, I call upon you to victoriously defeat and take with you these souls! Candor, Tyler is yours!"

Tyler stared at the creature covered in a black cloak. "You are one of them?" Tyler gasped.

"Regicide!" Candor bellowed.

Tyler filled with rage; it all made sense. "You—it was you that killed them! You were consumed by demons for killing a king: my grandfather! You committed regicide and that is what happened to you!"

Eljord laughed a deep, evil laugh. "Candor killed more than just your grandfather: he killed your grandmother, and most of their kingdom. He also killed the villagers from your pet's village; too bad he missed six of them. Oh, well, I helped him with four—the last two should be easy!" Eljord shot a Drade toward Weven and Danned, but Tyler was too quick: a shield appeared in front of them, and the Drade bounced back at Eljord, hitting him with enormous force. Tyler stared at him for a moment.

"He's a statue!" Weven growled.

Tyler ran up to Eljord's statue. He punched at it, angry and completely helpless. "He was our only hope of saving Moven! He was the only one who could reverse the Drade on the statues!" Tyler yelled through his tears of defeat.

"What have you done?" Candor screamed.

Tyler froze. All the creatures were slowly receding back into the ground. Candor was fighting to stay; he grabbed onto a statue, trying to resist the force that was pulling him back to the depths of darkness. His fingers slipped off the statue; kicking and screaming for Eljord, he disappeared into the ground. The bodies of the fallen soldiers that were lying on the ground were reduced to empty piles of armor.

"What just happened?" Keadon asked Tyler in a whisper.

"I'm not sure; I think Eljord's power was feeding the demons. Now that he is a statue, his powers are useless." Tyler turned and looked at his army as they all gathered their weapons and helped each other clean their wounds. They had just won the battle against Eljord; why were they not smiling? Why did they all look so defeated? Tyler picked up his sword and walked toward the statue of Moven. "It is not over yet! I will come back for you and figure out a way to help you." Tyler rested his head on Moven's stone shoulder. Tears streamed uncontrollably down his cheeks; he was overwhelmed with relief, anger, and the feeling of defeat for not being able to save Moven.

"Keadon!" Flain was shouting in her tiny voice.

Tyler didn't want to move yet, but from the sound of the commotion, he knew something was wrong. He stood up and saw everyone gathered over by the wall of Eljord's kingdom. They all turned around, looking at Tyler.

"What?" Tyler snapped, but no one answered. Tyler slowly started to walk over to them, until he remembered that Eljord had thrown Michael at the wall. Tyler felt a sharp pain in his chest and he ran over to the wall so fast, his feet barely touched the ground. "Move out of the way!" Tyler ordered.

"Tyler, we're sorry—there was nothing we could do!" Keadon said frantically. Tyler's army was gathered around, hiding Michael from Tyler.

"Move now!" Tyler yelled. Slowly, they all moved out of the way, exposing Michael's statue. "Michael!" Tyler gasped. Tyler approached the statue of his brother solemnly, reaching out his trembling hand to touch the hard, cold surface of his brother's now stone body. Tyler's body began to shake furiously; he clenched his fists so tightly, the palms of his hands began to bleed.

"Tyler, we will search until we find the reverse Drade. We will help your brother and Moven, we swear to you," Keadon said, putting his hand on Tyler's shoulder supportively, but removing it quickly. "Ouch! Tyler, you're burning up! Are you okay?"

"Tyler, come—we will return to your kingdom. You need some time to think. We will arrange for a troop to come back and bring Michael's and Moven's statues back to your castle. We have Nytstars who have studied Drades for years; they may be able to find the reverse," Shadow said firmly, but Tyler didn't move; he didn't seem to even acknowledge anyone. Still shaking, Tyler's eyes seemed to enlarge and turn black. His body became rigid and tense; dark clouds congregated above him.

"Tyler?" Keadon winced.

"Tyler, you need to control your anger!" Dronand yelled above the violent racket of the clouds. The ground began to shake; everyone was frozen with fear and uncertainty. Tyler seemed to be getting larger right before their eyes. "Tyler, Eljord was the one that did this, not us! We all need to leave here and return home!" Dronand yelled.

Tyler turned to him with an icy cold glare. Tyler was unrecognizable; his anger had taken him over. He ran his hand over Michael's stone-cold statue one last time. He let out a deafening scream. With his sword drawn, he ran toward the statue of Eljord, driving his sword right through the stone statue. There was a loud clap of thunder; lightning bolts shot through the dark clouds above Tyler and traveled down his sword and through the statue, splitting it in two. The lightning ran through Tyler's body, shaking him uncontrollably.

"Tyler!" Keadon yelled hysterically. Shadow ran toward him, trying to separate Tyler from his sword; his grip would not release. Weven, Danned, Vedin, and Dromand all tried to help Shadow, yet even with all of their strength, they could not pull Tyler free. Then, almost instantly, the lightning and thunder stopped. Tyler's body went limp and he fell to the ground.

"Tyler? Tyler, wake up!" Keadon frantically held his hand over Tyler's head, trying to use his powers to heal him, but with no visible wounds, there was nothing to heal.

"Keadon, look!" Flain gasped excitedly. Keadon spun around and saw Michael slowly beginning to transform back into himself. They looked around at all the statues; they too were transforming back to their prior states.

"He did it! Tyler reversed the Drade!" Keadon flew around to Michael and Moven excitedly.

"Tyler reversed the Drade!" Sara squealed as she ran to Michael, throwing her arms around him.

Moven turned to Tyler's still-lifeless body lying next to the broken statue of Eljord. Panic covered his face. Moven growled. Everybody stared at him, confused; they couldn't understand what he had said, but they could see he was panicked. Weven and Danned ran toward Tyler and picked up his limp body. Traydome squawked in the sky as he flew closer toward them. The Nythawk opened his giant claws and Weven and Danned lifted Tyler's body to him. Traydome grabbed him gently and flew off.

"What are you doing?" Michael snapped. "Where is he taking him?"

Moven stared at Shadow, then at Eljord's broken statue.

"Regicide!" Shadow said flatly. Everyone turned to the statue.

"It doesn't matter where you take him; you cannot escape the demons of regicide," Dronand snarled.

"What? Tyler sacrificed himself? He committed regicide to save me? And now he will be consumed by demons?"

Shadow nodded solemnly. They were all left feeling helpless. The King they had doubted, the King they had feared they could not trust, had paid the ultimate sacrifice to save his brother and friend. Moven, Weven, and Danned were reunited with their sisters and brother. Dronand explained to the hundreds of other statues that Tyler, their new King, had sacrificed himself, and killed Eljord. They all cheered in Tyler's honor.

Tyler's army left Eljord's kingdom and returned to Tyler's castle. They knew as soon as they saw Traydome resting on the grounds that Tyler was inside. Michael rushed into Tyler's room with Keadon right beside him. Neither was afraid of what they might see. They didn't care how Tyler looked; they were just hoping he was still there and had not yet been dragged into the depths of darkness. Outside his room, Laydin met them with a smile.

"Tyler will be happy to see you both. He is healing just fine, and he will be back to normal any day."

Michael and Keadon glanced at each other before they ran into Tyler's room.

"Finally—what took you both so long?" Tyler joked.

"You're okay?" Michael asked.

"I'm fine…you?"

Michael choked back his tears. "I'm fine." Michael and Tyler looked at Keadon and, together, asked, "You?"

Keadon burst into tears and flew around them both excitedly. "I'm fine," he sobbed.

Sara knocked unsurely on Tyler's door, opening it a crack. "Can I come in?" Tyler nodded and Michael awkwardly pulled her up a chair close to him. "How are you feeling?" she asked.

"I'm fine, but I shouldn't be," Tyler snapped.

"What do you mean, 'you shouldn't be'?"

"Think about it: I committed regicide. Why am I not consumed by demons? I should be, right? That's what happens, as far as I've been told...unless everyone lied."

"Tyler, you sound disappointed," Michael said, a little quietly.

"I heard the Dreamencers talking; Shadow thinks it's because you are too powerful for the demons. That's why you were able to break the Drade on the statues," Keadon explained.

"Well, it seemed a little too obvious—I mean, kill the creator of the Drade to reverse it? You would think that someone would have tried that before," Sara added.

"But it just doesn't make sense. That would mean that Tyler would have to be the most powerful Nytstar to have ever lived. Is that possible?" Michael said.

"No way, right? That's what you're thinking, Michael," Tyler snapped.

"I didn't mean it like that, Tyler. I just meant—well, think about it: the most powerful Nytstar ever to have lived? Doesn't it seem just a little impossible to you?"

"Dronand doesn't agree with Shadow, either. He thinks the answer is much simpler: he thinks Eljord didn't die," Keadon said, shooting a disapproving glare at Michael.

"Well, fancy that—you and your buddy Dronand both agree it's not possible for me to be that powerful."

"Enough, both of you! You have to stop all this fighting—you are driving me crazy!" Sara yelled as she left the room, slamming the door behind her.

"Well, what are you waiting for? Go after her," Tyler mocked.

"What is your problem, Tyler? You—"

"So, where do we start?" Keadon interrupted.

"Start what?" Michael and Tyler snapped in unison.

"Start our new mission to find out why you are not consumed by demons, Tyler. Although you could just be happy you're not and leave it at that—maybe the demons were too busy, or they forgot," Keadon laughed.

"I'm doing this alone, Keadon. I need to find the answers," Tyler insisted.

"No, you and Michael need to put your problems aside for now. Not that your constant fighting and arguing isn't entertaining and all, but the four of us will have a better chance at this if we can work together. We can't just sit by and let you do this on your own, Tyler—you know that. Besides, there is no way I'm going to miss an adventure this cool."

Tyler folded his arms across his chest and sighed. He knew Keadon was right: he needed their help.

"Whatever," Michael grumbled.

Tyler just gave Keadon a nod, refusing to even look at Michael.

CHAPTER SIXTEEN

GOING HOME

"So, what now?"

Michael shrugged. "Well, I guess we go home, back to the Lyt world. I know Lodiss will be back from London soon, and I have to make sure the Mysterious Blue is clean, and everything looks normal."

Tyler's face dropped. He wasn't sure he wanted to go back to the Lyt world, back to school with Mrs. Suzanne, Conner, and Chase.

"You're not coming back, are you?" Michael asked.

"I have to. How would we explain that to Mom and Dad?"

The door to Tyler's bedroom opened and Laydin walked in. "Excuse me, Your Majesty, but I think it is time for dinner. I had the cook prepare a meal for all of you."

Michael looked at Tyler. "We could stay one more night!"

Tyler almost smiled. "I'm starving!" Tyler got out of bed and they all walked down to the dining room together.

"Tyler, I wish you didn't have to go!" Keadon sighed.

"I don't have to go for long; I can come back as often as I want." Keadon nodded slightly. "Cheer up: I'll be back before you know it. I feel at home here."

When they opened up the doors to the dining room, they were all surprised to see a party waiting for them. There was a banner on the wall with the words "For Tyler, we fight; for peace, we win!" painted across it. Everyone bowed to Michael and Tyler when they entered; each guest took their turn to shake hands with the two of them. They were introduced to so many people, they would never remember them all.

"Tyler, I would like to introduce you to my mother, Queen Varlyanna," Keadon said.

Tyler stared at the most beautiful fairy he had ever seen. Her shiny blue hair flowed down to her feet; her eyes were a stunning mix of blue and silver; her dress was a deep pink, laced with blue. When she smiled, she was breathtaking. Tyler bowed to her and took her tiny, delicate hand and kissed it. "It is a pleasure to meet you, Your Highness," Tyler said.

"I am delighted to finally meet the young King who put my son's life in so much danger."

Tyler glanced at Keadon, who looked just as shocked as he was. "I am sorry, Your Highness. I didn't mean to put Keadon in any danger."

"I am sure you didn't. My son's mind is not easily changed once it has been made up. I hope he didn't cause you any trouble; he is too young to have any part in such a dangerous mission. He needs to learn a lot about being a fairy prince. Fairies are not right for battle; he needs to accept his size."

Tyler looked at Keadon, whose head was hung low. He looked quite upset. "Yes, Mother," he sighed.

"With all due respect, Your Highness, Keadon was a great asset to our journey. He saved all of our lives more than once; in fact, I believe if it hadn't been for Keadon, we would not have succeeded," Tyler stated. Keadon was beaming at Tyler; he puffed his chest out proudly and nodded at his mother.

"Really? I had no idea, Keadon—I am sorry. You are truly special." Queen Varlyanna smiled at Keadon and gave him a hug. She turned and curtsied to Tyler. "If you will excuse me, I need to go speak with someone." She curtsied again and flew away.

Moven walked up to Tyler, surrounded by his reunited siblings. "How can I ever repay you for what you did?" Moven said. Moven's sisters, Pide and Qeat, hugged Tyler tightly. "Thank you, Your Majesty! Thank you so very much! We are eternally grateful to you. We want to join your army; we want to be Dreamencers!"

Tyler was shocked. He had assumed that the army was not needed anymore, and he had never really thought those types of decisions were up to him. "Well, thank you. You will have to talk to whoever is in charge of that, though; I don't know how that works."

Moven stared at him, as did Weven, Danned, Yagger, Pide, and Qeat. "What?" Tyler asked, a little uneasy.

"You are in charge of all that, Tyler; it is your army. You are in charge of everything and everyone. You are King, remember!"

"I remember; I just don't know that I am the right king, that's all," Tyler mumbled.

Moven looked around to make sure no one had heard Tyler, then grabbed his arm and pulled him into a corner so they would not be heard. "Tyler, do not let anyone ever hear you talk like that. No matter what, you act like you know what you are doing; never let anyone think any different. You must never show weakness or it will be used against you."

Tyler was shocked. Eljord was dead; there was nothing to fear now. Tyler nodded but didn't have chance to ask Moven anything before he was whisked away by other party guests. For the rest of the night, the party went the same way: Tyler was whisked around the room, meeting as many people as he could and joining in with everyone as they danced, laughed, talked, ate all the wonderful foods the kitchen had prepared, and drank many drinks. For the night, Tyler forgot all about any worries he had about being King and the trouble between he and Michael.

"Tyler, I want to thank you: I just danced with my daughter for the first time. Thank you," Geoffrey said as he swayed back and forth a little. Sara and Michael giggled, tipping their hands to their mouths like drinking glasses and pointing to Geoffrey.

"You're welcome. I'm glad you're having a good time tonight."

"I like the wine!" Geoffrey stumbled.

"That's good," Tyler said, trying his best not to laugh, although Geoffrey probably wouldn't have noticed if had.

As the party drew to an end, the guests began to slowly leave, bowing to Tyler on their way out. Tyler realized how extremely tired he was; he said goodnight to the few remaining guests and went to his room, collapsing exhaustedly onto his bed.

"Tyler! Tyler, wake up!" Michael said, shaking Tyler slightly.

Tyler, startled, sat up in bed. "What happened? What's wrong?" Tyler said, panicked.

"Nothing's wrong, Tyler, but it's getting late. We need to go home."

Tyler rubbed his eyes. His room was still dark; at least, it was until Michael lit all the candles. "What time is it?"

"Its eleven AM; we're going home, remember? Did you sleep all night?"

Tyler wasn't sure; had he slept nightmare-free all night? Or maybe he was still asleep, and this was about to turn into a nightmare. Hesitantly, Tyler got out of bed and reached his hand out to touch Michael's shoulder, just to check if he was really there.

"You okay?" Michael asked, looking a bit worried.

"Yeah, I'm fine—and yes, I did sleep all night: no nightmares."

Michael smiled and gave Tyler a friendly little punch on the arm. "That's great, Ty!"

Tyler smiled; he felt great after the first nightmare-free night that he could ever remember. They met Sara and Keadon in the dining room for breakfast. There was no sign of the party the night before; the table was full of all kinds of delicious-looking breakfast treats. They ate all they could and joked and laughed together. After breakfast, they all said goodbye to Keadon and headed to the entrance room.

"We will be back—and soon!" Tyler promised Keadon.

"Take this with you," Keadon said, handing Tyler a very small black stone.

"What is it?"

"It's how we can reach each other. Keep it with you at all times if you're in trouble or you need me for anything. Just hold it tight; I will know."

"Does it work both ways?" Keadon nodded. "Thanks, Keadon. I will see you really soon…you know that, right? I promise. I couldn't stay away from this place—and my best friend. After all, I have never had a best friend before."

Keadon's face lit up and he puffed his chest out proudly.

Tyler, Michael, and Sara went into the room, and within moments, they were no longer in the Dark World. They had returned home.

They were in the Mysterious Blue, on the stairs. Sara came running up to them from her room. "It's like we never left! We were in the Dark World for ages—weeks—but here, it is the exact time we left. Amazing; I will never understand that."

"I'll never understand lots of things."

"Well, that's why we have Nomad, right?" Michael added.

"Something just doesn't feel right, though, you know? It all feels a little too easy. I wonder…"

"Daddy!" Sara suddenly yelled as she ran past Michael and Tyler. "Oh, I'm so glad you're back."

"It's great to be back; I just wish your mom was here, too."

"We'll find her, Geoffrey—I promise you that," Tyler said.

Michael and Tyler headed for the bus stop. "It feels strange knowing there is a whole other world out there—a world that you would rather be a part of," Michael whispered.

"Someday, I will be able to call the Dark World home," Tyler said as he stared out the bus window.

That night, Tyler lay awake in bed, thinking of his kingdom. He already missed Keadon and Moven; he couldn't wait to go back to the Dark World. He drifted off to sleep, dreaming of flying on the back of Traydome; he could almost feel the wind through his hair.

"You foolish, foolish boy—you didn't really think you could kill me, did you? You lay there, in your safe bed, in your safe Lyt world, while I destroy the Dark World." Tyler woke up with a start.

"Tyler, the phone is for you. I think it's Megan," Michael said, smiling, as he handed Tyler the phone.

Tyler rubbed his eyes, not too sure if he was dreaming or not. "Hello," Tyler mumbled into the phone as Michael left the room—though not before making kissy faces at Tyler—and headed to the kitchen for some breakfast.

Halfway through his cereal, Tyler entered the kitchen, dressed but still yawning.

"Good morning," Mrs. Leeds said, beaming at Tyler.

"I'm going out," Tyler said, turning around to leave the kitchen.

"Wait a minute—where are you going?"

"Out!" Tyler snapped.

"Tyler!" Michael yelled after him, but it was too late: Tyler had gone.

THE END